"YOU FEEL THIS BOOK ALONG YOUR SPINE. . . ."

—Kansas City Star

Tired of weeding peas at a penal farm, the tough, freewheeling McMurphy feigns insanity for a chance at the softer life of a mental institution. But he gets more than he's bargained for, much more. He is committed to the care of Big Nurse—a full-breasted, stiff-gaited tyrant who rules over her charges with chilling authority.

Her ward is a citadel of discipline. Strong-arm orderlies stand ready to quell even the feeblest insurrection. Her patients long ago gave up the struggle to assert themselves. Cowed, docile, they have surrendered completely to her unbridled authority.

Now, into their ranks charges McMurphy. The gambling Irishman sees at once what Big Nurse's game is. Appalled by the timidity of his fellow patients, he begins his one-man campaign to render her powerless. First in fun, and then in dire earnestness, he sets out to create havoc on her well-run ward . . . to make the gray halls ring with laughter, and anger, and life.

SIGNET Titles You'll Enjoy Reading

one
flew
over
the
cuckoo's
nest

by **KEN KESEY**

Ⓢ

A SIGNET BOOK from

NEW AMERICAN LIBRARY

TIMES MIRROR

To Vik Lovell
who told me dragons did not exist,
then led me to their lairs

COPYRIGHT © 1962 BY KEN KESEY

This is an authorized reprint of a hardcover edition published by
The Viking Press, Inc.

 SIGNET TRADEMARK REG. U.S. PAT. OFF. AND FOREIGN COUNTRIES
REGISTERED TRADEMARK—MARCA REGISTRADA
HECHO EN CHICAGO, U.S.A.

SIGNET, SIGNET CLASSICS, MENTOR, PLUME AND MERIDIAN BOOKS
are published by The New American Library, Inc.,
1301 Avenue of the Americas, New York, New York 10019

28 29 30 31

PRINTED IN THE UNITED STATES OF AMERICA

ABOUT THE AUTHOR

KEN KESEY was born in La Junta, Colorado, but his family later moved to Springfield, Oregon, where he attended public schools, and later the University of Oregon at Eugene. He has received the Woodrow Wilson scholarship to Stanford University and a Saxton Fellowship, and won the Fred Lowe Scholarship awarded to the outstanding wrestler in the Northwest. Mr. Kesey was king of the Merry Pranksters, a group which traveled the West Coast staging happenings; as a leader of this group, Mr. Kesey appeared as subject and star in the bestseller, THE ELECTRIC KOOL-AID ACID TEST, by Tom Wolfe.

At present he is "scratching his athlete's foot on his farm in Oregon, watching his kids and blueberries grow, and wondering how he could have written a novel that sold all those copies, produced all those plays and prompted a multi-million dollar movie that's going to fill all those theatre seats with all those paying patrons, yet have gleaned such a small sum for his own pocket." But he is more philosophic than bitter: "What the hell," he figures, "Colonel Sanders is probably broke, too . . ."

. . . one flew east, one flew west,
One flew over the cuckoo's nest.
                    —Children's folk rhyme

She knows what they been saying, and I can see she's furious clean out of control. She's going to tear the black bastards limb from limb, she's so furious. She's swelling up, swells till her back's splitting out the white uniform and she's let her arms section out long enough to wrap around the three of them five, six times. She looks around her with a swivel of her huge head. Nobody up to see, just old Broom Bromden the half-breed Indian back there hiding behind his mop and can't talk to call for help. So she really lets herself go and her painted smile twists, stretches to an open snarl, and she blows up bigger and bigger, big as a tractor, so big I can smell the machinery inside the way you smell a motor pulling too big a load. I hold my breath and figure, My God this time they're gonna do it! This time they let the hate build up too high and overloaded and they're gonna tear one another to pieces before they realize what they're doing!

But just as she starts crooking those sectioned arms around the black boys and they go to ripping at her underside with the mop handles, all the patients start coming out of the dorms to check on what's the hullabaloo, and she has to change back before she's caught in the shape of her hideous real self. By the time the patients get their eyes rubbed to where they can halfway see what the racket's about, all they see is the head nurse, smiling and calm and cold as usual, telling the black boys they'd best not stand in a group gossiping when it *is* Monday morning and there *is* such a lot to get done on the first morning of the week. . . .

". . . mean old Monday morning, you know, boys . . ."

"Yeah, Miz Ratched . . ."

". . . and we have quite a number of appointments this morning, so perhaps, if your standing here in a group talking isn't *too urgent* . . ."

"Yeah, Miz Ratched . . ."

She stops and nods at some of the patients come to stand around and stare out of eyes all red and puffy with sleep. She nods once to each. Precise, automatic gesture. Her face is smooth, calculated, and precision-made, like an expensive baby doll, skin like flesh-colored enamel, blend of white and cream and baby-blue eyes, small nose, pink little nostrils—everything working together except the color on her lips and fingernails, and the size of her bosom. A mistake was made somehow in manufacturing, putting those big, womanly breasts on what would of otherwise been a perfect work, and you can see how bitter she is about it.

The men are still standing and waiting to see what she was

onto the black boys about, so she remembers seeing me and says, "And since it *is* Monday, boys, why don't we get a good head start on the week by shaving poor Mr. Bromden first this morning, before the after-breakfast rush on the shaving room, and see if we can't avoid some of the—ah—disturbance he tends to cause, don't you think?"

Before anybody can turn to look for me I duck back in the mop closet, jerk the door shut dark after me, hold my breath. Shaving before you get breakfast is the worst time. When you got something under your belt you're stronger and more wide awake, and the bastards who work for the Combine aren't so apt to slip one of their machines in on you in place of an electric shaver. But when you shave *before* breakfast like she has me do some mornings—six-thirty in the morning in a room all white walls and white basins, and long-tube-lights in the ceiling making sure there aren't any shadows, and faces all round you trapped screaming behind the mirrors—then what chance you got against one of their machines?

I hide in the mop closet and listen, my heart beating in the dark, and I try to keep from getting scared, try to get my thoughts off someplace else—try to think back and remember things about the village and the big Columbia River, think about ah one time Papa and me were hunting birds in a stand of cedar trees near The Dalles. ... But like always when I try to place my thoughts in the past and hide there, the fear close at hand seeps in through the memory. I can feel that least black boy out there coming up the hall, smelling out for my fear. He opens out his nostrils like black funnels, his out-sized head bobbing this way and that as he sniffs, and he sucks in fear from all over the ward. He's smelling me now, I can hear him snort. He don't know where I'm hid, but he's smelling and he's hunting around. I try to keep still. ...

(Papa tells me to keep still, tells me that the dog senses a bird somewheres right close. We borrowed a pointer dog from a man in The Dalles. All the village dogs are no-'count mongrels, Papa says, fish-gut eaters and no class a-tall; this here dog, he got *insteek!* I don't say anything, but I already see the bird up in a scrub cedar, hunched in a gray knot of feathers. Dog running in circles underneath, too much smell around for him to point for sure. The bird safe as long as he keeps still. He's holding out pretty good, but the dog keeps sniffing and circling, louder and closer. Then the bird breaks, feathers springing, jumps out of the cedar into the birdshot from Papa's gun.)

The least black boy and one of the bigger ones catch me

before I get ten steps out of the mop closet, and drag me back to the shaving room. I don't fight or make any noise. If you yell it's just tougher on you. I hold back the yelling. I hold back till they get to my temples. I'm not sure it's one of those substitute machines and not a shaver till it gets to my temples; then I can't hold back. It's not a will-power thing any more when they get to my temples. It's a . . . *button,* pushed, says Air Raid Air Raid, turns me on so loud it's like no sound, everybody yelling at me, hands over their ears from behind a glass wall, faces working around in talk circles but no sound from the mouths. My sound soaks up all other sound. They start the fog machine again and it's snowing down cold and white all over me like skim milk, so thick I might even be able to hide in it if they didn't have a hold on me. I can't see six inches in front of me through the fog and the only thing I can hear over the wail I'm making is the Big Nurse whoop and charge up the hall while she crashes patients outta her way with that wicker bag. I hear her coming but I still can't hush my hollering. I holler till she gets there. They hold me down while she jams wicker bag and all into my mouth and shoves it down with a mop handle.

(A bluetick hound bays out there in the fog, running scared and lost because he can't see. No tracks on the ground but the ones he's making, and he sniffs in every direction with his cold red-rubber nose and picks up no scent but his own fear, fear burning down into him like steam.) It's gonna burn me just that way, finally telling about all this, about the hospital, and her, and the guys—and about McMurphy. I been silent so long now it's gonna roar out of me like floodwaters and you think the guy telling this is ranting and raving my *God;* you think this is too horrible to have really happened, this is too awful to be the truth! But, please. It's still hard for me to have a clear mind thinking on it. But it's the truth even if it didn't happen.

When the fog clears to where I can see, I'm sitting in the day room. They didn't take me to the Shock Shop this time. I remember they took me out of the shaving room and locked me in Seclusion. I don't remember if I got breakfast or not. Probably not. I can call to mind some mornings locked in Seclusion the black boys keep bringing seconds of everything—supposed to be for me, but they eat it instead—till all three of them get breakfast while I lie there on that pee-stinking mattress, watching them wipe up egg with toast. I can smell the grease and hear them chew the toast. Other mornings they bring me cold mush and force me to eat it without it even being salted.

This morning I plain don't remember. They got enough of those things they call pills down me so I don't know a thing till I hear the ward door open. That ward door opening means it's at least eight o'clock, means there's been maybe an hour and a half I was out cold in that Seclusion Room when the technicians could of come in and installed anything the Big Nurse ordered and I wouldn't have the slightest notion what.

I hear noise at the ward door, off up the hall out of my sight. That ward door starts opening at eight and opens and closes a thousand times a day, kashash, *click*. Every morning we sit lined up on each side of the day room, mixing jigsaw puzzles after breakfast, listen for a key to hit the lock, and wait to see what's coming in. There's not a whole lot else to do. Sometimes, at the door, it's a young resident in early so he can watch what we're like Before Medication. BM, they call it. Sometimes it's a wife visiting there on high heels with her purse held tight over her belly. Sometimes it's a clutch of grade school teachers being led on a tour by that fool Public Relation man who's always clapping his wet hands together and saying how overjoyed he is that mental hospitals have eliminated all the old-fashioned cruelty. "What a *cheery* atmosphere, don't you agree?" He'll bustle around the schoolteachers who are bunched together for safety, clapping his hands together. "Oh, when I think back on the old days, on the filth, the bad food, even, yes, brutality, oh, I realize, ladies, that we have come a long way in our campaign!" Whoever comes in

14

the door is usually somebody disappointing, but there's always a chance otherwise, and when a key hits the lock all the heads come up like there's strings on them.

This morning the lockworks rattle strange; it's not a regular visitor at the door. An Escort Man's voice calls down, edgy and impatient, "Admission, come sign for him," and the black boys go.

Admission. Everybody stops playing cards and Monopoly, turns toward the day-room door. Most days I'd be out sweeping the hall and see who they're signing in, but this morning, like I explain to you, the Big Nurse put a thousand pounds down me and I can't budge out of the chair. Most days I'm the first one to see the Admission, watch him creep in the door and slide along the wall and stand scared till the black boys come sign for him and take him into the shower room, where they strip him and leave him shivering with the door open while they all three run grinning up and down the halls looking for the Vaseline. "We *need* that Vaseline," they'll tell the Big Nurse, "for the thermometer." She looks from one to the other: "I'm *sure* you do," and hands them a jar holds at least a gallon, "but mind you boys don't group up in there." Then I see two, maybe all three of them in there, in that shower room with the Admission, running that thermometer around in the grease till it's coated the size of your finger, crooning, "Tha's right, mothah, that's right," and then shut the door and turn all the showers up to where you can't hear anything but the vicious hiss of water on the green tile. I'm out there most days, and I see it like that.

But this morning I have to sit in the chair and only listen to them bring him in. Still, even though I can't see him, I know he's no ordinary Admission. I don't hear him slide scared along the wall, and when they tell him about the shower he don't just submit with a weak little yes, he tells them right back in a loud, brassy voice that he's already plenty damn clean, thank you.

"They showered me this morning at the courthouse and last night at the jail. And I *swear* I believe they'd of washed my ears for me on the taxi ride over if they coulda found the vacilities. Hoo boy, seems like everytime they ship me someplace I gotta get scrubbed down before, after, and during the operation. I'm gettin' so the sound of water makes me start gathering up my belongings. And *get* back away from me with that thermometer, Sam, and give me a minute to look my new home over; I never been in a Institute of Psychology before."

The patients look at one another's puzzled faces, then back

to the door, where his voice is still coming in. Talking louder'n you'd think he needed to if the black boys were anywhere near him. He sounds like he's way above them, talking down, like he's sailing fifty yards overhead, hollering at those below on the ground. He sounds big. I hear him coming down the hall, and he sounds big in the way he walks, and he sure don't slide; he's got iron on his heels and he rings it on the floor like horseshoes. He shows up in the door and stops and hitches his thumbs in his pockets, boots wide apart, and stands there with the guys looking at him.

"Good *mornin*', buddies."

There's a paper Halloween bat hanging on a string above his head; he reaches up and flicks it so it spins around.

"Mighty nice fall day."

He talks a little the way Papa used to, voice loud and full of hell, but he doesn't look like Papa; Papa was a full-blood Columbia Indian—a chief—and hard and shiny as a gunstock. This guy is redheaded with long red sideburns and a tangle of curls out from under his cap, been needing cut a long time, and he's broad as Papa was tall, broad across the jaw and shoulders and chest, a broad white devilish grin, and he's hard in a different kind of way from Papa, kind of the way a baseball is hard under the scuffed leather. A seam runs across his nose and one cheekbone where somebody laid him a good one in a fight, and the stitches are still in the seam. He stands there waiting, and when nobody makes a move to say anything to him he commences to laugh. Nobody can tell exactly why he laughs; there's nothing funny going on. But it's not the way that Public Relation laughs, it's free and loud and it comes out of his wide grinning mouth and spreads in rings bigger and bigger till it's lapping against the walls all over the ward. Not like that fat Public Relation laugh. This sounds real. I realize all of a sudden it's the first laugh I've heard in years.

He stands looking at us, rocking back in his boots, and he laughs and laughs. He laces his fingers over his belly without taking his thumbs out of his pockets. I see how big and beat up his hands are. Everybody on the ward, patients, staff, and all, is stunned dumb by him and his laughing. There's no move to stop him, no move to say anything. He laughs till he's finished for a time, and he walks on into the day room. Even when he isn't laughing, that laughing sound hovers around him, the way the sound hovers around a big bell just quit ringing—it's in his eyes, in the way he smiles and swaggers, in the way he talks.

"My name is McMurphy, buddies, R. P. McMurphy, and

I'm a gambling fool." He winks and sings a little piece of a song: " '. . . and whenever I meet with a deck a cards I lays . . . my money . . . down,' " and laughs again.

He walks to one of the cards games, tips an Acute's cards up with a thick, heavy finger, and squints at the hand and shakes his head.

"Yessir, that's what I came to this establishment for, to bring you birds fun an' entertainment around the gamin' table. Nobody left in that Pendleton Work Farm to make my days interesting any more, so I requested a *transfer*, ya see. Needed some new blood. Hooee, look at the way this bird holds his cards, showin' to everybody in a block; man! I'll trim you babies like little lambs."

Cheswick gathers his cards together. The redheaded man sticks his hand out for Cheswick to shake.

"Hello, buddy; what's that you're playin'? Pinochle? Jesus, no wonder you don't care nothin' about showing your hand. Don't you have a straight deck around here? Well say, here we go, I brought along my own deck, just in case, has something in it other than face cards—and check the pictures, huh? Ever one different. Fifty-two positions."

Cheswick is pop-eyed already, and what he sees on those cards don't help his condition.

"Easy now, don't smudge 'em; we got lots of time, lots of games ahead of us. I like to use my deck here because it takes at least a week for the other players to get to where they can even see the *suit*. . . ."

He's got on work-farm pants and shirt, sunned out till they're the color of watered milk. His face and neck and arms are the color of oxblood leather from working long in the fields. He's got a primer-black motorcycle cap stuck in his hair and a leather jacket over one arm, and he's got on boots gray and dusty and heavy enough to kick a man half in two. He walks away from Cheswick and takes off the cap and goes to beating a dust storm out of his thigh. One of the black boys circles him with the thermometer, but he's too quick for them; he slips in among the Acutes and starts moving around shaking hands before the black boy can take good aim. The way he talks, his wink, his loud talk, his swagger all remind me of a car salesman or a stock auctioneer—or one of those pitchmen you see on a sideshow stage, out in front of his flapping banners, standing there in a striped shirt with yellow buttons, drawing the faces off the sawdust like a magnet.

"What happened, you see, was I got in a couple of hassles at the work farm, to tell the pure truth, and the court ruled that I'm a psychopath. And do you think I'm gonna argue with the court? Shoo, you can bet your bottom dollar I don't. If it gets me outta those damned pea fields I'll be whatever their little heart desires, be it psychopath or mad dog or werewolf, because I don't care if I never see another weedin' hoe to my dying day. Now they tell me a psychopath's a guy fights too much and fucks too much, but they ain't wholly right, do you think? I mean, whoever heard tell of a man gettin' too much poozle? Hello, buddy, what do they call you? My name's Mc-Murphy and I'll bet you two dollars here and now that you can't tell me how many spots are in that pinochle hand you're holding *don't* look. Two dollars; what d'ya say? God *damn*, Sam! can't you wait half a minute to prod me with that damn thermometer of yours?"

*T*he new man stands looking a minute, to get the set-up of the day room.

One side of the room younger patients, known as Acutes because the doctors figure them still sick enough to be fixed, practice arm wrestling and card tricks where you add and subtract and count down so many and it's a certain card. Billy Bibbit tries to learn to roll a tailormade cigarette, and Martini walks around, discovering things under the tables and chairs. The Acutes move around a lot. They tell jokes to each other and snicker in their fists (nobody ever dares let loose and laugh, the whole staff'd be in with notebooks and a lot of questions) and they write letters with yellow, runty, chewed pencils.

They spy on each other. Sometimes one man says something about himself that he didn't aim to let slip, and one of his buddies at the table where he said it yawns and gets up and sidles over to the big log book by the Nurses' Station and writes down the piece of information he heard—of therapeutic interest to the whole ward, is what the Big Nurse says the book is for, but I know she's just waiting to get enough evidence to have some guy reconditioned at the Main Building, overhauled in the head to straighten out the trouble.

The guy that wrote the piece of information in the log book, he gets a star by his name on the roll and gets to sleep late the next day.

Across the room from the Acutes are the culls of the Combine's product, the Chronics. Not in the hospital, these, to get fixed, but just to keep them from walking around the street giving the product a bad name. Chronics are in for good, the staff concedes. Chronics are divided into Walkers like me, can still get around if you keep them fed, and Wheelers and Vegetables. What the Chronics are—or most of us—are machines with flaws inside that can't be repaired, flaws born in, or flaws beat in over so many years of the guy running head-on into solid things that by the time the hospital found him he was bleeding rust in some vacant lot.

But there are some of us Chronics that the staff made a couple of mistakes on years back, some of us who were Acutes when we came in, and got changed over. Ellis is a Chronic came in an Acute and got fouled up bad when they overloaded him in that filthy brain-murdering room that the black boys call the "Shock Shop." Now he's nailed against the wall in the same condition they lifted him off the table for the last time, in the same shape, arms out, palms cupped, with the same horror on his face. He's nailed like that on the wall, like a stuffed trophy. They pull the nails when it's time to eat or time to drive him in to bed when they want him to move so's I can mop the puddle where he stands. At the old place he stood so long in one spot the piss ate the floor and beams away under him and he kept falling through to the ward below, giving them all kinds of census headaches down there when roll check came around.

Ruckly is another Chronic came in a few years back as an Acute, but him they overloaded in a different way: they made a mistake in one of their head installations. He was being a holy nuisance all over the place, kicking the black boys and biting the student nurses on the legs, so they took him away to be fixed. They strapped him to that table, and the last anybody saw of him for a while was just before they shut the door on him; he winked, just before the door closed, and told the black boys as they backed away from him, "You'll pay for this, you damn tarbabies."

And they brought him back to the ward two weeks later, bald and the front of his face an oily purple bruise and two little button-sized plugs stitched one above each eye. You can see by his eyes how they burned him out over there; his eyes are all smoked up and gray and deserted inside like blown fuses. All day now he won't do a thing but hold an old photograph up in front of that burned-out face, turning it over and over in his cold fingers, and the picture wore gray as his eyes on both sides with all his handling till you can't tell any more what it used to be.

The staff, now, they consider Ruckly one of their failures, but I'm not sure but what he's better off than if the installation had been perfect. The installations they do nowadays are generally successful. The technicians got more skill and experience. No more of the button holes in the forehead, no cutting at all—they go in through the eye sockets. Sometimes a guy goes over for an installation, leaves the ward mean and mad and snapping at the whole world and comes back a few weeks later with black-and-blue eyes like he'd been in a fist-fight, and he's the sweetest, nicest, best-behaved thing you ever saw. He'll maybe even go home in a month or two, a hat pulled low over the face of a sleepwalker wandering round in a simple, happy dream. A success, they say, but I say he's just another robot for the Combine and might be better off as a failure, like Ruckly sitting there fumbling and drooling over his picture. He never does much else. The dwarf black boy gets a rise out of him from time to time by leaning close and asking, "Say, Ruckly, what you figure your little wife is doing in town tonight?" Ruckly's head comes up. Memory whispers someplace in that jumbled machinery. He turns red and his veins clog up at one end. This puffs him up so he can just barely make a little whistling sound in his throat. Bubbles squeeze out the corner of his mouth, he's working his jaw so hard to say something. When he finally does get to where he can say his few words it's a low, choking noise to make your skin crawl— "Fffff*fuck* da wife! Fffff*fuck* da wife!" and passes out on the spot from the effort.

Ellis and Ruckly are the youngest Chronics. Colonel Matterson is the oldest, an old, petrified cavalry soldier from the First War who is given to lifting the skirts of passing nurses with his cane, or teaching some kind of history out of the text of his left hand to anybody that'll listen. He's the oldest on the ward, but not the one's been here longest—his wife brought him in only a few years back, when she got to where she wasn't up to tending him any longer.

I'm the one been here on the ward the longest, since the Second World War. I been here on the ward longer'n anybody. Longer'n any of the other patients. The Big Nurse has been here longer'n me.

The Chronics and the Acutes don't generally mingle. Each stays on his own side of the day room the way the black boys want it. The black boys say it's more orderly that way and let everybody know that's the way they'd like it to stay. They move us in after breakfast and look at the grouping and nod. "That's right, gennulmen, that's the way. Now you keep it that way."

Actually there isn't much need for them to say anything, because, other than me, the Chronics don't move around much, and the Acutes say they'd just as leave stay over on their own side, give reasons like the Chronic side smells worse than a dirty diaper. But I know it isn't the stink that keeps them away from the Chronic side so much as they don't like to be reminded that here's what could happen to *them* someday. The Big Nurse recognizes this fear and knows how to put it to use; she'll point out to an Acute, whenever he goes into a sulk, that you boys be good boys and cooperate with the staff policy which is engineered for your *cure,* or you'll end up over on *that* side.

(Everybody on the ward is proud of the way the patients cooperate. We got a little brass tablet tacked to a piece of maple wood that has printed on it: CONGRATULATIONS FOR GETTING ALONG WITH THE SMALLEST NUMBER OF PERSONNEL OF ANY WARD IN THE HOSPITAL. It's a prize for cooperation. It's hung on the wall right above the log book, right square in the middle between the Chronics and Acutes.)

This new redheaded Admission, McMurphy, knows right away he's not a Chronic. After he checks the day room over a minute, he sees he's meant for the Acute side and goes right for it, grinning and shaking hands with everybody he comes to. At first I see that he's making everybody over there feel uneasy, with all his kidding and joking and with the brassy way he hollers at that black boy who's still after him with a thermometer, and especially with that big wide-open laugh of his. Dials twitch in the control panel at the sound of it. The Acutes look spooked and uneasy when he laughs, the way kids look in a schoolroom when one ornery kid is raising too much hell with the teacher out of the room and they're all scared the teacher might pop back in and take it into her head to make them all stay after. They're fidgeting and twitching, responding to the dials in the control panel; I see McMurphy notices he's making them uneasy, but he don't let it slow him down.

"Damn, what a sorry-looking outfit. You boys don't look so crazy to me." He's trying to get them to loosen up, the way you see an auctioneer spinning jokes to loosen up the crowd before the bidding starts. "Which one of you claims to be the craziest? Which one is the biggest loony? Who runs these card games? It's my first day, and what I like to do is make a good impression straight off on the right man if he can prove to me he *is* the right man. Who's the bull goose loony here?"

He's saying this directly to Billy Bibbit. He leans down and glares so hard at Billy that Billy feels compelled to stutter out that he isn't the buh-buh-buh-bull goose loony yet, though he's next in luh-luh-line for the job.

McMurphy sticks a big hand down in front of Billy, and Billy can't do a thing but shake it. "Well, buddy," he says to Billy, "I'm truly glad you're next in luh-line for the job, but since I'm thinking about taking over this whole show myself, lock, stock, and barrel, maybe I better talk with the top man." He looks round to where some of the Acutes have stopped their card-playing, covers one of his hands with the other, and cracks all his knuckles at the sight. "I figure, you see, buddy, to be sort of the gambling baron on this ward, deal a wicked game of blackjack. So you better take me to your leader and we'll get it straightened out who's gonna be boss around here."

Nobody's sure if this barrel-chested man with the scar and the wild grin is play-acting or if he's crazy enough to be just like he talks, or both, but they are all beginning to get a big kick out of going along with him. They watch as he puts that big red hand on Billy's thin arm, waiting to see what Billy will say. Billy sees how it's up to him to break the silence, so he looks around and picks out one of the pinochle-players: "Harding," Billy says, "I guess it would b-b-be you. You're p-president of Pay-Pay-Patient's Council. This m-man wants to talk to you."

The Acutes are grinning now, not so uneasy any more, and glad that something out of the ordinary's going on. They all razz Harding, ask him if he's bull goose loony. He lays down his cards.

Harding is a flat, nervous man with a face that sometimes makes you think you seen him in the movies, like it's a face too pretty to just be a guy on the street. He's got wide, thin shoulders and he curves them in around his chest when he's trying to hide inside himself. He's got hands so long and white and dainty I think they carved each other out of soap, and sometimes they get loose and glide around in front of him free as two white birds until he notices them and traps them between his knees; it bothers him that he's got pretty hands.

He's president of the Patient's Council on account of he has a paper that says he graduated from college. The paper's framed and sits on his nightstand next to a picture of a woman in a bathing suit who also looks like you've seen her in the moving pictures—she's got very big breasts and she's holding the top of the bathing suit up over them with her fingers and looking sideways at the camera. You can see Harding sitting on a towel behind her, looking skinny in his bathing suit, like he's waiting for some big guy to kick sand on him. Harding brags a lot about having such a woman for a wife, says she's the sexiest woman in the world and she can't get enough of him nights.

When Billy points him out Harding leans back in his chair and assumes an important look, speaks up at the ceiling without looking at Billy or McMurphy. "Does this . . . gentleman have an appointment, Mr. Bibbit?"

"Do you have an appointment, Mr. McM-m-murphy? Mr. Harding is a busy man, nobody sees him without an ap-ap-pointment."

"This busy man Mr. Harding, is he the bull goose loony?"

He looks at Billy with one eye, and Billy nods his head up and down real fast; Billy's tickled with all the attention he's getting.

"Then you tell Bull Goose Loony Harding that R. P. McMurphy is waiting to see him and that this hospital ain't big enough for the two of us. I'm accustomed to being top man. I been a bull goose catskinner for every gyppo logging operation in the Northwest and bull goose gambler all the way from Korea, was even bull goose pea weeder on that pea farm at Pendleton—so I figure if I'm bound to be a loony, then I'm bound to be a stompdown dadgum good one. Tell this Harding that he either meets me man to man or he's a yaller skunk and better be outta town by sunset."

Harding leans farther back, hooks his thumbs in his lapels. "Bibbit, you tell this young upstart McMurphy that I'll meet him in the main hall at high noon and we'll settle this affair once and for all, libidos a-blazin'." Harding tries to drawl like McMurphy; it sounds funny with his high, breathy voice. "You might also warn him, just to be fair, that I have been bull goose loony on this ward for nigh onto two years, and that I'm crazier than any man alive."

"Mr. Bibbit, you might warn this Mr. Harding that I'm so crazy I admit to voting for Eisenhower."

"Bibbit! You tell Mr. McMurphy I'm so crazy I voted for Eisenhower *twice!*"

"And you tell Mr. Harding right back"—he puts both hands on the table and leans down, his voice getting low—"that I'm so crazy I plan to vote for Eisenhower again this *November.*"

"I take off my hat," Harding says, bows his head, and shakes hands with McMurphy. There's no doubt in my mind that McMurphy's won, but I'm not sure just what.

All the other Acutes leave what they've been doing and ease up close to see what new sort this fellow is. Nobody like him's ever been on the ward before. They're asking him where he's from and what his business is in a way I've never seen them do before. He says he's a dedicated man. He says he was just a wanderer and logging bum before the Army took him and taught him what his natural bent was; just like they taught some men to goldbrick and some men to goof off, he says, they taught him to play poker. Since then he's settled down and devoted himself to gambling on all levels. Just play poker and stay single and live where and how he wants to, if people would let him, he says, "but you know how society persecutes a dedicated man. Ever since I found my callin' I done time in so many small-town jails I could write a brochure. They say

I'm a habitual hassler. Like I fight some. Sheeut. They didn't mind so much when I was a dumb logger and got into a hassle; that's *excusable*, they say, that's a hard-workin' feller blowing off steam, they say. But if you're a gambler, if they know you to get up a back-room game now and then, all you have to do is split slantwise and you're a goddamned criminal. Hooee, it was breaking up the budget drivin' me to and from the pokey for a while there."

He shakes his head and puffs out his cheeks.

"But that was just for a period of time. I learned the ropes. To tell the truth, this 'sault and battery I was doing in Pendleton was the first hitch in close to a year. That's why I got busted. I was outa practice; this guy was able to get up off the floor and get to the cops before I left town. A very tough individual . . ."

He laughs again and shakes hands and sits down to arm wrestle every time that black boy gets too near him with the thermometer, till he's met everybody on the Acute side. And when he finishes shaking hands with the last Acute he comes right on over to the Chronics, like we aren't no different. You can't tell if he's really this friendly or if he's got some gambler's reason for trying to get acquainted with guys so far gone a lot of them don't even know their names.

He's there pulling Ellis's hand off the wall and shaking it just like he was a politician running for something and Ellis's vote was good as anybody's. "Buddy," he says to Ellis in a solemn voice, "my name is R. P. McMurphy and I don't like to see a full-grown man sloshin' around in his own water. Whyn't you go get dried up?"

Ellis looks down at the puddle around his feet in pure surprise. "Why, I thank you," he says and even moves off a few steps toward the latrine before the nails pull his hands back to the wall.

McMurphy comes down the line of Chronics, shakes hands with Colonel Matterson and with Ruckly and with Old Pete. He shakes the hands of Wheelers and Walkers and Vegetables, shakes hands that he has to pick up out of laps like picking up dead birds, mechanical birds, wonders of tiny bones and wires that have run down and fallen. Shakes hands with everybody he comes to except Big George the water freak, who grins and shies back from that unsanitary hand, so McMurphy just salutes him and says to his own right hand as he walks away, "Hand, how do you suppose that old fellow knew all the evil you been into?"

Nobody can make out what he's driving at, or why he's

making such a fuss with meeting everybody, but it's better'n mixing jigsaw puzzles. He keeps saying it's a necessary thing to get around and meet the men he'll be dealing with, part of a gambler's job. But he must know he ain't going to be dealing with no eighty-year-old organic who couldn't do any more with a playing card than put it in his mouth and gum it awhile. Yet he looks like he's enjoying himself, like he's the sort of guy that gets a laugh out of people.

I'm the last one. Still strapped in the chair in the corner. McMurphy stops when he gets to me and hooks his thumbs in his pockets again and leans back to laugh, like he sees something funnier about me than about anybody else. All of a sudden I was scared he was laughing because he knew the way I was sitting there with my knees pulled up and my arms wrapped around them, staring straight ahead as though I couldn't hear a thing, was all an act.

"Hooeee," he said, "look what we got here."

I remember all this part real clear. I remember the way he closed one eye and tipped his head back and looked down across that healing wine-colored scar on his nose, laughing at me. I thought at first that he was laughing because of how funny it looked, an Indian's face and black, oily Indian's hair on somebody like me. I thought maybe he was laughing at how weak I looked. But then's when I remember thinking that he was laughing because he wasn't fooled for one minute by my deaf-and-dumb act; it didn't make any difference *how* cagey the act was, he was onto me and was laughing and winking to let me know it.

"What's your story, Big Chief? You look like Sittin' Bull on a sitdown strike." He looked over to the Acutes to see if they might laugh about his joke; when they just sniggered he looked back to me and winked again. "What's your name, Chief?"

Billy Bibbit called across the room. "His n-n-name is Bromden. Chief Bromden. Everybody calls him Chief Buh-Broom, though, because the aides have him sweeping a l-large part of the time. There's not m-much else he can do, I guess. He's deaf." Billy put his chin in hands. "If I was d-d-deaf"—he sighed—"I would kill myself."

McMurphy kept looking at me. "He gets his growth, he'll be pretty good-sized, won't he? I wonder how tall he is."

"I think somebody m-m-measured him once at s-six feet seven; but even if he is big, he's scared of his own sh-sh-shadow. Just a bi-big deaf Indian."

"When I saw him sittin' here I *thought* he looked some Indian. But Bromden ain't an Indian name. What tribe is he?"

"I don't know, Billy said. "He was here wh-when I c-came."

"I have information from the doctor," Harding said, "that he is only half Indian, a Columbia Indian, I believe. That's a defunct Columbia Gorge tribe. The doctor said his father was the tribal leader, hence this fellow's title, 'Chief.' As to the 'Bromden' part of the name, I'm afraid my knowledge in Indian lore doesn't cover that."

McMurphy leaned his head down near mine where I had to look at him. "Is that right? You deef, Chief?"

"He's de-de-deef and dumb."

McMurphy puckered his lips and looked at my face a long time. Then he straightened back up and stuck his hand out.

"Well, what the hell, he can shake hands can't he? Deef or whatever. By God, Chief, you may be big, but you shake my hand or I'll consider it an insult. And it's not a good idea to insult the new bull goose loony of the hospital."

When he said that he looked back over to Harding and Billy and made a face, but he left that hand in front of me, big as a dinner plate.

I remember real clear the way that hand looked: there was carbon under the fingernails where he'd worked once in a garage; there was an anchor tattooed back from the knuckles; there was a dirty Band-Aid on the middle knuckle, peeling up at the edge. All the rest of the knuckles were covered with scars and cuts, old and new. I remember the palm was smooth and hard as bone from hefting the wooden handles of axes and hoes, not the hand you'd think could deal cards. The palm was callused, and the calluses were cracked, and dirt was worked in the cracks. A road map of his travels up and down the West. That palm made a scuffing sound against my hand. I remember the fingers were thick and strong closing over mine, and my hand commenced to feel peculiar and went to swelling up out there on my stick of an arm, like he was transmitting his own blood into it. It rang with blood and power. It blowed up near as big as his, I remember. . . .

"Mr. McMurry."

It's the Big Nurse.

"Mr. McMurry, could you come here please?"

It's the Big Nurse. That black boy with the thermometer has gone and got her. She stands there tapping that thermometer against her wrist watch, eyes whirring while she tries to gauge this new man. Her lips are in that triangle shape, like a doll's lips ready for a fake nipple.

"Aide Williams tells me, Mr. McMurry, that you've been somewhat difficult about your admission shower. Is this true?

Please understand, I appreciate the way you've taken it upon yourself to orient with the other patients on the ward, but everything in its own good time, Mr. McMurry. I'm sorry to interrupt you and Mr. Bromden, but you do understand: *everyone* . . . must follow the rules."

He tips his head back and gives that wink that she isn't fooling him any more than I did, that he's onto her. He looks up at her with one eye for a minute.

"Ya know, ma'am," he says, "ya know—that is the ex-*act* thing somebody *always* tells me about the rules . . ."

He grins. They both smile back and forth at each other, sizing each other up.

". . . just when they figure I'm about to do the dead oposite."

Then he lets go my hand.

*I*n the glass Station the Big Nurse has opened a package from a foreign address and is sucking into hypodermic needles the grass-and-milk liquid that came in vials in the package. One of the little nurses, a girl with one wandering eye that always keeps looking worried over her shoulder while the other one goes about its usual business, picks up the little tray of filled needles but doesn't carry them away just yet.

"What, Miss Ratched, is your opinion of this new patient? I mean, gee, he's good-looking and friendly and everything, but in my humble opinion he certainly takes *over*."

The Big Nurse tests a needle against her fingertip. "I'm afraid"—she stabs the needle down in the rubber-capped vial and lifts the plunger—"that is exactly what the new patient is planning: to take over. He is what we call a 'manipulator,' Miss Flinn, a man who will use everyone and everything to his own ends."

"Oh. But. I mean, in a mental hospital? What could his ends be?"

"Any number of things." She's calm, smiling, lost in the work of loading the needles. "Comfort and an easy life, for instance; the feeling of power and respect, perhaps; monetary gain—perhaps all of these things. Sometimes a manipulator's own ends are simply the actual *disruption* of the ward for the sake of disruption. There are such people in our society. A manipulator can influence the other patients and disrupt them to such an extent that it may take months to get everything running smooth once more. With the present permissive philosophy in mental hospitals, it's easy for them to get away with it. Some years back it was quite different. I recall some years back we had a man, a Mr. Taber, on the ward, and he was an *intolerable* Ward Manipulator. For a while." She looks up from her work, needle half filled in front of her face like a little wand. Her eyes get far-off and pleased with the memory. "Mistur Tay-bur," she says.

"But, gee," the other nurse says, "what on earth would *make* a man want to do something like disrupt the ward for, Miss Ratched? What possible motive . . . ?"

She cuts the little nurse off by jabbing the needle back into the vial's rubber top, fills it, jerks it out, and lays it on the tray. I watch her hand reach for another empty needle, watch it dart out, hinge over it, drop.

"You seem to forget, *Miss* Flinn, that this is an institution for the insane."

The Big Nurse tends to get real put out if something keeps her outfit from running like a smooth, accurate, precision-made machine. The slightest thing messy or out of kilter or in the way ties her into a little white knot of tight-smiled fury. She walks around with that same doll smile crimped between her chin and her nose and that same calm whir coming from her eyes, but down inside of her she's tense as steel. I know, I can feel it. And she don't relax a hair till she gets the nuisance attended to—what she calls "adjusted to sur-roundings."

Under her rule the ward Inside is almost completely ad-justed to surroundings. But the thing is she can't be on the ward all the time. She's got to spend some time Outside. So she works with an eye to adjusting the Outside world too. Working alongside others like her who I call the "Combine," which is a huge organization that aims to adjust the Outside as well as she has the Inside, has made her a real veteran at adjusting things. She was already the Big Nurse in the old place when I came in from the Outside so long back, and she'd been dedicating herself to adjustment for God knows how long.

And I've watched her get more and more skillful over the years. Practice has steadied and strengthened her until now she wields a sure power that extends in all directions on hair-like wires too small for anybody's eye but mine; I see her sit in the center of this web of wires like a watchful robot, tend her network with mechanical insect skill, know every second which wire runs where and just what current to send up to get the results she wants. I was an electrician's assistant in training camp before the Army shipped me to Germany and I had some electronics in my year in college is how I learned about the way these things can be rigged.

What she dreams of there in the center of those wires is a world of precision efficiency and tidiness like a pocket watch with a glass back, a place where the schedule is unbreakable and all the patients who aren't Outside, obedient under her beam, are wheelchair Chronics with catheter tubes run direct from every pantleg to the sewer under the floor. Year by year she accumulates her ideal staff: doctors, all ages and types, come and rise up in front of her with ideas of their own about the way a ward should be run, some with backbone enough to stand behind their ideas, and she fixes these doctors with dry-ice eyes day in, day out, until they retreat with unnatural chills. "I tell you I don't know *what* it is," they tell the guy in charge of personnel. "Since I started on that ward with that woman I feel like my veins are running ammonia. I shiver all the time, my kids won't sit in my lap, my wife won't sleep with me. I *insist* on a transfer—neurology bin, the alky tank, pediatrics, I just don't *care!*"

She keeps this up for years. The doctors last three weeks, three months. Until she finally settles for a little man with a big wide forehead and wide jowly cheeks and squeezed narrow across his tiny eyes like he once wore glasses that were way too small, wore them for so long they crimped his face in the middle, so now he has glasses on a string to his collar button; they teeter on the purple bridge of his little nose and they are always slipping one side or the other so he'll tip his head when he talks just to keep his glasses level. That's her doctor.

Her three daytime black boys she acquires after more years of testing and rejecting thousands. They come at her in a long black row of sulky, big-nosed masks, hating her and her chalk doll whiteness from the first look they get. She appraises them and their hate for a month or so, then lets them go because they don't hate enough. When she finally gets the three she wants—gets them one at a time over a number of years, weaving them into her plan and her network—she's damn positive they hate enough to be capable.

The first one she gets five years after I been on the ward, a twisted sinewy dwarf the color of cold asphalt. His mother was raped in Georgia while his papa stood by tied to the hot iron stove with plow traces, blood streaming into his shoes. The boy watched from a closet, five years old and squinting his eye to peep out the crack between the door and the jamb, and he never grew an inch after. Now his eyelids hang loose and thin from his brow like he's got a bat perched on the bridge of his nose. Eyelids like thin gray leather, he lifts them up just a bit whenever a new white man comes on the ward, peeks out from under them and studies the man up and down and nods just once like he's oh yes made positive certain of something he was already sure of. He wanted to carry a sock full of birdshot when he first came on the job, to work the patients into shape, but she told him they didn't do it that way

anymore, made him leave the sap at home and taught him her
own technique; taught him not to show his hate and to be
calm and wait, wait for a little advantage, a little slack, then
twist the rope and keep the pressure steady. All the time.
That's the way you get them into shape, she taught him.

The other two black boys come two years later, coming
to work only about a month apart and both looking so much
alike I think she had a replica made of the one who came
first. They are tall and sharp and bony and their faces are
chipped into expressions that never change, like flint arrow-
heads. Their eyes come to points. If you brush against their
hair it rasps the hide right off you.

All of them black as telephones. The blacker they are, she
learned from that long dark row that came before them, the
more time they are likely to devote to cleaning and scrubbing
and keeping the ward in order. For instance, all three of these
boys' uniforms are always spotless as snow. White and cold
and stiff as her own.

All three wear starched snow-white pants and white shirts
with metal snaps down one side and white shoes polished like
ice, and the shoes have red rubber soles silent as mice up and
down the hall. They never make any noise when they move.
They materialize in different parts of the ward every time a
patient figures to check himself in private or whisper some
secret to another guy. A patient'll be in a corner all by himself, when all of a sudden there's a squeak and frost forms
along his cheek, and he turns in that direction and there's a
cold stone mask floating above him against the wall. He just
sees the black face. No body. The walls are white as the white
suits, polished clean as a refrigerator door, and the black face
and hands seem to float against it like a ghost.

Years of training, and all three black boys tune in closer
and closer with the Big Nurse's frequency. One by one they
are able to disconnect the direct wires and operate on beams.
She never gives orders out loud or leaves written instructions
that might be found by a visiting wife or schoolteacher.
Doesn't need to any more. They are in contact on a high-
voltage wave length of hate, and the black boys are out there
performing her bidding before she even thinks it.

So after the nurse gets her staff, efficiency locks the ward
like a watchman's clock. Everything the guys think and say
and do is all worked out months in advance, based on the
little notes the nurse makes during the day. This is typed and
fed into the machine I hear humming behind the steel door
in the rear of the Nurses' Station. A number of Order Daily

Cards are returned, punched with a pattern of little square holes. At the beginning of each day the properly dated OD card is inserted in a slot in the steel door and the walls hum up: Lights flash on in the dorm at six-thirty: the Acutes up out of bed quick as the black boys can prod them out, get them to work buffing the floor, emptying ash trays, polishing the scratch marks off the wall where one old fellow shorted out a day ago, went down in an awful twist of smoke and smell of burned rubber. The Wheelers swing dead log legs out on the floor and wait like seated statues for somebody to roll chairs in to them. The Vegetables piss the bed, activating an electric shock and buzzer, rolls them off on the tile where the black boys can hose them down and get them in clean greens. . . .

Six-forty-five the shavers buzz and the Acutes line up in alphabetical order at the mirrors, A, B, C, D. . . . The walking Chronics like me walk in when the Acutes are done, then the Wheelers are wheeled in. The three old guys left, a film of yellow mold on the loose hide under their chins, they get shaved in their lounge chairs in the day room, a leather strap across the forehead to keep them from flopping around under the shaver.

Some mornings—Mondays especially—I hide and try to buck the schedule. Other mornings I figure it's cagier to step right into place between A and C in the alphabet and move the route like everybody else, without lifting my feet—powerful magnets in the floor maneuver personnel through the ward like arcade puppets. . . .

Seven o'clock the mess hall opens and the order of line-up reverses: the Wheelers first, then the Walkers, then the Acutes pick up trays, corn flakes, bacon and eggs, toast—and this morning a canned peach on a piece of green, torn lettuce. Some of the Acutes bring trays to the Wheelers. Most Wheelers are just Chronics with bad legs, they feed themselves, but there's these three of them got no action from the neck down whatsoever, not much from the neck up. These are called Vegetables. The black boys push them in after everybody else is sat down, wheel them against a wall, and bring them identical trays of muddy-looking food with little white diet cards attached to the trays. Mechanical Soft, reads the diet cards for these toothless three: eggs, ham, toast, bacon, all chewed thirty-two times apiece by the stainless-steel machine in the kitchen. I see it purse sectioned lips, like a vacuum-cleaner hose, and spurt a clot of chewed-up ham onto a plate with a barnyard sound.

The black boys stoke the sucking pink mouths of the Vegetables a shade too fast for swallowing, and the Mechanical Soft squeezes out down their little knobs of chins onto the greens. The black boys cuss the Vegetables and ream the mouths bigger with a twisting motion of the spoon, like coring a rotten apple: "This ol' fart Blastic, he's comin' to pieces befo' my very eyes. I can't tell no more if I'm feeding him bacon puree or chunks of his own fuckin' tongue." ...

Seven-thirty back to the day room. The Big Nurse looks out through her special glass, always polished till you can't tell it's there, and nods at what she sees, reaches up and tears a sheet off her calendar one day closer to the goal. She pushes a button for things to start. I hear the wharrup of a big sheet of tin being shook someplace. Everybody come to order. Acutes: sit on your side of the day room and wait for cards and Monopoly games to be brought out. Chronics: sit on your side and wait for puzzles from the Red Cross box. Ellis: go to your place at the wall, hands up to receive the nails and pee running down your leg. Pete: wag your head like a puppet. Scanlon: work your knobby hands on the table in front of you, constructing a make-believe bomb to blow up a make-believe world. Harding: begin talking, waving your dove hands in the air, then trap them under your armpits because grown men aren't supposed to wave their pretty hands that way. Sefelt: begin moaning about your teeth hurting and your hair falling out. Everybody: breath in ... and out ... in perfect order; hearts all beating at the rate the OD cards have ordered. Sound of matched cylinders.

Like a cartoon world, where the figures are flat and outlined in black, jerking through some kind of goofy story that might be real funny if it weren't for the cartoon figures being real guys. ...

Seven-forty-five the black boys move down the line of Chronics taping catheters on the ones that will hold still for it. Catheters are second-hand condoms the ends clipped off and rubber-banded to tubes that run down pantlegs to a plastic sack marked DISPOSABLE NOT TO BE RE-USED, which it is my job to wash out at the end of each day. The black boys anchor the condom by taping it to the hairs; old Catheter Chronics are hairless as babies from tape removal. ...

Eight o'clock the walls whirr and hum into full swing. The speaker in the ceiling says, "Medications," using the Big Nurse's voice. We look in the glass case where she sits, but she's nowhere near the microphone; in fact, she's ten feet away from the microphone, tutoring one of the little nurses how to prepare a neat drug tray with pills arranged orderly. The Acutes line up at the glass door, A, B, C, D, then the Chronics, then the Wheelers (the Vegetables get theirs later, mixed in a spoon of applesauce). The guys file by and get a capsule in a paper cup—throw it to the back of the throat and get the cup filled with water by the little nurse and wash the capsule down. On rare occasions some fool might ask what he's being required to swallow.

"Wait just a shake, honey; what are these two little red capsules in here with my vitamin?"

I know him. He's a big, griping Acute, already getting the reputation of being a troublemaker.

"It's just medication, Mr. Taber, good for you. Down it goes, now."

"But I mean what *kind* of medication. Christ, I can see that they're pills—"

"Just swallow it all, shall we, Mr. Taber—just for me?" She takes a quick look at the Big Nurse to see how the little flirting technique she is using is accepted, then looks back at the Acute. He still isn't ready to swallow something he don't know what is, not even just for her.

"Miss, I don't like to create trouble. But I don't like to swallow something without knowing what it is, neither. How do I know this isn't one of those funny pills that makes me something I'm not?"

"Don't get upset, Mr. Taber—"

"Upset? All I want to *know*, for the lova Jesus—"

But the Big Nurse has come up quietly, locked her hand on his arm, paralyzes him all the way to the shoulder. "That's all right, Miss Flinn," she says. "If Mr. Taber chooses to act like a child, he may have to be treated as such. We've tried to be kind and considerate with him. Obviously, that's not the answer. Hostility, hostility, that's the thanks we get. You can go, Mr. Taber, if you don't wish to take your medication orally."

"All I wanted to *know*, for the—"

"You can go."

He goes off, grumbling, when she frees his arm, and spends the morning moping around the latrine, wondering about those capsules. I got away once holding one of those same red capsules under my tongue, played like I'd swallowed it, and crushed it open later in the broom closet. For a tick of time, before it all turned into white dust, I saw it was a miniature electronic element like the ones I helped the Radar Corps work with in the Army, microscopic wires and grids and transistors, this one designed to dissolve on contact with air. . . .

Eight-twenty the cards and puzzles go out. . . .

Eight-twenty-five some Acute mentions he used to watch his sister taking her bath; the three guys at the table with him fall all over each other to see who gets to write it in the log book. . . .

Eight-thirty the ward door opens and two technicians trot in, smelling like grape wine; technicians always move at a fast walk or a trot because they're always leaning so far forward they have to move fast to keep standing. They always lean forward and they always smell like they sterilized their instruments in wine. They pull the lab door to behind them, and I sweep up close and can make out voices over the vicious zzzth-zzzth-zzzth of steel on whetstone.

"What we got already at this ungodly hour of the morning?"

"We got to install an Indwelling Curiosity Cutout in some nosy booger. Hurry-up job, she says, and I'm not even sure we got one of the gizmos in stock."

"We might have to call IBM to rush one out for us; let me check back in Supply—"

"Hey; bring out a bottle of that pure grain while you're back there: it's gettting so I can't install the simplest frigging component but what I need a bracer. Well, what the hell, it's better'n garage work. . . ."

Their voices are forced and too quick on the comeback to be real talk—more like cartoon comedy speech. I sweep away before I'm caught eavesdropping.

The two big black boys catch Taber in the latrine and drag him to the mattress room. He gets one a good kick in the shins. He's yelling bloody murder. I'm surprised how helpless he looks when they hold him, like he was wrapped with bands of black iron.

They push him face down on the mattress. One sits on his head, and the other rips his pants open in back and peels the cloth until Taber's peach-colored rear is framed by the ragged lettuce-green. He's smothering curses into the mattress and the black boy sitting on his head saying, "Tha's right, Mistuh Taber, tha's right. . . . " The nurse comes down the hall, smearing Vaseline on a long needle, pulls the door shut so they're out of sight for a second, then comes right back out, wiping the needle on a shred of Taber's pants. She's left the Vaseline jar in the room. Before the black boy can close the door after her I see the one still sitting on Taber's head, dab-

bing at him with a Kleenex. They're in there a long time before
the door opens up again and they come out, carrying him
across the hall to the lab. His greens are ripped clear off now
and he's wrapped up in a damp sheet. . . .

Nine o'clock young residents wearing leather elbows talk
to Acutes for fifty minutes about what they did when they
were little boys. The Big Nurse is suspicious of the crew-cut
looks of these residents, and that fifty minutes they are on the
ward is a tough time for her. While they are around, the machinery goes to fumbling and she is scowling and making
notes to check the records of these boys for old traffic viola-
tions and the like. . . .

Nine-fifty the residents leave and the machinery hums up
smooth again. The nurse watches the day room from her glass
case; the scene before her takes on that blue-steel clarity
again, that clean orderly movement of a cartoon comedy.

Taber is wheeled out of the lab on a Gurney bed.

"We had to give him another shot when he started coming
up during the spine tap," the technician tells her. "What do
you say we take him right on over to Building One and buzz
him with EST while we're at it—that way not waste the extra
Seconal?"

"I think it is an excellent suggestion. Maybe after that take
him to the electroencephalograph and check his head—we
may find evidence of a need for brain work."

The technicians go trotting off, pushing the man on the
Gurney, like cartoon men—or like puppets, mechanical puppets in one of those Punch and Judy acts where it's supposed
to be funny to see the puppet beat up by the Devil and swallowed headfirst by a smiling alligator. . . .

Ten o'clock the mail comes up. Sometimes you get the torn
envelope. . . .

Ten-thirty Public Relation comes in with a ladies' club following him. He claps his fat hands at the day-room door. "Oh,
hello guys; stiff lip, stiff lip . . . look around, girls; isn't it
clean, so bright? This is Miss Ratched. I chose this ward because it's *her* ward. She's, girls, just like a mother. Not that
I mean age, but you girls understand . . ."

Public Relation's shirt collar is so tight it bloats his face up
when he laughs, and he's laughing most of the time I don't
ever know what at, laughing high and fast like he wishes he
could stop but can't do it. And his face bloated up red and
round as a balloon with a face painted on it. He got no hair
on his face and none on his head to speak of; it looks like he

glued some on once but it kept slipping off and getting in his cuffs and his shirt pocket and down his collar. Maybe that's why he keeps his collar so tight, to keep the little pieces of hair from falling down in there.

Maybe that's why he laughs so much, because he isn't able to keep all the pieces out.

He conducts these tours—serious women in blazer jackets, nodding to him as he points out how much things have improved over the years. He points out the TV, the big leather chairs, the sanitary drinking fountains; then they all go have coffee in the Nurse's Station. Sometimes he'll be by himself and just stand in the middle of the day room and clap his hands (you can *hear* they are wet), clap them two or three times till they stick, then hold them prayerlike together under one of his chins and start spinning. Spin round and around there in the middle of the floor, looking wild and frantic at the TV, the new pictures on the walls, the sanitary drinking fountain. And laughing.

What he sees that's so funny he don't ever let us in on, and the only thing I can see funny is him spinning round and around out there like a rubber toy—if you push him over he's weighted on the bottom and straightaway rocks back upright, goes to spinning again. He never, never looks at the men's faces. . . .

Ten-forty, -forty-five, -fifty, patients shuttle in and out to appointments in ET or OT or PT, or in queer little rooms somewhere where the walls are never the same size and the floors aren't level. The machinery sounds about you reach a steady cruising speed.

The ward hums the way I heard a cotton mill hum once when the football team played a high school in California. After a good season one year the boosters in the town were so proud and carried away that they paid to fly us to California to play a championship high-school team down there. When we flew into the town we had to go visit some local industry. Our coach was one for convincing folks that athletics was educational because of the learning afforded by travel, and every trip we took he herded the team around to creameries and beet farms and canneries before the game. In California it was the cotton mill. When we went in the mill most of the team took a look and left to go sit in the bus over stud games on suitcases, but I stayed inside over in a corner out of the way of the Negro girls running up and down the aisles of machines. The mill put me in a kind of dream, all the humming and clicking and rattling of people and machinery, jerking around in a pattern. That's why I stayed when the others left, that, and because it reminded me somehow of the men in the tribe who'd left the village in the last days to do work on the gravel crusher for the dam. The frenzied pattern, the faces hypnotized by routine . . . I wanted to go out in the bus with the team, but I couldn't.

It was morning in early winter and I still had on the jacket they'd given us when we took the championship—a red and green jacket with leather sleeves and a football-shaped emblem sewn on the back telling what we'd won—and it was making a lot of the Negro girls stare. I took it off, but they kept staring. I was a whole lot bigger in those days.

One of the girls left her machine and looked back and forth up the aisles to see if the foreman was around, then came over to where I was standing. She asked if we was going to play the high school that night and she told me she had a brother played tailback for them. We talked a piece about football and the like and I noticed how her face looked blurred, like there was a mist between me and her. It was the cotton fluff sifting from the air.

I told her about the fluff. She rolled her eyes and ducked her mouth to laugh in her fist when I told her how it was like looking at her face out on a misty morning duck-hunting. And she said, "Now what in the everlovin' world would you want with me out alone in a duck blind?" I told her she could take care of my gun, and the girls all over the mill went to giggling in their fists. I laughed a little myself, seeing how clever I'd been. We were still talking and laughing when she grabbed both my wrists and dug in. The features of her face snapped into brilliant focus; I saw she was terrified of something.

"Do," she said to me in a whisper, "do take me, big boy. Outa this here mill, outa this town, outa this life. Take me to some ol' duck blind someplace. Someplace *else*. Huh, big boy, huh?"

Her dark, pretty face glittered there in front of me. I stood with my mouth open, trying to think of some way to answer her. We were locked together this way for maybe a couple of seconds; then the sound of the mill jumped a hitch, and something commenced to draw her back away from me. A string somewhere I didn't see hooked on that flowered red skirt and was tugging her back. Her fingernails peeled down my hands and as soon as she broke contact with me her face switched out of focus again, became soft and runny like melting chocolate behind that blowing fog of cotton. She laughed and spun around and gave me a look of her yellow leg when the skirt billowed out. She threw me a wink over her shoulder as she ran back to her machine where a pile of fiber was spilling off the table to the floor; she grabbed it up and ran featherfooted down the aisle of machines to dump the fiber in a hopper; then she was out of sight around the corner.

All those spindles reeling and wheeling and shuttles jumping around and bobbins wringing the air with string, whitewashed walls and steel-gray machines and girls in flowered skirts skipping back and forth, and the whole thing webbed with flowing white lines stringing the factory together—it all stuck with me and every once in a while something on the ward calls it to mind.

Yes. This is what I know. The ward is a factory for the Combine. It's for fixing up mistakes made in the neighborhoods and in the schools and in the churches, the hospital is. When a completed product goes back out into society, all fixed up good as new, *better* than new sometimes, it brings joy to the Big Nurse's heart; something that came in all twisted different is now a functioning, adjusted component, a credit to the whole outfit and a marvel to behold. Watch him sliding across the land with a welded grin, fitting into some nice little neighborhood where they're just now digging trenches along the street to lay pipes for city water. He's happy with it. He's adjusted to surroundings finally. . . .

"Why, I've never seen anything to beat the change in Maxwell Taber since he's got back from that hospital; a little black and blue around the eyes, a little weight lost, and, you know what? he's a *new man*. Gad, modern American science . . ."

And the light is on in his basement window way past midnight every night as the Delayed Reaction Elements the technicians installed lend nimble skills to his fingers as he bends over the doped figure of his wife, his two little girls just four and six, the neighbor he goes bowling with Mondays; he adjusts them like he was adjusted. This is the way they spread it.

When he finally runs down after a pre-set number of years, the town loves him dearly and the paper prints his picture helping the Boy Scouts last year on Graveyard Cleaning Day, and his wife gets a letter from the principal of the high school how Maxwell Wilson Taber was an inspirational figure to the youth of our fine community.

Even the embalmers, usually a pair of penny-pinching tightwads, are swayed. "Yeah, look at him there: old Max Taber, he was a good sort. What do you say we use that expensive thirty-weight at no extra charge to his wife. No, what the dickens, let's make it on the house."

A successful Dismissal like this is a product brings joy to the Big Nurse's heart and speaks good of her craft and the whole industry in general. Everybody's happy with a Dismissal.

But an Admission is a different story. Even the best-behaved Admission is bound to need some work to swing into routine, and, also, you never can tell when just that *certain* one might come in who's free enough to foul things up right and left, really make a hell of a mess and constitute a threat to the whole smoothness of the outfit. And, like I explain, the Big Nurse gets real put out if anything keeps her outfit from running smooth.

*B*efore noontime they're at the fog machine again but they haven't got it turned up full; it's not so thick but what I can see if I strain real hard. One of these days I'll quit straining and let myself go completely, lose myself in the fog the way some of the other Chronics have, but for the time being I'm interested in this new man—I want to see how he takes to the Group Meeting coming up.

Ten minutes to one the fog dissolves completely and the black boys are telling Acutes to clear the floor for the meeting. All the tables are carried out of the day room to the tub room across the hall—leaves the floor, McMurphy says, like we was aiming to have us a little dance.

The Big Nurse watches all this through her window. She hasn't moved from her spot in front of that one window for three solid hours, not even for lunch. The day-room floor gets cleared of tables, and at one o'clock the doctor comes out of his office down the hall, nods once at the nurse as he goes past where she's watching out her window, and sits in his chair just to the left of the door. The patients sit down when he does; then the little nurses and the residents straggle in. When everybody's down, the Big Nurse gets up from behind her window and goes back to the rear of the Nurses' Station to that steel panel with dials and buttons on it, sets some kind of automatic pilot to run things while she's away, and comes out into the day room, carrying the log book and a basketful of notes. Her uniform, even after she's been here half a day, is still starched so stiff it don't exactly bend any place; it cracks sharp at the joints with a sound like a frozen canvas being folded.

She sits just to the right of the door.

Soon as she's sat down, Old Pete Bancini sways to his feet and starts in wagging his head and wheezing. "I'm tired. Whew. O Lord. Oh, I'm *awful* tired . . ." the way he always does whenever there's a new man on the ward who might listen to him.

The Big Nurse doesn't look over at Pete. She's going through the papers in her basket. "Somebody go sit beside Mr. Bancini," she says. "Quiet him down so we can start the meeting."

Billy Bibbit goes. Pete has turned facing McMurphy and is lolling his head from side to side like a signal light at a railroad crossing. He worked on the railroad thirty years; now he's wore clean out but still's functioning on the memory.

"I'm ti-i-uhd," he says, wagging his face at McMurphy.

"Take it easy, Pete," Billy says, lays a freckled hand on Pete's knee.

". . . Awful tired . . ."

"I know, Pete"—pats the skinny knee, and Pete pulls back his face, realizes nobody is going to heed his complaint today.

The nurse takes off her wrist watch and looks at the ward clock and winds the watch and sets it face toward her in the basket. She takes a folder from the basket.

"Now. Shall we get into the meeting?"

She looks around to see if anybody else is about to interrupt her, smiling steady as her head turns in her collar. The guys won't meet her look; they're all looking for hangnails. Except McMurphy. He's got himself an armchair in the corner, sits in it like he's claimed it for good, and he's watching her every move. He's still got his cap on, jammed tight down on his red head like he's a motorcycle racer. A deck of cards in his lap opens for a one-handed cut, then clacks shut with a sound blown up loud by the silence. The nurse's swinging eyes hang on him for a second. She's been watching him play poker all morning and though she hasn't seen any money pass hands she suspects he's not exactly the type that is going to be happy with the ward rule of gambling for matches only. The deck whispers open and clacks shut again and then disappears somewhere in one of those big palms.

The nurse looks at her watch again and pulls a slip of paper out of the folder she's holding, looks at it, and returns it to the folder. She puts the folder down and picks up the log book. Ellis coughs from his place on the wall; she waits until he stops.

"Now. At the close of Friday's meeting . . . we were discussing Mr. Harding's problem . . . concerning his young wife. He had stated that his wife was extremely well endowed in the bosom and that this made him uneasy because she drew stares from men on the street." She starts opening to places in the log book; little slips of paper stick out of the top of the book to mark the pages. "According to the notes listed by various patients in the log, Mr. Harding has been heard to say that she 'damn well gives the bastards reason to stare.' He has also been heard to say that he may give *her* reason to seek further sexual attention. He has been heard to say, 'My dear sweet but illiterate wife thinks any word or gesture that does not smack of brickyard brawn and brutality is a word or gesture of weak dandyism.' "

She continues reading silently from the book for a while, then closes it.

"He has also stated that his wife's ample bosom at times gives him a feeling of inferiority. So. Does anyone care to touch upon this subject further?"

Harding shuts his eyes, and nobody else says anything. McMurphy looks around at the other guys, waiting to see if anybody is going to answer the nurse, then holds his hand up and snaps his fingers, like a school kid in class; the nurse nods at him.

"Mr.—ah—McMurry?"

"Touch upon what?"

"What? Touch—"

"You ask, I believe, 'Does anyone care to touch upon—' "

"Touch upon the—subject, Mr. McMurry, the subject of Mr. Harding's problem with his wife."

"Oh. I thought you mean touch upon her—something else."

"Now what could you—"

But she stops. She was almost flustered for a second there. Some of the Acutes hide grins, and McMurphy takes a huge stretch, yawns, winks at Harding. Then the nurse, calm as anything, puts the log book back in the basket and takes out another folder and opens it and starts reading.

"McMurry, Randle Patrick. Committed by the state from the Pendleton Farm for Correction. For diagnosis and possible treatment. Thirty-five years old. Never married. Distinguished Service Cross in Korea, for leading an escape from a Communist prison camp. A dishonorable discharge, afterward, for insubordination. Followed by a history of street brawls and barroom fights and a series of arrests for Drunkenness, Assault and Battery, Disturbing the Peace, re*peated* gambling, and one arrest—for Rape."

"Rape?" The doctor perks up.

"Statutory, with a girl of—"

"Whoa. Couldn't make that stick," McMurphy says to the doctor. "Girl wouldn't testify."

"With a child of fifteen."

"Said she was *seventeen*, Doc, and she was *plenty* willin'."

"A court doctor's examination of the child proved entry, re*peated* entry, the record states—"

"So willin', in fact, I took to sewing my pants shut."

"The child refused to testify in spite of the doctor's findings.

part 1

*T*hey're out there.
Black boys in white suits up before me
to commit sex acts in the hall and get it mopped up before I
can catch them.

They're mopping when I come out the dorm, all three of
them sulky and hating everything, the time of day, the place
they're at here, the people they got to work around. When
they hate like this, better if they don't see me. I creep along
the wall quiet as dust in my canvas shoes, but they got special sensitive equipment detects my fear and they all look up,
all three at once, eyes glittering out of the black faces like
the hard glitter of radio tubes out of the back of an old radio.

"Here's the Chief. The *soo*-pah Chief, fellas. Ol' Chief
Broom. Here you go, Chief Broom. . . ."

Stick a mop in my hand and motion to the spot they aim
for me to clean today, and I go. One swats the backs of my
legs with a broom handle to hurry me past.

"Haw, you look at 'im shag it? Big enough to eat apples off
my head an' he mine me like a baby."

9

They laugh and then I hear them mumbling behind me, heads close together. Hum of black machinery, humming hate and death and other hospital secrets. They don't bother not talking out loud about their hate secrets when I'm nearby because they think I'm deaf and dumb. Everybody thinks so. I'm cagey enough to fool them that much. If my being half Indian ever helped me in any way in this dirty life, it helped me being cagey, helped me all these years.

I'm mopping near the ward door when a key hits it from the other side and I know it's the Big Nurse by the way the lockworks cleave to the key, soft and swift and familiar she been around locks so long. She slides through the door with a gust of cold and locks the door behind her and I see her fingers trail across the polished steel—tip of each finger the same color as her lips. Funny orange. Like the tip of a soldering iron. Color so hot or so cold if she touches you with it you can't tell which.

She's carrying her woven wicker bag like the ones the Umpqua tribe sells out along the hot August highway, a bag shape of a tool box with a hemp handle. She's had it all the years I been here. It's a loose weave and I can see inside it; there's no compact or lipstick or woman stuff, she's got that bag full of a thousand parts she aims to use in her duties today—wheels and gears, cogs polished to a hard glitter, tiny pills that gleam like porcelain, needles, forceps, watchmakers pliers, rolls of copper wire . . .

She dips a nod at me as she goes past. I let the mop push me back to the wall and smile and try to foul her equipment up as much as possible by not letting her see my eyes—they can't tell so much about you if you got your eyes closed.

In my dark I hear her rubber heels hit the tile and the stuff in her wicker bag clash with the jar of her walking as she passes me in the hall. She walks stiff. When I open my eyes she's down the hall about to turn into the glass Nurses' Station where she'll spend the day sitting at her desk and looking out her window and making notes on what goes on out in front of her in the day room during the next eight hours. Her face looks pleased and peaceful with the thought.

Then . . . she sights those black boys. They're still down there together, mumbling to one another. They didn't hear her come on the ward. They sense she's glaring down at them now, but it's too late. They should of knew better'n to group up and mumble together when she was due on the ward. Their faces bob apart, confused. She goes into a crouch and advances on where they're trapped in a huddle at the end of the corridor

There seemed to be intimidation. Defendant left town shortly after the trial."

"Hoo boy, I *had* to leave. Doc, let me tell you"—he leans forward with an elbow on a knee, lowering his voice to the doctor across the room—"that little hustler would of actually burnt me to a frazzle by the time she reached legal sixteen. She got to where she was tripping me and beating me to the floor."

The nurse closes up the folder and passes it across the doorway to the doctor. "Our new Admission, Doctor Spivey," just like she's got a man folded up inside that yellow paper and can pass him on to be looked over. "I thought I might brief you on his record later today, but as he seems to insist on asserting himself in the Group Meeting, we might as well dispense with him now."

The doctor fishes his glasses from his coat pocket by pulling on the string, works them on his nose in front of his eyes. They're tipped a little to the right, but he leans his head to the left and brings them level. He's smiling a little as he turns through the folder, just as tickled by this new man's brassy way of talking right up as the rest of us, but, just like the rest of us, he's careful not to let himself come right out and laugh. The doctor closes the folder when he gets to the end, and puts his glasses back in his pocket. He looks to where McMurphy is still leaned out at him from across the day room.

"You've—it seems—no other psychiatric history, Mr. Mc-Murry?"

"McMurphy, Doc."

"Oh? But I thought—the nurse was saying—"

He opens the folder again, fishes out those glasses, looks the record over for another minute before he closes it, and puts his glasses back in his pocket. "Yes. McMurphy. That is correct. I beg your pardon."

"It's okay, Doc. It was the lady there that started it, made the mistake. I've known some people inclined to do that. I had this uncle whose name was Hallahan, and he went with a woman once who kept acting like she couldn't remember his name right and calling him Hooligan just to get his goat. It went on for months before he stopped her. Stopped her good, too."

"Oh? How did he stop her?" the doctor asks.

McMurphy grins and rubs his nose with his thumb. "Ah-ah, now, I can't be tellin' that. I keep Unk Hallahan's method a strict secret, you see, in case I need to use it myself someday."

He says it right at the nurse. She smiles right back at him, and he looks over at the doctor. "Now; what was you asking about my record, Doc?"

"Yes. I was wondering if you've any previous psychiatric history. Any analysis, any time spent in any other institution?"

"Well, counting state *and* county coolers—"

"*Mental* institutions."

"Ah. No, if that's the case. This is my first trip. But I *am* crazy, Doc. I swear I am. Well here—let me show you here. I believe that other doctor at the work farm . . ."

He gets up, slips the deck of cards in the pocket of his jacket, and comes across the room to lean over the doctor's shoulder and thumb through the folder on his lap. "Believe he wrote something, back at the back here somewhere . . ."

"Yes? I missed that. Just a moment." The doctor fishes his glasses out again and puts them on and looks to where McMurphy is pointing.

"Right here, Doc. The nurse left this part out while she was *summarizing* my record. Where it says, 'Mr. McMurphy has evidenced re*peated*'—I just want to make sure I'm understood completely, Doc—'*repeated* outbreaks of passion that suggest the possible diagnosis of psychopath.' He told me that 'psychopath' means I fight and fuh—pardon me, ladies—means I am he put it *over*zealous in my sexual relations. Doctor, is that real serious?"

He asks it with such a little-boy look of worry and concern all over his broad, tough face that the doctor can't help bending his head to hide another little snicker in his collar, and his glasses fall from his nose dead center back in his pocket. All of the Acutes are smiling too, now, and even some of the Chronics.

"I mean that overzealousness, Doc, have you ever been troubled by it?"

The doctor wipes his eyes. "No, Mr. McMurphy, I'll admit I haven't. I am interested, however, that the doctor at the work farm added this statement: 'Don't overlook the possibility that this man might be feigning psychosis to escape the drudgery of the work farm.'" He looks up at McMurphy. "And what about that, Mr. McMurphy?"

"Doctor"—he stands up to his full height, wrinkles his forehead, and holds out both arms, open and honest to all the wide world—"do I look like a sane man?"

The doctor is working so hard to keep from giggling again he can't answer. McMurphy pivots away from the doctor and asks the same thing of the Big Nurse: "*Do* I?" Instead of answering she stands up and takes the manila folder away from the doctor and puts it back in the basket under her watch. She sits back down.

"Perhaps, Doctor, you should advise Mr. McMurry on the protocol of these Group Meetings."

"Ma'am," McMurphy says, "have I told you about my uncle Hallahan and the woman who used to screw up his name?"

She looks at him for a long time without her smile. She has the ability to turn her smile into whatever expression she wants to use on somebody, but the look she turns it into is no different, just a calculated and mechanical expression to serve her purpose. Finally she says, "I beg your pardon. Mack-Murph-y." She turns back to the doctor. "Now, Doctor, if you would explain . . ."

The doctor folds his hands and leans back. "Yes. I suppose what I should do is explain the complete *theory* of our Therapeutic Community, while we're at it. Though I usually save it until later. Yes. A good idea, Miss Ratched, a fine idea."

"Certainly the theory too, doctor, but what I had in mind was the rule that the patients remain seated during the course of the meeting."

"Yes. Of course. Then I will explain the theory. Mr. Mc-Murphy, one of the first things is that the patients remain seated during the course of the meeting. It's the only way, you see, for us to maintain order."

"Sure, Doctor. I just got up to show you that thing in my record book."

He goes over to his chair, gives another big stretch and yawn, sits down, and moves around for a while like a dog coming to rest. When he's comfortable, he looks over at the doctor, waiting.

"As to the *theory* . . ." The doctor takes a deep, happy breath.

"Ffffuck da wife," Ruckly says. McMurphy hides his mouth behind the back of his hand and calls across the ward to Ruckly in a scratchy whisper, "Whose wife?" and Martini's head snaps up, eyes wide and staring. "Yeah," he says, "whose wife? Oh. Her? Yeah, I see her. *Yeah.*"

"I'd give a lot to have that man's eyes," McMurphy says of Martini and then doesn't say anything all the rest of the meeting. Just sits and watches and doesn't miss a thing that happens or a word that's said. The doctor talks about his theory until the Big Nurse finally decides he's used up time enough and asks him to hush so they can get on to Harding, and they talk the rest of the meeting about that.

McMurphy sits forward in his chair a couple of times during

the meeting like he might have something to say, but he decides better and leans back. There's a puzzled expression coming over his face. Something strange is going on here, he's finding out. He can't quite put his finger on it. Like the way nobody will laugh. Now he thought sure there would be a laugh when he asked Ruckly, "Whose wife?" but there wasn't even a sign of one. The air is pressed in by the walls, too tight for laughing. There's something strange about a place where the men won't let themselves loose and laugh, something strange about the way they all knuckle under to that smiling flour-faced old mother there with the too-red lipstick and the too-big boobs. And he thinks he'll just wait a while to see what the story is in this new place before he makes any kind of play. That's a good rule for a smart gambler; look the game over awhile before you draw yourself a hand.

I've heard that theory of the Therapeutic Community enough times to repeat it forwards and backwards—how a guy has to learn to get along in a group before he'll be able to function in a normal society; how the group can help the guy by showing him where he's out of place; how society is what decides who's sane and who isn't, so you got to measure up. All that stuff. Every time we get a new patient on the ward the doctor goes into the theory with both feet; it's pretty near the only time he takes things over and runs the meeting. He tells how the goal of the Therapeutic Community is a democratic ward, run completely by the patients and their votes, working toward making worth-while citizens to turn back Outside onto the street. Any little gripe, any grievance, anything you want changed, he says, should be brought up before the group and discussed instead of letting it fester inside of you. Also you should feel at ease in your surroundings to the extent you can freely discuss emotional problems in front of patients and staff. Talk, he says, discuss, confess. And if you hear a friend say something during the course of your everyday conversation, then list it in the log book for the staff to see. It's not, as the movies call it, "squealing," it's helping your fellow. Bring these old sins into the open where they can be washed by the sight of all. And participate in Group Discussion. Help yourself and your friends probe into the secrets of the subconscious. There should be no need for secrets among friends.

Our intention, he usually ends by saying, is to make this as much like your own democratic, free neighborhoods as possible—a little world Inside that is a made-to-scale prototype of the big world Outside that you will one day be taking your place in again.

He's maybe got more to say, but about this point the Big Nurse usually hushes him, and in the lull old Pete stands up and wigwags that battered copper-pot head and tells everybody how tired he is, and the nurse tells somebody to go hush him up too, so the meeting can continue, and Pete is generally hushed and the meeting goes on.

Once, just one time that I can remember, four or five years back, did it go any different. The doctor had finished his spiel, and the nurse had opened right up with, "Now. Who will start? Let out those old secrets." And she'd put all the Acutes in a trance by sitting there in silence for twenty minutes after the question, quiet as an electric alarm about to go off, waiting for somebody to start telling something about themselves. Her eyes swept back and forth over them as steady as a turning beacon. The day room was clamped silent for twenty long minutes, with all of the patients stunned where they sat. When twenty minutes had passed, she looked at her watch and said, "Am I to take it that there's not a man among you that has committed some act that he has never admitted?" She reached in the basket for the log book. "Must we go over past history?"

That triggered something, some acoustic device in the walls, rigged to turn on at just the sound of those words coming from her mouth. The Acutes stiffened. Their mouths opened in unison. Her sweeping eyes stopped on the first man along the wall.

His mouth worked. "I robbed a cash register in a service station."

She moved to thte next man.

"I tried to take my little sister to bed."

Her eyes clicked to the next man; each one jumped like a shooting-gallery target.

"I—one time—wanted to take my brother to bed."

"I killed my cat when I was six. Oh, God forgive me, I stoned her to death and said my neighbor did it."

"I lied about trying. I did take my sister!"

"So did I! So did I!"

"And me! And *me!*"

It was better than she'd dreamed. They were all shouting to outdo one another, going further and further, no way of stopping, telling things that wouldn't ever let them look one another in the eye again. The nurse nodding at each confession and saying Yes, yes, yes.

Then old Pete was on his feet. "I'm *tired!*" was what he

shouted, a strong, angry copper tone to his voice that no one had ever heard before.

Everyone hushed. They were somehow ashamed. It was as if he had suddenly said something that was real and true and important and it had put all their childish hollering to shame. The Big Nurse was furious. She swiveled and glared at him, the smile dripping over her chin; she'd just had it going so good.

"Somebody see to poor Mr. Bancini," she said.

Two or three got up. They tried to soothe him, pat him on his shoulder. But Pete wasn't being hushed. "Tired! Tired!" he kept on.

Finally the nurse sent one of the black boys to take him out of the day room by force. She forgot that the black boys didn't hold any control over people like Pete.

Pete's been a Chronic all his life. Even though he didn't come into the hospital till he was better than fifty, he'd always been a Chronic. His head has two big dents, one on each side, where the doctor who was with his mother at borning time pinched his skull trying to pull him out. Pete had looked out first and seen all the delivery-room machinery waiting for him and somehow realized what he was being born into, and had grabbed on to everything handy in there to try to stave off being born. The doctor reached in and got him by the head with a set of dulled ice tongs and jerked him loose and figured everything was all right. But Pete's head was still too new, and soft as clay, and when it set, those two dents left by the tongs stayed. And this made him simple to where it took all his straining effort and concentration and will power just to do the tasks that came easy to a kid of six.

But one good thing—being simple like that put him out of the clutch of the Combine. They weren't able to mold him into a slot. So they let him get a simple job on the railroad, where all he had to do was sit in a little clapboard house way out in the sticks on a lonely switch and wave a red lantern at the trains if the switch was one way, and a green one if it was the other, and a yellow one if there was a train someplace up ahead. And he did it, with main force and a gutpower they couldn't mash out of his head, out by himself on that switch. And he never had any controls installed.

That's why the black boy didn't have any say over him. But the black boy didn't think of that right off any more than the nurse did when she ordered Pete removed from the day room. The black boy walked right up and gave Pete's arm a jerk toward the door, just like you'd jerk the reins on a plow horse to turn him.

"Tha's right, Pete. Less go to the dorm. You disturbin' ever'-body."

Pete shook his arm loose. "I'm *tired*," he warned.

"C'mon, old man, you makin' a fuss. Less us go to bed and be still like a good boy."

"Tired . . ."

"I said you goin' to the dorm, old man!"

The black boy jerked at his arm again, and Pete stopped wigwagging his head. He stood up straight and steady, and his eyes snapped clear. Usually Pete's eyes are half shut and all murked up, like there's milk in them, but this time they came clear as blue neon. And the hand on that arm the black boy was holding commenced to swell up. The staff and most of the rest of the patients were talking among themselves, not paying any attention to this old guy and his old song about being tired, figuring he'd be quieted down as usual and the meeting would go on. They didn't see the hand on the end of that arm pumping bigger and bigger as he clenched and un-clenched it. I was the only one saw it. I saw it swell and clench shut, flow in front of my eyes, become smooth—hard. A big rusty iron ball at the end of a chain. I stared at it and waited, while the black boy gave Pete's arm another jerk toward the dorm.

"Ol' man, I say you got—"

He saw the hand. He tried to edge back away from it, saying, "You a good boy, Peter," but he was a shade too late. Pete had that big iron ball swinging all the way from his knees. The black boy whammed flat against the wall and stuck, then slid down to the floor like the wall there was greased. I heard tubes pop and short all over inside that wall, and the plaster cracked just the shape of how he hit.

The other two—the least one and the other big one—stood stunned. The nurse snapped her fingers, and they sprang into motion. Instant movement, sliding across the floor. The little one beside the other like an image in a reducing mirror. They were almost to Pete when it suddenly struck them what the other boy should of known, that Pete wasn't wired under con-trol like the rest of us, that he wasn't about to mind just be-cause they gave him an order or gave his arm a jerk. If they were to take him they'd have to take him like you take a wild bear or bull, and with one of their number out cold against the baseboards, the other two black boys didn't care for the odds.

This thought got them both at once and they froze, the big one and his tiny image, in exactly the same position, left foot forward, right hand out, halfway between Pete and the Big Nurse. That iron ball swinging in front of them and that snow-white anger behind them, they shook and smoked and I could hear gears grinding. I could see them twitch with confusion, like machines throttled full ahead and with the brake on.

Pete stood there in the midlde of the floor, swinging that ball back and forth at his side, all leaned over to its weight. Everybody was watching him now. He looked from the big black boy to the little one, and when he saw they weren't about to come any closer he turned to the patients.

"You see—it's a lotta baloney," he told them, "it's all a lotta baloney."

The Big Nurse had slid from her chair and was working toward her wicker bag leaning at the door. "Yes, yes, Mr. Bancini," she crooned, "now if you'll just be calm—"

"That's all it is, nothin' but a lotta baloney." His voice lost its copper strength and became strained and urgent like he didn't have much time to finish what he had to say. "Ya see, I can't help it, can't—don't ya see. I was born dead. Not you. You wasn't born dead. Ahhhh, it's been hard . . ."

He started to cry. He couldn't make the words come out right anymore; he opened and closed his mouth to talk but he couldn't sort the words into sentences any more. He shook his head to clear it and blinked at the Acutes:

"Ahhhh, I . . . tell . . . ya . . . I tell *you*."

He began slumping over again, and his iron ball shrank back to a hand. He held it cupped out in front of him like he was offering something to the patients.

"I can't help it. I was born a miscarriage. I had so many insults I died. I was born dead. I can't help it. I'm tired. I'm give out trying. You got chances. I had so many insults I was born dead. You got it easy. I was born dead an' life was hard. I'm tired. I'm tired out talking and standing up. I been dead fifty-five *years*."

The Big Nurse got him clear across the room, right through his greens. She jumped back without gettng the needle pulled out after the shot and it hung there from his pants like a little tail of glass and steel, old Pete slumping farther and farther forward, not from the shot but from the effort; the last couple of minutes had worn him out finally and completely, once and for all—you could just look at him and tell he was finished.

So there wasn't really any need for the shot; his head had already commenced to wag back and forth and his eyes were

murky. By the time the nurse eased back in to get the needle
he was bent so far forward he was crying directly on the floor
without wetting his face, tears spotting a wide area as he
swung his head back and forth, spatting, spatting, in an even
pattern on the day-room floor, like he was sowing them.
"Ahhhhh," he said. He didn't flinch when she jerked the needle
out.

He had come to life for maybe a minute to try to tell us
something, something none of us cared to listen to or tried to
understand, and the effort had drained him dry. That shot in
his hip was as wasted as if she'd squirted it in a dead man—
no heart to pump it, no vein to carry it up to his head, no brain
up there for it to mortify with its poison. She'd just as well
shot it in a dried-out old cadaver.

"I'm . . . tired . . ."

"Now. I think if you two boys are *brave* enough, Mr.
Bancini will go to bed like a good fellow."

". . . awful tired."

"And Aide Williams is coming around, Doctor Spivey. See
to him, won't you. Here. His watch is broken and he's cut
his arm."

Pete never tried anything like that again, and he never will.
Now, when he starts acting up during a meeting and they
try to hush him, he always hushes. He'll still get up from time
to time and wag his head and let us know how tired he is, but
it's not a complaint or excuse or warning any more—he's finished with that; it's like an old clock that won't tell time but
won't stop neither, with the hands bent out of shape and the
face bare of numbers and the alarm bell rusted silent, an old,
worthless clock that just keeps ticking and cuckooing without
meaning nothing.

The group is still tearing into poor Harding when two o'clock
rolls around.

At two o'clock the doctor begins to squirm around in his
chair. The meetings are uncomfortable for the doctor unless
he's talking about his theory; he'd rather spend his time down
in his office, drawing on graphs. He squirms around and finally
clears his throat, and the nurse looks at her watch and tells
us to bring the tables back in from the tub room and we'll
resume this discussion again at one tomorrow. The Acutes click
out of their trance, look for an instant in Harding's direction.
Their faces burn with a shame like they have just woke
up to the fact they been played for suckers again. Some of
them go to the tub room across the hall to get the tables, some

wander over to the magazine racks and show a lot of interest in the old *McCall's* magazines, but what they're all really doing is avoiding Harding. They've been maneuvered again into grilling one of their friends like he was a criminal and they were all prosecutors and judge and jury. For forty-five minutes they been chopping a man to pieces, almost as if they enjoyed it, shooting questions at him: What's he *think* is the matter with him that he can't please the little lady; why's he *insist* she has never had anything to do with another man; how's he expect to get well if he doesn't answer *honestly?*— questions and insinuations till now they feel bad about it and they don't want to be made more uncomfortable by being near him.

McMurphy's eyes follow all of this. He doesn't get out of his chair. He looks puzzled again. He sits in his chair for a while, watching the Acutes, scuffing that deck of cards up and down the red stubble on his chin, then finally stands up from his arm chair, yawns and stretches and scratches his belly button with a corner of a card, then puts the deck in his pocket and walks over to where Harding is off by himself, sweated to his chair.

McMurphy looks down at Harding a minute, then laps his big hand over the back of a nearby wooden chair, swings it around so the back is facing Harding, and straddles it like he'd straddle a tiny horse. Harding hasn't noticed a thing. McMurphy slaps his pockets till he finds his cigarettes, and takes one out and lights it; he holds it out in front of him and frowns at the tip, licks his thumb and finger, and arranges the fire to suit him.

Each man seems unaware of the other. I can't even tell if Harding's noticed McMurphy at all. Harding's got his thin shoulders folded nearly together around himself, like green wings, and he's sitting very straight near the edge of his chair, with his hands trapped between his knees. He's staring straight ahead, humming to himself, trying to look calm—but he's chewing at his cheeks, and this gives him a funny skull grin, not calm at all.

McMurphy puts his cigarette back between his teeth and folds his hands over the wooden chair back and leans his chin on them, squinting one eye against the smoke. He looks at Harding with his other eye a while, then starts talking with that cigarette wagging up and down in his lips.

"Well say, buddy, is this the way these leetle meetings usually go?"

"Usually go?" Harding's humming stops. He's not chewing

his cheeks any more but he still stares ahead, past McMurphy's shoulder.

"Is this the usual *pro*-cedure for these Group Ther'py shindigs? Bunch of chickens at a peckin' party?"

Harding's head turns with a jerk and his eyes find McMurphy, like it's the first time he knows that anybody's sitting in front of him. His face creases in the middle when he bites his cheeks again, and this makes it look like he's grinning. He pulls his shoulders back and scoots to the back of the chair and tries to look relaxed.

"A 'pecking party'? I fear your quaint down-home speech is wasted on me, my friend. I have not the slightest inclination what you're talking about."

"Why then, I'll just explain it to you." McMurphy raises his voice; though he doesn't look at the other Acutes listening behind him, it's them he's talking to. "The flock gets sight of a spot of blood on some chicken and they all go to *peckin'* at it, see, till they rip the chicken to shreds, blood and bones and feathers. But usually a couple of the *flock* gets spotted in the fracas, then it's their turn. And a few more gets spots and gets pecked to death, and more and more. Oh, a peckin' party can wipe out the whole flock in a matter of a few hours, buddy, I seen it. A mighty awesome sight. The only way to prevent it—with chickens—is to clip blinders on them. So's they can't see."

Harding laces his long fingers around a knee and draws the knee toward him, leaning back in the chair. "A pecking party. That certainly is a pleasant analogy, my friend."

"And that's just exactly what that meeting I just set through reminded me of, buddy, if you want to know the dirty truth. It reminded me of a flock of dirty chickens."

"So that makes me the chicken with the spot of blood, friend?"

"That's right, buddy."

They're still grinning at each other, but their voices have dropped so low and taut I have to sweep over closer to them with my broom to hear. The other Acutes are moving up closer too.

"And you want to know somethin' else, buddy? You want to know who pecks that first peck?"

Harding waits for him to go on.

"It's that old nurse, that's who."

There's a whine of fear over the silence. I hear the machinery in the walls catch and go on. Harding is having a tough time holding his hands still, but he keeps trying to act calm.

"So," he says, "it's as simple as that, as stupidly simple as that. You're on our ward six hours and have already simplified all the work of Freud, Jung, and Maxwell Jones and summed it up in one analogy: it's a 'peckin' party.' "

"I'm not talking about Fred Yoong and Maxwell Jones, buddy, I'm just talking about that crummy meeting and what that nurse and those other bastards did to you. Did in spades."

"*Did* to me?"

"That's right, *did*. Did you every chance they got. Did you coming and did you going. You must of done something to make a passle of enemies here in this place, buddy, because it seems there's sure a passle got it in for you."

"Why, this is incredible. You completely disregard, completely overlook and disregard the fact that what the fellows were doing today was for my own benefit? That any question or discussion raised by Miss Ratched or the rest of the staff is done solely for therapeutic reasons? You must not have heard a word of Doctor Spivey's theory of the Therapeutic Community, or not have had the education to comprehend it if you did. I'm disappointed in you, my friend, oh, very disappointed. I had judged from our encounter this morning that you were more intelligent—an illiterate clod, perhaps, certainly a backwoods braggart with no more sensitivity than a goose, but basically intelligent nevertheless. But, observant and insightful though I usually am, I still make mistakes."

"The hell with you, buddy."

"Oh, yes; I forgot to add that I noticed your primitive brutality also this morning. Psychopath with definite sadistic tendencies, probably motivated by an unreasoning egomania. Yes. As you see, all these natural talents certainly qualify you as a competent therapist and render you quite capable of criticizing Miss Ratched's meeting procedure, in spite of the fact that she is a highly regarded psychiatric nurse with twenty years in the field. Yes, with your talent, my friend, you could work subconscious miracles, soothe the aching id and heal the wounded superego. You could probably bring about a cure for the whole ward, Vegetables and all, in six short months, ladies and gentlemen or your money back."

Instead of rising to the argument, McMurphy just keeps on looking at Harding, finally asks in a level voice, "And you really think this crap that went on in the meeting today is bringing about some kinda cure, doing some kinda good?"

"What other reason would we have for submitting ourselves to it, my friend? The staff desires our cure as much as we do. They aren't monsters. Miss Ratched may be a strict middle-aged lady, but she's not some kind of giant monster of the poultry clan, bent on sadistically pecking out our eyes. You can't believe that of her, can you?"

"No, buddy, not that. She ain't peckin' at your *eyes.* That's not what she's peckin' at."

Harding flinches, and I see his hands begin to creep out from between his knees like white spiders from between two moss-covered tree limbs, up the limbs toward the joining at the trunk.

"Not our eyes?" he says. "Pray, then, where *is* Miss Ratched pecking, my friend?"

McMurphy grinned. "Why, don't you *know,* buddy?"

"No, of course I don't know! I mean, if you insi—"

"At your balls, buddy, at your everlovin' *balls.*"

The spiders reach the joining at the trunk and settle there, twitching. Harding tries to grin, but his face and lips are so white the grin is lost. He stares at McMurphy. McMurphy takes the cigarette out of his mouth and repeats what he said.

"Right at your balls. No, that nurse ain't some kinda monster chicken, buddy, what she is is a ball-cutter. I've seen a thousand of 'em, old and young, men and women. Seen 'em all over the country and in the homes—people who try to make you weak so they can get you to toe the line, to follow their rules, to live like they want you to. And the best way to do this, to get you to knuckle under, is to weaken you by gettin' you where it hurts the worst. You ever been kneed in the nuts in a brawl, buddy? Stops you cold, don't it? There's nothing worse. It makes you sick, it saps every bit of strength you got. If you're up against a guy who wants to win by making you weaker instead of making himself stronger, then watch for his knee, he's gonna go for your vitals. And that's what that old buzzard is doing, going for your vitals."

Harding's face is still colorless, but he's got control of his hands again; they flip loosely before him, trying to toss off what McMurphy has been saying:

"Our dear Miss Ratched? Our sweet, smiling, tender angel of mercy, Mother Ratched, a ball-cutter? Why, friend, that's *most* unlikely."

"Buddy, don't give me that tender little mother crap. She may be a mother, but she's big as a damn barn and tough as knife metal. She fooled me with that kindly little old mother bit for maybe three minutes when I came in this morning, but no longer. I don't think she's really fooled any of you guys for any six months or a year, neither. Hooo*wee,* I've seen some bitches in my time, but she takes the cake."

"A bitch? But a moment ago she was a ball-cutter, then a

buzzard—or was it a chicken? Your metaphors are bumping
into each other, my friend."

"The hell with that; she's a bitch and a buzzard and a ball-
cutter, and don't kid me, you know what I'm talking about."

Harding's face and hands are moving faster than ever now,
a speeded film of gestures, grins, grimaces, sneers. The more he
tries to stop it, the faster it goes. When he lets his hands and
face move like they want to and doesn't try to hold them back,
they flow and gesture in a way that's real pretty to watch, but
when he worries about them and tries to hold back he becomes
a wild, jerky puppet doing a high-strung dance. Everything is
moving faster and faster, and his voice is speeding up to match.

"Why, see here, my friend Mr. McMurphy, my psychopathic
sidekick, our Miss Ratched is a veritable angel of mercy and
why just *every*one knows it. She's unselfish as the wind, toil-
ink thanklessly for the good of all, day after day, five long
days a week. That takes heart, my friend, heart. In fact, I
have been informed by sources—I am not at liberty to disclose
my sources, but I might say that Martini is in contact with the
same people a good part of the time—that she even *further*
serves mankind on her weekends off by doing generous volunteer work about town. Preparing a rich array of charity—
canned goods, cheese for the binding effect, soap—and pre-
senting it to some poor young couple having a difficult time
financially." His hands flash in the air, molding the picture
he is describing. "Ah, look: There she is, our nurse. Her
gentle knock on the door. The ribboned basket. The young
couple overjoyed to the point of speechlessness. The husband
open-mouthed, the wife weeping openly. She appraises their
dwelling. Promises to send them money for—scouring powder, yes. She places the basket in the center of the floor. And
when our angel leaves—throwing kisses, smiling ethereally—
she is so *intoxicated* with the sweet milk of human kindness
that her deed has generated within her large bosom, that she
is beside herself with generosity. Be-*side* herself, do you hear?
Pausing at the door, she draws the timid young bride to one
side and offers her twenty dollars of her own: 'Go, you poor
unfortunate underfed child, go, and buy yourself a *decent*
dress. I *realize* your husband can't afford it, but here, take
this, and *go*.' And the couple is forever indebted to her benevo-
lence."

He's been talking faster and faster, the cords stretching out
in his neck. When he stops talking, the ward is completely
silent. I don't hear anything but a faint reeling rhythm, what
I figure is a tape recorder somewhere getting all of this.

Harding looks around, sees everybody's watching him, and he does his best to laugh. A sound comes out of his mouth like a nail being crowbarred out of a plank of green pine; Eee-eee-eee. He can't stop it. He wrings his hands like a fly and clinches his eyes at the awful sound of that squeaking. But he can't stop it. It gets higher and higher until finally, with a suck of breath, he lets his face fall into his waiting hands.

"Oh the bitch, the bitch, the bitch," he whispers through his teeth.

McMurphy lights another cigarette and offers it to him; Harding takes it without a word. McMurphy is still watching Harding's face in front of him there, with a kind of puzzled wonder, looking at it like it's the first human face he ever laid eyes on. He watches while Harding's twitching and jerking slows down and the face comes up from the hands.

"You are right," Harding says, "about all of it." He looks up at the other patients who are watching him. "No one's ever dared come out and say it before, but there's not a man among us that doesn't think it, that doesn't feel just as you do about her and the whole business—feel it somewhere down deep in his scared little soul."

McMurphy frowns and asks, "What about that little fart of a doctor? He might be a little slow in the head, but not so much as not to be able to see how she's taken over and what she's doing."

Harding takes a long pull off the cigarette and lets the smoke drift out with his talk. "Doctor Spivey ... is exactly like the rest of us, McMurphy, completely conscious of his inadequacy. He's a frightened, desperate, ineffectual little rabbit, totally incapable of running this ward without our Miss Ratched's help, and he knows it. And, worse, she *knows* he knows it and reminds him every chance she gets. Every time she finds he's made a little slip in the bookwork or in, say, the charting you can just imagine her in there grinding his nose in it."

"That's right," Cheswick says, coming up beside McMurphy, "grinds our noses in our mistakes."

"Why doesn't he fire her?"

"In this hospital," Harding says, "the doctor doesn't hold the power of hiring and firing. That power goes to the supervisor, and the supervisor is a woman, a dear old friend of Miss Ratched's; they were Army nurses together in the thirties. We are victims of a matriarchy here, my friend, and the doctor is just as helpless against it as we are. He knows that all Ratched has to do is pick up that phone you see sitting at her elbow and call the supervisor and mention, oh, say, that the doctor seems to be making a *great* number of requisitions for Demerol—"

"Hold it, Harding, I'm not up on all this shop talk."

"Demerol, my friend, is a synthetic opiate, twice as addictive as heroin. Quite common for doctors to be addicted to it."

"That little fart? Is he a dope addict?"

"I'm certain I don't know."

"Then where does she get off with accusing him of—"

"Oh, you're not paying attention, my friend. She *doesn't* accuse. She merely needs to insinuate, insinuate anything, don't you see? Didn't you notice today? She'll call a man to the door of the Nurses' Station and stand there and ask him about a Kleenex found under his bed. No more, just ask. And he'll feel like he's lying to her, whatever answer he gives. If he says he was cleaning a pen with it, she'll say, 'I see, a pen,' or if he says he has a cold in his nose, she'll say, 'I see, a cold,' and she'll nod her neat little gray coiffure and smile her neat little smile and turn and go back into the Nurses' Station, leave him standing there wondering just what *did* he use that Kleenex for."

He starts to tremble again, and his shoulders fold back around him.

"No. She doesn't need to accuse. She has a genius for insinuation. Did you ever hear her, in the course of our discussion today, ever *once* hear her accuse me of anything? Yet it seems I have been accused of a multitude of things, of jealousy and paranoia, of not being man enough to satisfy my wife, of having relations with male friends of mine, of holding my cigarette in an affected manner, even—it seems to me—accused of having nothing between my legs but a patch of hair —and *soft* and *downy* and *blond hair at that!* Ball-cutter? Oh, you *underestimate* her!"

Harding hushes all of a sudden and leans forward to take McMurphy's hand in both of his. His face is tilted oddly, edged, jagged purple and gray, a busted wine bottle.

"This world . . . belongs to the strong, my friend! The ritual of our existence is based on the strong getting stronger by devouring the weak. We must face up to this. No more than right that it should be this way. We must learn to accept it as a law of the natural world. The rabbits accept their role in the ritual and recognize the wolf as the strong. In defense, the rabbit becomes sly and frightened and elusive and he digs holes and hides when the wolf is about. And he endures, he goes on. He knows his place. He most certainly doesn't challenge the wolf to combat. Now, would that be wise? Would it?"

He lets go McMurphy's hand and leans back and crosses his legs, takes another long pull off the cigarette. He pulls the cigarette from his thin crack of a smile, and the laugh starts up again—eee-eee-eee, like a nail coming out of a plank.

"Mr. McMurphy ... my friend ... I'm not a chicken, I'm a rabbit. The doctor is a rabbit. Cheswick there is a rabbit. Billy Bibbit is a rabbit. All of us in here are rabbits of varying ages and degrees, hippity-hopping through our Walt Disney world. Oh, don't misunderstand me, we're not in here *because* we are rabbits—we'd be rabbits wherever we were —we're all in here because we can't *adjust* to our rabbithood. We *need* a good strong wolf like the nurse to teach us our place."

"Man, you're talkin' like a fool. You mean to tell me that you're gonna sit back and let some old blue-haired woman talk you into being a rabbit?"

"Not talk me into it, no. I was born a rabbit. Just look at me. I simply need the nurse to make me *happy* with my role."

"You're no damned rabbit!"

"See the ears? the wiggly nose? the cute little button tail?"

"You're talking like a crazy ma—"

"Like a crazy man? How astute."

"Damn it, Harding, I didn't mean it like that. You ain't crazy that way. I mean—hell, I been surprised how sane you guys all are. As near as I can tell you're not any crazier than the average asshole on the street—"

"Ah yes, the asshole on the street."

"But not, you know, crazy like the movies paint crazy people. You're just hung up and—kind of—"

"Kind of rabbit-like, isn't that it?"

"Rabbits, *hell!* Not a thing like rabbits, goddammit."

"Mr. Bibbit, hop around for Mr. McMurphy here. Mr. Cheswick, show him how *furry* you are."

Billy Bibbit and Cheswick change into hunched-over white rabbits, right before my eyes, but they are too ashamed to do any of the things Harding told them to do.

"Ah, they're bashful, McMurphy. Isn't that sweet? Or, perhaps, the fellows are ill at ease because they didn't stick up for their friend. Perhaps they are feeling guilty for the way they once again let her victimize them into being her interrogators. Cheer up, friends, you've no reason to feel ashamed. It is all as it should be. It's not the rabbit's place to stick up for his fellow. That would have been foolish. No, you were wise, cowardly but wise."

"Look here, Harding," Cheswick says.

"No, no, Cheswick. Don't get irate at the truth."

"Now look here; there's been times when I've said the same things about old lady Ratched that McMurphy has been saying."

"Yes, but you said them very quietly and took them all back later. You are a rabbit too, don't try to avoid the truth. That's why I hold no grudge against you for the questions you asked me during the meeting today. You were only playing your role. If you had been on the carpet, or you Billy, or you Fredrickson, I would have attacked you just as cruelly as you attacked me. We mustn't be ashamed of our behavior; it's the way we little animals were meant to behave."

McMurphy turns in his chair and looks the other Acutes up and down. "I ain't so sure but what they should be ashamed. Personally, I thought it was damned crummy the way they swung in on her side against you. For a minute there I thought I was back in a Red Chinese prison camp . . ."

"Now by God, McMurphy," Cheswick says, "you listen here."

McMurphy turns and listens, but Cheswick doesn't go on. Cheswick never goes on; he's one of these guys who'll make a big fuss like he's going to lead an attack, holler charge and stomp up and down a minute, take a couple steps, and quit. McMurphy looks at him where he's been caught off base again after such a tough-sounding start, and says to him, "A hell of a lot like a Chinese prison camp."

Harding holds up his hands for peace. "Oh, no, no, that isn't right. You mustn't condemn us, my friend. No. In fact . . ."

I see that sly fever come into Harding's eye again; I think he's going to start laughing, but instead he takes his cigarette out of his mouth and points it at McMurphy—in his hand it looks like one of his thin, white fingers, smoking at the end.

". . . you too, Mr. McMurphy, for all your cowboy bluster and your sideshow swagger, you too, under that crusty surface, are probably just as soft and fuzzy and rabbit-souled as we are."

"Yeah, you bet. I'm a little cottontail. Just what is it makes me a rabbit, Harding? My psychopathic tendencies? Is it my fightin' tendencies, or my fuckin' tendencies? Must be the fuckin', mustn't it? All that whambam-thank-you-ma'am. Yeah, that whambam, that's probably what makes me a rabbit—"

"Wait; I'm afraid you've raised a point that requires some deliberation. Rabbits are noted for that certain trait, aren't they? Notorious, in fact, for their whambam. Yes. Um. But in any case, the point you bring up simply indicates that you are a healthy, functioning and adequate rabbit, whereas most of us in here even lack the sexual ability to make the grade as adequate rabbits. Failures, we are—feeble, stunted, weak little creatures in a weak little race. Rabbits, *sans* whambam; a pathetic notion."

"Wait a minute; you keep twistin' what I say—"

"No. You were right. You remember, it was you that drew our attention to the place where the nurse was concentrating her pecking? That was true. There's not a man here that isn't afraid he is losing or has already lost his whambam. We comical little creatures can't even achieve masculinity in the rabbit world, that's how weak and inadequate we are. Hee. We are —the *rabbits,* one might say, of the rabbit world!"

He leans forward again, and that strained, squeaking laugh of his that I been expecting begins to rise from his mouth, his hands flipping around, his face twitching.

"Harding! Shut your damned mouth!"

It's like a slap. Harding is hushed, chopped off cold with his mouth still open in a drawn grin, his hands dangling in a cloud of blue tobacco smoke. He freezes this way a second; then his eyes narrow into sly little holes and he lets them slip over to McMurphy, speaks so soft that I have to push my broom up right next to his chair to hear what he says.

"Friend . . . *you* . . . may be a wolf."

"Goddammit, I'm no wolf and you're no rabbit. *Hoo,* I never heard such—"

"You have a very wolfy roar."

With a loud hissing of breath, McMurphy turns from Harding to the rest of the Acutes standing around. "Here; all you guys. What the hell is the matter with you? You ain't as crazy as all this, thinking you're some animal."

"No," Cheswick says and steps in beside McMurphy. "No, by God, not me. I'm not any rabbit."

"That's the boy, Cheswick. And the rest of you, let's just knock it off. Look at you, talking yourself into running scared from some fifty-year-old woman. What is there she can do to you, anyway?"

"Yeah, what?" Cheswick says and glares around at the others.

"She can't have you whipped. She can't burn you with hot irons. She can't tie you to the rack. They got laws about that sort of thing nowadays; this ain't the Middle Ages. There's not a thing in the world that she can—"

"You s-s-*saw* what she c-can do to us! In the m-m-meeting

today." I see Billy Bibbit has changed back from a rabbit. He leans toward McMurphy, trying to go on, his mouth wet with spit and his face red. Then he turns and walks away. "Ah, it's n-no use. I should just k-k-kill myself."

McMurphy calls after him. "Today? What did I see in the meeting today? Hell's bells, all I saw today was her asking a couple of questions, and nice, easy questions at that. Questions ain't bonebreakers, they ain't sticks and stones."

Billy turns back. "But the wuh-wuh-*way* she asks them—"

"You don't have to answer, do you?"

"If you d-don't answer she just smiles and m-m-makes a note in her little book and then she—she—oh, *hell!*"

Scanlon comes up beside Billy. "If you don't answer her questions, Mack, you *admit* it just by keeping quiet. It's the way those bastards in the government get you. You can't beat it. The only thing to do is blow the whole business off the face of the whole bleeding earth—blow it all up."

"Well, when she asks one of those questions, why don't you tell her to up and go to hell?"

"Yeah," Cheswick says, shaking his fist, "tell her to up and go to hell."

"So then what, Mack? She'd just come right back with 'Why do you seem so *upset* by that par-tik-uler question, Patient McMurphy?' "

"So, you tell her to go to hell again. Tell them all to go to hell. They still haven't hurt you."

The Acutes are crowding closer around him. Fredrickson answers this time. "Okay, you tell her that and you're listed as Potential Assaultive and shipped upstairs to the Disturbed ward. I had it happen. Three times. Those poor goofs up there don't even get off the ward to go to the Saturday afternoon movie. They don't even have a TV."

"And, my friend, if you *continue* to demonstrate such hostile tendencies, such as telling people to go to hell, you get lined up to go to the Shock Shop, perhaps even on to greater things, an operation, an—"

"Damn it, Harding, I told you I'm not up on this talk."

"The Shock Shop, Mr. McMurphy, is jargon for the EST machine, the Electro Shock Therapy. A device that might be said to do the work of the sleeping pill, the electric chair, *and* the torture rack. It's a clever little procedure, simple, quick, nearly painless it happens so fast, but no one ever wants another one. Ever."

"What's this thing do?"

"You are strapped to a table, shaped, ironically, like a cross, with a crown of electric sparks in place of thorns. You are touched on each side of the head with wires. Zap! Five cents' worth of electricity through the brain and you are jointly administered therapy and a punishment for your hostile go-to-hell behavior, on top of being put out of everyone's way for six hours to three days, depending on the individual. Even when you do regain consciousness you are in a state of disorientation for days. You are unable to think coherently. You can't recall things. Enough of these treatments and a man could turn out like Mr. Ellis you see over there against the wall. A drooling, pants-wetting idiot at thirty-five. Or turn into a mindless organism that eats and eliminates and yells 'fuck the wife,' like Ruckly. Or look at Chief Broom clutching to his namesake there beside you."

Harding points his cigarette at me, too late for me to back off. I make like I don't notice. Go on with my sweeping.

"I've heard that the Chief, years ago, received more than two hundred shock treatments when they were really the vogue. Imagine what this could do to a mind that was already slipping. Look at him: a giant janitor. There's your Vanishing American, a six-foot-eight sweeping machine, scared of its own shadow. That, my friend, is what we can be threatened with."

McMurphy looks at me a while, then turns back to Harding. "Man, I tell you, how come you stand for it? What about this democratic-ward manure that the doctor was giving me? Why don't you take a vote?"

Harding smiles at him and takes another slow drag on his cigarette. "Vote what, my friend? Vote that the nurse may not ask any more questions in Group Meeting? Vote that she shall not *look* at us in a certain way? You tell me, Mr. McMurphy, what do we vote on?"

"Hell, I don't care. Vote on anything. Don't you see you have to do something to show you still got some guts? Don't you see you can't let her take over completely? Look at you here: you say the Chief is scared of his own shadow, but I never saw a scareder-looking bunch in my life than you guys."

"Not me!" Cheswick says.

"Maybe not you, buddy, but the rest are even scared to open up and *laugh*. You know, that's the first thing that got me about this place, that there wasn't anybody laughing. I haven't heard a real laugh since I came through that door, do you know that? Man, when you lose your laugh you lose your *footing*. A man go around lettin' a woman whup him down till he can't laugh any more, and he loses one of the biggest edges he's got on his side. First thing you know he'll begin to think she's tougher than he is and—"

"Ah. I believe my friend is catching on, fellow rabbits. Tell me, Mr. McMurphy, how does one go about showing a woman who's boss, I mean other than laughing at her? How does he show her who's king of the mountain? A man like you should be able to tell us that. You don't slap her around, do you? No, then she calls the law. You don't lose your temper and shout at her; she'll win by trying to placate her big ol' angry boy: 'Is us wittle man getting *fussy?* Ahhhhh?' Have you ever tried to keep up a noble and angry front in the face of such consolation? So you see, my friend, it is somewhat as you stated: man has but *one* truly effective weapon against the juggernaut of modern matriarchy, but it certainly is not laughter. One weapon, and with every passing year in this hip, motivationally researched society, more and more people are discovering how to render that weapon useless and conquer those who have hitherto been the conquerors—"

"Lord, Harding, but you do come on," McMurphy says.

"—and do you think, for all your acclaimed psychopathic powers, that you could effectively use your weapon against our champion? Do you think you could use it against Miss Ratched, McMurphy? Ever?"

And sweeps one of his hands toward the glass case. Everybody's head turns to look. She's in there, looking out through her window, got a tape recorder hid out of sight somewhere, getting all this down—already planning how to work it into the schedule.

The nurse sees everybody looking at her and she nods and they all turn away. McMurphy takes off his cap and runs his hands into that red hair. Now everybody is looking at him; they're waiting for him to make an answer and he knows it. He feels he's been trapped some way. He puts the cap back on and rubs the stitch marks on his nose.

"Why, if you mean do I think I could get a bone up over that old buzzard, no, I don't believe I could. . . ."

"She's not all that homely, McMurphy. Her face is quite handsome and well preserved. And in spite of all her attempts to *conceal* them, in that sexless get-up, you can still make out the evidence of some rather extraordinary breasts. She must have been a rather beautiful young woman. Still—for the sake of argument, could you get it up over her even if she wasn't old, even if she was young and had the beauty of Helen?"

"I don't know Helen, but I see what you're drivin' at. And

you're by God right. I couldn't get it up over old frozen face in there even if she had the beauty of Marilyn Monroe."

"There you are. She's won."

That's it. Harding leans back and everybody waits for what McMurphy's going to say next. McMurphy can see he's backed up against the wall. He looks at the faces a minute, then shrugs and stands up from his chair.

"Well, what the hell, it's no skin off my nose."

"That's true, it's no skin off your nose."

"And I damn well don't want to have some old fiend of a nurse after me with three thousand volts. Not when there's nothing in it for me but the adventure."

"No. You're right."

Harding's won the argument, but nobody looks too happy. McMurphy hooks his thumbs in his pockets and tries a laugh.

"No sir, I never heard of anybody offering a twenty-bone bounty for bagging a ball-cutter."

Everybody grins at this with him, but they're not happy. I'm glad McMurphy is going to be cagey after all and not get sucked in on something he can't whip, but I know how the guys feel; I'm not so happy myself. McMurphy lights another cigarette. Nobody's moved yet. They're all still standing there, grinning and uncomfortable. McMurphy rubs his nose again and looks away from the bunch of faces hung out there around him, looks back at the nurse and chews his lip.

"But you say . . . she don't send you up to that other ward unless she gets your goat? Unless she makes you crack in some way and you end up cussing her out or busting a window or something like that?"

"Unless you do something like that."

"You're sure of that, now? Because I'm getting just the shadiest notion of how to pick up a good purse off you birds in here. But I don't want to be a sucker about it. I had a hell of a time getting outa that other hole; I don't want to be jumping outa the fryin' pan into the fire."

"Absolutely certain. She's powerless unless you do something to honestly deserve the Disturbed Ward or EST. If you're tough enough to keep her from getting to you, she can't do a thing."

"So if I behave myself and don't cuss her out—"

"Or cuss one of the aides out."

"—or cuss one of the aides out or tear up jack some way around here, she can't do nothing to me?"

"Those are the rules we play by. Of course, she always wins, my friend, always. She's impregnable herself, and with the element of time working for her she eventually gets inside everyone. That's why the hospital regards her as its top nurse and grants her so much authority; she's a master of forcing the trembling libido out into the open—"

"The hell with that. What I want to know is am I safe to try to beat her at her own game? If I come on nice as pie to her, whatever else I in-*sinuate*, she ain't gonna get in a tizzy and have me electrocuted?"

"You're safe as long as you keep control. As long as you don't lose your temper and give her actual reason to request the restriction of the Disturbed Ward, or the therapeutic benefits of Electro Shock, you are safe. But that entails first and foremost keeping one's temper. And you? With your red hair and black record? Why delude yourself?"

"Okay. *All* right." McMurphy rubs his palms together. "Here's what I'm thinkin'. You birds seem to think you got quite the champ in there, don't you? Quite the—what did you call her?—sure, impregnable woman. What I want to know is how many of you are dead *sure* enough to put a little money on her?"

"Dead sure enough . . . ?"

"Just what I said: any of you sharpies here willing to take my five bucks that says that I can get the best of that woman —before the week's up—without her getting the best of me? One week, and if I don't have her to where she don't know whether to shit or go blind, the bet is yours."

"You're *betting* on this?" Cheswick is hopping from foot to foot and rubbing his hands together like McMurphy rubs his.

"You're damned right."

Harding and some of the others say that they don't get it.

"It's simple enough. There ain't nothing noble or complicated about it. I like to gamble. And I like to win. And I think I can win this gamble, okay? It got so at Pendleton the guys wouldn't even lag pennies with me on account of I was such a winner. Why, one of the big reasons I got myself sent here was because I needed some new suckers. I'll tell you something: I found out a few things about this place before I came out here. Damn near half of you guys in here pull compensation, three, four hundred a month and not a thing in the world to do with it but let it draw dust. I thought I might take advantage of this and maybe make both our lives a little more richer. I'm starting level with you. I'm a gambler and I'm not in the habit of losing. And I've never seen a woman I thought was more man than me, I don't care whether I can get it up for her or not. She may have the element of time, but I got a pretty long winning streak goin' myself."

He pulls off his cap, spins it on his finger, and catches it behind his back in his other hand, neat as you please.

"Another thing: I'm in this place because that's the way I planned it, pure and simple, because it's a better place than a work farm. As near as I can tell I'm no loony, or never knew it if I was. Your nurse don't know this; she's not going to be looking out for somebody coming at her with a trigger-quick mind like I obviously got. These things give me an edge I like. So I'm saying five bucks to each of you that wants it if I can't put a betsy bug up that nurse's butt within a week."

"I'm still not sure I—"

"Just that. A bee in her butt, a burr in her bloomers. Get her goat. Bug her till she comes apart at those neat little seams, and shows, just one time, she ain't so unbeatable as you think. One week. I'll let you be the judge whether I win or not."

Harding takes out a pencil and writes something on the pinochle pad.

"Here. A lien on ten dollars of that money they've got drawing dust under my name over in Funds. It's worth twice that to me, my friend, to see this unlikely miracle brought off."

McMurphy looks at the paper and folds it. "Worth it to any of the rest of you birds?" Other Acutes line up now, taking turns at the pad. He takes the pieces of paper when they're finished, stacking them on his palm, pinned under a big stiff thumb. I see the pieces of paper crowd up in his hand. He looks them over.

"You trust me to hold the bets, buddies?"

"I believe we can be safe in doing that," Harding says. "You won't be going any place for a while."

O ne Christmas at midnight on the button, at the old place, the ward door blows open with a crash, in comes a fat man with a beard, eyes ringed red by the cold and his nose just the color of a cherry. The black boys get him cornered in the hall with flashlights. I see he's all tangled in the tinsel Public Relation has been stringing all over the place, and he's stumbling around in it in the dark. He's shading his red eyes from the flashlights and sucking on his mustache.

"Ho ho ho," he says. "I'd like to stay but I must be hurrying along. Very tight schedule, ya know. Ho ho. Must be going. . . ."

The black boys move in with the flashlights. They kept him with us six years before they discharged him, clean-shaven and skinny as a pole.

The Big Nurse is able to set the wall clock at whatever speed she wants by just turning one of those dials in the steel door; she takes a notion to hurry things up, she turns the speed up, and those hands whip around that disk like spokes in a wheel. The scene in the picture-screen windows goes through rapid changes of light to show morning, noon, and night—throb off and on furiously with day and dark, and everybody is driven like mad to keep up with that passing of fake time; awful scramble of shaves and breakfasts and appointments and lunches and medications and ten minutes of night so you barely get your eyes closed before the dorm light's screaming at you to get up and start the scramble again, go like a sonofabitch this way, going through the full schedule of a day maybe twenty times an hour, till the Big Nurse sees everybody is right up to the breaking point, and she slacks off on the throttle, eases off the pace on that clock-dial, like some kid been fooling with the moving-picture projection machine and finally got tired watching the film run at ten times its natural speed, got bored with all that silly scampering and insect squeak of talk and turned it back to normal.

She's given to turning up the speed this way on days like,

say, when you got somebody to visit you or when the VFW brings down a smoker show from Portland—times like that, times you'd like to hold and have stretch out. That's when she speeds things up.

But generally it's the other way, the slow way. She'll turn that dial to a dead stop and freeze the sun there on the screen so it don't move a scant hair for weeks, so not a leaf on a tree or a blade of grass in the pasture shimmers. The clock hands hang at two minutes to three and she's liable to let them hang there till we rust. You sit solid and you can't budge, you can't walk or move to relieve the strain of sitting, you can't swallow and you can't breathe. The only thing you can move is your eyes and there's nothing to see but petrified Acutes across the room waiting on one another to decide whose play it is. The old Chronic next to me has been dead six days, and he's rotting to the chair. And instead of fog sometimes she'll let a clear chemical gas in through the vents, and the whole ward is set solid when the gas changes into plastic.

Lord knows how long we hang this way.

Then, gradually, she'll ease the dial up a degree, and that's worse yet. I can take hanging dead still better'n I can take that sirup-slow hand of Scanlon across the room, taking three days to lay down a card. My lungs pull for the thick plastic air like getting it through a pinhole. I try to go to the latrine and I feel buried under a ton of sand, squeezing my bladder till green sparks flash and buzz across my forehead.

I strain with every muscle and bone to get out of that chair and go to the latrine, work to get up till my arms and legs are all ashake and my teeth hurt. I pull and pull and all I gain is maybe a quarter-inch off the leather seat. So I fall back and give up and let the pee pour out, activating a hot salt wire down my left leg that sets off humiliating alarms, sirens, spotlights, everybody up yelling and running around and the big black boys knocking the crowd aside right and left as the both of them rush headlong at me, waving awful mops of wet copper wires cracking and spitting as they short with the water.

About the only time we get any let-up from this time control is in the fog; then time doesn't mean anything. It's lost in the fog, like everything else. (They haven't really fogged the place full force all day today, not since McMurphy came in. I bet he'd yell like a bull if they fogged it.)

When nothing else is going on, you usually got the fog or the time control to contend with, but today something's happened: there hasn't been any of these things worked on us all day, not since shaving. This afternoon everything is matching up. When the swing shift comes on duty the clock says four-thirty, just like it should. The Big Nurse dismisses the black boys and takes a last look around the ward. She slides a long silver hatpin out of the iron-blue knot of hair back of her head, takes off her white cap and sets it careful in a cardboard box (there's mothballs in that box), and drives the hatpin back in the hair with a stab of her hand.

Behind the glass I see her tell everyone good evening. She hands the little birthmarked swing-shift nurse a note; then her hand reaches out to the control panel in the steel door, clacks on the speaker in the day room: "Good evening, boys. Behave yourselves." And turns the music up louder than ever. She rubs the inside of her wrist across her window; a disgusted look shows the fat black boy who just reported on duty that he better get to cleaning it, and he's at the glass with a paper towel before she's so much as locked the ward door behind her.

The machinery in the walls whistles, sighs, drops into a lower gear.

Then, till night, we eat and shower and go back to sit in the day room. Old Blastic, the oldest Vegetable, is holding his stomach and moaning. George (the black boys call him Rub-a-dub) is washing his hands in the drinking fountain. The Acutes sit and play cards and work at getting a picture on our TV set by carrying the set every place the cord will reach, in search of a good beam.

The speakers in the ceiling are still making music. The music from the speakers isn't transmitted in on a radio beam is why the machinery don't interfere. The music comes off a long tape from the Nurses' Station, a tape we all know so well by heart that there don't any of us consciously hear it except new men like McMurphy. He hasn't got used to it yet. He's dealing blackjack for cigarettes, and the speaker's right over the card table. He's pulled his cap way forward till he has to lean his head back and squint from under the brim to see his cards. He holds a cigarette between his teeth and talks around it like a stock auctioneer I saw once in a cattle auction in The Dalles.

". . . hey-ya, hey-ya, come on, come on," he says, high, fast; "I'm waitin' on you suckers, you hit or you sit. Hit, you say? well well well and with a king up the boy wants a hit. Whad-daya know. So comin' at you and *too* bad, a little lady for the lad and he's over the wall and down the road, up the hill and dropped his load. Comin' at you, Scanlon, and I *wish some idiot in that nurses' hothouse would turn down that frigging music!* Hooee! Does that thing play night and day, Harding? I never heard such a driving racket in my life."

Harding gives him a blank look. "Exactly what noise is it you're referring to, Mr. McMurphy?"

"That damned *radio*. Boy. It's been going ever since I come in this morning. And don't come on with some baloney that you don't hear it."

Harding cocks his ear to the ceiling. "Oh, yes, the so-called music. Yes, I suppose we do hear it if we concentrate, but then one can hear one's own heartbeat too, if he concentrates hard enough." He grins at McMurphy. "You see, that's a recording playing up there, my friend. We seldom hear the radio. The world news might not be therapeutic. And we've all heard that recording so many times now it simply slides out of our hearing, the way the sound of a waterfall soon becomes an unheard sound to those who live near it. Do you think if you lived near a waterfall you could hear it very long?"

(I still hear the sound of the falls on the Columbia, always will—always—hear the whoop of Charley Bear Belly stabbed himself a big chinook, hear the slap of fish in the water, laughing naked kids on the bank, the women at the racks . . . from a long time ago.)

"Do they leave it on all the time, like a waterfall?" McMurphy says.

"Not when we sleep," Cheswick says, "but all the rest of the time, and that's the truth."

"The hell with that. I'll tell that coon over there to turn it off or get his fat little ass kicked!"

He starts to stand up, and Harding touches his arm. "Friend, that is exactly the kind of statement that gets one branded assaultive. Are you so eager to forfeit the bet?"

McMurphy looks at him. "That's the way it is, huh? A pressure game? Keep the old pinch on?"

"That's the way it is."

He slowly lowers himself back into his seat, saying, "Horse muh-noo-ur."

Harding looks about at the other Acutes around the card table. "Gentlemen, already I seem to detect in our redheaded challenger a most unheroic decline of his TV-cowboy stoicism."

He looks at McMurphy across thte table, smiling, McMurphy nods at him and tips his head back for the wink and licks his big thumb. "Well sir, ol' Professor Harding sounds like he's

getting cocky. He wins a couple of splits and he goes to comin'
on like a wise guy. Well well well; there he sits with a deuce
showing and here's a pack of Mar-boros says he backs down.
. . . *Whups,* he sees me, okeedokee, Perfessor, here's a trey,
he wants another, gets another deuce, try for the big five,
Perfessor? Try for that big double pay, or play it safe? Another pack says you won't. Well well well, the Perfessor sees
me, this tells the tale, *too* bad, another lady and the Perfessor
flunks his exams. . . ."

The next song starts up from the speaker, loud and clangy
and a lot of accordion. McMurphy takes a look up at the
speaker, and his spiel gets louder and louder to match it.

". . . hey-ya hey-ya, okay, *next,* goddammit, you hit or you
sit . . . comin' at ya . . . !"

Right up to the lights out at nine-thirty.

I could of watched McMurphy at that blackjack table all
night, the way he dealt and talked and roped them in and led
them smack up to the point where they were *just about* to
quit, then backed down a hand or two to give them confidence
and bring them along again. Once he took a break for a cigarette and tilted back in his chair, his hands folded behind his
head, and told the guys, "The secret of being a top-notch con
man is being able to know what the mark *wants,* and how to
make him think he's getting it. I learned that when I worked
a season on a skillo wheel in a carnival. You *fe-e-el* the sucker
over with your eyes when he comes up and you say, 'Now
here's a bird that needs to feel tough.' So every time he snaps
at you for taking him you quake in your boots, scared to
death, and tell him, 'Please, sir. No trouble. The next roll is on
the house, sir.' So the both of you are getting what you want."

He rocks forward, and the legs of his chair come down with
a crack. He picks up the deck, zips his thumb over it, knocks
the edge of it against the table top, licks his thumb and finger.

"And what I deduce you marks need is a big fat pot to
temptate you. Here's ten packages on the next deal. Hey-*yah,*
comin' at you, guts ball from here on out. . . ."

And throws back his head and laughs out loud at the way
the guys hustled to get their bets down.

That laugh banged around the day room all evening, and
all the time he was dealing he was joking and talking and trying to get the players to laugh along with him. But they were
all afraid to loosen up; it'd been too long. He gave up trying
and settled down to serious dealing. They won the deal off

him a time or two, but he always bought it back or fought it back, and the cigarettes on each side of him grew in bigger and bigger pyramid stacks.

Then just before nine-thirty he started letting them win, lets them win it all back so fast they don't hardly remember losing. He pays out the last couple of cigarettes and lays down the deck and leans back with a sigh and shoves the cap out of his eyes, and the game is done.

"Well, sir, win a few, lose the rest is what I say." He shakes his head so forlorn. "I don't know—I was always a pretty shrewd customer at twenty-one, but you birds may just be too *tough* for me. You got some kinda uncanny *knack*, makes a man leery of playing against such sharpies for real money tomorrow."

He isn't even kidding himself into thinking they fall for that. He let them win, and every one of us watching the game knows it. So do the players. But there still isn't a man raking his pile of cigarettes—cigarettes he didn't really win but only won back because they were his in the first place—that doesn't have a smirk on his face like he's the toughest gambler on the whole Mississippi.

The fat black boy and a black boy named Geever run us out of the day room and commence turning lights off with a little key on a chain, and as the ward gets dimmer and darker the eyes of the little birthmarked nurse in the station get bigger and brighter. She's at the door of the glass station, issuing nighttime pills to the men that shuffle past her in a line, and she's having a hard time keeping straight who gets poisoned with what tonight. She's not even watching where she pours the water. What has distracted her attention this way is that big redheaded man with the dreadful cap and the horrible-looking scar, coming her way. She's watching McMurphy walk away from the card table in the dark day room, his one horny hand twisting the red tuft of hair that sticks out of the little cup at the throat of his work-farm shirt, and I figure by the way she rears back when he reaches the door of the station that she's probably been warned about him beforehand by the Big Nurse. ("Oh, one more thing before I leave it in your hands tonight, Miss Pilbow; that new man sitting over there, the one with the garish red sideburns and facial lacerations—I've reason to believe he is a sex maniac.")

McMurphy sees how she's looking so scared and big-eyed at him, so he sticks his head in the station door where she's issuing pills, and gives her a big friendly grin to get acquainted on. This flusters her so she drops the water pitcher on her foot. She gives a cry and hops on one foot, jerks her hand, and the pill she was about to give me leaps out of the little cup and right down the neck of her uniform where that birthmark stain runs like a river of wine down into a valley.

"Let me give you a hand, ma'am."

And that very hand comes through the station door, scarred and tattooed and the color of raw meat.

"Stay back! There are two aides on the ward with me!"

She rolls her eyes for the black boys, but they are off tying Chronics in bed, nowhere close enough to help in a hurry. McMurphy grins and turns the hand over so she can see he isn't holding a knife. All she can see is the light shining off the slick, waxy, callused palm.

"All I mean to *do*, miss, is to—"

"Stay back! Patients aren't allowed to enter the— Oh, stay back, I'm a *Catholic!*" and straightaway jerks at the gold chain around her neck so a cross flies out from between her bosoms, slingshots the lost pill up in the air! McMurphy strikes at the air right in front of her face. She screams and pops the cross in her mouth and clinches her eyes shut like she's about to get socked, stands like that, paper-white except for that stain which turns darker than ever, as though it sucked the blood from all the rest of her body. When she finally opens her eyes again there's that callused hand right in front of her with my little red capsule sitting in it.

"—*was* to pick up your waterin' can you dropped." He holds that out in the other hand.

Her breath comes out in a loud hiss. She takes the can from him. "Thank you. Good night, good night," and closes the door in the next man's face, no more pills tonight.

In the dorm McMurphy tosses the pill on my bed. "You want your sourball, Chief?"

I shake my head at the pill, and he flips it off the bed like it was a bug pestering him. It hops across the floor with a cricket scrabble. He goes to getting ready for bed, pulling off his clothes. The shorts under his work pants are coal black satin covered with big white whales with red eyes. He grins when he sees I'm looking at the shorts. "From a co-ed at Oregon State, Chief, a Literary major." He snaps the elastic with his thumb. "She gave them to me because she said I was a symbol."

His arms and neck and face are sunburned and bristled with curly orange hairs. He's got tattoos on each shoulder; one says "Fighting Leathernecks" and has a devil with a red eye and red horns and an M-1 rifle, and the other is a poker hand fanned out across his muscle—aces and eights. He puts his roll of clothes on the nightstand next to my bed and goes to punching at his pillow. He's been assigned the bed right next to mine.

He gets between the sheets and tells me I better hit the sack myself, that here comes one of those black boys to douse the lights on us. I look around, and the black boy named Geever is coming, and I kick off my shoes and get in bed just as he walks up to tie a sheet across me. When he's finished with me he takes a last look around and giggles and flips the dorm lights off.

Except for the white powder of light from the Nurses' Station out in the hall, the dorm is dark. I can just make out McMurphy next to me, breathing deep and regular, the covers over him rising and falling. The breathing gets slower and slower, till I figure he's been asleep for a while. Then I hear a soft, throaty sound from his bed, like the chuckle of a horse. He's still awake and he's laughing to himself about something.

He stops laughing and whispers, "Why, you sure did give a jump when I told you that coon was coming, Chief. I thought somebody told me you was deef."

*F*irst time for a long, long time I'm in bed without taking that little red capsule (if I hide to keep from taking it, the night nurse with the birthmark sends the black boy named Geever out to hunt me down, hold me captive with his flashlight till she can get the needle ready), so I fake sleep when the black boy's coming past with his light.

When you take one of these red pills you don't just go to sleep; you're paralyzed with sleep, and all night long you can't wake, no matter what goes on around you. That's why the staff gives me the pills; at the old place I took to waking up at night and catching them performing all kinds of horrible crimes on the patients sleeping around me.

I lie still and slow my breathing, waiting to see if something is going to happen. It is dark my lord and I hear them slipping around out there in their rubber shoes; twice they peek in the dorm and run a flashlight over everybody. I keep my eyes shut and keep awake. I hear a wailing from up on Disturbed, loo loo *looo*—got some guy wired to pick up code signals.

"Oh, a beer, I think, fo' the long night ahead," I hear a black boy whisper to the other. Rubber shoes squeak off toward the Nurses' Station, where the refrigerator is. "You like a beer, sweet thing with a birthmark? Fo' the long night ahead?"

The guy upstairs hushes. The low whine of the devices in the walls gets quieter and quieter, till it hums down to nothing. Not a sound across the hospital—except for a dull, padded rumbling somewhere deep in the guts of the building, a sound that I never noticed before—a lot like the sound you hear when you're standing late at night on top of a big hydroelectric dam. Low, relentless, brute power.

The fat black boy stands out there in the hall where I can see him, looking all around and giggling. He walks toward the dorm door, slow, wiping the wet gray palms in his armpits. The light from the Nurses' Station throws his shadow on the dorm wall big as an elephant, gets smaller as he walks to the dorm door and looks in. He giggles again and unlocks the

78

fuse box by the door and reaches in. "Tha's right, babies, sleep tight."

Twists a knob, and the whole floor goes to slipping down away from him standing in the door, lowering into the building like a platform in a grain elevator!

Not a thing but the dorm floor moves, and we're sliding away from the walls and door and the windows of the ward at a hell of a clip—beds, bedstands, and all. The machinery— probably a cog-and-track affair at each corner of the shaft—is greased silent as death. The only sound I hear is the guys breathing, and that drumming under us getting louder the farther down we go. The light of the dorm door five hundred yards back up this hole is nothing but a speck, dusting the square sides of the shaft with a dim powder. It gets dimmer and dimmer till a faraway scream comes echoing down the sides of the shaft— "Stay *back!*"—and the light goes out altogether.

The floor reaches some kind of solid bottom far down in the ground and stops with a soft jar. It's dead black, and I can feel the sheet around me choking off my wind. Just as I get the sheet untied, the floor starts sliding forward with a little jolt. Some kind of castors under it I can't hear. I can't even hear the guys around me breathing, and I realize all of a sudden it's because that drumming's gradually got so loud I can't hear anything else. We must be square in the middle of it. I go to clawing at that damned sheet tied across me and just about have it loose when a whole wall slides up, reveals a huge room of endless machines stretching clear out of sight, swarming with sweating, shirtless men running up and down catwalks, faces blank and dreamy in firelight thrown from a hundred blast furnaces.

It—everything I see—looks like it sounded, like the inside of a tremendous dam. Huge brass tubes disappear upward in the dark. Wires run to transformers out of sight. Grease and cinders catch on everything, staining the couplings and motors and dynamos red and coal black.

The workers all move at the same smooth sprint, an easy, fluid stride. No one's in a hurry. One will hold up a second, spin a dial, push a button, throw a switch, and one side of his face flashes white like lightning from the spark of the connecting switch, and run on, up steel steps and along a corrugated iron catwalk—pass each other so smooth and close I hear the slap of wet sides like the slap of a salmon's tail on water—stop again, throw lightning from another switch, and run on again.

They twinkle in all directions clean on out of sight, these flash pictures of the dreamy doll faces of the workmen.

A workman's eyes snap shut while he's going at full run, and he drops in his tracks; two of his buddies running by grab him up and lateral him into a furnace as they pass. The furnace whoops a ball of fire and I hear the popping of a million tubes like walking through a field of seed pods. This sound mixes with the whirr and clang of the rest of the machines.

There's a rhythm to it, like a thundering pulse.

The dorm floor slides on out of the shaft and into the machine room. Right away I see what's straight above us—one of those trestle affairs like you find in meat houses, rollers on tracks to move carcasses from the cooler to the butcher without much lifting. Two guys in slacks, white shirts with the sleeves turned back, and thin black ties are leaning on the catwalk above our beds, gesturing to each other as they talk, cigarettes in long holders tracing lines of red light. They're talking but you can't make out the words above the measured roar rising all around them. One of the guys snaps his fingers, and the nearest workman veers in a sharp turn and sprints to his side. The guy points down at one of the beds with his cigarette holder, and the worker trots off to the steel stepladder and runs down to our level, where he goes out of sight between two transformers huge as potato cellars.

When that worker appears again he's pulling a hook along the trestle overhead and taking giant strides as he swings along it. He passes my bed and a furnace whooping somewhere suddenly lights his face up right over mine, a face handsome and brutal and waxy like a mask, wanting nothing. I've seen a million faces like it.

He goes to the bed and with one hand grabs the old Vegetable Blastic by the heel and lifts him straight up like Blastic don't weight more'n a few pounds; with the other hand the worker drives the hook through the tendon back of the heel, and the old guy's hanging there upside down, his moldy face blown up big, scared, the eyes scummed with mute fear. He keeps flapping both arms and the free leg till his pajama top falls around his head. The worker grabs the top and bunches and twists it like a burlap sack and pulls the trolley clicking back over the trestle to the catwalk and looks up to where those two guys in white shirts are standing. One of the guys takes a scalpel from a holster at his belt. There's a chain welded to the scalpel. The guy lowers it to the worker, loops the other end of the chain around the railing so the worker can't run off with a weapon.

The worker takes the scalpel and slices up the front of old Blastic with a clean swing and the old man stops thrashing around. I expect to be sick, but there's no blood or innards falling out like I was looking to see—just a shower of rust and ashes, and now and again a piece of wire or glass. Worker's standing there to his knees in what looks like clinkers.

A furnace got its mouth open somewhere, licks up somebody.

I think about jumping up and running around and waking up McMurphy and Harding and as many of the guys as I can, but there wouldn't be any sense in it. If I shook somebody awake he'd say, Why you crazy idiot, what the hell's eating you? And then probably help one of the workers lift me onto one of those hooks himself, saying, How about let's see what the insides of an *Indian* are like?

I hear the high, cold, whistling wet breath of the fog machine, see the first wisps of it come seeping out from under McMurphy's bed. I hope he knows enough to hide in the fog.

I hear a silly prattle reminds me of somebody familiar, and I roll enough to get a look down the other way. It's the hairless Public Relation with the bloated face, that the patients are always arguing about why it's bloated. "I'll say he *does*," they'll argue. "Me, I'll say he doesn't; you ever hear of a guy *really* who wore one?" "Yeh, but you ever hear of a guy like *him*, before?" The first patient shrugs and nods, "Interesting point."

Now he's stripped except for a long undershirt with fancy monograms sewed red on front and back. And I see once and for all (the undershirt rides up his back some as he comes walking past, giving me a peek) that he definitely *does* wear one, laced so tight it might blow up any second.

And dangling from the stays he's got half a dozen withered objects, tied by the hair like scalps.

He's carrying a little flask of something that he sips from to keep his throat open for talking, and a camphor hanky he puts in front of his nose from time to time to stop out the stink. There's a clutch of schoolteachers and college girls and the like hurrying after him. They wear blue aprons and their hair in pin curls. They are listening to him give a brief lecture on the tour.

He thinks of something funny and has to stop his lecture long enough for a swig from the flask to stop the giggling. During the pause one of his pupils stargazes around and sees the gutted Chronic dangling by his heel. She gasps and jumps back. The Public Relation turns and catches sight of the corpse and rushes to take one of those limp hands and give it a spin. The student shrinks forward for a cautious look, face in a trance.

"You *see?* You *see?*" He squeals and rolls his eyes and spews stuff from his flask he's laughing so hard. He's laughing till I think he'll explode.

When he finally drowns the laughing he starts back along the row of machines and goes into his lecture again. He stops suddenly and slaps his forehead—"Oh, scatterbrained *me!*"— and comes running back to the hanging Chronic to rip off another trophy and tie it to his girdle.

Right and left there are other things happening just as bad— crazy, horrible things too goofy and outlandish to cry about and too much true to laugh about—but the fog is getting thick enough I don't have to watch. And somebody's tugging at my arm. I know already what will happen: somebody'll drag me out of the fog and we'll be back on the ward and there won't be a sign of what went on tonight and if I was fool enough to try and tell anybody about it they'd say, Idiot, you just had a nightmare; things as crazy as a big machine room down in the bowels of a dam where people get cut up by robot workers don't exist.

· But if they don't exist, how can a man see them?

It's Mr. Turkle that pulls me out of the fog by the arm, shaking me and grinning. He says, "You havin' a bad dream, Mistuh Bromden." He's the aide works the long lonely shift from 11 to 7, an old Negro man with a big sleepy grin on the end of a long wobbly neck. He smells like he's had a little to drink. "Back to sleep now, Mistuh Bromden."

Some nights he'll untie the sheet from across me if it's so tight I squirm around. He wouldn't do it if he thought the day crew knew it was him, because they'd probably fire him, but he figures the day crew will think it was me untied it. I think he really does it to be kind, to help—but he makes sure he's safe first.

This time he doesn't untie the sheet but walks away from me to help two aides I never saw before and a young doctor lift old Blastic onto the stretcher and carry him out, covered with a sheet—handle him more careful than anybody ever handled him before in all his life.

C ome morning, McMurphy is up before I am, the first time anybody been up before me since Uncle Jules the Wallwalker was here. Jules was a shrewd old white-haired Negro with a theory the world was being tipped over on its side during the night by the black boys; he used to slip out in the early mornings, aiming to catch them tipping it. Like Jules, I'm up early in the mornings to watch what machinery they're sneaking onto the ward or installing in the shaving room, and usually it's just me and the black boys in the hall for fifteen minutes before the next patient is out of bed. But this morning I hear McMurphy out there in the latrine as I come out of the covers. Hear him singing! Singing so you'd think he didn't have a worry in the world. His voice is clear and strong slapping up against the cement and steel.

" 'Your horses are hungry, that's what she did say.' " He's enjoying the way the sound rings in the latrine. " 'Come sit down beside me, an' feed them some hay.' " He gets a breath, and his voice jumps a key, gaining pitch and power till it's joggling the wiring in all the walls. " 'My horses ain't hungry, they won't eat your hay-ay-aeee.' " He holds the note and plays with it, then swoops down with the rest of the verse to finish it off. " 'So fare-thee-well, darlin', I'm gone on my way.' "

Singing! Everybody's thunderstruck. They haven't heard such a thing in years, not on this ward. Most of the Acutes in the dorm are up on their elbows, blinking and listening. They look at one another and raise their eyebrows. How come the black boys haven't hushed him up out there? They never let anybody raise that much racket before, did they? How come they treat this new guy different? He's a man made outa skin and bone that's due to get weak and pale and die, just like the rest of us. He lives under the same laws, gotta eat, bumps up against the same troubles; these things make him just as vulnerable to the Combine as anybody else, don't they?

But the new guy *is* different, and the Acutes can see it, different from anybody been coming on this ward for the past ten years, different from anybody they ever met outside. He's just as vulnerable, maybe, but the Combine didn't get him.

" 'My wagons are loaded,' " he sings, " 'my whip's in my hand. . . .' "

How'd he manage to slip the collar? Maybe, like old Pete, the Combine missed getting to him soon enough with controls. Maybe he growed up so wild all over the country, batting around from one place to another, never around one town longer'n a few months when he was a kid so a school never got much a hold on him, logging, gambling, running carnival wheels, traveling lightfooted and fast, keeping on the move so much that the Combine never had a chance to get anything installed. Maybe that's it, he never gave the Combine a chance, just like he never gave the black boy a chance to get to him with the thermometer yesterday morning, because a moving target is hard to hit.

No wife wanting new linoleum. No relatives pulling at him with watery old eyes. No one to *care* about, which is what makes him free enough to be a good con man. And maybe the reason the black boys don't rush into that latrine and put a stop to his singing is because they *know* he's out of control, and they remember that time with old Peter and what a man out of control can do. And they can see that McMurphy's a lot bigger than old Pete; if it comes down to getting the best of him, it's going to take all three of them and the Big Nurse waiting on the sidelines with a needle. The Acutes nod at one another; that's the reason, they figure, that the black boys haven't stopped his singing where they would stop any of the rest of us.

I come out of the dorm into the hall just as McMurphy comes out of the latrine. He's got his cap on and not much else, just a towel grabbed around his hips. He's holding a toothbrush in his other hand. He stands in the hall, looking up and down, rocking up on his toes to keep off the cold tile as much as he can. Picks him out a black boy, the least one, and walks up to him and whaps him on the shoulder just like they'd been friends all their lives.

"Hey there, old buddy, what's my chance of gettin' some toothpaste for brushin' my grinders?"

The black boy's dwarf head swivels and comes nose to knuckle with that hand. He frowns at it, then takes a quick check where's the other two black boys just in case, and tells McMurphy they don't open the cabinet till six-forty-five. "It's a policy," he says.

"Is that right? I mean, is that where they keep the toothpaste? In the cabinet?"

"Tha's right, locked in the cabinet."

The black boys tries to go back to polishing the baseboards, but that hand is still lopped over his shoulder like a big red clamp.

"Locked in the cabinet, is it? Well well well, now why do you reckon they keep the toothpaste locked up? I mean, it ain't like it's dangerous, is it? You can't poison a man with it, can you? You couldn't brain some guy with the tube, could you? What reason you suppose they have for puttin' something as harmless as a little tube of toothpaste under lock and key?"

"It's ward policy, Mr. McMurphy, tha's the reason," And when he sees that this last reason don't affect McMurphy like it should, he frowns at that hand on his shoulder and adds, "What you s'pose it'd be like if *evahbody* was to brush their teeth whenever they took a notion to brush?"

McMurphy turns loose the shoulder, tugs at the tuft of red wool at his neck, and thinks this over. "Uh-huh, uh-huh, I think I can see what you're drivin' at: ward policy is for those that can't brush after every meal."

"My *gaw*, don't you *see?*"

"Yes, now, I do. You're saying people'd be brushin' their teeth whenever the spirit moved them."

"Tha's right, tha's why we—"

"And, lordy, can you imagine? Teeth bein' brushed at six-thirty, six-twenty—who can tell? maybe even six o'clock. Yeah, I can see your point."

He winks past the black boy at me standing against the wall.

"I gotta get this baseboard cleaned, McMurphy."

"Oh. I didn't mean to keep you from your job." He starts to back away as the black boy bends to his work again. Then he comes forward and leans over to look in the can at the black boy's side. "Well, look here; what do we have here?"

The black boy peers down. "Look where?"

"Look here in this old can, Sam. What is the stuff in this old can?"

"Tha's . . . soap powder."

"Well, I generally use paste, but"—McMurphy runs his toothbrush down in the powder and swishes it around and pulls it out and taps it on the side of the can—"but this will do fine for me. I thank you. We'll look into that ward policy business later."

And he heads back to the latrine, where I can hear his singing garbled by the piston beat of his toothbrushing.

That black boy's standing there looking after him with his scrub rag hanging limp in his gray hand. After a minute he blinks and looks around and sees I been watching and comes over and drags me down the hall by the drawstring on my pajamas and pushes me to a place on the floor I just did yesterday.

"There! Damn you, right there! That's where I want you workin', not gawkin' around like some big useless cow! There! There!"

And I lean over and go to mopping with my back to him so he won't see me grin. I feel good, seeing McMurphy get that black boy's goat like not many men could. Papa used to be able to do it—spraddle-legged, dead-panned, squinting up at the sky that first time the government men showed up to negotiate about buying off the treaty. "Canada honkers up there," Papa says, squinting up. Government men look, rattling papers. "What are you—? In July? There's no—uh—geese this time of year. Uh, no geese."

They had been talking like tourists from the East who figure you've got to talk to Indians so they'll understand. Papa didn't seem to take any notice of the way they talked. He kept looking at the sky. "Geese up there, white man. You know it. Geese this year. And last year. And the year before and the year before."

The men looked at one another and cleared their throats. "Yes. Maybe true, Chief Bromden. Now. Forget geese. Pay attention to contract. What we offer could greatly benefit you—your people—change the lives of the red man."

Papa said, ". . . and the year before and the year before and the year before . . ."

By the time it dawned on the government men that they were being poked fun at, all the council who'd been sitting on the porch of our shack, putting pipes in the pockets of their red and black plaid wool shirts and taking them back out again, grinning at one another and at Papa—they had all busted up laughing fit to kill. Uncle R & J Wolf was rolling on the ground, gasping with laughter and saying, "You know it, white man."

It sure did get their goat; they turned without saying a word and walked off toward the highway, red-necked, us laughing behind them. I forget sometimes what laughter can do.

The Big Nurse's key hits the lock, and the black boy is up to her soon as she's in the door, shifting from foot to foot like a kid asking to pee. I'm close enough I hear McMurphy's name come into his conversation a couple of times, so I know he's telling her about McMurphy brushing his teeth, completely

forgetting to tell her about the old Vegetable who died during the night. Waving his arms and trying to tell her what that
fool redhead's been up to already, so early in the morning—
disrupting things, goin' contrary to ward policy, can't she *do*
something?

She glares at the black boy till he stops fidgeting, then looks
up the hall to where McMurphy's singing is booming out of
the latrine door louder than ever. " 'Oh, your parents don't like
me, they say I'm too po-o-or; they say I'm not worthy to enter
your door.' "

Her face is puzzled at first; like the rest of us, it's been so
long since she's heard singing it takes her a second to recognize what it is.

" 'Hard livin's my pleasure, my money's my o-o-own, an'
them that don't like me, they can leave me alone.' "

She listens a minute more to make sure she isn't hearing
things; then she goes to puffing up. Her nostrils flare open, and
every breath she draws she gets bigger, as big and tough-looking's I seen her get over a patient since Taber was here. She
works the hinges in her elbows and fingers. I hear a small
squeak. She starts moving, and I get back against the wall, and
when she rumbles past she's already big as a truck, trailing that
wicker bag behind in her exhaust like a semi behind a Jimmy
Diesel. Her lips are parted, and her smile's going out before
her like a radiator grill. I can smell the hot oil and magneto
spark when she goes past, and every step hits the floor she
blows up a size bigger, blowing and puffing, roll down anything in her path! I'm scared to think *what* she'll do.

Then, just as she's rolling along at her biggest and meanest,
McMurphy steps out of the latrine door right in front of her,
holding that towel around his hips—stops her *dead!* She shrinks
to about head-high to where that towel covers him, and he's
grinning down on her. Her own grin is giving way, sagging at
the edges.

"Good morning, Miss Rat-shed! How's things on the outside?"

"You can't run around here—in a *towel!*"

"No?" He looks down at the part of the towel she's eye to
eye with, and it's wet and skin tight. "Towels against ward
policy too? Well, I guess there's nothin' to do exce—"

"*Stop*! don't you dare. You get back in that dorm and get
your clothes on this *instant!*"

She sounds like a teacher bawling out a student, so Mc-
Murphy hangs his head like a student and says in a voice
sounds like he's about to cry, "I can't do that, ma'am. I'm

afraid some thief in the night boosted my clothes whilst I slept. I sleep awful sound on the mattresses you have here."

"Somebody boosted . . . ?"

"Pinched. Jobbed. Swiped. Stole," he says happily. "You know, man, like somebody boosted my threads." Saying this tickles him so he goes into a little barefooted dance before her.

"Stole your clothes?"

"That looks like the whole of it."

"But—prison clothes? Why?"

He stops jigging around and hangs his head again. "All I know is that they were there when I went to bed and gone when I got up. Gone slick as a whistle. Oh, I do *know* they were nothing but prison clothes, coarse and faded and uncouth, ma'am, well I know it—and prison clothes may not seem like much to those as has *more*. But to a nude man—"

"That outfit," she says, realizing, "was *supposed* to be picked up. You were issued a uniform of green convalescents this morning."

He shakes his head and sighs, but still don't look up. "No. No, I'm afraid I wasn't. Not a thing this morning but the cap that's on my head and—"

"Williams," she hollers down to the black boy who's still at the ward door like he might make a run for it. "Williams, can you come here a moment?"

He crawls to her like a dog to a whipping.

"Williams, why doesn't this patient have an issue of convalescents?"

The black boy is relieved. He straightens up and grins, raises that gray hand and points down the other end of the hall to one of the big ones. "Mistuh Washington over there is 'signed to the laundry duty this mornin'. Not me. No."

"Mr. *Washington!*" She nails him with his mop poised over the bucket, freezes him there. "Will you come here a moment!"

The mop slides without a sound back in the bucket, and with slow, careful movements he leans the handle against the wall. He turns around and looks down at McMurphy and the least black boy and the nurse. He looks then to his left and to his right, like she might be yelling at somebody else.

"Come down here!"

He puts his hands in his pockets and starts shuffling down the hall to her. He never walks very fast, and I can see how if he don't get a move on she might freeze him and shatter him all to hell by just looking; all the hate and fury and frustration she was planning to use on McMurphy is beaming out down the hall at the black boy, and he can feel it blast against him like a blizzard wind, slowing him more than ever. He has to lean into it, pulling his arms around him. Frost forms in his hair and eyebrows. He leans farther forward, but his steps are getting slower; he'll never make it.

Then McMurphy takes to whistling "Sweet Georgia Brown," and the nurse looks away from the black boy just in time. Now she's madder and more frustrated than ever, madder'n I ever saw her get. Her doll smile is gone, stretched tight and thin as a red-hot wire. If some of the patients could be out to see her now, McMurphy could start collecting his bets.

The black boy finally gets to her, and it took him two hours. She draws a long breath. "Washington, why wasn't this man issued a change of greens this morning? Couldn't you see he had nothing on but a towel?"

"And my cap," McMurphy whispers, tapping the brim with his finger.

"Mr. Washington?"

The big black boy looks at the little one who pointed him out, and the little black boy commences to fidget again. The big boy looks at him a long time with those radio-tube eyes, plans to square things with *him* later; then the head turns and he looks McMurphy up and down, taking in the hard, heavy shoulders, the lopsided grin, the scar on the nose, the hand clamping the towel in place, and then he looks at the nurse.

"I guess—" he starts out.

"You *guess!* You'll do more than *guess!* You'll get him a uniform this instant, Mr. Washington, or spend the next two weeks working on Geriatrics Ward! Yes. You may need a month of bedpans and slab baths to refresh your appreciation of just how little work you aides have to do on this ward. If this was one of the other wards, who do you think would be scouring the hall all day? Mr. Bromden here? No, you know who it would be. We excuse you aides from most of your housekeeping duties to enable you to see to the patients. And that means seeing that they don't parade around exposed. What do you think would have happened if one of the young nurses had come in early and found a patient running round the halls without a uniform? What do you think!"

The big black boy isn't too sure what, but he gets her drift and ambles off to the linen room to get McMurphy a set of greens—probably ten sizes too small—and ambles back and holds it out to him with a look of the clearest hate I ever saw. McMurphy just looks confused, like he don't know how to take the outfit the black boy's handing to him, what with one hand holding the toothbrush and the other hand holding up

the towel. He finally winks at the nurse and shrugs and un-
wraps the towel, drapes it over her shoulder like she was a
wooden rack.

I see he had his shorts on under the towel all along.

I think for a fact that she'd rather he'd of been stark naked
under that towel than had on those shorts. She's glaring at
those big white whales leaping round on his shorts in pure
wordless outrage. That's more'n she can take. It's a full minute
before she can pull herself together enough to turn on the
least black boy; her voice is shaking out of control, she's so
mad.

"Williams . . . I believe . . . you were supposed to have
the windows of the Nurses' Station polished by the time I arrived this morning." He scuttles off like a black and white bug.
"And you, Washington—and you . . ." Washington shuffles
back to his bucket in almost a trot. She looks around again,
wondering who else she can light into. She spots me, but by
this time some of the other patients are out of the dorm and
wondering about the little clutch of us here in the hall. She
closes her eyes and concentrates. She can't have them see her
face like this, white and warped with fury. She uses all the
power of control that's in her. Gradually the lips gather together again under the little white nose, run together, like the
red-hot wire had got hot enough to melt, shimmer a second,
then click solid as the molten metal sets, growing cold and
strangely dull. Her lips part, and her tongue comes between
them, a chunk of slag. Her eyes open again, and they have that
strange dull and cold and flat look the lips have, but she goes
into her good-morning routine like there was nothing different
about her, figuring the patients'll be too sleepy to notice.

"Good morning, Mr. Sefelt, are your teeth any better? Good
morning, Mr. Fredrickson, did you and Mr. Sefelt have a good
night last night? You bed right next to each other, don't you?
Incidentally, it's been brought to my attention that you two
have made some arrangement with your medication—you are
letting Bruce have your medication, aren't you, Mr. Sefelt?
We'll discuss that later. Good morning, Billy; I saw your
mother on the way in, and she told me to be sure to tell you
she thought of you all the time and *knew* you wouldn't disap-
point her. Good morning, Mr. Harding—why, look, your fingertips are red and raw. Have you been chewing your fingernails again?"

Before they could answer, even if there was some answer to
make, she turns to McMurphy still standing there in his shorts.
Harding looks at the shorts and whistles.

"And you, Mr. McMurphy," she says, smiling, sweet as sugar, "if you are finished showing off your manly physique and your gaudy underpants. I think you had better go back in the dorm and put on your greens."

He tips his cap to her and to the patients ogling and poking fun at his white-whale shorts, and goes to the dorm without a word. She turns and starts off in the other direction, her flat red smile going out before her; before she's got the door closed on her glass station, his singing is rolling from the dorm door into the hall again.

" 'She took me to her parlor, and coo-oo-ooled me with her fan' "—I can hear the whack as he slaps his bare belly—" 'whispered low in her mamma's ear, I luh-uhvvv that gamblin' man.' "

Sweeping the dorm soon's it's empty, I'm after dust mice under his bed when I get a smell of something that makes me realize for the first time since I been in the hospital that this big dorm full of beds, sleeps forty grown men, has always been sticky with a thousand other smells—smells of germicide, zinc ointment, and foot powder, smell of piss and sour old-man manure, of Pablum and eyewash, of musty shorts and socks musty even when they're fresh back from the laundry, the stiff odor of starch in the linen, the acid stench of morning mouths, the banana smell of machine oil, and sometimes the smell of singed hair—but never before now, before he came in, the man smell of dust and dirt from the open fields, and sweat, and work.

All through breakfast McMurphy's talking and laughing a mile a minute. After this morning he thinks the Big Nurse is going to be a snap. He don't know he just caught her off guard and, if anything, made her strengthen herself.

He's being the clown, working at getting some of the guys to laugh. It bothers him that the best they can do is grin weakly and snigger sometimes. He prods at Billy Bibbit, sitting across the table from him, says in a secret voice, "Hey, Billy boy, you remember that time in Seattle you and me picked up those two twitches? One of the best rolls I ever had."

Billy's eyes bob up from his plate. He opens his mouth but can't say a thing. McMurphy turns to Harding.

"We'd never have brought it off, neither, picking them up on the spur of the moment that way, except that they'd heard tell of Billy Bibbit. Billy 'Club' Bibbit, he was known as in them days. Those girls were about to take off when one looked at him and says 'Are you *the* renowned Billy Club Bibbit? Of the famous fourteen inches?' And Billy ducked his head and blushed—like he's doin' now—and we were a shoo-in. And I remember, when we got them up to the hotel, there was this woman's voice from over near Billy's bed, says, 'Mister Bibbit, I'm disappointed in you; I heard that you had four—four—for goodness *sakes!*'"

And whoops and slaps his leg and gooses Billy with his thumb till I think Billy will fall in a dead faint from blushing and grinning.

McMurphy says that as a matter of fact a couple of sweet twitches like those two is the *only* thing this hospital does lack. The bed they give a man here, finest he's ever slept in, and what a fine table they do spread. He can't figure why everybody's so glum about being locked up here.

"Look at me now," he tells the guys and lifts a glass to the light, "getting my first glass of orange juice in six months. Hooee, that's good. I ask you, what did I get for breakfast at that work farm? What was I served? Well, I can describe what it *looked* like, but I sure couldn't hang a name on it; morning noon and night it was burnt black and had potatoes in it and looked like roofing glue. I know one thing; it wasn't orange juice. Look at me now: bacon, toast, butter, eggs—coffee the little honey in the kitchen even asks me if I like it black or white thank you—and a great! big! cold glass of orange juice. Why, you couldn't *pay* me to leave this place!"

He gets seconds on everything and makes a date with the girl pours coffee in the kitchen for when he gets discharged, and he compliments the Negro cook on sunnysiding the best eggs he ever ate. There's bananas for the corn flakes, and he gets a handful, tells the black boy that he'll filch him one 'cause he looks so starved, and the black boy shifts his eyes to look down the hall to where the Nurse is sitting in her glass case, and says it ain't allowed for the help to eat with the patients.

"Against ward policy?"

"Tha's right."

"Tough luck"—and peels three bananas right under the black boy's nose and eats one after the other, tells the boy that any time you want one snuck outa the mess hall for you, Sam, you just give the word.

When McMurphy finishes his last banana he slaps his belly and gets up and heads for the door, and the big black boy blocks the door and tells him the rule that patients sit in the mess hall till they all leave at seven-thirty. McMurphy stares at him like he can't believe he's hearing right, then turns and looks at Harding. Harding nods his head, so McMurphy shrugs and goes back to his chair. "I sure don't want to go against that goddamned policy."

The clock at the end of the mess hall shows it's a quarter after seven, lies about how we only been sitting here fifteen minutes when you can tell it's been at least an hour. Everybody is finished eating and leaned back, watching the big hand to move to seven-thirty. The black boys take away the Vegetables' splattered trays and wheel the two old men down to get hosed off. In the mess hall about half the guys lay their heads on their arms, figuring to get a little sleep before the black boys get back. There's nothing else to do, with no cards or magazines or picture puzzles. Just sleep or watch the clock.

But McMurphy can't keep still for that; he's got to be up to something. After about two minutes of pushing food scraps around his plate with his spoon, he's ready for more excitement. He hooks his thumbs in his pockets and tips back and one-eyes that clock up on the wall. Then he rubs his nose.

"You know—that old clock up there puts me in mind of the *targets* at the target range at Fort Riley. That's where I got my first medal, a sharpshooter medal. Dead-Eye McMurphy.

Who wants to lay me a pore little dollar that I can't put this dab of butter square in the center of the face of that clock up there, or at least *on* the face?"

He gets three bets and takes up his butter pat and puts it on his knife, gives it a flip. It sticks a good six inches or so to the left of the clock, and everybody kids him about it until he pays his bets. They're still riding him about did he mean Dead-Eye or Dead-Eyes when the least black boy gets back from hosing Vegetables and everybody looks into his plate and keeps quiet. The black boy senses something is in the air, but he can't see what. And he probably never would of known except old Colonel Matterson is gazing around, and *he* sees the butter stuck up on the wall and this causes him to point up at it and go into one of his lessons, explaining to us all in his patient, rumbling voice, just like what he said made sense.

"The but-ter . . . is the Re-pub-li-can party. . . ."

The black boy looks where the colonel is pointing, and there that butter is, easing down the wall like a yellow snail. He blinks at it but he doesn't say a word, doesn't even bother looking around to make certain who flipped it up there.

McMurphy is whispering and nudging the Acutes sitting around him, and in a minute they all nod, and he lays three dollars on the table and leans back. Everybody turns in his chair and watches that butter sneak on down the wall, starting, hanging still, shooting ahead and leaving a shiny trail behind it on the paint. Nobody says a word. They look at the butter, then at the clock, then back at the butter. The clock's moving now.

The butter makes it down to the floor about a half minute before seven-thirty, and McMurphy gets back all the money he lost.

The black boy wakes up and turns away from the greasy stripe on the wall and says we can go, and McMurphy walks out of the mess hall, folding his money in his pocket. He puts his arms around the black boy's shoulders and half walks, half carries him, down the hall toward the day room. "The day's half gone, Sam, ol' buddy, an' I'm just barely breaking even. I'll have to hustle to catch up. How about breaking out that deck of cards you got locked securely in that cabinet, and I'll see if I can make myself heard over that loudspeaker."

Spends most of that morning hustling to catch up by dealing more blackjack, playing for IOUs now instead of cigarettes. He moves the blackjack table two or three times to try to get out from under the speaker. You can tell it's getting on his nerves. Finally he goes to the Nurses' Station and raps on a pane of glass till the Big Nurse swivels in her chair and opens the door, and he asks her how about turning that infernal noise off for a while. She's calmer than ever now, back in her seat behind her pane of glass; there's no heathen running around half-naked to unbalance her. Her smile is settled and solid. She closes her eyes and shakes her head and tells McMurphy very pleasantly, No.

"Can't you even ease down the volume? It ain't like the whole state of Oregon needed to hear Lawrence Welk play 'Tea for Two' three times every hour, all day long! If it was soft enough to hear a man shout his bets across the table I might get a game of poker going—"

"You've been told, Mr. McMurphy, that it's against the policy to gamble for money on the ward."

"Okay, then down soft enough to gamble for matches, for fly buttons—just turn the damn thing down!"

"Mr. McMurphy"—she waits and lets her calm school-teacher tone sink in before she goes on; she knows every Acute on the ward is listening to them—"do you want to know what I think? I think you are being very selfish. Haven't you noticed there are others in this hospital besides yourself? There are old men here who couldn't hear the radio at all if it were lower, old fellows who simply aren't capable of reading, or working puzzles—or playing cards to win other men's cigarettes. Old fellows like Matterson and Kittling, that music coming from the loudspeaker is all they have. And you want to take that away from them. We like to hear suggestions and requests whenever we can, but I should think you might at least give some thought to others before you make your requests."

He turns and looks over at the Chronic side and sees there's something to what she says. He takes off his cap and runs his hand in his hair, finally turns back to her. He knows as well as she does that all the Acutes are listening to everything they say.

"Okay—I never thought about that."

"I thought you hadn't."

He tugs at that little tuft of red showing out of the neck of his greens, then says. "Well, hey; what do you say to us taking the card game someplace else? Some other room? Like, say, that room you people put the tables in during that meeting. There's nothing in there all the rest of the day. You could un-lock that room and let the card-players go in there, and leave the old men out here with their radio—a good deal all around."

She smiles and closes her eyes again and shakes her head gently. "Of course, you take the suggestion up with the rest of the staff at some time, but I'm afraid everyone's feelings will correspond with mine: we do not have adequate coverage for two day rooms. There isn't enough personnel. And I wish you wouldn't lean against the glass there, please; your hands are oily and staining the window. That means extra work for some of the other men."

He jerks his hand away, and I see he starts to say something and then stops, realizing she didn't leave him anything else to say, unless he wants to start cussing at her. His face and neck are red. He draws a long breath and concentrates on his will power, the way she did this morning, and tells her that he is very sorry to have bothered her, and goes back to the card table.

Everybody on the ward can feel that it's started.

At eleven o'clock the doctor comes to the day-room door and calls over to McMurphy that he'd like to have him come down to his office for an interview. "I interview all new admissions on the second day."

McMurphy lays down his cards and stands up and walks over to the doctor. The doctor asks him how his night was, but McMurphy just mumbles an answer.

"You look deep in thought today, Mr. McMurphy."

"Oh, I'm a thinker all right," McMurphy says, and they walk off together down the hall. When they come back what seems like days later, they're both grinning and talking and happy about something. The doctor is wiping tears off his glasses and looks like he's actually been laughing, and McMurphy is back as loud and full of brass and swagger as ever. He's that way all through lunch, and at one o'clock he's the first one in his seat for the meeting, his eyes blue and ornery from his place in the corner.

The Big Nurse comes into the day room with her covey of student nurses and her basket of notes. She picks the log book up from the table and frowns into it a minute (nobody's informed on anybody all day long), then goes to her seat beside the door. She picks up some folders from the basket on her lap and riffles through them till she finds the one on Harding.

"As I recall, we were making quite a bit of headway yesterday with Mr. Harding's problem—"

"Ah—before we go into that," the doctor says, "I'd like to interrupt a moment, if I might. Concerning a talk Mr. Mc-

Murphy and I had in my office this morning. Reminiscing, actually. Talking over old times. You see Mr. McMurphy and I find we have something in common—we went to the same high school."

The nurses look at one another and wonder what's got into this man. The patients glance at McMurphy grinning from his corner and wait for the doctor to go on. He nods his head.

"Yes, the same high school. And in the course of our reminiscing we happened to bring up the carnivals the school used to sponsor—marvelous, noisy, gala occasions. Decorations, crepe streamers, booths, games—it was always one of the prime events of the year. I—as I mentioned to McMurphy—was the chairman of the high-school carnival both my junior and senior years—wonderful carefree years . . ."

It's got real quiet in the day room. The doctor raises his head, peers around to see if he's making a fool of himself. The Big Nurse is giving him a look that shouldn't leave any doubts about it, but he doesn't have on his glasses and the look misses him.

"Anyway—to put an end to this maudlin display of nostalgia —in the course of our conversation McMurphy and I wondered what would be the attitude of some of the men toward a carnival here on the ward?"

He puts on his glasses and peers around again. Nobody's jumping up and down at the idea. Some of us can remember Taber trying to engineer a carnival a few years back, and what happened to it. As the doctor waits, a silence rears up from out of the nurse and looms over everybody, daring anybody to challenge it. I know McMurphy can't because he was in on the planning of the carnival, and just as I'm thinking that nobody will be fool enough to break that silence, Cheswick, who sits right next to McMurphy, gives a grunt and is on his feet, rubbing his ribs, before he knows what happened.

"Uh—I personally believe, see"—he looks down at McMurphy's fist on the chair arm beside him, with that big stiff thumb sticking straight up out of it like a cow prod—"that a carnival is a real good idea. Something to break the monotony."

"That's right, Charley," the doctor says, appreciating Cheswick's support, "and not altogether without therapeutic value."

"Certainly not," Cheswick says, looking happier now. "No. Lots of therapeutics in a carnival. You bet."

"It would b-b-be fun," Billy Bibbit says.

"Yeah, that too," Cheswick says. "We could do it, Doctor Spivey, sure we could. Scanlon can do his human bomb act, and I can make a ring toss in Occupational Therapy."

"I'll tell fortunes," Martini says and squints at a spot above his head.

"I'm rather good at diagnosing pathologies from palm reading, myself," Harding says.

"Good, good," Cheswick says and claps his hands. He's never had anybody support anything he said before.

"Myself," McMurphy drawls, "I'd be honored to work a skillo wheel. Had a little experience . . ."

"Oh, there are numerous possibilities," the doctor says, sitting up straight in his chair and really warming to it. "Why, I've got a million ideas. . . ."

He talks full steam ahead for another five minutes. You can tell a lot of the ideas are ideas he's already talked over with McMurphy. He describes games, booths, talks of selling tickets, then stops as suddenly as though the Nurse's look had hit him right between the eyes. He blinks at her and asks, "What do you think of the idea, Miss Ratched? Of a carnival? Here, on the ward?"

"I agree that it may have a number of therapeutic possibilities," she says, and waits. She lets that silence rear up from her again. When she's sure nobody's going to challenge it, she goes on. "But I also believe that an idea like this should be discussed in staff meeting before a decision is reached. Wasn't that your idea, Doctor?"

"Of course. I merely thought, understand, I would feel out some of the men first. But certainly, a staff meeting first. Then we'll continue our plans."

Everybody knows that's all there is to the carnival.

The Big Nurse starts to bring things back into hand by rattling the folio she's holding. "Fine. Then if there is no other new business—and if Mr. Cheswick will be seated—I think we might go right on into the discussion. We have"—she takes her watch from the basket and looks at it—"forty-eight minutes left. So, as I—"

"Oh. Hey, wait. I remember there is some other new business." McMurphy has his hand up, fingers snapping. She looks at the hand for a long time before she says anything.

"Yes, Mr. McMurphy?"

"Not me, Doctor Spivey has. Doc, tell 'em what you come up with about the hard-of-hearing guys and the radio."

The nurse's head gives one little jerk, barely enough to see, but my heart is suddenly roaring. She puts the folio back in the basket, turns to the doctor.

"Yes," says the doctor. "I very nearly forgot." He leans back and crosses his legs and puts his fingertips together; I can see he's still in good spirits about his carnival. "You see, Mc-Murphy and I were talking about that age-old problem we have on this ward: the mixed population, the young and the old together. It's not the most ideal surroundings for our Therapeutic Community, but Administration says there's no helping it with the Geriatric Building overloaded the way it is. I'll be the first to admit it's not an absolutely pleasant situation for anyone concerned. In our talk, however, McMurphy and I did happen to come up with an idea which might make things more pleasant for both age groups. McMurphy mentioned that he had noticed some of the old fellows seemed to have difficulty hearing the radio. He suggested the speaker be turned up louder so the Chronics with auditory weaknesses could hear it. A very humane suggestion, I think."

McMurphy gives a modest wave of his hand, and the doctor nods at him and goes on.

"But I told him I had received previous complaints from some of the younger men that the radio is already so loud it hinders conversation and reading. McMurphy said he hadn't thought of this, but mentioned that it did seem a shame that those who wished to read couldn't get off by themselves where it was quiet and leave the radio for those who wished to listen. I agreed with him that it did seem a shame and was ready to drop the matter when I happened to think of the old tub room where we store the tables during the ward meeting. We don't use the room at all otherwise; there's no longer a need for the hydrotherapy it was designed for, now that we have the new drugs. So how would the group like to have that room as a sort of second day room, a *game* room, shall we say?"

The group isn't saying. They know whose play it is next. She folds Harding's folio back up and puts it on her lap and crosses her hands over it, looking around the room just like somebody might dare have something to say. When it's clear nobody's going to talk till she does, her head turns again to the doctor. "It sounds like a fine plan, Doctor Spivey, and I appreciate Mr. McMurphy's interest in the other patients, but I'm terribly afraid we don't have the personnel to cover a second day room."

And is so certain that this should be the end of it she starts to open the folio again. But the doctor has thought this through more than she figured.

"I thought of that, too, Miss Ratched. But since it will be largely the Chronic patients who remain here in the day room with the speaker—most of whom are restricted to lounges or wheel chairs—one aide and one nurse in here should easily be able to put down any riots or uprisings that might occur, don't you think?"

She doesn't answer, and she doesn't care much for his joking about riots and uprisings either, but her face doesn't change. The smile stays.

"So the other two aides and nurses can cover the men in the tub room, perhaps even better than here in a larger area. What do you think, men? Is it a workable idea? I'm rather enthused about it myself, and I say we give it a try, see what it's like for a few days. If it doesn't work, well, we've still got the key to lock it back up, haven't we?"

"Right!" Cheswick says, socks his fist into his palm. He's still standing, like he's afraid to get near that thumb of Mc-Murphy's again. "Right, Doctor Spivey, if it don't work, we've still got the key to lock it back up. You bet."

The doctor looks around the room and sees all the other Acutes nodding and smiling and looking so pleased with what he takes to be him and his idea that he blushes like Billy Bibbit and has to polish his glasses a time or two before he can go on. It tickles me to see the little man so happy with himself. He looks at all the guys nodding, and nods himself and says, "Fine, fine," and settles his hands on his knees. "Very good. Now. If that's decided—I seem to have forgotten what we were planning to talk about this morning?"

The nurse's head gives that one little jerk again, and she bends over her basket, picks up a folio. She fumbles with the papers, and it looks like her hands are shaking. She draws out a paper, but once more, before she can start reading out of it, McMurphy is standing and holding up his hand and shifting from foot to foot, giving a long, thoughtful, "Saaaay," and her fumbling stops, freezes as though the sound of his voice froze her just like her voice froze that black boy this morning. I get that giddy feeling inside me again when she freezes. I watch her close while McMurphy talks.

"Saaaaay, Doctor, what I been dyin' to know is what did this dream I dreamt the other night mean? You see, it was like I was *me*, in the dream, and then again kind of like I *wasn't* me—like I was somebody else that looked like me—like—like my *daddy!* Yeah, that's who it was. It was my daddy because sometimes when I saw me—him—I saw there was this iron bolt through the jawbone like daddy used to have—"

"Your father has an iron *bolt* through his jawbone?"

"Well, not any more, but he did once when I was a kid. He went around for about ten months with this big metal bolt going in *here* and coming out *here!* God, he was a regular

Frankenstein. He'd been clipped on the jaw with a pole ax when he got into some kinda hassle with this pond man at the logging mill—Hey! Let me tell you how *that* incident came about. . . ."

Her face is still calm, as though she had a cast made and painted to just the look she wants. Confident, patient, and unruffled. No more little jerk, just that terrible cold face, a calm smile stamped out of red plastic; a clean, smooth forehead, not a line in it to show weakness or worry; flat, wide, painted-on green eyes, painted on with an expression that says I can wait, I might lose a yard now and then but I can wait, and be patient and calm and confident, because I know there's no real losing for me.

I thought for a minute there I saw her whipped. Maybe I did. But I see now that it don't make any difference. One by one the patients are sneaking looks at her to see how she's taking the way McMurphy is dominating the meeting, and they see the same thing. She's too big to be beaten. She covers one whole side of the room like a Jap statue. There's no moving her and no help against her. She's lost a little battle here today, but it's a minor battle in a big war that she's been winning and that she'll go on winning. We mustn't let McMurphy get our hopes up any different, lure us into making some kind of dumb play. She'll go on winning, just like the Combine, because she has all the power of the Combine behind her. She don't lose on her losses, but she wins on ours. To beat her you don't have to whip her two out of three or three out of five, but every time you meet. As soon as you let down your guard, as soon as you lose *once*, she's won for good. And eventually we all got to lose. Nobody can help that.

Right now, she's got the fog machine switched on, and it's rolling in so fast I can't see a thing but her face, rolling in thicker and thicker, and I feel as hopeless and dead as I felt happy a minute ago, when she gave that little jerk—even more hopeless than ever before, on account of I know now there is no real help against her or her Combine. McMurphy can't help any more than I could. Nobody can help. And the more I think about how nothing can be helped, the faster the fog rolls in.

And I'm glad when it gets thick enough you're lost in it and can let go, and be safe again.

There's a Monopoly game going on in the day room. They've been at it for three days, houses and hotels everywhere, two tables pushed together to take care of all the deeds and stacks of play money. McMurphy talked them into making the game interesting by paying a penny for every dollar the bank issues them; the monopoly box is loaded with change.

"It's your roll, Cheswick."

"Hold it a minute before he rolls. What's a man need to buy thum hotels?"

"You need four houses on every lot of the same color, Martini. Now let's *go,* for Christsakes."

"Hold it a minute."

There's a flurry of money from that side of the table, red and green and yellow bills blowing in every direction.

"You buying a hotel or you playing happy new year, for Christsakes?"

"It's your dirty roll, Cheswick."

"Snake eyes? Hoooeee, Cheswicker, where does that put you? That don't put you on my Marvin Gardens by any chance? That don't mean you have to pay me, let's see, three hundred and fifty dollars?"

"Boogered."

"What's thum other things? Hold it a minute. What's thum other things *all* over the board?"

"Martini, you been seeing them other things all over the board for two days. No wonder I'm losing my ass. McMurphy, I don't see how you can concentrate with Martini sitting there hallucinating a mile a minute."

"Cheswick, you never mind about Martini. He's doing real good. You just come on with that three fifty, and Martini will take care of himself; don't we get rent from him every time one of his 'things' lands on our property?"

"Hold it a minute. There's so many of thum."

"That's okay, Mart. You just keep us posted whose property they land on. You're still the man with the dice, Cheswick. You rolled a double, so you roll again. Atta boy. *Faw!* a big six."

"Takes me to . . . Chance: 'You Have Been Elected Chairman of the Board; Pay Every Player—' Boogered and double boogered!"

"Whose hotel is this here for Christsakes on the Reading Railroad?"

"My friend, that, as anyone can see, is not a hotel; it's a depot."

"Now *hold* it a minute—"

McMurphy surrounds his end of the table, moving cards, rearranging money, evening up his hotels. There's a hundred-dollar bill sticking out of the brim of his cap like a press card; mad money, he calls it.

"Scanlon? I believe it's your turn, buddy."

"Gimme those dice. I'll blow this board to pieces. Here we go. Lebenty Leben, count me over eleven, Martini."

"Why, all right."

"Not that one, you crazy bastard; that's not my piece, that's my *house*."

"It's the same color."

"What's this little house doing on the Electric Company?"

"That's a power station."

"Martini, those ain't the dice you're shaking—"

"Let him be; what's the difference?"

"Those are a couple of houses!"

"*Faw*. And Martini rolls a big, let me see, a big nineteen. Good goin', Mart; that puts you—Where's your piece, buddy?"

"Eh? Why here it is."

"He had it in his mouth, McMurphy. Excellent. That's two moves over the second and third bicuspid, four moves to the board, which takes you on to—to Baltic Avenue, Martini. Your own and only property. How fortunate can a man get, friends? Martini has been playing three days and lit on his property practically every time."

"Shut up and roll, Harding. It's your turn."

Harding gathers the dice up with his long fingers, feeling the smooth surfaces with his thumb as if he was blind. The fingers are the same color as the dice and look like they were carved by his other hand. The dice rattle in his hand as he shakes it. They tumble to a stop in front of McMurphy.

"*Faw*. Five, six, seven. Tough luck, buddy. That's another o' my vast holdin's. You owe me—oh, two hundred dollars should about cover it."

"Pity."

The game goes round and round, to the rattle of dice and the shuffle of play money.

*T*here's long spells—three days, years—
when you can't see a thing, know where
you are only by the speaker sounding overhead like a bell
buoy clanging in the fog. When I can see, the guys are usually
moving around as unconcerned as though they didn't notice
so much as a mist in the air. I believe the fog affects their
memory some way it doesn't affect mine.

Even McMurphy doesn't seem to know he's been fogged in.
If he does, he makes sure not to let on that he's bothered by it.
He's making sure none of the staff sees him bothered by anything; he knows that there's no better way in the world to
aggravate somebody who's trying to make it hard for you than
by acting like you're not bothered.

He keeps up his high-class manners around the nurses and
the black boys in spite of anything they might say to him, in
spite of every trick they pull to get him to lose his temper. A
couple of times some stupid rule gets him mad, but he just
makes himself act more polite and mannerly than ever till he
begins to see how funny the whole thing is—the rules, the dis-
approving looks they use to enforce the rules, the ways of talking to you like you're nothing but a three-year-old—and when
he sees how funny it is he goes to laughing, and this aggravates
them no end. He's safe as long as he can laugh, he thinks, and
it works pretty fair. Just once he loses control and shows he's
mad, and then it's not because of the black boys or the Big
Nurse and something they did, but it's because of the patients,
and something they *didn't* do.

It happened at one of the group meetings. He got mad at
the guys for acting too cagey—too chicken-shit, he called it.
He'd been taking bets from all of them on the World Series
coming up Friday. He'd had it in mind that they would get
to watch the games on TV, even though they didn't come on
during regulation TV time. During the meeting a few days before he asks if it wouldn't be okay if they did the cleaning work
at night, during TV time, and watched the games during the
afternoon. The nurse tells him no, which is about what he
expected. She tells him how the schedule has been set up for a

104

delicately balanced reason that would be thrown into turmoil by the switch of routines.

This doesn't surprise him, coming from the nurse; what does surprise him is how the Acutes act when he asks them what they think of the idea. Nobody says a thing. They're all sunk back out of sight in little pockets of fog. I can barely see them.

"Now look here," he tells them, but they don't look. He's been waiting for somebody to say something, answer his question. Nobody acts like they've heard it. "Look here, damn it," he says when nobody moves, "there's at least twelve of you guys I know of myself got a leetle personal *interest* who wins these games. Don't you guys care to watch them?"

"I don't know, Mack," Scanlon finally says, "I'm pretty used to seeing that six-o'clock news. And if switching times would really mess up the schedule as bad as Miss Ratched says—"

"The hell with the schedule. You can get back to the bloody schedule next week, when the Series is over. What do you say, buddies? Let's take a vote on watching the TV during the afternoon instead of at night. All those in favor?"

"Ay," Cheswick calls out and gets to his feet.

"I mean all those in favor raise their hands. Okay, all those in favor?"

Cheswick's hand comes up. Some of the other guys look around to see if there's any other fools. McMurphy can't believe it.

"Come on now, what is this crap? I thought you guys could vote on policy and that sort of thing. Isn't that the way it is, Doc?"

The doctor nods without looking up.

"Okay then; now who wants to watch those games?"

Cheswick shoves his hand higher and glares around. Scanlon shakes his head and then raises his hand, keeping his elbow on the arm of the chair. And nobody else. McMurphy can't say a word.

"If that's settled, then," the nurse says, "perhaps we should get on with the meeting."

"Yeah," he says, slides down in his chair till the brim of his cap nearly touches his chest. "Yeah, perhaps we should get on with the sonofabitchin' meeting at that."

"Yeah," Cheswick says, giving all the guys a hard look and sitting down, "yeah, get on with the godblessed meeting." He nods stiffly, then settles his chin down on his chest, scowling. He's pleased to be sitting next to McMurphy, feeling brave like this. It's the first time Cheswick ever had somebody along with him on his lost causes.

After the meeting McMurphy won't say a word to any of them, he's so mad and disgusted. It's Billy Bibbit who goes up to him.

"Some of us have b-been here for fi-fi-five years, Randle," Billy says. He's got a magazine rolled up and is twisting at it with his hands; you can see the cigarette burns on the backs of his hands. "And some of us will b-be here maybe th-that muh-muh-much longer, long after you're g-g-gone, long after this Wo-world Series is over. And ... don't you see ..." He throws down the magazine and walks away. "Oh, what's the use of it anyway."

McMurphy stares after him, that puzzled frown knotting his bleached eyebrows together again.

He argues for the rest of the day with some of the other guys about why they didn't vote, but they don't want to talk about it, so he seems to give up, doesn't say anything about it again till the day before the Series starts. "Here it is Thursday," he says, sadly shaking his head.

He's sitting on one of the tables in the tub room with his feet on a chair, trying to spin his cap around one finger. Other Acutes mope around the room and try not to pay any attention to him. Nobody'll play poker or blackjack with him for money any more—after the patients wouldn't vote he got mad and skinned them so bad at cards that they're all so in debt they're scared to go any deeper—and they can't play for cigarettes because the nurse has started making the men keep their cartons on the desk in the Nurses Station, where she doles them out one pack a day, says its for their health, but everybody knows it's to keep McMurphy from winning them all at cards. With no poker or blackjack, it's quiet in the tub room, just the sound of the speaker drifting in from the day room. It's so quiet you can hear that guy upstairs in Disturbed climbing the wall, giving out an occasional signal, loo loo *looo*, a bored, uninterested sound, like a baby yells to yell itself to sleep.

"Thursday," McMurphy says again.

"*Looooo*," yells that guy upstairs.

"That's Rawler," Scanlon says, looking up at the ceiling. He don't want to pay any attention to McMurphy. "Rawler the Squawler. He came through this ward a few years back. Wouldn't keep still to suit Miss Ratched, you remember, Billy? Loo loo loo all the time till I thought I'd go nuts. What they should do with that whole bunch of dingbats up there is toss a couple of grenades in the dorm. They're no use to any-body—"

"And tomorrow is Friday," McMurphy says. He won't let Scanlon change the subject.

"Yeah," Cheswick says, scowling around the room, "tomorrow is Friday."

Harding turns a page of his magazine. "And that will make nearly a week our friend McMurphy has been with us without succeeding in throwing over the government, is that what you're saying, Cheswickle? Lord, to think of the chasm of apathy in which we have fallen—a shame, a pitiful shame."

"The hell with that," McMurphy says. "What Cheswick means is that the first Series game is gonna be played on TV tomorrow, and what are we gonna be doin'? Mopping up this damned nursery again."

"Yeah," Cheswick says. "Ol' Mother Ratched's Therapeutic Nursery."

Against the wall of the tub room I get a feeling like a spy; the mop handle in my hands is made of metal instead of wood (metal's a better conductor) and it's hollow; there's plenty of room inside it to hide a miniature microphone. If the Big Nurse is hearing this, she'll really get Cheswick. I take a hard ball of gum from my pocket and pick some fuzz off it and hold it in my mouth till it softens.

"Let me see again," McMurphy says. "How many of you birds will vote with me if I bring up that time switch again?"

About half the Acutes nod yes, a lot more than would really vote. He puts his hat back on his head and leans his chin in his hands.

"I tell ya, I can't figure it out. Harding, what's wrong with *you*, for crying out loud? You afraid if you raise your hand that old buzzard'll cut it off."

Harding lifts one thin eyebrow. "Perhaps I am; perhaps I *am* afraid she'll cut if off if I raise it."

"What about you, Billy? Is that what you're scared of?"

"No. I don't think she'd d-d-*do* anything, but"—he shrugs and sighs and climbs up on the big panel that controls the nozzles on the shower, perches up there like a monkey—"but I just don't think a vote wu-wu-would do any good. Not in the l-long run. It's just no use, M-Mack."

"Do any *good*? Hooee! It'd do you birds some good just to get the exercise lifting that arm."

"It's still a risk, my friend. She always has the capacity to make things worse for us. A baseball game isn't worth the risk," Harding says.

"Who the hell says so? Jesus, I haven't missed a World Series in years. Even when I was in the cooler one September they let us bring in a TV and watch the *Series;* they'd of had a riot on their hands if they hadn't. I just may have to kick that damned door down and walk to some bar downtown to see the game, just me and my buddy Cheswick."

"Now there's a suggestion with a lot of merit," Harding says, tossing down his magazine. "Why not bring that up for vote in group meeting tomorrow? 'Miss Ratched, I'd like to move that the ward be transported *en masse* to the Idle Hour for beer and television.' "

"I'd second the motion," Cheswick says. "Damn right."

"The hell with that in mass business," McMurphy says. "I'm tired of looking at you bunch of old ladies; when me and Cheswick bust outta here I think by God I'm gonna nail the door shut behind me. You guys better stay behind; your mamma probably wouldn't let you cross the street."

"Yeah? Is that it?" Fredrickson has come up behind McMurphy. "You're just going to raise one of those big he-man boots of yours and *kick* down the door? A real tough guy."

McMurphy don't hardly look at Fredrickson; he's learned that Fredrickson might act hard-boiled now and then, but it's an act that folds under the slightest scare.

"What about it, he-man," Fredrickson keeps on, "are you going to kick down that door and show us how tough you are?"

"No, Fred, I guess not. I wouldn't want to scuff up my boot."

"Yeah? Okay, you been talking so big, just how *would* you go about busting out of here?"

McMurphy takes a look around him. "Well, I guess I could knock the mesh outa one of these windows with a chair when and if I took a notion. . . ."

"Yeah? You could, could you? Knock it right out? Okay, let's see you try. Come on, he-man, I'll bet you ten dollars you can't do it."

"Don't bother trying, Mack," Cheswick says. "Fredrickson knows you'll just break a chair and end up on Disturbed. The first day we arrived over here we were given a demonstration about these screens. They're specially made. A technician picked up a chair just like that one you've got your feet on and beat the screen till the chair was no more than kindling wood. Didn't hardly dent the screen."

"Okay then," McMurphy says, taking a look around him. I can see he's getting more interested. I hope the Big Nurse isn't hearing this; he'll be up on Disturbed in an hour. "We need something heavier. How about a table?"

"Same as the chair. Same wood, same weight."

"All right, by God, let's just figure out what I'd have to toss through that screen to bust out. And if you birds don't think I'd do it if I ever got the urge, then you got another think coming. Okay—something bigger'n a table or a chair . . . Well, if it was night I might throw that fat coon through it; he's heavy enough."

"Much too soft," Harding says. "He'd hit the screen and it would dice him like an eggplant."

"How about one of the beds?"

"A bed is too big even if you could lift it. It wouldn't go through the window."

"I could lift it all right. Well, hell, right over there you are: that thing Billy's sittin' on. That big control panel with all the handles and cranks. That's hard enough, ain't it? And it damn well should be heavy enough."

"Sure," Fredrickson says. "That's the same as you kicking your foot through the steel door at the front."

"What would be wrong with using the panel? It don't look nailed down."

"No, it's not bolted—there's probably nothing holding it but a few wires—but *look* at it, for Christsakes."

Everybody looks. The panel is steel and cement, half the size of one of the tables, probably weighs four hundred pounds.

"Okay, I'm looking at it. It don't look any bigger than hay bales I've bucked up onto truck beds."

"I'm afraid, my friend, that this contrivance will weigh a bit more than your bales of hay."

"About a quarter-ton more, I'd bet," Fredrickson says.

"He's right, Mack," Cheswick says. "It'd be awful heavy."

"Hell, are you birds telling me I can't *lift* that dinky little gizmo?"

"My friend, I don't recall anything about psychopaths being able to move mountains in addition to their other noteworthy assets."

"Okay, you say I can't lift it. Well *by* God . . ."

McMurphy hops off the table and goes to peeling off his green jacket; the tattoos sticking half out of his T-shirt jump around the muscles on his arms.

"Then who's willing to lay five bucks? Nobody's gonna convince me I can't do something till I try it. Five bucks . . ."

"McMurphy, this is as foolhardy as your bet about the nurse."

"Who's got five bucks they want to lose? You hit or you sit. . . ."

The guys all go to signing liens at once; he's beat them so many times at poker and blackjack they can't wait to get back at him, and this is a certain sure thing. I don't know what he's driving at; broad and big as he is, it'd take three of him to move that panel, and he knows it. He can just look at it and see he probably couldn't even tip it, let alone lift it. It'd take a giant to lift if off the ground. But when the Acutes all get their IOUs signed, he steps up to the panel and lifts Billy Bibbit down off it and spits in his big callused palms and slaps them together, rolls his shoulders.

"Okay, stand outa the way. Sometimes when I go to exertin' myself I use up all the air nearby and grown men faint from suffocation. Stand back. There's liable to be crackin' cement and flying steel. Get the women and kids someplace safe. Stand back. . . ."

"By golly, he might do it," Cheswick mutters.

"Sure, maybe he'll talk if off the floor," Fredrickson says.

"More likely he'll acquire a beautiful hernia," Harding says. "Come now, McMurphy, quit acting like a fool; there's no man can lift that thing."

"Stand back, sissies, you're using my oxygen."

McMurphy shifts his feet a few times to get a good stance, and wipes his hands on his thighs again, then leans down and gets hold of the levers on each side of the panel. When he goes to straining, the guys go to hooting and kidding him. He turns loose and straightens up and shifts his feet around again.

"Giving up?" Fredrickson grins.

"Just *limbering* up. Here goes the real effort"—and grabs those levers again.

And suddenly nobody's hooting at him any more. His arms commence to swell, and the veins squeeze up to the surface. He clinches his eyes, and his lips draw away from his teeth. His head leans back, and tendons stand out like coiled ropes running from his heaving neck down both arms to his hands. His whole body shakes with the strain as he tries to lift something he *knows* he can't lift, something *everybody* knows he can't lift.

But, for just a second, when we hear the cement grind at our feet, we think, by golly, he might do it.

Then his breath exploded out of him, and he falls back limp against the wall. There's blood on the levers where he tore his hands. He pants for a minute against the wall with his eyes shut. There's no sound but his scraping breath; nobody's saying a thing.

He opens his eyes and looks around at us. One by one he looks at the guys—even at me—then he fishes in his pockets for all the IOUs he won the last few days at poker. He bends over the table and tries to sort them, but his hands are froze into red claws, and he can't work the fingers.

Finally he throws the whole bundle on the floor—probably forty or fifty dollars' worth from each man—and turns to walk out of the tub room. He stops at the door and looks back at everybody standing around.

"But I tried, though," he says. "Goddammit, I sure as hell did that much, now, didn't I?"

And walks out and leaves those stained pieces of paper on the floor for whoever wants to sort through them.

A visiting doctor covered with gray cobwebs on his yellow skull is addressing the resident boys in the staff room.

I come sweeping past him. "Oh, and what's this here." He gives me a look like I'm some kind of bug. One of the residents points at his ears, signal that I'm deaf, and the visiting doctor goes on.

I push my broom up face to face with a big picture Public Relation brought in one time when it was fogged so thick I didn't see him. The picture is a guy fly-fishing somewhere in the mountains, looks like the Ochocos near Paineville—snow on the peaks showing over the pines, long white aspen trunks lining the stream, sheep sorrel growing in sour green patches. The guy is flicking his fly in a pool behind a rock. It's no place for a fly, it's a place for a single egg on a number-six hook—he'd do better to drift the fly over those riffles downstream.

There's a path running down through the aspen, and I push my broom down the path a ways and sit down on a rock and look back out through the frame at that visiting doctor talking with the residents. I can see him stabbing some point in the palm of his hand with his finger, but I can't hear what he says because of the crash of the cold, frothy stream coming down out of the rocks. I can smell the snow in the wind where it blows down off the peaks. I can see mole burrows humping along under the grass and buffalo weed. It's a real nice place to stretch your legs and take it easy.

You forget—if you don't sit down and make the effort to think back—forget how it was at the old hospital. They didn't have nice places like this on the walls for you to climb into. They didn't have TV or swimming pools or chicken twice a month. They didn't have nothing but walls and chairs, confinement jackets it took you hours of hard work to get out of. They've learned a lot since then. "Come a long way," says fat-faced Public Relation. They've made life look very pleasant with paint and decorations and chrome bathroom fixtures. "A man that would want to run away from a place as nice as this," says fat-faced Public Relation, "why, there'd be something wrong with him."

Out in the staff room the visiting authority is hugging his elbows and shivering like he's cold while he answers questions the resident boys ask him. He's thin and meatless, and his clothes flap around his bones. He stand there, hugging his elbows and shivering. Maybe he feels the cold snow wind off the peaks too.

*I*t's getting hard to locate my bed at night, have to crawl around on my hands and knees feeling underneath the springs till I find my gobs of gum stuck there. Nobody complains about all the fog. I know why, now: as bad as it is, you can slip back in it and feel safe. That's what McMurphy can't understand, us wanting to be safe. He keeps trying to drag us out of the fog, out in the open where we'd be easy to get at.

*T*here's a shipment of frozen parts come in downstairs—hearts and kidneys and brains and the like. I can hear them rumble into cold storage down the coal chute. A guy sitting in the room someplace I can't see is talking about a guy up on Disturbed killing himself. Old Rawler. Cut both nuts off and bled to death, sitting right on the can in the latrine, half a dozen people in there with him didn't know it till he fell off to the floor, dead.

What makes people so impatient is what I can't figure; all the guy had to do was wait.

I know how they work it, the fog machine. We had a whole platoon used to operate fog machines around airfields overseas. Whenever intelligence figured there might be a bombing attack, or if the generals had something secret they wanted to pull—out of sight, hid so good that even the spies on the base couldn't see what went on—they fogged the field.

It's a simple rig: you got an ordinary compressor sucks water out of one tank and a special oil out of another tank, and compresses them together, and from the black stem at the end of the machine blooms a white cloud of fog that can cover a whole airfield in ninety seconds. The first thing I saw when I landed in Europe was the fog those machines make. There were some interceptors close after our transport, and soon as it hit ground the fog crew started up the machines. We could look out the transport's round, scratched windows and watch the jeeps draw the machines up close to the plane and watch the fog boil out till it rolled across the field and stuck against the windows like wet cotton.

You found your way off the plane by following a little referees' horn the lieutenant kept blowing, sounded like a goose honking. Soon as you were out of the hatch you couldn't see no more than maybe three feet in any direction. You felt like you were out on that airfield all by yourself. You were safe from the enemy, but you were awfully alone. Sounds died and dissolved after a few yards, and you couldn't hear any of the rest of your crew, nothing but that little horn squeaking and honking out of a soft furry whiteness so thick that your body just faded into white below the belt; other than that brown shirt and brass buckle, you couldn't see nothing but white, like from the waist down you were being dissolved by the fog too.

And then some guy wandering as lost as you would all of a sudden be right before your eyes, his face bigger and clearer than you ever saw a man's face before in your life. Your eyes were working so hard to see in that fog that when something did come in sight every detail was ten times as clear as usual, so clear both of you had to look away. When a man showed

116

up you didn't want to look at his face and he didn't want to look at yours, because it's painful to see somebody so clear that it's like looking inside him, but then neither did you want to look away and lose him completely. You had a choice: you could either strain and look at things that appeared in front of you in the fog, painful as it might be, or you could relax and lose yourself.

When they first used that fog machine on the ward, one they bought from Army Surplus and hid in the vents in the new place before we moved in, I kept looking at anything that appeared out of the fog as long and hard as I could, to keep track of it, just like I used to do when they fogged the airfields in Europe. Nobody'd be blowing a horn to show the way, there was no rope to hold to, so fixing my eyes on something was the only way I kept from getting lost. Sometimes I got lost in it anyway, got in too deep, trying to hide, and every time I did, it seemed like I always turned up at that same place, at that same metal door with the row of rivets like eyes and no number, just like the room behind the door drew me to it, no matter how hard I tried to stay away, just like the current generated by the fiends in that room was conducted in a beam along the fog and pulled me back along it like a robot. I'd wander for days in the fog, scared I'd never see another thing, then there'd be that door, opening to show me the mattress padding on the other side to stop out the sounds, the men standing in a line like zombies among shiny copper wires and tubes pulsing light, and the bright scrape of arcing electricity. I'd take my place in the line and wait my turn at the table. The table shaped like a cross, with shadows of a thousand murdered men printed on it, silhouette wrists and ankles running under leather straps sweated green with use, a silhouette neck and head running up to a silver band goes across the forehead. And a technician at the controls beside the table looking up from his dials and down the line and pointing at me with a rubber glove. "Wait, I *know* that big bastard there—better rabbit-punch him or call for some more help or something. He's an awful case for thrashing around."

So I used to try not to get in too deep, for fear I'd get lost and turn up at the Shock Shop door. I looked hard at anything that came into sight and hung on like a man in a blizzard hangs on a fence rail. But they kept making the fog thicker and thicker, and it seemed to me that, no matter how hard I tried, two or three times a month I found myself with that door opening in front of me to the acid smell of sparks and ozone. In spite of all I could do, it was getting tough to keep from getting lost.

Then I discovered something: I don't have to end up at that door if I stay still when the fog comes over me and just keep quiet. The trouble was I'd been finding that door my own self because I got scared of being lost so long and went to hollering so they could track me. In a way, I was hollering for them *to* track me; I had figured that anything was better'n being lost for good, even the Shock Shop. Now, I don't know. Being lost isn't so bad.

All this morning I been waiting for them to fog us in again. The last few days they been doing it more and more. It's my idea they're doing it on account of McMurphy. They haven't got him fixed with controls yet, and they're trying to catch him off guard. They can see he's due to be a problem; a half a dozen times already he's roused Cheswick and Harding and some of the others to where it looked like they might actually stand up to one of the black boys—but always, just the time it looked like the patient might be helped, the fog would start, like it's starting now.

I heard the compressor start pumping in the grill a few minutes back, just as the guys went to moving tables out of the day room for the therapeutic meeting, and already the mist is oozing across the floor so thick my pants legs are wet. I'm cleaning the windows in the door of the glass station, and I hear the Big Nurse pick up the phone and call the doctor to tell him we're just about ready for the meeting, and tell him perhaps he'd best keep an hour free this afternoon for a Staff meeting. "The reason being," she tells him, "I think it is past time to have a discussion of the subject of Patient Randle McMurphy and whether he should be on this ward or not." She listens a minute, and tells him, "I don't think it's wise to let him go on upsetting the patients the way he has the last few days."

That's why she's fogging the ward for the meeting. She don't usually do that. But now she's going to do something with McMurphy today, probably ship him to Disturbed. I put down my window rag and go to my chair at the end of the line of Chronics, barely able to see the guys getting into their chairs and the doctor coming through the door wiping his glasses like he thinks the blurred look comes from his steamed lenses instead of the fog.

It's rolling in thicker than I ever seen it before.

I can hear them out there, trying to go on with the meeting, talking some nonsense about Billy Bibbit's stutter and how it came about. The words come to me like through water, it's so

thick. In fact it's so much like water it floats me right up out
of my chair and I don't know which end is up for a while.
Floating makes me a little sick to the stomach at first. I can't
see a thing. I never had it so thick it floated me like this.

The words get dim and loud, off and on, as I float around,
but as loud as they get, loud enough sometimes I know I'm
right next to the guy that's talking, I still can't see a thing.

I recognize Billy's voice, stuttering worse than ever because
he's nervous. ". . . fuh-fuh-flunked out of college be-be-cause
I quit ROTC. I c-c-couldn't take it. Wh-wh-wh-whenever the
officer in charge of class would call roll, call 'Bibbit,' I couldn't
answer. You were s-s-supposed to say heh-heh-heh . . ."
He's choking on the word, like it's a bone in his throat. I hear
him swallow and start again. "You were supposed to say,
'Here sir,' and I never c-c-could get it out."

His voice gets dim; then the Big Nurse's voice comes cutting
from the left. "Can you recall, Billy, when you first had
speech trouble? When did you first stutter, do you remember?"

I can't tell is he laughing or what. "Fir-first stutter? First
stutter? The first word I said I st-stut-tered:m-m-m-m-mam-
ma."

Then the talking fades out altogether; I never knew that to
happen before. Maybe Billy's hid himself in the fog too. Maybe all the guys finally and forever crowded back into the fog.

A chair and me float past each other. It's the first thing I've
seen. It comes sifting out of the fog off to my right, and for
a few seconds it's right beside my face, just out of my reach.
I been accustomed of late to just let things alone when they
appear in the fog, sit still and not try to hang on. But this
time I'm scared, the way I used to be scared. I try with all
I got to pull myself over to the chair and get hold of it, but
there's nothing to brace against and all I can do is thrash the
air, all I can do is watch the chair come clear, clearer than ever
before to where I can even make out the fingerprint where a
worker touched the varnish before it was dry, looming out for
a few seconds, then fading on off again. I never seen it where
things floated around this way. I never seen it this thick before, thick to where I can't get down to the floor and get on
my feet if I wanted to and walk around. That's why I'm so
scared; I feel I'm going to float off someplace for good this time.

I see a Chronic float into sight a little below me. It's old
Colonel Matterson, reading from the wrinkled scripture of that
long yellow hand. I look close at him because I figure it's the
last time I'll ever see him. His face is enormous, almost more
than I can bear. Every hair and wrinkle of him is big, as though

I was looking at him with one of those microscopes. I see him so clear I see his whole life. The face is sixty years of southwest Army camps, rutted by iron-rimmed caisson wheels, worn to the bone by thousands of feet on two-day marches.

He holds out that long hand and brings it up in front of his eyes and squints into it, brings up his other hand and underlines the words with a finger wooden and varnished the color of a gunstock by nicotine. His voice is deep and slow and patient, and I see the words come out dark and heavy over his brittle lips when he reads.

"No . . . The flag is . . . Ah-mer-ica. America is . . . the plum. The peach. The wah-ter-mel-on. America is . . . the gumdrop. The pump-kin seed. America is . . . tell-ah-vision."

It's true. It's all wrote down on that yellow hand. I can read it along with him myself.

"Now . . . The cross is . . . Mex-i-co." He looks up to see if I'm paying attention, and when he sees I am he smiles at me and goes on. "Mexico is . . . the wal-nut. The hazelnut. The ay-corn. Mexico is . . . the rain-bow. The rain-bow is . . . wooden. Mexico is . . . woo-den."

I can see what he's driving at. He's been saying this sort of thing for the whole six years he's been here, but I never paid him any mind, figured he was no more than a talking statue, a thing made out of bone and arthritis, rambling on and on with these goofy definitions of his that didn't make a lick of sense. Now, at last, I see what he's saying. I'm trying to hold him for one last look to remember him, and that's what makes me look hard enough to understand. He pauses and peers up at me again to make sure I'm getting it, and I want to yell out to him Yes, I see: Mexico *is* like a walnut; it's brown and hard and you feel it with your eye and it *feels* like the walnut! You're making sense, old man, a sense of your own. You're not crazy the way they think. Yes . . . I see . . .

But the fog's clogged my throat to where I can't make a sound. As he sifts away I see him bend back over that hand.

"Now . . . The green sheep is . . . Can-a-da. Canada is . . . the fir tree. The wheat field. The cal-en-dar . . ."

I strain to see him drifting away. I strain so hard my eyes ache and I have to close them, and when I open them again the colonel is gone. I'm floating by myself again, more lost than ever.

This is the time, I tell myself. I'm going for good.

There's old Pete, face like a searchlight. He's fifty yards off to my left, but I can see him plain as though there wasn't any fog at all. Or maybe he's up right close and real small, I can't be sure. He tells me once about how tired he is, and just his saying it makes me see his whole life on the railroad, see him working to figure out how to read a watch, breaking a sweat while he tries to get the right button in the right hole of his railroad overalls, doing his absolute damnedest to keep up with a job that comes so easy to the others they can sit back in a chair padded with cardboard and read mystery stories and girlie books. Not that he ever really figured to keep up —he knew from the start he couldn't do that—but he had to try to keep up, just to keep them in sight. So for forty years he was able to live, if not right in the world of men, at least on the edge of it.

I can see all that, and be hurt by it, the way I was hurt by seeing things in the Army, in the war. The way I was hurt by seeing what happened to Papa and the tribe. I thought I'd got over seeing those things and fretting over them. There's no sense in it. There's nothing to be done.

"I'm tired," is what he says.

"I know you're tired, Pete, but I can't do you no good fretting about it. You know I can't."

Pete floats on the way of the old colonel.

Here comes Billy Bibbit, the way Pete come by. They're all filing by for a last look. I know Billy can't be more'n a few feet away, but he's so tiny he looks like he's a mile off. His face is out to me like the face of a beggar, needing so much more'n anybody can give. His mouth works like a little doll's mouth.

"And even when I pr-proposed, I flubbed it. I said 'Huh-honey, will you muh-muh-muh-muh-muh ...' till the girl broke out l-laughing."

Nurse's voice, I can't see where it comes from: "Your mother has spoken to me about this girl, Billy. Apparently she was quite a bit beneath you. What would you speculate it was about her that frightened you so, Billy?"

"I was in luh-love with her."

I can't do nothing for you either, Billy. You know that. None of us can. You got to understand that as soon as a man goes to help somebody, he leaves himself wide open. He *has* to be cagey, Billy, you should know that as well as anyone. What could I do? I can't fix your stuttering. I can't wipe the razor-blade scars off your wrists or the cigarette burns off the back of your hands. I can't give you a new mother. And as far as the nurse riding you like this, rubbing your nose in your weakness till what little dignity you got left is gone and you shrink up to nothing from humiliation, I can't do anything about that, either. At Anzio, I saw a buddy of mine tied to a tree fifty yards from me, screaming for water, his face blistered in the sun. They wanted me to try to go out and help him. They'd of cut me in half from the farmhouse over there.

Put your face away, Billy.

They kept filing past.

It's like each face was a sign like one of those "I'm Blind" signs the dago accordion players in Portland hung around their necks, only these signs say "I'm tired" or "I'm scared" or "I'm dying of a bum liver" or "I'm all bound up with machinery and people *pushing* me alla time." I can read all the signs, it don't make any difference how little the print gets. Some of the faces are looking around at one another and could read the other fellow's if they would, but what's the sense? The faces blow past in the fog like confetti.

I'm further off than I've ever been. This is what it's like to be dead. I guess this is what it's like to be a Vegetable; you lose yourself in the fog. You don't move. They feed your body till it finally stops eating; then they burn it. It's not so bad. There's no pain. I don't feel much of anything other than a touch of chill I figure will pass in time.

I see my commanding officer pinning notices on the bulletin board, what we're to wear today. I see the US Department of Interior bearing down on our little tribe with a gravel-crushing machine.

I see Papa come loping out of a draw and slow up to try and take aim at a big six-point buck springing off through the cedars. Shot after shot puffs out of the barrel, knocking dust all around the buck. I come out of the draw behind Papa and bring the buck down with my second shot just as it starts climbing the rimrock. I grin at Papa.

I never knew you to miss a shot like that before, Papa.

Eye's gone, boy. Can't hold a bead. Sights on my gun just now was shakin' like a dog shittin' peach pits.

Papa, I'm telling you: that cactus moon of Sid's is gonna make you old before your time.

A man drinks that cactus moon of Sid's, boy, he's already old before his time. Let's go gut that animal out before the flies blow him.

That's not even happening now. You see? There's nothing you can do about a happening out of the past like that.

Look there, my man . . .

I hear whispers, black boys.

Look there, that old fool Broom, slipped off to sleep.

Tha's right, Chief Broom, tha's right. You sleep an' keep outa trouble Yasss.

I'm not cold any more. I think I've about made it. I'm off to where the cold can't reach me I can stay off here for good. I'm not scared any more. They can't reach me. Just the words reach me, and those're fading.

Well ... in as much as Billy has decided to walk out on the discussion, does anyone else have a problem to bring before the group?

As a matter of fact, ma'am, there does happen to be something ...

That's that McMurphy. He's far away. He's still trying to pull people out of the fog. Why don't he leave me be?

". . . remember that vote we had a day or so back—about the TV time? Well, today's Friday and I thought I might just bring it up again, just to see if anybody else has picked up a little guts."

"Mr. McMurphy, the purpose of this meeting is therapy, group therapy, and I'm not certain these petty grievances—"

"Yeah, yeah, the hell with that, we've heard it before. Me and some of the rest of the guys decided—"

"One moment, Mr. McMurphy, let me pose a question to the group: do any of you feel that Mr. McMurphy is perhaps imposing his personal desires on some of you too much? I've been thinking you might be happier if he were moved to a different ward."

Nobody says anything for a minute. Then someone says, "Let him vote, why dontcha? Why ya want to ship him to Disturbed just for bringing up a vote? What's so wrong with changing time?"

"Why, Mr. Scanlon, as I recall, you refused to eat for three days until we allowed you to turn the set on at six instead of six-thirty."

"A man needs to see the world news, don't he? God, they coulda bombed Washington and it'd been a week before we'd of heard."

"Yes? And how do you feel about relinquishing your world news to watch a bunch of men play baseball?"

"We can't have both, huh? No, I suppose not. Well, what the dickens—I don't guess they'll bomb us this week."

"Let's let him have the vote, Miss Ratched."

"Very well. But I think this is ample evidence of how much he is upsetting some of you patients. What is it you are proposing, Mr. McMurphy?"

"I'm proposing a revote on watching the TV in the afternoon."

"You're certain one more vote will satisfy you? We have more important things—"

"It'll satisfy me. I just'd kind of like to see which of these birds has any guts and which doesn't."

"It's that kind of talk, Doctor Spivey, that makes me wonder if the patients wouldn't be more content if Mr. McMurphy were moved."

"Let him call the vote, why dontcha?"

"Certainly, Mr. Cheswick. A vote is now before the group. Will a show of hands be adequate, Mr. McMurphy, or are you going to insist on a secret ballot?"

"I want to see the hands. I want to see the hands that don't go up, too."

"Everyone in favor of changing the television time to the afternoon, raise his hand."

The first hand that comes up, I can tell, is McMurphy's, because of the bandage where that control panel cut into him when he tried to lift it. And then off down the slope I see them, other hands coming up out of the fog. It's like ... that big red hand of McMurphy's is reaching into the fog and dropping down and dragging the men up by their hands, dragging them blinking into the open. First one, then another, then the next. Right on down the line of Acutes, dragging them out of the fog till there they stand, all twenty of them, raising not just for watching TV, but against the Big Nurse, against her trying to send McMurphy to Disturbed, against the way she's talked and acted and beat them down for years.

Nobody says anything. I can feel how stunned everybody is, the patients as well as the staff. The nurse can't figure what happened; yesterday, before he tried lifting that panel, there wasn't but four or five men might of voted. But when she talks she don't let it show in her voice how surprised she is.

"I count only twenty, Mr. McMurphy."

"Twenty? Well, why not? Twenty is all of us there—" His voice hangs as he realizes what she means. "Now hold on just a goddamned minute, lady—"

"I'm afraid the vote is defeated."

"Hold on just one goddamned *minute!*"

"There are forty patients on the ward, Mr. McMurphy. Forty patients, and only twenty voted. You must have a majority to change the ward policy. I'm afraid the vote is closed."

The hands are coming down across the room. The guys know they're whipped, are trying to slip back into the safety of the fog. McMurphy is on his feet.

"Well, I'll be a sonofabitch. You mean to tell me that's how you're gonna pull it? Count the votes of those old birds over there too??"

"Didn't you explain the voting procedure to him Doctor?"

"I'm afraid—a majority *is* called for, McMurphy. She's right, she's right."

"A majority, Mr. McMurphy; it's in the ward constitution."

"And I suppose the way to change the damned constitution is with a majority vote. Sure. Of all the chicken-shit things I've ever seen, this by God takes the *cake!*"

"I'm sorry, Mr. McMurphy, but you'll find it written in the policy if you'd care for me to—"

"So this's how you work this democratic bullshit—hell's bells!"

"You seem upset, Mr. McMurphy. Doesn't he seem upset, Doctor? I want you to note this."

"Don't give me that noise, lady. When a guy's getting screwed he's got a right to holler. And we've been damn well screwed."

"Perhaps, Doctor, in view of the patient's condition, we should bring this meeting to a close early today—"

"Wait! Wait a minute, let me talk to some of those old guys."

"The vote is closed, Mr. McMurphy."

"Let me talk to 'em."

He's coming across the day room at us. He gets bigger and bigger, and he's burning red in the face. He reaches into the fog and tries to drag Ruckly to the surface because Ruckly's the youngest.

"What about you, buddy? You want to watch the World Series? Baseball? Baseball games? Just raise that hand up there—"

Fffffffuck da wife."

"All right, forget it. You, partner, how about you? What was your name—Ellis? What do you say, Ellis, to watching a ball game on TV? Just raise your hand. . . ."

Ellis's hands are nailed to the wall, can't be counted as a vote.

"I said the voting is closed, Mr. McMurphy. You're just making a spectacle of yourself."

He don't pay any attention to her. He comes on down the line of Chronics. "C'mon, c'mon, just one vote from you birds, just raise a hand. Show her you can still do it."

"I'm tired," says Pete and wags his head.

"The night is . . . the Pacific Ocean." The Colonel is reading off his hand, can't be bothered with voting.

"*One* of you guys, for cryin' out loud! This is where you get the edge, don't you see that? We have to do this—or we're *whipped!* Don't a one of you clucks know what I'm talking about enough to give us a hand? You, Gabriel? George? No? You, Chief, what about you?

He's standing over me in the mist. Why won't he leave me be?

"Chief, you're our last bet."

The Big Nurse is folding her papers; the other nurses are standing up around her. She finally gets to her feet.

"The meeting is adjourned, then," I hear her say. "And I'd like to see the staff down in the staff room in about an hour. So, if there is nothing el—"

It's too late to stop it now. McMurphy did something to it that first day, put some kind of hex on it with his hand so it won't act like I order it. There's no sense in it, any fool can see; I wouldn't do it on my own. Just by the way the nurse is staring at me with her mouth empty of words I can see I'm in for trouble, but I can't stop it. McMurphy's got hidden wires hooked to it, lifting it slow just to get me out of the fog and into the open where I'm fair game. He's doing it, wires ...

No. That's not the truth. I lifted it myself.

McMurphy whoops and drags me standing, pounding my back.

"Twenty-one! The Chief's vote makes it twenty-one! And by God if that ain't a majority I'll eat my hat!"

"Yippee," Cheswick yells. The other Acutes are coming across toward me.

"The meeting was closed," she says. Her smile is still there, but the back of her neck as she walks out of the day room and into the Nurses' Station, is red and swelling like she'll blow apart any second.

But she don't blow up, not right off, not until about an hour later. Behind the glass her smile is twisted and queer, like we've never seen before. She just sits. I can see her shoulders rise and fall as she breathes.

McMurphy looks up at the clock and he says it's time for the game. He's over by the drinking fountain with some of the other Acutes, down on his knees scouring off the baseboard. I'm sweeping out the broom closet for the tenth time that day. Scanlon and Harding, they got the buffer going up and down the hall, polishing the new wax into shining figure eights. McMurphy says again that he guesses it must be game time and he stands up, leaves the scouring rag where it lies. Nobody else stops work. McMurphy walks past the window where she's glaring out at him and grins at her like he knows he's got her whipped now. When he tips his head back and winks at her she gives that little sideways jerk of her head.

Everybody keeps on at what he's doing, but they all watch out of the corners of their eyes while he drags his armchair out to in front of the TV set, then switches on the set and sits down. A picture swirls onto the screen of a parrot out on the baseball field singing razorblade songs. McMurphy gets up and turns up the sound to drown out the music coming down from the speaker in the ceiling, and he drags another chair in front of him and sits down and crosses his feet on the chair and leans back and lights a cigarette. He scratches his belly and yawns.

"Hoo-*weee!* Man, all I need me now is a can of beer and a red-hot."

We can see the nurse's face get red and her mouth work as she stares at him. She looks around for a second and sees everybody watching what she's going to do— even the black boys and the little nurses sneaking looks at her, and the residents beginning to drift in for the staff meeting, they're watching. Her mouth clamps shut. She looks back at McMurphy and waits till the razor-blade song is finished; then she gets up and goes to the steel door where the controls are, and she flips a switch and the TV picture swirls back into the gray. Nothing is left on the screen but a little eye of light beading right down on McMurphy sitting there.

That eye don't faze him a bit. To tell the truth, he don't even let on he knows the picture is turned off; he puts his cigarette between his teeth and pushes his cap forward in his red hair till he has to lean back to see out from under the brim.

And sits that way, with his hands crossed behind his head and his feet stuck out in a chair, a smoking cigarette sticking out from under his hatbrim—watching the TV screen.

The nurse stands this as long as she can; then she comes to the door of the Nurses' Station and calls across to him he'd better help the men with the housework. He ignores her.

"I said, Mr. McMurphy, that you are supposed to be working during these hours." Her voice has a tight whine like an electric saw ripping through pine. "Mr. McMurphy, I'm *warning* you!"

Everybody's stopped what he was doing. She looks around her, then takes a step out of the Nurses' Station toward Mc-Murphy.

"You're committed, you realize. You are ... under the *jurisdiction* of me ... the staff." She's holding up a fist, all those red-orange fingernails burning into her palm. "Under jurisdiction and *control*—"

Harding shuts off the buffer, and leaves it in the hall, and goes pulls him a chair up alongside McMurphy and sits down and lights him a cigarette too.

"Mr. Harding! You return to your scheduled duties!"

I think how her voice sounds like it hit a nail, and this strikes me so funny I almost laugh.

"Mr. Har-*ding!*"

Then Cheswick goes and gets him a chair, and then Billy Bibbit goes, and then Scanlon and then Fredrickson and Sefelt, and then we all put down our mops and brooms and scouring rags and we all go pull us chairs up.

"You *men*—Stop this. *Stop!*"

And we're all sitting there lined up in front of that blanked-out TV set, watching the gray screen just like we could see the baseball game clear as day, and she's ranting and screaming behind us.

If somebody'd of come in and took a look, men watching a blank TV, a fifty-year-old woman hollering and squealing at the back of their heads about discipline and order and re-criminations, they'd of thought the whole bunch was crazy as loons.

part 2

*J*ust at the edge of my vision I can see that white enamel face in the Nurses' Station, teetering over the desk, see it warp and flow as it tries to pull back into shape. The rest of the guys are watching too, though they're trying to act like they aren't. They're trying to act like they still got their eyes on nothing but that blank TV in front of us, but anyone can see they're all sneaking looks at the Big Nurse behind her glass there, just the same as I am. For the first time she's on the other side of the glass and getting a taste of how it feels to be watched when you wish more than anything else to be able to pull a green shade between your face and all the eyes that you can't get away from.

The residents, the black boys, all the little nurses, they're watching her too, waiting for her to go down the hall where it's time for the meeting she herself called, and waiting to see how she'll act now that it's known she can be made to lose control. She knows they're watching, but she don't move. Not even when they start strolling down to the staff room without her. I notice all the machinery in the wall is quiet, like it's still waiting for her to move.

There's no more fog any place.

All of a sudden I remember I'm supposed to clean the staff room. I always go down and clean the staff room during these meetings they have, been doing it for years. But now I'm too scared to get out of my chair. The staff always let me clean the room because they didn't think I could hear, but now that they saw me lift my hand when McMurphy told me to, won't they know I can hear? Won't they figure I been hearing all these years, listening to secrets meant only for their ears? What'll they do to me in that staff room if they know that?

Still, they expect me to be in there. If I'm not, they'll know for sure that I can hear, be way ahead of me, thinking, You see? He isn't in here cleaning, don't that prove it? It's obvious what's to be done. . . .

I'm just getting the full force of the dangers we let ourselves in for when we let McMurphy lure us out of the fog.

There's a black boy leaning against the wall near the door, arms crossed, pink tongue tip darting back and forth over his lips, watching us sitting in front of the TV set. His eyes dart back and forth like his tongue and stop on me, and I see his leather eyelids raise a little. He watches me for a long time, and I know he's wondering about the way I acted in the group meeting. Then he comes off the wall with a lurch, breaking contact, and goes to the broom closet and brings back a bucket of soapy water and a sponge, drags my arm up and hangs the bucket bale over it, like hanging a kettle on a fireplace boom.

"Le's go, Chief," he says. "Le's get up and get to your duties."

I don't move. The bucket rocks on my arm. I don't make a sign I heard. He's trying to trick me. He asks me again to get up, and when I don't move he rolls his eyes up to the ceiling and sighs, reaches down and takes my collar, and tugs a little, and I stand up. He stuffs the sponge in my pocket and points up the hall where the staff room is, and I go.

And while I'm walking up the hall with the bucket, zoom, the Big Nurse comes past me with all her old calm speed and power and turns into the door. That makes me wonder.

Out in the hall all by myself, I notice how clear it is—no fog any place. It's a little cold where the nurse just went past, and the white tubes in the ceiling circulate frozen light like rods of glowing ice, like frosted refrigerator coils rigged up to glow white. The rods stretch down to the staff-room door where the nurse just turned in at the end of the hall—a heavy steel door like the door of the Shock Shop in Building One, except there are numbers printed on this one, and this one has a little glass peephole up head-high to let the staff peek out at who's knocking. As I get closer I see there's light seeping out this peephole, green light, bitter as bile. The staff meeting is about to start in there, is why there's this green seepage; it'll be all over the walls and windows by the time the meeting is halfway through, for me to sponge off and squeeze in my bucket, use the water later to clear the drains in the latrine.

Cleaning the staff room is always bad. The things I've had to clean up in these meetings nobody'd believe, horrible things, poisons manufactured right out of skin pores and acids in the air strong enough to melt a man. I've seen it.

I been in some meetings where the table legs strained and contorted and the chairs knotted and the walls gritted against one another till you could of wrung sweat out the room. I been in meetings where they kept talking about a patient so long that the patient materialized in the flesh, nude on the coffee table in front of them, vulnerable to any fiendish notion they took; they'd have him smeared around in an awful mess before they were finished.

That's why they have me at the staff meetings, because they can be such a messy affair and somebody has to clean up, and since the staff room is open only during the meeting it's got to be somebody they think won't be able to spread the word what's going on. That's me. I been at it so long, sponging and dusting and mopping this staff room and the old wooden one at the other place, that the staff usually don't even notice me; I move around in my chores, and they see right through me like I wasn't there—the only thing they'd miss if I didn't show up would be the sponge and the water bucket floating around.

But this time when I tap at the door and the Big Nurse looks through the peephole she looks dead at me, and she takes longer than ordinary unlocking that door to let me in. Her face has come back into shape, strong as ever, it seems to me. Everybody else goes ahead spooning sugar in their coffee and borrowing cigarettes, the way they do before every meeting, but there's a tenseness in the air. I think it's because of me at first. Then I notice that the Big Nurse hasn't even sat down, hasn't even bothered to get herself a cup of coffee.

She lets me slip through the door and stabs me again with both eyes as I go past her, closes that door when I'm in and locks it, and pivots around and glares at me some more. I know she's suspicious. I thought she might be too upset by the way McMurphy defied her to pay any attention to me, but she don't look shook at all. She's clear-headed and wondering now just how *did* Mr. Bromden hear that Acute McMurphy asking

him to raise his hand on that vote? She's wondering how did he
know to lay down his mop and go sit with the Acutes in front
of that TV set? None of the other Chronics did that. She's
wondering if it isn't time we did some checking on our Mr.
Chief Bromden.

I put my back to her and dig into the corner with my sponge.
I lift the sponge up above my head so everybody in the room
can see how it's covered with green slime and how hard I'm
working; then I bend over and rub harder than ever. But
hard as I work and hard as I try to act like I'm not aware of her
back there, I can still feel her standing at the door and drilling
into my skull till in a minute she's going to break through, till
I'm just about to give up and yell and tell them everything if
she don't take those eyes off me.

Then she realizes that she's being stared at too—by all the
rest of the staff. Just like she's wondering about me, they are
wondering about her and what she's planning to do about that
redhead back down there in the day room. They're watching
to see what she'll say about him, and they don't care anything
about some fool Indian on his hands and knees in the corner.
They're waiting for her so she quits looking at me and goes
and draws a cup of coffee and sits down, stirs sugar in it so
careful the spoon never touches the side of the cup.

It's the doctor who starts things off. "Now, people, if we
can get things rolling?"

He smiles around at the residents sipping coffee. He's trying
not to look at the Big Nurse. She's sitting there so silent it
makes him nervous and fidgety. He grabs out his glasses and
puts them on for a look at his watch, goes to winding it while
he talks.

"Fifteen after. It's past time we started. Now. Miss Ratched,
as most of you know, called this get-together. She phoned me
before the Therapeutic Community meeting and said that in
her opinion McMurphy was due to constitute a disturbance on
the ward. Ever so intuitive, considering what went on a few
minutes ago, don't you think?"

He stops winding his watch on account of it's tight enough
another twist is going to spray it all over the place, and he sits
there smiling at it, drumming the back of his hand with pink
little fingers, waiting. Usually at about this point in the meeting
she'll take over, but she doesn't say anything.

"After today," the doctor goes on, "no one can say that this
is an ordinary man we're dealing with. No, certainly not. And
he *is* a disturbing factor, that's obvious. So—ah—as I see it,
our course in this discussion is to decide what action to take

in dealing with him. I believe the nurse called this meeting—correct me if I'm off base here, Miss Ratched—to talk the situation out and unify the staff's opinion of what should be done about Mr. McMurphy?"

He gives her a pleading look, but she still doesn't say anything. She's lifted her face toward the ceiling, checking for dirt most likely, and doesn't appear to have heard a thing he's been saying.

The doctor turns to the line of residents across the room; all of them got the same leg crossed and coffee cup on the same knee. "You fellows," the doctor says, "I realize you haven't had adequate time to arrive at a proper diagnosis of the patient, but you *have* had a chance at observing him in action. What do *you* think?"

The question pops their heads up. Cleverly, he's put them on the carpet too. They all look from him to the Big Nurse. Some way she has regained all her old power in a few short minutes. Just sitting there, smiling up at the ceiling and not saying anything, she has taken control again and made everyone aware that she's the force in here to be dealt with. If these boys don't play it just right they're liable to finish their training up in Portland at the alky hospital. They begin to fidget around like the doctor.

"He's quite a disturbing influence, all right." The first boy plays it safe.

They all sip their coffee and think about that. Then the next one says, "And he could constitute an actual danger."

"That's true, that's true," the doctor says.

The boy thinks he may have found the key and goes on. "Quite a danger, in fact," he says and moves forward in his chair. "Keep in mind that this man performed violent acts for the sole purpose of getting away from the work farm and into the comparative luxury of this hospital."

"*Planned* violent acts," the first boy says.

And the third boy mutters, "Of course, the very nature of this plan could indicate that he is simply a shrewd con man, and not mentally ill at all."

He glances around to see how this strikes her and sees she still hasn't moved or given any sign. But the rest of the staff sits there glaring at him like he's said some awful vulgar thing. He sees how he's stepped way out of bounds and tries to bring it off as a joke by giggling and adding, "You know, like 'He Who Marches Out Of Step Hears Another Drum ' "—but it's too late. The first resident turns on him after setting down his cup of coffee and reaching in his pocket for a pipe big as your fist.

"Frankly, Alvin," he says to the third boy, "I'm disappointed in you. Even if one hadn't read his history all one should need to do is pay attention to his behavior on the ward to realize how absurd the suggestion is. This man is not only very very sick, but I believe he is definitely a Potential Assaultive. I think that is what Miss Ratched was suspecting when she called this meeting. Don't you recognize the arch type of psychopath? I've never heard of a clearer case. This man is a Napoleon, a Genghis Khan, Attila the Hun."

Another one joins in. He remembers the nurse's comments about Disturbed. "Robert's right, Alvin. Didn't you see the way the man acted out there today? When one of his schemes was thwarted he was up out of his chair, on the verge of violence. You tell us, Doctor Spivey, what do his records say about violence?"

"There is a marked disregard for discipline and authority," the doctor says.

"Right. His history shows, Alvin, that time and again he has acted out his hostilities against authority figures—in school, in the service, in *jail!* And I think that his performance after the voting furor today is as conclusive an indication as we can have of what to expect in the future." He stops and frowns into his pipe, puts it back in his mouth, and strikes a match and sucks the flame into the bowl with a loud popping sound. When it's lit he sneaks a look up through the yellow cloud of smoke at the Big Nurse; he must take her silence as agreement because he goes on, more enthusiastic and certain than before.

"Pause for a minute and imagine, Alvin," he says, his words cottony with smoke, imagine what will happen to one of us when we're alone in Individual Therapy with Mr. McMurphy. Imagine you are approaching a particularly painful break-through and he decides he's just had all he can take of you—how would he put it?—your 'damn fool collitch-kid pryin'!' You tell him he mustn't get hostile and he says 'to hell with that,' and tell him to calm down, in an authoritarian voice, of course, and here he comes, all two hundred and ten red-headed psychopathic Irishman pounds of him, right across the interviewing table at you. Are you—are any of us, for that matter—prepared to deal with Mr. McMurphy when these moments arise?"

He puts his size-ten pipe back in the corner of his mouth and spreads his hands on his knees and waits. Everybody's thinking about McMurphy's thick red arms and scarred hands and how his neck comes out of his T-shirt like a rusty wedge. The resident named Alvin has turned pale at the thought, like that yellow pipe smoke his buddy was blowing at him had stained his face.

"So you believe it would be wise," the doctor asks, "to send him up to Disturbed?"

"I believe it would be at the very least safe," the guy with the pipe answers, closing his eyes.

"I'm afraid I'll have to withdraw my suggestion and go along with Robert," Alvin tells them all, "if only for my own protection."

They all laugh. They're all more relaxed now, certain they've come round to the plan she was wanting. They all have a sip of coffee on it except the guy with the pipe, and he has a big to-do with the thing going out all the time, goes through a lot of matches and sucking and puffing and popping of his lips. It finally smokes up again to suit him, and he says, a little proudly, "Yes, Disturbed Ward for ol' Red McMurphy, I'm afraid. You know what I think, observing him these few days?"

"Schizophrenic reaction?" Alvin asks.

Pipe shakes his head.

"Latent Homosexual with Reaction Formation?" the third one says.

Pipe shakes his head again and shuts his eyes. "No," he says and smiles round the room, *"Negative Oedipal."*

They all congratulate him.

"Yes, I think there is a lot pointing to it," he says. "But whatever the final diagnosis is, we must keep one thing in mind: we're not dealing with an ordinary man."

"You—are very, very wrong, Mr Gideon."

It's the Big Nurse.

Everybody's head jerks toward her—mine too, but I check myself and pass the motion off like I'm trying to scrub a speck I just discovered on the wall above my head. Everybody's confused all to hell for sure now. They figured they were proposing just what she'd want, just what she was planning to propose in the meeting herself. I thought so too. I've seen her send men half the size of McMurphy up to Disturbed for no more reason than there was a chance they might spit on somebody; now she's got this bull of a man who's bucked her and everybody else on the staff, a guy she all but said was on his way off the ward earlier this afternoon, and she says no.

"No. I don't agree. Not at all." She smiles around at all of them. "I don't agree that he should be sent up to Disturbed, which would simply be an easy way of passing our problem on to another ward, and I don't agree that he is some kind of extraordinary being—some kind of 'super' psychopath."

She waits but nobody is about to disagree. For the first time she takes a sip of her coffee; the cup comes away from her mouth with that red-orange color on it. I stare at the rim of the cup in spite of myself; she *couldn't* be wearing lipstick that color. That color on the rim of the cup must be from heat, touch of her lips set it smoldering.

"I'll admit that my first thought when I began to recognize Mr. McMurphy for the disturbing force that he is was that he should most definitely be sent up to Disturbed. But now I believe it is too late. Would removing him undo the harm that he has done to our ward? I don't believe it would, not after this afternoon. I believe if he were sent to Disturbed now it would be exactly what the patients would expect. He would be a martyr to them. They would never be given the opportunity to see that this man is not an—as you put it, Mr. Gideon—'extraordinary person.' "

She takes another sip and sets the cup on the table; the whack of it sounds like a gavel; all three residents sit bolt upright.

"No. He isn't extraordinary. He is simply a man and no more, and is subject to all the fears and all the cowardice and all the timidity that any other man is subject to. Given a few more days, I have a very strong feeling that he will prove this, to us as well as the rest of the patients. If we keep him on the ward I am certain his brashness will subside, his self-made rebellion will dwindle to nothing, and"—she smiles, knowing something nobody else does—"that our redheaded hero will cut himself down to something patients will all recognize and lose respect for: a braggart and a blowhard of the type who may climb up on a soapbox and shout for a following, the way we've all seen Mr. Cheswick do, then back down the moment there is any real danger to him personally."

"Patient McMurphy"—the boy with the pipe feels he should try to defend his position and save face just a little bit—"does not strike me as a coward."

I expect her to get mad, but she doesn't; she just gives him that let's-wait-and-see look and says, "I didn't say he was exactly a coward, Mr. Gideon; oh, no. He's simply very fond of someone. As a psychopath, he's much too fond of a Mr. Randle Patrick McMurphy to subject him to any needless danger." She gives the boy a smile that puts his pipe out for sure this time. "If we just wait for a while, our hero will—what is it you college boys say?—give up his bit? Yes?"

The following scenes are from the Fantasy Films production, *ONE FLEW OVER THE CUCKOO'S NEST,* starring Jack Nicholson.

McMurphy (Jack Nicholson) arrives at the hospital, exaggerating his mental condition.

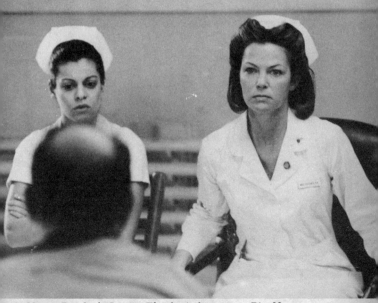

Nurse Ratched (Louise Fletcher), known as Big Nurse, represents the Establishment, as she sternly questions a patient.

McMurphy shows the patients a deck of porno cards.

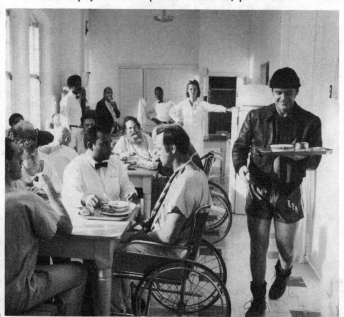

Wearing unusual hospital gear, McMurphy enlivens the mess hall.

Chief Bromden (Will Sampson) gets coaching in basketball.

Candy (Marya Small), a lively girl friend of McMurphy's, is "escort" for a group of the men on a rare fishing trip.

In the day room, McMurphy in a pensive moment.

McMurphy manages to slip Candy and her friend Rose (Louise Moritz) into the hospital for a party that includes Turkle (Scatman Crothers).

McMurphy wets down the patients arguing over a game of Monopoly.

The patients watch McMurphy's antics with amusement. (L. to r., Sefelt (William Duell), Cheswick (Sydney Lassick), Scanlon (Delos Smith, Jr.), Martini (Danny Devito), Frederickson (Vincent Schiavelli), Harding (William Redfield).

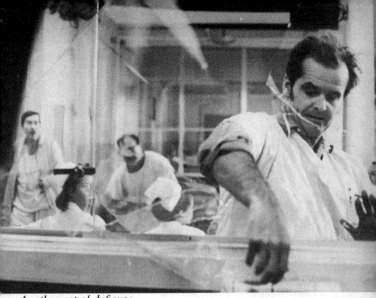

Another act of defiance.

McMurphy finally explodes and attacks the Big Nurse.

McMurphy and Chief Bromden discussing their escape.

"... one flew east, one flew west,
One flew over the cuckoo's nest."

"But that may take weeks'" the boy starts.

"We have weeks," she says. She stands up, looking more pleased with herself than I've seen her look since Mc-Murphy came to trouble her a week ago. "We have weeks, or months, or even years if need be. Keep in mind that Mr. Mc-Murphy is committed. The length of time he spends in this hospital is entirely up to us. Now, if there is nothing else . . ."

The way the Big Nurse acted so confident in that staff meeting, that worried me for a while, but it didn't make any difference to McMurphy. All weekend, and the next week, he was just as hard on her and her black boys as he ever was, and the patients were loving it. He'd won his bet; he'd got the nurse's goat the way he said he would, and had collected on it, but that didn't stop him from going right ahead and acting like he always had, hollering up and down the hall, laughing at the black boys, frustrating the whole staff, even going so far as to step up to the Big Nurse in the hall one time and ask her, if she didn't mind tellin', just what was the actual inch-by-inch measurement on them great big ol' breasts that she did her best to conceal but never could. She walked right on past, ignoring him just like she chose to ignore the way nature had tagged her with those outsized badges of femininity, just like she was above him, and sex, and everything else that's weak and of the flesh.

When she posted work assignments on the bulletin board, and he read that she'd given him latrine duty, he went to her office and knocked on that window of hers and personally thanked her for the honor, and told her he'd think of her every time he swabbed out a urinal. She told him that wasn't necessary; just do his work and that would be sufficient, thank you.

The most work he did on them was to run a brush around the bowls once or twice apiece, singing some song as loud as he could in time to the swishing brush; then he'd splash in some Clorox and he'd be through. "That's clean enough," he'd tell the black boy who got after him for the way he hurried through his job, "maybe not clean enough for *some* people, but myself I plan to piss in 'em, not eat lunch out of 'em." And when the Big Nurse gave in to the black boy's frustrated pleading and came in to check McMurphy's cleaning assignment personally, she brought a little compact mirror and she held it under the rim of the bowls. She walked along shaking her head and saying, "Why, this is an outrage . . an outrage . . ." at every bowl. McMurphy sidled right along beside her, winking down his nose and saying in answer, "No; that's a toilet bowl . . . a *toilet* bowl."

But she didn't lose control again, or even act at all like she might. She would get after him about the toilets, using that same terrible, slow, patient pressure she used on everybody, as he stood there in front of her, looking like a little kid getting a bawling out, hanging his head, and the toe of one boot on top of the other, saying, "I *try* and *try* ma'am, but I'm afraid I'll never make my mark as head man of the crappers."

Once he wrote something on a slip of paper, strange writing that looked like a foreign alphabet, and stuck it up under one of those toilet bowl rims with a wad of gum; when she came to that toilet with her mirror she gave a short gasp at what she read reflected and dropped her mirror in the toilet. But she didn't lose control That doll's face and that doll's smile were forged in confidence. She stood up from the toilet bowl and gave him a look that would peel paint and told him it was his job to make the latrine *cleaner,* not dirtier.

Actually, there wasn't much cleaning of any kind getting done on the ward. As soon as it came time in the afternoon when the schedule called for house duties, it was also time for the baseball games to be on TV, and everybody went and lined the chairs up in front of the set and they didn't move out of them until dinner. It didn't make any difference that the power was shut off in the Nurses' Station and we couldn't see a thing but that blank gray screen, because McMurphy'd entertain us for hours, sit and talk and tell all kinds of stories, like how he made a thousand dollars in one month driving a truck for a gyppo outfit and then lost every penny of it to some Canadian in an ax-throwing contest, or how he and a buddy slick-tongued a guy into riding a brahma bull at a rodeo in Albany, into riding him while he wore a blindfold: "Not the bull, I mean, the *guy* had on the blindfold." They told the guy that the blindfold would keep him from getting dizzy when the bull went to spinning; then, when they got a bandanna wrapped around his eyes to where he couldn't see, they set him on that bull backward. McMurphy told it a couple of times and slapped his thigh with his hat and laughed everytime he remembered it. "Blindfolded and backwards ... And I'm a sonofagun if he didn't stay the limit and won the purse. And I was second; if he'd been throwed I'd of took first and a neat little purse. I swear the next time I pull a stunt like that I'll blindfold the damn bull instead."

Whack his leg and throw back his head and laugh and laugh, digging his thumb into the ribs of whoever was sitting next to him, trying to get him to laugh too.

There was times that week when I'd hear that full-throttled

laugh, watch him scratching his belly and stretching and yawn-ing and leaning back to wink at whoever he was joking with, everything coming to him just as natural as drawing breath, and I'd quit worrying about the Big Nurse and the Combine behind her. I'd think he was strong enough being his own self that he would never back down the way she was hoping he would. I'd think, maybe he truly is something extraordinary. He's what he is, that's it. Maybe that makes him strong enough, being what he is. The Combine hasn't got to him in all these years; what makes that nurse think she's gonna be able to do it in a few weeks? He's not gonna let them twist him and manu-facture him.

And later, hiding in the latrine from the black boys, I'd take a look at my own self in the mirror and wonder how it was possible that anybody could manage such an enormous thing as being what he was. There'd be my face in the mirror, dark and hard with big, high cheekbones like the cheek underneath them had been hacked out with a hatchet, eyes all black and hard and mean-looking, just like Papa's eyes or the eyes of all those tough mean-looking Indians you see on TV, and I'd think, That ain't me, that ain't my face. It wasn't even me when I was trying to be that face. I wasn't even really me then; I was just being the way I looked, the way people wanted. It don't seem like I ever been me. How can McMurphy be what he is?

I was seeing him different than when he first came in; I was seeing more to him than just big hands and red sideburns and a broken-nosed grin. I'd see him do things that didn't fit with his face or hands, things like painting a picture at OT with real paints on a blank paper with no lines or numbers anywhere on it to tell him where to paint, or like writing letters to somebody in a beautiful flowing hand. How could a man who looked like him paint pictures or write letters to people or be upset and worried like I saw him once when he got a letter back? These were the kind of things you expected from Billy Bibbit or Harding. Harding had hands that looked like they should have done paintings though they never did; Harding trapped his hands and forced them to work sawing planks for doghouses. McMurphy wasn't like that. He hadn't let what he looked like run his life one way or the other, any more than he'd let the Combine mill him into fitting where they wanted him to fit.

I was seeing lots of things different. I figured the fog ma-chine had broke down in the walls when they turned it up too high for that meeting on Friday, so now they weren't able to circulate fog and gas and foul up the way things looked. For the first time in years I was seeing people with none of that black outline they used to have, and one night I was even able to see out the windows.

Like I explained, most nights before they ran me to bed they gave me this pill, knocked me out and kept me out. Or if something went haywire with the dose and I woke up, my eyes were all crusted over and the dorm was full of smoke, wires in the walls loaded to the limit, twisting and sparking death and hate in the air—all too much for me to take so I'd ram my head under the pillow and try to get back to sleep. Every time I peeked back out there would be the smell of burning hair and a sound like sidemeat on a hot griddle.

But this one night, a few nights after the big meeting, I woke up and the dorm was clean and silent; except for the soft breathing of the men and the stuff rattling around loose under the brittle ribs of the two old Vegetables, it was dead quiet. A window was up, and the air in the dorm was clear and had a taste to it made me feel kind of giddy and drunk, gave me this sudden yen to get up out of bed and do something.

I slid from between the sheets and walked barefoot across the cold tile between the beds. I felt the tile with my feet and wondered how many times, how many thousand times, had I run a mop over this same tile floor and never felt it at all. That mopping seemed like a dream to me, like I couldn't exactly believe all those years of it had really happened. Only that cold linoleum under my feet was real right then, only that moment.

I walked among the guys heaped in long white rows like snowbanks, careful not to bump into somebody, till I came to the wall with the windows. I walked down the windows to one where the shade popped softly in and out with the breeze, and I pressed my forehead up against the mesh. The wire was cold and sharp, and I rolled my head against it from side to side to feel it with my cheeks, and I smelled the breeze. It's fall coming, I thought, I can smell that sour-molasses smell of silage, clanging the air like a bell—smell somebody's been burning oak leaves, left them to smolder overnight because they're too green.

It's fall coming, I kept thinking, fall coming; just like that was the strangest thing ever happened. Fall. Right outside here it was spring a while back, then it was summer, and now it's fall—that's sure a curious idea.

I realized I still had my eyes shut. I had shut them when I put my face to the screen, like I was scared to look outside. Now I had to open them. I looked out the window and saw for the first time how the hospital was out in the country. The moon was low in the sky over the pastureland; the face of it was scarred and scuffed where it had just torn up out of the snarl of scrub oak and madrone trees on the horizon. The stars up close to the moon were pale; they got brighter and braver the farther they got out of the circle of light ruled by the giant moon. It called to mind how I noticed the exact same thing when I was off on a hunt with Papa and the uncles and I lay rolled in blankets Grandma had woven, lying off a piece from where the men hunkered around the fire as they passed a quart jar of cactus liquor in a silent circle. I watched that big Oregon prairie moon above me put all the stars around it to shame. I kept awake watching, to see if the moon ever got dimmer or the stars got brighter, till the dew commenced to drift onto my cheeks and I had to pull a blanket over my head.

Something moved on the grounds down beneath my window—cast a long spider of shadow out across the grass as it ran out of sight behind a hedge. When it ran back to where I could get a better look, I saw it was a dog, a young, gangly mongrel slipped off from home to find out about things went on after dark. He was sniffing digger squirrel holes, not with a notion to go digging after one but just to get an idea what they were up to at this hour. He'd run his muzzle down a hole, butt up in the air and tail going, then dash off to another. The moon glistened around him on the wet grass, and when he ran he left tracks like dabs of dark paint spattered across the blue shine of the lawn. Galloping from one particularly interesting hole to the next, he became so took with what was coming off—the moon up there, the night, the breeze full of smells so wild makes a young dog drunk—that he had to lie down on his back and roll. He twisted and thrashed around like a fish, back bowed and belly up, and when he got to his feet and shook himself a spray came off him in the moon like silver scales.

He sniffed all the holes over again one quick one, to get the smells down good, then suddenly froze still with one paw lifted and his head tilted, listening. I listened too, but I couldn't hear anything except the popping of the window shade. I listened for a long time. Then, from a long way off, I heard a high, laughing gabble, faint and coming closer. Canada honkers going south for the winter. I remembered all the hunting and belly-crawling I'd ever done trying to kill a honker, and that I never got one.

I tried to look where the dog was looking to see if I could find the flock, but it was too dark. The honking came closer and

closer till it seemed like they must be flying right through the
dorm, right over my head. Then they crossed the moon—a
black, weaving necklace, drawn into a V by that lead goose.
For an instant that lead goose was right in the center of that
circle, bigger than the others, a black cross opening and closing,
then he pulled his V out of sight into the sky once more.

I listened to them fade away till all I could hear was my
memory of the sound. The dog could still hear them a long
time after me. He was still standing with his paw up; he hadn't
moved or barked when they flew over. When he couldn't hear
them any more either, he commenced to lope off in the direction they had gone, toward the highway, loping steady and
solemn like he had an appointment. I held my breath and I
could hear the flap of his big paws on the grass as he loped;
then I could hear a car speed up out of a turn. The headlights
loomed over the rise and peered ahead down the highway. I
watched the dog and the car making for the same spot of pavement.

The dog was almost to the rail fence at the edge of the
grounds when I felt somebody slip up behind me. Two people.
I didn't turn, but I knew it was the black boy named Geever
and the nurse with the birthmark and the crucifix. I heard a
whir of fear start up in my head. The black boy took my arm
and pulled me around. "I'll get 'im," he says.

"It's chilly at the window there, Mr. Bromden," the nurse
tells me. "Don't you think we'd better climb back into our nice
toasty bed?"

"He cain't hear," the black boy tells her. "I'll take him. He's
always untying his sheet and roaming 'round."

And I move and she draws back a step and says, "Yes,
please do," to the black boy. She's fiddling with the chain runs
down her neck. At home she locks herself in the bathroom out
of sight, strips down, and rubs that crucifix all over that stain
running from the corner of her mouth in a thin line down
across her shoulders and breasts. She rubs and rubs and hails
Mary to beat thunder, but the stain stays. She looks in the
mirror, sees it's darker'n ever. Finally take a wire brush used
to take paint off boats and scrubs the stain away, puts a night-
gown on over the raw, oozing hide, and crawls in bed.

But she's too full of the stuff. While she's asleep it rises in
her throat and into her mouth, drains out of that corner of her
mouth like purple spit and down her throat, over her body.
In the morning she sees how she's stained again and somehow
she figures it's not really from inside her—how could it be? a
good Catholic girl like her?—and she figures it's on account of

working evenings among a whole wardful of people like me. It's all our fault, and she's going to get us for it if it's the last thing she does. I wish McMurphy'd wake up and help me.

"You get him tied in bed, Mr. Geever, and I'll prepare a medication."

*I*n the group meetings there were gripes coming up that had been buried so long the thing being griped about had already changed. Now that McMurphy was around to back them up, the guys started letting fly at everything that had ever happened on the ward they didn't like.

"Why does the dorms have to be locked on the weekends?" Cheswick or somebody would ask. Can't a fellow even have the weekends to himself?"

"Yeah, Miss Ratched," McMurphy would say. "Why?"

"If the dorms were left open, we have learned from past experience, you men would return to bed after breakfast."

"Is that a mortal sin? I mean, *normal* people get to sleep late on the weekends."

"You men are in this hospital," she would say like she was repeating it for the hundredth time, "because of your proven inability to adjust to society. The doctor and I believe that every minute spent in the company of others, with some exceptions, is therapeutic, while every minute spent brooding alone only increases your separation."

"Is that the reason that there has to be at least eight guys together before they can be taken off the ward to OT or PT or one of them Ts?"

"That is correct."

"You mean it's sick to want to be off by yourself?"

"I didn't say that—"

"You mean if I go into latrine to relieve myself I should take along at least seven buddies to keep me from brooding on the can?"

Before she could come up with an answer to that, Cheswick bounced to his feet and hollered at her, "Yeah, is that what you mean?" and the other Acutes sitting around the meeting would say, "Yeah, yeah, is that what you mean?"

She would wait till they all died down and the meeting was quiet again, then say quietly, "If you men can calm yourself enough to act like a group of adults at a discussion instead of children on the playground, we will ask the doctor if he thinks it would be beneficial to consider a change in the ward policy at this time. Doctor?"

Everybody knew the kind of answer the doctor would make, and before he even had the chance Cheswick would be off on another complaint. "Then what about our cigarettes, Miss Ratched?"

"Yeah, what about that," the Acutes grumbled.

McMurphy turned to the doctor and put the question straight to *him* this time before the nurse had a chance to answer. "Yeah, Doc, what about our cigarettes? How does she have the right to keep the cigarettes—*our* cigarettes— piled up on her desk in there like she owned them, bleed a pack out to us now and again whenever she feels like it. I don't care much about the idea of buying a carton of cigarettes and having somebody tell me when I can smoke them."

The doctor tilted his head so he could look at the nurse through his glasses. He hadn't heard about her taking over the extra cigarettes to stop the gambling. "What's this about cigarettes, Miss Ratched? I don't believe I've heard—"

"I feel, Doctor, that three and four and sometimes five packages of cigarettes a day are entirely too many for a man to smoke. That is what seemed to be happening last week— after Mr. McMurphy's arrival—and that is why I thought it might be best to impound the cartons the men purchased at the canteen and allow each man only one pack a day."

McMurphy leaned forward and whispered loudly to Cheswick, "Hear tell her next decision is about trips to the can; not only does a guy have to take his seven buddies into the latrine with him but he's also limited to two trips a day, to be taken when she says so."

And leaned back in his chair and laughed so hard that nobody else could say anything for nearly a minute.

McMurphy was getting a lot of kick out of the ruckus he was raising, and I think was a little surprised that he wasn't getting a lot of pressure from the staff too, especially surprised that the Big Nurse wasn't having any more to say to him than she was. "I thought the old buzzard was tougher than this," he said to Harding after one meeting. "Maybe all she needed to straighten her out was a good bringdown. The thing is"— he frowned—"she acts like she still holds all the cards up that white sleeve of hers."

He went on getting a kick out of it till about Wednesday of the next week. Then he learned why the Big Nurse was so sure of her hand. Wednesday's the day they pack everybody up who hasn't got some kind of rot and move to the swimming pool, whether we want to go or not. When the fog was on the ward I used to hide in it to get out of going. The pool always scared me; I was always afraid I'd step in over my head and drown, be sucked off down the drain and clean out to sea. I used to be real brave around water when I was a kid on the Columbia; I'd walk the scaffolding around the falls with all the other men, scrambling around with water roaring green and white all around me and the mist making rainbows, without even any hobnails like the men wore. But when I saw my Papa start getting scared of things, I got scared too, got so I couldn't even stand a shallow pool.

We came out of the locker room and the pool was pitching and splashing and full of naked men; whooping and yelling bounced off the high ceiling the way it always does in indoor swimming pools. The black boys herded us into it. The water was a nice warm temperature but I didn't want to get away from the side (the black boys walk along the edge with long bamboo poles to shove you away from the side if you try to grab on) so I stayed close to McMurphy on account of I knew they wouldn't try to make him go into deep water if he didn't want to.

He was talking to the lifeguard, and I was standing a few feet away. McMurphy must of been standing in a hole because he was having to tread water where I was just standing on the bottom. The lifeguard was standing on the edge of the pool; he had a whistle and a T-shirt on with his ward number on it. He and McMurphy had got to talking about the difference between hospital and jail, and McMurphy was saying how much better the hospital was. The lifeguard wasn't so sure. I heard him tell McMurphy that, for one thing, being committed ain't like being sentenced. "You're sentenced in a jail, and you got a date ahead of you when you *know* you're gonna be turned loose," he said.

McMurphy stopped splashing around like he had been. He swam slowly to the edge of the pool and held there, looking up at the lifeguard. "And if you're committed?" he asked after a pause.

The lifeguard raised his shoulders in a musclebound shrug and tugged at the whistle around his neck. He was an old pro-footballer with cleat marks in his forehead, and every so often when he was off his ward a signal would click back of his eyes and his lips'd go to spitting numbers and he'd drop to all fours in a line stance and cut loose on some strolling nurse, drive a shoulder in her kidneys just in time to let the halfback shoot past through the hole behind him. That's why he was up on

Disturbed; whenever he wasn't lifeguarding he was liable to do something like that.

He shrugged again at McMurphy's question, then looked back and forth to see if any black boys were around, and knelt close to the edge of the pool. He held his arm out for McMurphy to look at.

"You see this cast?"

McMurphy looked at the big arm. "You don't have a cast on that arm, buddy."

The lifeguard just grinned. "Well, that cast's on there because I got a bad fracture in the last game with the Browns. I can't get back in togs till the fracture knits and I get the cast off. The nurse on my ward tells me she's curing the arm in secret. Yeah, man, she says if I go easy on that arm, don't exert it or nothing, she'll take the cast off and I can get back with the ball club."

He put his knuckles on the wet tile, went into a three-point stance to test how the arm was coming along. McMurphy watched him a minute, then asked how long he'd been waiting for them to tell him his arm was healed so he could leave the hospital. The lifeguard raised up slowly and rubbed his arm. He acted hurt that McMurphy had asked that, like he thought he was being accused of being soft and licking his wounds. "I'm committed," he said. "I'd of left here before now if it was up to me. Maybe I couldn't play first string, with this bum arm, but I could of folded towels, couldn't I? I could of done *something*. That nurse on my ward, she keeps telling the doctor I ain't ready. Not even to fold towels in the crummy old locker room, I ain't ready."

He turned and walked over to his lifeguard chair, climbed up the chair ladder like a drugged gorilla, and peered down at us, his lower lip pushed way out. "I was picked up for drunk and disorderly, and I been here eight years and eight months," he said.

McMurphy pushed backward from the edge of the pool and trod water and thought this over: he'd had a six months' sentence at the work farm with two months finished, four more to go—and four more months was the most he wanted to spend locked up any place. He'd been close to a month in this nuthouse and it might be a lot better than a work farm, what with good beds and orange juice for breakfast, but it wasn't better to the point that he'd want to spend a couple of years here.

He swam over to the steps at the shallow end of he pool and sat there the rest of the period, tugging that little tuft of wool at his throat and frowning. Watching him sitting there frowning all to himself, I remembered what the Big Nurse had said in the meeting, and I began to feel afraid.

When they blew the whistle for us to leave the pool and we all were straggling toward the locker room, we ran into this other ward coming into the swimming pool for their period, and in the footbath at the shower you had to go through was this one kid from the other ward. He had a big spongy pink head and bulgy hips and legs—like somebody'd grabbed a balloon full of water and squeezed it in the middle—and he was lying on his side in the footbath, making noises like a sleepy seal. Cheswick and Harding helped him stand up, and he lay right back down in the footbath. The head bobbed around in the disinfectant. McMurphy watched them lift him standing again.

"What the devil is he?" he asked.

"He has hydrocephalus," Harding told him. "Some manner of lymph disorder, I believe. Head fills up with liquid. Give us a hand helping him stand up."

They turned the kid loose, and he lay back down in the footbath again; the look on his face was patient and helpless and stubborn; his mouth sputtered and blew bubbles in the milky-looking water. Harding repeated his request to McMurphy to give them a hand, and he and Cheswick bent down to the kid again. McMurphy pushed past them and stepped across the kid into the shower.

"Let him lay," he said, washing himself down in the shower. "Maybe he don't like deep water."

I could see it coming. The next day he surprised everybody on the ward by getting up early and polishing that latrine till it sparkled, and then went to work on the hall floors when the black boys asked him to. Surprised everybody but the Big Nurse; she acted like it was nothing surprising at all.

And that afternoon in the meeting when Cheswick said that everybody'd agreed that there should be some kind of showdown on the cigarette situation, saying, "I ain't no little kid to have cigarettes kept from me like cookies! We want something done about it, ain't that right, Mack?" and waited for McMurphy to back him up, all he got was silence.

He looked over at McMurphy's corner. Everybody did. McMurphy was there, studying the deck of cards that slid in and out of sight in his hands. He didn't even look up. It was awfully quiet; there was just that slap of greasy cards and Cheswick's heavy breathing.

"I want something *done!*" Cheswick suddenly yelled again.

"I ain't no little kid!" He stamped his foot and looked around him like he was lost and might break out crying any minute. He clenched both fists and held them at his chubby round chest. His fists made little pink balls against the green, and they were clenched so hard he was shaking.

He never had looked big; he was short and too fat and had a bald spot in the back of his head that showed like a pink dollar, but standing there by himself in the center of the day room like that he looked tiny. He looked at McMurphy and got no look back, and went down the line of Acutes looking for help. Each time a man looked away and refused to back him up, and the panic in his face doubled. His looking finally came to a stop at the Big Nurse. He stamped his foot again.

"I want something *done!* Hear me? I want *something* done! Something! Something! Some—"

The two big black boys clamped his arms from behind, and the least one threw a strap around him. He sagged like he'd been punctured, and the two big ones dragged him up to Disturbed; you could hear the soggy bounce of him going up the steps. When they came back and sat down, the Big Nurse turned to the line of Acutes across the room and looked at them. Nothing had been said since Cheswick left.

"Is there any more discussion," she said, "on the rationing of cigarettes?"

Looking down the canceled row of faces hanging against the wall across the room from me, my eyes finally came to McMurphy in his chair in the corner, concentrating on improving his one-handed card cut . . . and the white tubes in the ceiling begin to pump their refrigerated light again . . . I can feel it, beams all the way into my stomach.

After McMurphy doesn't stand up for us any longer, some of the Acutes talk and say he's still outsmarting the Big Nurse, say that he got word she was about to send him to Disturbed and decided to toe the line a while, not give her any reason. Others figure he's letting her relax, then he's going to spring something new on her, something wilder and more ornery than ever. You can hear them talking in groups, wondering.

But me, I *know* why. I heard him talk to the lifeguard. He's finally getting cagey, is all. The way Papa finally did when he came to realize that he couldn't beat that group from town who wanted the government to put in the dam because of the money and the work it would bring, and because it would get rid of the village: Let that tribe of fish Injuns take their stink and their two hundred thousand dollars the government is paying them and go some place else with it! Papa had done the smart thing signing the papers; there wasn't anything to gain by bucking it. The government would of got it anyhow, sooner or later; this way the tribe would get paid good. It was the smart thing. McMurphy was doing the smart thing. I could see that. He was giving in because it was the smartest thing to do, not because of any of these other reasons the Acutes were making up. He didn't say so, but I knew and I told myself it was the smart thing to do. I told myself that over and over: It's safe. Like hiding. It's the smart thing to do, nobody could say any different. I know what he's doing.

Then one morning all the Acutes know too, know his real reason for backing down and that the reasons they been making up were just lies to kid themselves. He never says a thing about the talk he had with the lifeguard, but they know. I figure the nurse broadcast this during the night along all the little lines in the dorm floor, because they know all at once. I can tell by the way they look at McMurphy that morning when he comes into the day room. Not looking like they're mad with him, or even disappointed, because they can understand as well as I can that the only way he's going to get the Big Nurse to lift his commitment is by acting like she wants, but still looking at him like they wished things didn't have to be this way.

Even Cheswick could understand it and didn't hold anything against McMurphy for not going ahead and making a big fuss over the cigarettes. He came back down from Disturbed on the same day that the nurse broadcast the information to the beds, and he told McMurphy himself that he could understand how he acted and that it was surely the sharpest thing to do, considering, and that if he'd thought about Mack being committed he'd never have put him on the spot like he had the other day. He told McMurphy this while we were all being taken over to the swimming pool. But just as soon as we got to the pool he said he did wish *something* mighta been done, though, and dove into the water. And got his fingers stuck some way in the grate that's over the drain at the bottom of the pool, and neither the big lifeguard nor McMurphy nor the two black boys could pry him loose, and by the time they got a screwdriver and undid the grate and brought Cheswick up, with the grate still clutched by his chubby pink and blue fingers, he was drowned.

*U*p ahead of me in the lunch line I see a tray sling in the air, a green plastic cloud raining milk and peas and vegetable soup. Sefelt's jittering out of the line on one foot with his arms both up in the air, falls backward in a stiff arch, and the whites of his eyes come by me upside down. His head hits the tile with a crack like rocks under water, and he holds the arch, like a twitching, jerking bridge. Fredrickson and Scanlon make a jump to help, but the big black boy shoves them back and grabs a flat stick out of his back pocket, got tape wrapped around it and covered with a brown stain. He pries Sefelt's mouth open and shoves the stick between his teeth, and I hear the stick splinter with Sefelt's bite. I can taste the slivers. Sefelt's jerks slow down ad get more powerful, working and building up to big stiff kicks that lift him to a bridge, then falling—lifting and falling, slower and slower, till the Big Nurse comes in and stands over him and he melts limp all over the floor in a gray puddle.

She folds her hands in front of her, might hold a candle, and looks down at what's left of him oozing out of the cuffs of his pants and shirt. "Mr. Sefelt?" she says to the black boy.

"Tha's right—*uhn.*" The black boy is jerking to get his stick back. "Mistuh *See-fel'.*"

"And Mr. Sefelt has been asserting he needs *no more medication.*" She nods her head, steps back a step out of the way of him spreading toward her white shoes. She raises her head and looks around her at the circle of Acutes that've come up to see. She nods again and repeats, ". . . needs *no more medication.*" Her face is smiling, pitying, patient, and disgusted all at once—a trained expression.

McMurphy's never seen such a thing. "What's he got wrong with him?" he asks.

She keeps her eye on the puddle, not turning to McMurphy. "Mr. Sefelt is an epileptic, Mr. McMurphy. This means he may be subject to seizures like this at any time if he doesn't follow medical advice. He knows better. We'd told him this would happen when he didn't take his medication. Still, he will insist on acting foolish."

Fredrickson comes out of the line with his eyebrows bris-

152

tling. He's a sinewy, bloodless guy with blond hair and stringy blond eyebrows and a long jaw, and he acts tough every so often the way Cheswick used to try to do—roar and rant and cuss out one of the nurses, say he's gonna *leave* this stinkin' place! They always let him yell and shake his fist till he quiets down, then ask him if you are *through*, Mr. Fredrickson, we'll go start typing the release—then make a book in the Nurses' Station how long it'll be till he's tapping at the glass with a guilty look and asking to apologize and how about just *forgetting* those hotheaded things he said, just pigeonhole those old forms for a day or so, okay?

He steps up to the nurse, shaking his fist at her. "Oh, is that it? Is that it, huh? You gonna crucify old Seef just as if he was doing it to *spite* you or something?"

She lays a comforting hand on his arm, and his fist unrolls.

"It's okay, Bruce. Your friend will be all right. Apparently hasn't been swallowing his Dilantin. I simply don't know what he is doing with it."

She knows as well as anybody; Sefelt holds the capsules in his mouth and gives them to Fredrickson later. Sefelt doesn't like to take them because of what he calls "disastrous side effects," and Fredrickson likes a double dose because he's scared to death of having a fit. The nurse knows this, you can tell by her voice, but to look at her there, so sympathetic and kind, you'd think she was ignorant of anything at all between Fredrickson and Sefelt.

"Yeahhh," says Fredrickson, but he can't work his attack up again. "Yeah, well, you don't need to act like it was as simple as just take the stuff or don't take it. You know how Seef worries about what he looks like and how women think he's ugly and all that, and you know how he thinks the Dilantin—"

"I know," she says and touches his arm again. "He also blames his falling hair on the drug. Poor old fellow."

"He's not that old!"

"I know, Bruce. Why do you get so *upset*? I've never understood what went on between you and your friend that made you get so *defensive!*"

"Well, heck, anyway!" he says and jams his fists in his pockets.

The nurse bends over and brushes a little place clean on the floor and puts her knee on it and starts kneading Sefelt back to some shape. She tells the black boy to stay with the poor old fellow and she'll go send a Gurney down for him; wheel him into the dorm and let him sleep the rest of the day. When she stands she gives Fredrickson a pat on the arm, and he grumbles, "Yeah, I have to take Dilantin too, you know. That's why I know what Seef has to face. I mean, that's why I—well, heck—."

"I understand, Bruce, what *both* of you must go through, but don't you think anything is better than *that?*"

Fredrickson looks where she points. Sefelt has pulled back halfway normal, swelling up and down with big wet, rattling breaths. There's a punk-knot rising on the side of his head where he landed, and a red foam around the black boy's stick where it goes into his mouth, and his eyes are beginning to roll back into the whites. His hands are nailed out to each side with the palms up and the fingers jerking open and shut, just the way I've watched men jerk at the Shock Shop strapped to the crossed table, smoke curling up out of the palms from the current. Sefelt and Fredrickson never been to the Shock Shop. They're manufactured to generate their own voltage, store it in their spines and can be turned on remote from the steel door in the Nurses' Station if they get out of line—be right in the best part of a dirty joke and stiffen like the jolt hit square in the small of the back. It saves the trouble of taking them over to that room.

The nurse gives Fredrickson's arm a little shake like he'd gone to sleep, and repeats, "Even if you take into consideration the harmful effects of the medicine, don't you think it's better than *that?*"

As he stares down at the floor, Fredrickson's blond eyebrows are raised like he's seeing for the first time just how *he* looks at least once a month. The nurse smiles and pats his arm and heads for the door, glares at the Acutes to shame them for gathering around watching such a thing; when she's gone, Fredrickson shivers and tries to smile.

"I don't know *what* I got mad at the old girl about—I mean, she didn't do anything to give me a reason to blow up like that, did she?"

It isn't that he wants an answer; it's more sort of realizing that he can't put his finger on a reason. He shivers again and starts to slip back away from the group. McMurphy comes up and asks him in a low voice what *is* it they take?

"Dilantin, McMurphy, an anti-convulsant, if you must know."

"Don't it work or something?"

"Yeah, I guess it works all right—if you take it."

"Then what's the sweat about taking it or not?"

"Look, if you must know! Here's the dirty sweat about taking it." Fredrickson reaches up and grabs his lower lip between his thumb and finger, pulls it down to show gums ragged and pink and bloodless around long shiny teeth. "Your *gungs*," he says, hanging onto the lip. "Dilantin gnakes your gungs rot. And a seizure gnakes you grit your teeth. And you—"

There's a noise on the floor. They look to where Sefelt is moaning and wheezing, just as the black boy draws two teeth out with his taped stick.

Scanlon takes his tray and walks away from the bunch, saying, "Hell of a life. Damned if you do and damned if you don't. Puts a man in one confounded *bind*, I'd say."

McMurphy says, "Yeah. I see what you mean," looking down into Sefelt's gathering face. His face has commenced to take on that same haggard, puzzled look of pressure that the face on the floor has.

Whatever it was went haywire in the mechanism, they've just about got it fixed again. The clean, calculated arcade movement is coming back: six-thirty out of bed, seven into the mess hall, eight the puzzles come out for the Chronics and the cards for the Acutes . . . in the Nurses' Station I can see the white hands of the Big Nurse float over the controls.

T hey take me with the Acutes sometimes, and sometimes they don't. They take me once with them over to the library and I walk over to the technical section, stand there looking at the titles of books on electronics, books I recognize from that year I went to college; I remember inside the books are full of schematic drawings and equations and theories—hard, sure, safe things.

I want to look at one of the books, but I'm scared to. I'm scared to do anything. I feel like I'm floating in the dusty yellow air of the library, halfway to the bottom, halfway to the top. The stacks of books teeter above me, crazy, zig-zagging, running all different angles to one another. One shelf bends a little to the left, one to the right. Some of them are leaning over me, and I don't see how the books keep from falling out. It goes up and up this way, clear out of sight, the rickety stacks nailed together with slats and two-by-fours. Propped up with poles, leaning against ladders, on all sides of me. If I pulled one book out, lord knows what awful thing might result.

I hear somebody walk in, and it's one of the black boys from our ward and he's got Harding's wife with him. They're talking and grinning to each other as they come into the library.

"See here, Dale," the black boy calls over to Harding where he's reading a book, "look here who come to visit you. I tole her it wun't visitin' hours but you know she jus' sweet-talk me into bringin' her right on over here anyhow." He leaves her standing in front of Harding and goes off, saying mysteriously, "Don't you forget now, you hear?"

She blows the black boy a kiss, then turns to Harding, slinging her hips forward. "Hello, Dale."

"Honey," he says, but he doesn't make any move to take the couple of steps to her. He looks around him at everybody watching.

She's as tall as he is. She's got on high-heeled shoes and is carrying a black purse, not by the strap, but holding it the way you hold a book. Her fingernails are red as drops of blood against the shiny black patent-leather purse.

"Hey, Mack," Harding calls to McMurphy, who's sitting across the room, looking at a book of cartoons. "If you'll curtail your literary pursuits a moment I'll introduce you to my counterpart and Nemesis; I would be trite and say, 'to my better half,' but I think that phrase indicates some kind of basically equal division, don't you?"

He tries to laugh, and his two slim ivory fingers dip into his shirt pocket for cigarettes, fidget around getting the last one from the package. The cigarette shakes as he places it between his lips. He and his wife haven't moved toward each other yet.

McMurphy heaves up out of his chair and pulls his cap off as he walks over. Harding's wife looks at him and smiles, lifting one of her eyebrows. "Afternoon, Miz Harding," McMurphy says.

She smiles back bigger than before and says, "I hate Mrs. Harding, Mack; why don't you call me Vera?"

They all three sit back down on the couch where Harding was sitting, and he tells his wife about McMurphy and how McMurphy got the best of the Big Nurse, and she smiles and says that it doesn't surpise her a bit. While Harding's telling the story he gets enthusiastic and forgets about his hands, and they weave the air in front of him into a picture clear enough to see, dancing the story to the tune of his voice like two beautiful ballet women in white. His hands can be anything. But as soon as the story's finished he notices McMurphy and his wife are watching the hands, and he traps them between his knees. He laughs about this, and his wife says to him, "Dale, when are you going to learn to laugh instead of making that mousy little squeak?"

It's the same thing that McMurphy said about Harding's laugh on that first day, but it's different somehow; where McMurphy saying it calmed Harding down, her saying it makes him more nervous than ever.

She asks for a cigarette, and Harding dips his fingers in his pocket again and it's empty. "We've been rationed," he says, folding his thin shoulders forward like he was trying to hide the half-smoked cigarette he was holding, "to one pack a day. That doesn't seem to leave a man any margin for chivalry, Vera my dearest."

"Oh Dale, you never do have enough, do you?"

His eyes take on that sly, fevered skittishness as he looks at her and smiles. "Are we speaking symbolically, or are we still dealing with the concrete here-and-now cigarettes? No matter; you know the answer to the question, whichever way you intended it."

"I didn't intend nothing by it except what I said, Dale—"

"You didn't intend *any*thing by it, sweetest; your use of 'didn't' and 'nothing' constitutes a double negative. McMurphy, Vera's English rivals yours for illiteracy. Look, honey, you understand that between 'no' and 'any' there is—"

"All right! That's enough! I meant it both ways. I meant it any way you want to take it. I meant you don't have enough of nothing *period!*"

"Enough of *anything*, my bright little child."

She glares at Harding a second, then turns to McMurphy sitting beside her. "You, Mack, what about you. Can you handle a simple little thing like offering a girl a cigarette?"

His package is already lying in his lap. He looks down at it like he wishes it wasn't, then says, "Sure I always got cigarettes. Reason is, I'm a bum. I bum them whenever I get the chance is why my pack lasts longer than Harding's here. He smokes only his own. So you can see he's more likely to run out than—"

"You don't have to apologize for my inadequacies, my friend. It neither fits your character nor complements mine."

"No, it doesn't," the girl says. "All you have to do is light my cigarette."

And she leans so far forward to his match that even clear across the room I could see down her blouse.

She talks some more about some of Harding's friends who she wishes would quit dropping around the house looking for him. "You know the type, don't you, Mack?" she says. "The hoity-toity boys with the nice long hair combed so perfectly and the limp little wrists that flip so nice." Harding asks her if it was only him that they were dropping around to see, and she says any man that drops around to see her flips more than his damned limp wrists.

She stands suddenly and says it's time for her to go. She takes McMurphy's hand and tells him she hopes she sees him again sometime and she walks out of the library. McMurphy can't say a word. At the clack of her high heels everybody's head comes up again, and they watch her walk down the hall till she turns out of sight.

"What do you think?" Harding says.

McMurphy starts. "She's got one hell of a set of chabobs," is all he can think of. "Big as Old Lady Ratched's."

"I didn't mean physically, my friend, I mean what do you—"

"Hell's bells, Harding!" McMurphy yells suddenly. "I don't know what to think! What do you want out of me? A marriage counsellor? All I know is this: nobody's very big in the first place, and it looks to me like everybody spends their whole life tearing everybody else down. I know what you want me to think; you want me to feel sorry for you, to think she's a real bitch. Well, you didn't make her feel like any queen either. Well, screw you and 'what do you think?' I've got worries of my own without getting hooked with yours. So just quit!" He glares around the library at the other patients. "Alla you! Quit *bugging* me, goddammit!"

And sticks his cap back on his head and walks back to his cartoon magazine across the room. All the Acutes are looking at each other with their mouths open. What's he hollering at *them* about? Nobody's been bugging him. Nobody's asked him for a thing since they found out that he was trying to behave to keep his commitment from being extended. Now they're surprised at the way he just blew up at Harding and can't figure the way he grabs the book up from the chair and sits down and holds it up close in front of his face—either to keep people from looking at him or to keep from having to look at people.

That night at supper he apologizes to Harding and says he don't know what hung him up so at the library. Harding says perhaps it was his wife: she frequently hangs people up. McMurphy sits staring into his coffee and says, "I don't know, man. I just met her this afternoon. So she sure the hell isn't the one's been giving me bad dreams this last miserable week."

"Why, Mis-tur McMurphy," Harding cries, trying to talk like the little resident boy who comes to the meetings, "you simply must tell us about these dreams. Ah, wait until I get my pencil and pad." Harding is trying to be funny to relieve the strain of the apology. He picks up a napkin and a spoon and acts like he's going to take notes. "Now. Pre-cisely, what was it you saw in these—ah—dreams?"

McMurphy don't crack a smile. "I don't know, man. Nothing but faces, I guess—just faces."

The next morning Martini is behind the control panel in the tub room, playing like he's a jet pilot. The poker game stops to grin at his act.

"EeeeeeaahHOOoomeerr. Ground to air, ground to air: object sighted four-oh-sixteen-hundred—appears to be enemy missile. Proceed at once! EeeahhOOOmmmm."

Spins a dial, shoves a lever forward and leans with the bank of the ship. He cranks a needle to "ON FULL" at the side of the panel, but no water comes out of the nozzles set around the square tile booth in front of him. They don't use hydrotherapy any more, and nobody's turned the water on. Brand-new chrome equipment and steel panel never been used. Except for the chrome the panel and shower look just like the hydrotherapy outfits they used at the old hospital fifteen years ago: nozzles capable of reaching parts of the body from every angle, a technician in a rubber apron standing on the other side of the room manipulating the controls on that panel, dictating which nozzles squirt where, how hard, how hot—spray opened soft and soothing, then squeezed sharp as a needle—you hung up there between the nozzles in canvas straps, soaked and limp and wrinkled while the technician enjoyed his toy.

"EeeeaaooOOOoommm. . . . Air to ground, air to ground; missile sighted; coming into my sights now. . . ."

Martini bends down and aims over the panel through the ring of nozzles. He closes one eye and peeps through the ring with the other eye.

"On target! Ready . . . Aim . . . Fi—!"

His hands jerk back from the panel and he stands bolt upright, hair flying and both eyes bulging out at the shower booth so wild ad scared all the card-players spin around in their chairs to see if they can see it too—but they don't see anything in there but the buckles hanging among the nozzles on stiff new canvas straps.

Martini turns and looks straight at McMurphy. No one else. "Didn't you see thum? Didn't you?"

"See who, Mart? I don't see anything."

"In all those straps? Didn't you?"

McMurphy turns and squints at the shower. "Nope. Not a thing."

"Hold it a minute. They need you to see thum," Martini says.

"Damn you, Martini, I told you I can't see them! Understand? Not a blessed thing!"

"Oh," Martini says. He nods his head and turns from the shower booth. "Well, I didn't see thum either. I's just kidding you."

McMurphy cuts the deck and shuffles it with a buzzing snap. "Well—I don't care for that sort of kiddin', Mart." He cuts to shuffle again, and the cards splash everywhere like the deck exploded between his two trembling hands.

I remember it was a Friday again, three weeks after we voted on TV, and everybody who could walk was herded over to Building One for what they try to tell us is chest X-rays for TB, which I know is a check to see if everybody's machinery is functioning up to par.

We're benched in a long row down a hall leading to a door marked X-RAY. Next to X-ray is a door marked EENT where they check our throats during the winter. Across the hall from us is another bench, and it leads to that metal door. With the line of rivets. And nothing marked on it at all. Two guys are dozing on the bench between two black boys, while another victim inside is getting his treatment and I can hear him screaming. The door opens inward with a whoosh, and I can see the twinkling tubes in the room. They wheel the victim out still smoking, and I grip the bench where I sit to keep from being sucked through that door. A black boy and a white one drag one of the other guys on the bench to his feet, and he sways and staggers under the drugs in him. They usually give you red capsules before Shock. They push him through the door, and the technicians get him under each arm. For a second I see the guy realizes where they got him, and he stiffens both heels into the cement floor to keep from being pulled to the table—then the door pulls shut, phumph, with metal hitting a mattress, and I can't see him any more.

"Man, what they got going on in there?" McMurphy asks Harding.

"In there? Why, that's right, isn't it? You haven't had the pleasure. Pity. An experience no human should be without." Harding laces his fingers behind his neck and leans back to look at the door. "That's the Shock Shop I was telling you about some time back, my friend, the EST, Electro-Shock Therapy. Those fortunate souls in there are being given a free trip to the moon. No, on second thought, it isn't completely free. You pay for the service with brain cells instead of money, and everyone has simply billions of brain cells on deposit. You won't miss a few."

He frowns at the one lone man left on the bench. "Not a very large clientele today, it seems, nothing like the crowds

162

of yesteryear. But then, *c'est la vie*, fads come and go. And I'm afraid we are witnessing the sunset of EST. Our dear head nurse is one of the few with the heart to stand up for a grand old Faulknerian tradition in the treatment of the rejects of sanity: Brain Burning."

The door opens. A Gurney comes whirring out, nobody pushing it, takes the corner on two wheels and disappears smoking up the hall. McMurphy watches them take the last guy in and close the door.

"What they do is"—McMurphy listens a moment—"take some bird in there and shoot *electricity* through his skull?"

"That's a concise way of putting it."

"What the hell *for?*"

"Why, the patient's good, of course. Everything done here is for the patient's good. You may sometimes get the impression, having lived only on our ward, that the hospital is a vast efficient mechanism that would function quite well if the patient were not imposed on it, but that's not true. EST isn't always used for punitive measures, as our nurse uses it, and it isn't pure sadism on the staff's part, either. A number of supposed Irrecoverables were brought back into contact with shock, just as a number were helped with lobotomy and leucotomy. Shock treatment has some advantages; it's cheap, quick, entirely painless. It simply induces a seizure."

"What a life," Sefelt moans. "Give some of us pills to stop a fit, give the rest shock to start one."

Harding leans forward to explain it to McMurphy. "Here's how it came about: two psychiatrists were visiting a slaughterhouse, for God knows what perverse reason, and were watching cattle being killed by a blow between the eyes with a sledgehammer. They noticed that not all the cattle were killed, that some would fall to the floor in a state that greatly resembled an epileptic convulsion. 'Ah, *zo*,' the first doctor says. 'Ziz is exactly vot ve need for our patients—zee induced *fit!*' His colleague agreed, of course. It was known that men coming out of an epileptic convulsion were inclined to be calmer and more peaceful for a time, and that violent cases completely out of contact were able to carry on rational conversations after a convulsion. No one knew why; they still don't. But it was obvious that if a seizure could be induced in non-epileptics, great benefits might result. And here, before them, stood a man inducing seizures every so often with remarkable aplomb."

Scanlon says he thought the guy used a hammer instead of a bomb, but Harding says he will ignore that completely, and he goes ahead with the explanation.

"A hammer *is* what the butcher used. And it was here that the colleague had some reservations. After all, a man wasn't a cow. Who knows when the hammer might slip and break a nose? Even knock out a mouthful of teeth? Then where would they be, with the high cost of dental work? If they were going to knock a man in the head, they needed to use something surer and more accurate than a hammer; they finally settled on electricity."

"Jesus, didn't they think it might do some damage? Didn't the public raise Cain about it?"

"I don't think you fully understand the public, my friend; in this country, when something is out of order, then the quickest way to get it fixed is the best way."

McMurphy shakes his head. "Hoo-*wee!* Electricity through the head. Man, that's like electrocuting a guy for murder."

"The reasons for both activities are much more closely related than you might think; they are both cures."

"And you say it don't *hurt?*"

"I personally guarantee it. Completely painless. One flash and you're unconscious immediately. No gas, no needle, no sledgehammer. Absolutely painless. The thing is, no one ever wants another one. You . . . change. You forget things. It's as if"—he presses his hands against his temples, shutting his eyes—"it's as if the jolt sets off a wild carnival wheel of images, emotions, memories. These wheels, you've seen them; the barker takes your bet and pushes a button. *Chang!* With light and sound and numbers round and round in a whirlwind, and maybe you win with what you end up with and maybe you lose and have to play again. Pay the man for another spin, son, pay the man."

"Take it easy, Harding."

The door opens and the Gurney comes back out with the guy under a sheet, and the technicians go out for coffee. Mc-Murphy runs his hand through his hair. "I don't seem able to get all this stuff that's happening straight in my mind."

"What's that? This shock treatment?"

"Yeah. No, not just that. All this . . ." He waves his hand in a circle. "All these things going on."

Harding's hand touches McMurphy's knee. "Put your troubled mind at ease, my friend. In all likelihood you needn't concern yourself with EST. It's almost out of vogue and only used in the extreme cases nothing else seems to reach, like lobotomy."

"Now lobotomy, that's chopping away part of the brain?"

"You're right again. You're becoming very sophisticated in

the jargon. Yes; chopping away the brain. Frontal-lobe castration. I guess if she can't cut below the belt she'll do it above the eyes."

"You mean Ratched."

"I do indeed."

"I didn't think the nurse had the say-so on this kind of thing."

"She does indeed."

McMurphy acts like he's glad to get off talking about shock and lobotomy and get back to talking about the Big Nurse. He asks Harding what he figures is wrong with her. Harding and Scanlon and some of the others have all kinds of ideas. They talk for a while about whether she's the root of all the trouble here or not, and Harding says she's the root of most of it. Most of the other guys think so too, but McMurphy isn't so sure any more. He says he thought so at one time but now he don't know. He says he don't think getting her out of the way would really make much difference; he says that there's something bigger making all this mess and goes on to try to say what he thinks it is. He finally gives up when he can't explain it.

McMurphy doesn't know it, but he's onto what I realized a long time back, that it's not just the Big Nurse by herself, but it's the whole Combine, the nation-wide Combine that's the really big force, and the nurse is just a high-ranking official for them.

The guys don't agree with McMurphy. They say they *know* what the trouble with things is, then get in an argument about that. They argue till McMurphy interrupts them.

"Hell's bells, listen at you," McMurphy says. "All I hear is gripe, gripe, gripe. About the nurse or the staff or the hospital. Scanlon wants to bomb the whole outfit. Sefelt blames the drugs. Fredrickson blames his family trouble. Well, you're all just passing the buck."

He says that the Big Nurse is just a bitter, icy-hearted old woman, and all this business trying to get him to lock horns with her is a lot of bull—wouldn't do anybody any good, especially him. Getting shut of her wouldn't be getting shut of the real deep-down hang-up that's causing the gripes.

"You think not?" Harding says. "Then since you are suddenly so lucid on the problem of mental health, what *is* this trouble? What *is* this deep-down hang-up, as you so cleverly put it."

"I tell you, man, I don't know. I never seen the beat of it."
He sits still for a minute, listening to the hum from the X-ray

room; then he says, "But if it was no more'n you say, if it was, say, just this old nurse with her sex worries, then the solution to all your problems would be to just throw her down and solve her worries, wouldn't it?"

Scanlon claps his hands. "Hot damn! That's it. You're nominated, Mack, you're just the stud to handle the job."

"Not me. No sir. You got the wrong boy."

"Why not? I thought you's the super-stud with all that whambam."

"Scanlon, buddy, I plan to stay as clear of that old buzzard as I possibly can."

"So I've been noticing," Harding says, smiling. "What's happened between the two of you? You had her on the ropes for a period there; then you let up. A sudden compassion for our angel of mercy?"

"No; I found out a few things, that's why. Asked around some different places. I found out why you guys all kiss her ass so much and bow and scrape and let her walk all over you. I got wise to what you were using me for."

"Oh? That's interesting."

"You're blamed right it's interesting. It's interesting to me that you bums didn't tell me what a risk I was running, twisting her tail that way. Just because I don't like her ain't a sign I'm gonna bug her into adding another year or so to my sentence. You got to swallow your pride sometimes and keep an eye out for old Number One."

"Why, friends, you don't suppose there's anything to this rumor that our Mr. McMurphy has conformed to policy merely to aid his chances of an early release?"

"You know what I'm talking about, Harding. Why didn't you tell me she could keep me committed in here till she's good and ready to turn me loose?"

"Why, I had *forgotten* you were committed." Harding's face folds in the middle over his grin. "Yes. You're becoming sly. Just like the rest of us."

"You damn betcha I'm becoming sly. Why should it be me goes to bat at these meetings over these piddling little gripes about keeping the dorm door open and about cigarettes in the Nurses' Station? I couldn't figure it at first, why you guys were coming to me like I was some kind of savior. Then I just happened to find out about the way the nurses have the big say as to who gets discharged and who doesn't. And I got wise awful damned fast. I said, 'Why, those slippery bastards have *conned* me, snowed me into holding their bag. If that don't beat all, conned ol' R. P. McMurphy.' " He tips his head back and grins at the line of us on the bench. "Well, I don't mean nothing personal, you understand, buddies, but screw that noise. I want out of here just as much as the rest of you. I got just as much to lose hassling that old buzzard as *you* do."

He grins and winks down his nose and digs Harding in the ribs with his thumb, like he's finished with the whole thing but no hard feelings, when Harding says something else.

"No. You've got more to lose than I do, my friend."

Harding's grinning again, looking with that skitterish sideways look of a jumpy mare, a dipping, rearing motion of the head. Everybody moves down a place. Martini comes away from the X-ray screen, buttoning his shirt and muttering, "I wouldn't of believed it if I hadn't saw it," and Billy Bibbit goes to the black glass to take Martini's place.

"You have more to lose than I do," Harding says again. "I'm voluntary. I'm not committed."

McMurphy doesn't say a word. He's got that same puzzled look on his face like there's something isn't right, something he can't put his finger on. He just sits there looking at Harding, and Harding's rearing smile fades and he goes to fidgeting around from McMurphy staring at him so funny. He swallows and says, "As a matter of fact, there are only a few men on the ward who *are* committed. Only Scanlon and—well, I guess some of the Chronics. And you. Not many commitments in the whole hospital. No, not many at all."

Then he stops, his voice dribbling away under McMurphy's eyes. After a bit of silence McMurphy says softly, "Are you bullshitting me?" Harding shakes his head. He looks frightened. McMurphy stands up in the hall and says, "Are you guys *bullshitting* me!"

Nobody'll say anything. McMurphy walks up and down in front of that bench, running his hand around in that thick hair. He walks all the way to the back of the line, then all the way to the front, to the X-ray machine. It hisses and spits at him.

"You, Billy—you *must* be committed, for Christsakes!"

Billy's got his back to us, his chin up on the black screen, standing on tiptoe. No, he says into the machinery.

"Then *why? Why?* You're just a young guy! You oughta be out running around in a convertible, bird-dogging girls. All of this"—he sweeps his hand around him again—"why do you stand for it?"

Billy doesn't say anything, and McMurphy turns from him to another couple of guys.

"Tell me why. You gripe, you bitch for *weeks* on end about

how you can't stand this place, can't stand the nurse or anything about her, and all the time you ain't committed. I can
understand it with some of those old guys on the ward. They're
nuts. But you, you're not exactly the everyday man on the
street, but you're not *nuts.*"

They don't argue with him. He moves on to Sefelt.

"Sefelt, what about you? There's nothing wrong with you but
you have fits. Hell, I had an uncle who threw conniptions twice
as bad as yours and saw visions from the Devil to boot, but he
didn't lock himself in the nuthouse. You could get along outside if you had the guts—"

"Sure!" It's Billy, turned from the screen, his face boiling
tears. "Sure!" he screams again. "If we had the g-guts! I could
go outside to-today, if I had the guts. My m-m-mother is a
good friend of M-Miss Ratched, and I could get an AMA
signed this afternoon, if I had the guts!"

He jerks his shirt up from the bench and tries to pull it on,
but he's shaking too hard. Finally he slings it from him and
turns back to McMurphy.

"You think I wuh-wuh-wuh-*want* to stay in here? You think
I wouldn't like a con-con-vertible and a guh-guh-girl friend? But
did you ever have people l-l-laughing at you? No, because
you're so b-big and so *tough!* Well, I'm not big and tough.
Neither is Harding. Neither is F-Fredrickson. Neither is Suh-
Sefelt. Oh—oh, you—you t-talk like we stayed in here because
we liked it! Oh—it's n-no use . . ."

He's crying and stuttering too hard to say anything else, and
he wipes his eyes with the backs of his hands so he can see.
One of the scabs pulls off his hand, and the more he wipes
the more he smears blood over his face and in his eyes. Then
he starts running blind, bouncing down the hall from side to
side with his face a smear of blood, a black boy right after
him.

McMurphy turns round to the rest of the guys and opens
his mouth to ask something else, and then closes it when he
sees how they're looking at him. He stands there a minute with
the row of eyes aimed at him like a row of rivets; then he says,
"Hell's bells," in a weak sort of way, and he puts his cap back
on and pulls it down hard and goes back to his place on the
bench. The two technicians come back from coffee and go
back in that room across the hall; when the door whooshes
open you can smell the acid in the air like when they recharge
a battery. McMurphy sits there, looking at that door.

"I don't seem able to get it straight in my mind. . . ."

*C*rossing the grounds back to the ward, McMurphy lagged back at the tail end of the bunch with his hands in the pockets of his greens and his cap tugged low on his head, brooding over a cold cigarette. Everybody was keeping pretty quiet. They'd got Billy calmed down, and he was walking at the front of the group with a black boy on one side and that white boy from the Shock Shop on the other side.

I dropped back till I was walking beside McMurphy and I wanted to tell him not to fret about it, that nothing could be done, because I could see that there was some thought he was worrying over in his mind like a dog worries at a hole he don't know what's down, one voice saying, Dog, that hole is none of your affair—it's too big and too black and there's a spoor all over the place says bears or something just as bad. And some other voice coming like a sharp whisper out of way back in his breed, not a smart voice, nothing cagey about it, saying, *Sic* 'im, dog, *sic* 'im!

I wanted to tell him not to fret about it, and I was just about to come out and say it when he raised his head and shoved his hat back and speeded up to where the least black boy was walking and slapped him on the shoulder and asked him, "Sam, what say we stop by the canteen here a second so I can pick me up a carton or two of cigarettes."

I had to hurry to catch up, and the run made my heart ring a high, excited pitch in my head. Even in the canteen I still heard that sound my heart had knocked ringing in my head, though my heart had slowed back to normal. The sound reminded me of how I used to feel standing in the cold fall Friday night out on a football field, waiting for the ball to be kicked and the game to get going. The ringing would build and build till I didn't think I could stand still any longer; then the kick would come and it would be gone and the game would be on its way. I felt that same Friday-night ringing now, and felt the same wild, stomping-up-and-down impatience. And I was seeing sharp and high-pitched too, the way I did before a game and the way I did looking out of the dorm window a while back: everything was sharp and clear and solid like I forgot

169

it could be. Lines of toothpaste and shoelaces, ranks of sunglasses and ballpoint pens guaranteed right on them to write a lifetime on butter under water, all guarded against shoplifters by a big-eyed force of Teddy bears sitting high on a shelf over the counter.

McMurphy came stomping up to the counter beside me and hooked his thumbs in his pockets and told the salesgirl to give him a couple of cartons of Marlboros. "Maybe make it three cartons," he said, grinning at her. "I plan to do a lot of smokin'."

The ringing didn't stop until the meeting that afternoon. I'd been half listening to them work on Sefelt to get him to face up to the reality of his problems so he could adjust ("It's the Dilantin!" he finally yells. "Now, Mr. Sefelt, if you're to be helped, you must be honest," she says. "But, it's *got* to be the Dilantin that does it; don't it make my *gums* soft?" She smiles. "Jim, you're forty-five years old . . .") when I happened to catch a look at McMurphy sitting in his corner. He wasn't fiddling with a deck of cards or dozing into a magazine like he had been during all the meetings the last two weeks. And he wasn't slouched down. He was sitting up stiff in his chair with a flushed, reckless look on his face as he looked back and forth from Sefelt to the Big Nurse. As I watched, the ringing went higher. His eyes were blue stripes under those white eyebrows, and they shot back and forth just the way he watched cards turning up around a poker table. I was certain that any minute he was going to do some crazy thing to get him up on Disturbed for sure. I'd seen the same look on other guys before they'd climbed all over a black boy. I gripped down on the arm of my chair and waited, scared it would happen, and, I began to realize, just a little scared it wouldn't.

He kept quiet and watched till they were finished with Sefelt; then he swung half around in his chair and watched while Fredrickson, trying some way to get back at them for the way they had grilled his friend, griped for a few loud minutes about the cigarettes being kept in the Nurses' Station. Fredrickson talked himself out and finally flushed and apologized like always and sat back down. McMurphy still hadn't made any kind of move. I eased up where I'd been gripping the arm of the chair, beginning to think I'd been wrong.

There was just a couple of minutes left in the meeting. The Big Nurse folded up her papers and put them in the basket and set the basket off her lap on the floor, then let her eyes swing to McMurphy for just a second like she wanted to check if he was awake and listening. She folded her hands in her lap and looked down at the fingers and drew a deep breath, shaking her head.

"Boys, I've given a great deal of thought to what I am about to say. I've talked it over with the doctor and with the rest of the staff, and, as much as we regretted it, we all came to the same conclusion—that there should be some manner of punishment meted out for the unspeakable behavior concerning the house duties three weeks ago." She raised her hand and looked around. "We waited this long to say anything, hoping that you men would take it upon yourselves to apologize for the rebellious way you acted. But not a one of you has shown the slightest sign of remorse."

Her hand went up again to stop any interruptions that might come—the movement of a tarot-card reader in a glass arcade case.

"Please understand: We do not impose certain rules and restrictions on you without a great deal of thought about their therapeutic value. A good many of you are in here because you could not adjust to the rules of society in the Outside World, because you refused to face up to them, because you tried to circumvent them and avoid them. At some time—perhaps in your childhood—you may have been allowed to get away with flouting the rules of society. When you broke a rule you knew it. You wanted to be dealt with, *needed* it, but the punishment did not come. That foolish lenience on the part of your parents may have been the germ that grew into your present illness. I tell you this hoping you will understand that it is *entirely* for your own good that we enforce discipline and order."

She let her head twist around the room. Regret for the job she has to do was worked into her face. It was quiet except for that high fevered, delirious ringing in my head.

"It's difficult to enforce discipline in these surroundings. You must be able to see that. What can we do to you? You can't be arrested. You can't be put on bread and water. You must see that the staff has a problem; what *can* we do?"

Ruckly had an idea what they could do, but she didn't pay any attention to it. The face moved with a ticking noise till the features achieved a different look. She finally answered her own question.

"We must take away a privilege. And after careful consideration of the circumstances of this rebellion, we've decided that there would be a certain justice in taking away the privilege of the tub room that you men have been using for your card games during the day. Does this seem unfair?"

Her head didn't move. She didn't look. But one by one everybody else looked at him sitting there in his corner. Even the old Chronics, wondering why everybody had turned to look in one direction, stretched out their scrawny necks like birds and turned to look at McMurphy—faces turned to him, full of a naked, scared hope.

That single thin note in my head was like tires speeding down a pavement.

He was sitting straight up in his chair, one big red finger scratching lazily at the stitchmarks run across his nose. He grinned at everybody looking at him and took his cap by the brim and tipped it politely, then looked back at the nurse.

"So, if there is no discussion on this ruling, I think the hour is almost over . . ."

She paused again, took a look at him herself. He shrugged his shoulders and with a loud sigh slapped both hands down on his knees and pushed himself standing out of the chair. He stretched and yawned and scratched the nose again and started strolling across the day-room floor to where she sat by the Nurses' Station, heisting his pants with his thumbs as he walked. I could see it was too late to keep him from doing whatever fool thing he had in mind, and I just watched, like everybody else. He walked with long steps, too long, and he had his thumbs hooked in his pockets again. The iron in his boot heels cracked lightning out of the tile. He was the logger again, the swaggering gambler, the big redheaded brawling Irishman, the cowboy out of the TV set walking down the middle of the street to meet a dare.

The Big Nurse's eyes swelled out white as he got close. She hadn't reckoned on him doing anything. This was supposed to be her final victory over him, supposed to establish her rule once and for all. But here he comes and he's big as a house!

She started popping her mouth and looking for her black boys, scared to death, but he stopped before he got to her. He stopped in front of her window and he said in his slowest, deepest drawl how he figured he could use one of the smokes he bought this mornin', then ran his hand through the glass.

The glass came apart like water splashing, and the nurse threw her hands to her ears. He got one of the cartons of cigarettes with his name on it and took out a pack, then put it back and turned to where the Big Nurse was sitting like a chalk statue and very tenderly went to brushing the slivers of glass off her head and shoulders.

"I'm sure *sorry*, ma'am," he said. "Gawd but I am. That window glass was so spick and span I com-*pletely* forgot it was there."

It took just a couple of seconds. He turned and left her sitting there with her face shifting and jerking and walked back across the day room to his chair, lighting up a cigarette.

The ringing that was in my head had stopped.

part 3

After that, McMurphy had things his way for a good long while. The nurse was biding her time till another idea come to her that would put her on top again. She knew she'd lost one big round and was losing another, but she wasn't in any hurry. For one thing, she wasn't about to recommend release; the fight could go on as long as she wanted, till he made a mistake or till he just gave out, or until she could come up with some new tactic that would put her back on top in everybody's eyes.

A good lot happened before she came up with that new tactic. After McMurphy was drawn out of what you might call a short retirement and had announced he was back in the hassle by breaking out her personal window, he made things on the ward pretty interesting. He took part in every meeting, every discussion—drawling, winking, joking his best to wheedle a skinny laugh out of some Acute who'd been scared to grin since he was twelve. He got together enough guys for a basketball team and some way talked the doctor into letting him bring a ball back from the gym to get the team used to handling it.

The nurse objected, said the next thing they'd be playing soccer in the day room and polo games up and down the hall, but the doctor held firm for once and said let them go. "A number of the players, Miss Ratched, have shown marked progress since that basketball team was organized; I think it has proven its therapeutic value."

She looked at him a while in amazement. So he was doing a little muscle-flexing too. She marked the tone of his voice for later, for when her time came again, and just nodded and went to sit in her Nurses' Station and fiddle with the controls on her equipment. The janitors had put a cardboard in the frame over her desk till they could get another window pane cut to fit, and she sat there behind it every day like it wasn't even there, just like she could still see right into the day room. Behind that square of cardboard she was like a picture turned to the wall.

She waited, without comment, while McMurphy continued to run around the halls in the mornings in his white-whale shorts, or pitched pennies in the dorms, or ran up and down the hall blowing a nickle-plated ref's whistle, teaching Acutes the fast break from ward door to the Seclusion Room at the other end, the ball pounding in the corridor like cannon shots and McMurphy roaring like a sergeant, "Drive, you puny mothers, *drive!*"

When either one spoke to the other it was always in the most polite fashion. He would ask her nice as you please if he could use her fountain pen to write a request for an Unaccompanied Leave from the hospital, wrote it out in front of her on her desk, and handed her the request and the pen back at the same time with such a nice, "Thank you," and she would look at it and say just as polite that she would "take it up with the staff"—which took maybe three minutes—and come back to tell him she certainly was sorry but a pass was not considered therapeutic at this time. He would thank her again and walk out of the Nurses' Station and blow that whistle loud enough to break windows for miles, and holler, "Practice, you mothers, get that ball and let's get a little sweat rollin'."

He's been on the ward a month, long enough to sign the bulletin board in the hall to request a hearing in group meeting about an Accompanied Pass. He went to the bulletin board with her pen and put down under TO BE ACCOMPANIED BY: "A twitch I know from Portland named Candy Starr,"—and ruined the pen point on the period. The pass request was brought up in group meeting a few days later, the same day, in fact, that workmen put a new glass window in front of the

Big Nurse's desk, and after his request had been turned down on the grounds that this Miss Starr didn't seem like the most wholesome person for a patient to go pass with, he shrugged and said that's how she bounces I guess, and got up and walked to the Nurses' Station, to the window that still had the sticker from the glass company down in the corner, and ran his fist through it again—explained to the nurse while blood poured from his fingers that he thought the cardboard had been left out and the frame was open. "When did they sneak that danged glass in there? Why that thing is a *menace!*"

The nurse taped his hand in the station while Scanlon and Harding dug the cardboard out of the garbage and taped it back in the frame, using adhesive from the same roll the nurse was bandaging McMurphy's wrist and fingers with. McMurphy sat on a stool, grimacing something awful while he got his cuts tended, winking at Scanlon and Harding over the nurse's head. The expression on her face was calm and blank as enamel, but the strain was beginning to show in other ways. By the way she jerked the adhesive tight as she could, showing her remote patience wasn't what it used to be.

We got to go to the gym and watch our basketball team —Harding, Billy Bibbit, Scanlon, Fredrickson, Martini, and McMurphy whenever his hand would stop bleeding long enough for him to get in the game—play a team of aides. Our two big black boys played for the aides. They were the best players on the court, running up and down the floor together like a pair of shadows in red trunks, scoring basket after basket with mechanical accuracy. Our team was too short and too slow, and Martini kept throwing passes to men that nobody but him could see, and the aides beat us by twenty points. But something happened that let most of us come away feeling there'd been a kind of victory, anyhow: in one scramble for the ball our big black boy named Washington got cracked with somebody's elbow, and his team had to hold him back as he stood straining to where McMurphy was sitting on the ball— not paying the least bit of heed to the thrashing black boy with red pouring out of his big nose and down his chest like paint splashed on a blackboard and hollering to the guys holding him, "He beggin' for it! The sonabitch jus' *beggin*' for it!"

McMurphy composed more notes for the nurse to find in the latrine with her mirror. He wrote long outlandish tales about himself in the log book and signed them Anon. Sometimes he slept till eight o'clock. She would reprimand him, without heat at all, and he would stand and listen till she was finished and then destroy her whole effect by asking something like did she wear a B cup, he wondered, or a C cup, or any ol' cup at all?

The other Acutes were beginning to follow his lead. Harding began flirting with all the student nurses, and Billy Bibbit completely quit writing what he used to call his "observations" in the log book, and when the window in front of her desk got replaced again, with a big X across it in whitewash to make sure McMurphy didn't have any excuse for not knowing it was there, Scanlon did it in by accidentally bouncing our basketball through it before the whitewashed X was even dry. The ball punctured, and Martini picked it off the floor like a dead bird and carried it to the nurse in the station, where she was staring at the new splash of broken glass all over her desk, and asked couldn't she please fix it with tape or something? Make it well again? Without a word she jerked it out of his hand and stuffed it in the garbage.

So, with basketball season obviously over, McMurphy decided fishing was the thing. He requested another pass after telling the doctor he had some friends at the Siuslaw Bay at Florence who would like to take eight or nine of the patients out deep-sea fishing if it was okay with the staff, and he wrote on the request list out in the hall that this time he would be accompanied by "two sweet old aunts from a little place outside of Oregon City." In the meeting his pass was granted for the next weekend. When the nurse finished officially noting his pass in her roll book, she reached into her wicker bag beside her feet and drew out a clipping that she had taken from the paper that morning, and read out loud that although fishing off the coast of Oregon was having a peak year, the salmon were running quite late in the season and the sea was rough and dangerous. And she would suggest the men give that some thought.

"Good idea," McMurphy said. He closed his eyes and sucked a deep breath through his teeth. "Yes sir! The salt smell o' the poundin' sea, the crack o' the bow against the waves— braving the elements, where men are men and boats are boats. Miss Ratched, you've talked me into it. I'll call and rent that boat this very night. Shall I sign you on?"

Instead of answering she walked to the bulletin board and pinned up the clipping.

The next day he started signing up the guys that wanted to go and that had ten bucks to chip in on boat rent, and the nurse started steadily bringing in clippings from the newspapers that told about wrecked boats and sudden storms on the coast. McMurphy pooh-poohed her and her clippings, saying that his two aunts had spent most of their lives bouncing around the waves in one port or another with this sailor or that, and they both guaranteed the trip was safe as pie, safe as pudding, not a thing to worry about. But the nurse still knew her patients. The clippings scared them more than Mc-Murphy'd figured. He'd figured there would be a rush to sign up, but he'd had to talk and wheedle to get the guys he did. The day before the trip he still needed a couple more before he could pay for the boat.

I didn't have the money, but I kept getting this notion that I wanted to sign the list. And the more he talked about fishing for Chinook salmon the more I wanted to go. I knew it was a fool thing to want; if I signed up it'd be the same as coming right out and telling everybody I wasn't deaf. If I'd been hearing all this talk about boats and fishing it'd show I'd been hearing everything else that'd been said in confidence around me for the past ten years. And if the Big Nurse found out about that, that I'd heard all the scheming and treachery that had gone on when she didn't think anybody was listening, she'd hunt me down with an electric saw, fix me where she *knew* I was deaf and dumb. Bad as I wanted to go, it still made me smile a little to think about it: I had to keep on acting deaf if I wanted to hear at all.

I lay in bed the night before the fishing trip and thought it over, about my being deaf, about the years of not letting on I heard what was said, and I wondered if I could ever act any other way again. But I remembered one thing: it wasn't me that started acting deaf; it was people that first started acting like I was too dumb to hear or see or say anything at all.

It hadn't been just since I came in the hospital, either; people first took to acting like I couldn't hear or talk a long time before that. In the Army anybody with more stripes acted that way toward me. That was the way they figured you were supposed to act around someone looked like I did. And even as far back as grade school I can remember people saying that they didn't think I was listening, so they quit listening to the things I was saying. Lying there in bed, I tried to think back when I first noticed it. I think it was once when we were still living in the village on the Columbia. It was summer. . . .

. . . and I'm about ten years old and I'm out in front of the shack sprinkling salt on salmon for the racks behind the house, when I see a car turn off the highway and come lumbering across the ruts through the sage, towing a load of red dust behind it as solid as a string of boxcars.

I watch the car pull up the hill and stop down a piece from our yard, and the dust keeps coming, crashing into the rear of it and busting in every direction and finally settling on the sage and soapweed round about and making it look like chunks of red, smoking wreckage. The car sits there while the dust settles, shimmering in the sun. I know it isn't tourists with cameras because they never drive this close to the village. If they want to buy fish they buy them back at the highway; they don't come to the village because they probably think we still scalp people and burn them around a post. They don't know some of our people are lawyers in Portland, probably wouldn't believe it if I told them. In fact, one of my uncles became a real lawyer and Papa says he did it purely to prove he could, when he'd rather poke salmon in the fall than anything. Papa says if you don't watch it people will force you one way or the other, into doing what they think you should do, or into just being mule-stubborn and doing the opposite out of spite.

The doors of the car open all at once and three people get out, two out of the front and one out of the back. They come climbing up the slope toward our village and I see the first two are men in blue suits, and the behind one, the one that got out of the back, is an old white-haired woman in an outfit so stiff and heavy it must be armor plate. They're puffing and sweating by the time they break out of the sage into our bald yard.

The first man stops and looks the village over. He's short and round and wearing a white Stetson hat. He shakes his head at the rickety clutter of fishracks and secondhand cars and chicken coops and motorcycles and dogs.

"Have you ever in all your born days seen the like? Have you now? I swear to heaven, have you *ever?*"

He pulls off the hat and pats his red rubber ball of a head with a handkerchief, careful, like he's afraid of getting one or the other mussed up—the handkerchief or the dab of damp stringy hair.

"Can you imagine people wanting to live this way? Tell me, John, can you?" He talks loud on account of not being used to the roar of the falls.

John's next to him, got a thick gray mustache lifted tight up under his nose to stop out the smell of the salmon I'm working on. He's sweated down his neck and cheeks, and he's sweated clean out through the back of his blue suit. He's making notes in a book, and he keeps turning in a circle, looking at our shack, our little garden, at Mama's red and green and yellow Saturday-night dresses drying out back on a stretch of bedcord—keeps turning till he makes a full circle and comes back to me, looks at me like he just sees me for the first time, and me not but two yards away from him. He bends toward me and squints and lifts his mustache up to his nose again like it's me stinking instead of the fish.

"Where do you suppose his parents are?" John asks. "Inside the house? Or out on the falls? We might as well talk this over with the man while we're out here."

"I, for one, am not going inside that hovel," the fat guy says.

"That hovel," John says through his mustache, "is where the Chief lives, Breckenridge, the man we are here to deal with, the noble leader of these people."

"Deal with? Not me, not my job. They pay me to appraise, not fraternize."

This gets a laugh out of John.

"Yes, that's true. But someone should inform them of the government's plans."

"If they don't already know, they'll know soon enough."

"It would be very simple to go in and talk with him."

"Inside in that squalor? Why, I'll just bet you anything that place is acrawl with black widows. They say these 'dobe shacks always house a regular civilization in the walls between the sods. And *hot*, lord-a-mercy, I hope to tell you. I'll wager it's a regular oven in there. Look, look how overdone little Hiawatha is here. Ho. Burnt to a fair turn, he is."

He laughs and dabs at his head and when the woman looks at him he stops laughing. He clears his throat and spits into the dust and then walks over and sits down in the swing Papa built for me in the juniper tree, and sits there swinging back and forth a little bit and fanning himself with his Stetson.

What he said makes me madder the more I think about it. He and John go ahead talking about our house and village and property and what they are worth, and I get the notion they're talking about these things around me because they don't know I speak English. They are probably from the East someplace, where people don't know anything about Indians but what they see in the movies. I think how ashamed they're going to be when they find out I know what they are saying.

I let them say another thing or two about the heat and the house; then I stand up and tell the fat man, in my very best schoolbook language, that our sod house is likely to be cooler than any one of the houses in town, *lots* cooler! "I know for a *fact* that it's cooler'n that school I go to and even cooler'n that movie house in The Dalles that advertises on that sign drawn with icicle letters that it's 'cool inside'!"

And I'm just about to go and tell them, how, if they'll come
on in, I'll so get Papa from the scaffolds on the falls, when I
see that they don't look like they'd heard me talk at all. They
aren't even looking at me. The fat man is swinging back and
forth, looking off down the ridge of lava to where the men are
standing their places on the scaffolding in the falls, just plaid-
shirted shapes in the mist from this distance. Every so often
you can see somebody shoot out an arm and take a step forward like a swordfighter, and then hold up his fifteen-foot
forked spear for somebody on the scaffold above him to pull
off the flopping salmon. The fat guy watches the men standing in their places in the fifty-foot veil of water, and bats his
eyes and grunts every time one of them makes a lunge for a
salmon.

The other two, John and the woman, are just standing. Not
a one of the three acts like they heard a thing I said; in fact
they're all looking off from me like they'd as soon I wasn't
there at all.

And everything stops and hangs this way for a minute.

I get the funniest feeling that the sun is turned up brighter
than before on the three of them. Everything else looks like
it usually does—the chickens fussing around in the grass on
top of the 'dobe houses, the grasshoppers batting from bush to
bush, the flies being stirred into black clouds around the fish
racks by the little kids with sage flails, just like every other
summer day. Except the sun, on these three strangers, is all of
a sudden way the hell brighter than usual and I can see the . . .
seams where they're put together. And, almost, see the apparatus inside them take the words I just said and try to fit
the words in here and there, this place and that, and when they
find the words don't have any place ready-made where they'll
fit, the machinery disposes of the words like they weren't even
spoken.

The three are stock still while this goes on. Even the swing's
stopped, nailed out at a slant by the sun, with the fat man
petrified in it like a rubber doll. Then Papa's guinea hen wakes
up in the juniper branches and sees we got strangers on the
premises and goes to barking at them like a dog, and the spell
breaks.

The fat man hollers and jumps out of the swing and sidles
away through the dust, holding his hat up in front of the sun
so's he can see what's up there in the juniper tree making such
a racket. When he sees it's nothing but a speckled chicken he
spits on the ground and puts his hat on.

"I, myself, sincerely *feel*," he says, "that whatever offer we make on this . . . metropolis will be quite sufficient."

"Could be. I still think we should make some effort to speak with the Chief—"

The old woman interrupts him by taking one ringing step forward. "No." This is the first thing she's said. "No," she says again in a way that reminds me of the Big Nurse. She lifts her eyebrows and looks the place over. Her eyes spring up like the numbers in a cash register; she's looking at Mamma's dresses hung so carefully on the line, and she's nodding her head.

"No. We don't talk with the Chief today. Not yet. I think . . . that I agree with Breckenridge for once. Only for a different reason. You recall the record we have shows the wife is not Indian but white? White. A woman from town. Her name is Bromden. He took her name, not she his. Oh, yes, I think if we just leave now and go back into town, and, of course, spread the word with the townspeople about the government's plans so they understand the advantages of having a hydroelectric dam and a lake instead of a cluster of shacks beside a falls, *then* type up an offer—and mail it to the wife, you see, by mistake? I feel our job will be a great deal easier."

She looks off to the men on the ancient, rickety, zigzagging scaffolding that has been growing and branching out among the rocks of the falls for hundreds of years.

"Whereas if we meet now with the husband and make some abrupt offer, we may run up against an un*told* amount of Navaho stubbornness and love of—I suppose we must call it home."

I start to tell them he's *not* Navaho, but think what's the use if they don't listen? They don't care what tribe he is.

The woman smiles and nods at both the men, a smile and a nod to each, and her eyes ring them up, and she begins to move stiffly back to their car, talking in a light, young voice.

"As my sociology professor used to emphasize, 'There is generally one person in every situation you must never underestimate the power *of*.' "

And they get back in the car and drive away, with me standing there wondering if they ever even *saw* me.

I was kind of amazed that I'd remembered that. It was the first time in what seemed to me centuries that I'd been able to remember much about my childhood. It fascinated me to discover I could still do it. I stay in bed awake, remembering other happenings, and just about that time, while I was half in a kind of dream, I heard a sound under my bed like a mouse with a walnut. I leaned over the edge of the bed and saw the shine of metal biting off pieces of gum I knew by heart. The black boy named Geever had found where I'd been hiding my chewing gum; was scraping the pieces off into a sack with a long, lean pair of scissors open like jaws.

I jerked back up under the covers before he saw me looking. My heart was banging in my ears, scared he'd seen me. I wanted to tell him to get away, to mind his own business and leave my chewing gum alone, but I couldn't even let on I heard. I lay still to see if he'd caught me bending over to peek under the bed at him, but he didn't give any sign—all I heard was the zzzth-zzzth of his scissors and pieces falling into the sack, reminded me of hailstones the way they used to rattle on our tar-paper roof. He clacked his tongue and giggled to himself.

"Um-ummm. Lord gawd amighty. Hee. I wonder how many times this muthuh chewed some o' this stuff? Just as *hard*."

McMurphy heard the black boy muttering to himself and woke and rolled up to one elbow to look at what he was up to at this hour down on his knees under my bed. He watched the black boy a minute, rubbing his eyes to be sure of what he was seeing, just like you see little kids rub their eyes; then he sat up completely.

"I will be a sonofabitch if he ain't in here at eleven-thirty at night, fartin' around in the dark with a pair of scissors and a paper sack." The black boy jumped and swung his flashlight up in McMurphy's eyes. "Now tell me, Sam: what the devil are you collectin' that needs the cover of night?"

"Go back to sleep, McMurphy. It don't concern nobody else."

McMurphy let his lips spread in a slow grin, but he didn't look away from the light. The black boy got uneasy after about half a minute of shining that light on McMurphy sitting there, on that glossy new-healed scar and those teeth and that tattooed panther on his shoulder, and took the light away. He bent back to his work, grunting and puffing like it was a mighty effort prying off dried gum.

"One of the duties of a night aide," he explained between grunts, trying to sound friendly, "is to keep the bedside area cleaned up."

"In the dead of night?"

"McMurphy, we got a thing posted called a *Job* Description, say cleanliness is a *twenty-fo'-hour job*!"

"You might of done your twenty-four hours worth before we got in bed, don't you think, instead of sittin' out there watching TV till ten-thirty. Does Old Lady Ratched know you boys watch TV most of your shift? What do you reckon she'd do if she found out about that?"

The black boy got up and sat on the edge of my bed. He tapped the flashlight against his teeth, grinning and giggling. The light lit his face up like a black jack o'lantern.

"Well, let me tell you about this gum," he said and leaned close to McMurphy like an old chum. "You see, for years I been wondering where Chief Bromden got his chewin' gum—never havin' any money for the canteen, never havin' anybody give him a stick that I saw, never askin' Public Relations—so I *watched*, and I *waited*. And look here." He got back on his knees and lifted the edge of my bedspread and shined the light under. "How 'bout that? I bet they's pieces of gum under here been used a *thousand* times!"

This tickled McMurphy. He went to giggling at what he saw. The black boy held up the sack and rattled it, and they laughed some more about it. The black boy told McMurphy good night and rolled the top of the sack like it was his lunch and went off somewhere to hide it for later.

"Chief?" McMurphy whispered. "I want you to tell me something." And he started to sing a little song, a hillbilly song, popular a long time ago: " 'Oh, does the Spearmint lose its flavor on the bedpost overnight?' "

At first I started getting real mad. I thought he was making fun of me like other people had.

" 'When you chew it in the morning,' " he sang in a whisper, " 'will it be too hard to bite?' "

But the more I thought about it the funnier it seemed to me. I tried to stop it but I could feel I was about to laugh—not at McMurphy's singing, but at my own self.

" 'This question's got me goin', won't somebody set me right; does the Spearmint lose its flavor on the bedpost over niiiite?' "

He held out that last note and twiddled it down me like a feather. I couldn't help but start to chuckle, and this made me scared I'd get to laughing and not be able to stop. But just then McMuphy jumped off his bed and went to rustling through his nightstand, and I hushed. I clenched my teeth, wondering what to do now. It'd been a long time since I'd let anyone hear me do any more than grunt or bellow. I heard him shut the bedstand, and it echoed like a boiler door. I heard him say, "Here," and something lit on my bed. Little. Just the size of a lizard or a snake . . .

"Juicy Fruit is the best I can do for you at the moment,

Chief. Package I won off Scanlon pitchin' pennies." And he got back in bed.

And before I realized what I was doing, I told him Thank you.

He didn't say anything right off. He was up on his elbow, watching me the way he'd watched the black boy, waiting for me to say something else. I picked up the package of gum from the bedspread and held it in my hand and told him Thank you.

It didn't sound like much because my throat was rusty and my tongue creaked. He told me I sounded a little out of practice and laughed at that. I tried to laugh with him, but it was a squawking sound, like a pullet trying to crow. It sounded more like crying than laughing.

He told me not to hurry, that he had till six-thirty in the morning to listen if I wanted to practice. He said a man been still long as me probably had a considerable lot to talk about, and he lay back on his pillow and waited. I thought for a minute for something to say to him, but the only thing that came to my mind was the kind of thing one man can't say to another because it sounds wrong in words. When he saw I couldn't say anything he crossed his hands behind his head and started talking himself.

"Ya know, Chief, I was just rememberin' a time down in the Willamette Valley—I was pickin' beans outside of Eugene and considering myself damn lucky to get the job. It was in the early thirties so there wasn't many kids able to get jobs. I got the job by proving to the bean boss I could pick just as fast and clean as any of the adults. Anyway, I was the only kid in the rows. Nobody else around me but grown-ups. And after I tried a time or two to talk to them I saw they weren't for listening to me—scrawny little patchquilt redhead anyhow. So I hushed. I was so peeved at them not listening to me I kept hushed the livelong four weeks I picked that field, workin' right along side of them, listening to them prattle on about this uncle or that cousin. Or if somebody didn't show up for work, gossip about him. Four weeks and not a peep out of me. Till I think by God they forgot I *could* talk, the mossbacked old bastards. I bided my time. Then, on the last day, I opened up and went to telling them what a petty bunch of farts they were. I told each one just how his buddy had drug him over the coals when he was absent. Hooee, did they listen then! They finally got to arguing with each other and created such a shitstorm I lost my quarter-cent-a-pound bonus I had comin' for not missin' a day because I already had a bad reputation around town and the bean boss claimed the disturbance was likely my fault even if he couldn't prove it. I cussed him out too. My shootin' off my mouth that time probably cost me twenty dollars or so. Well worth it, too."

He chuckled a while to himself, remembering, then turned his head on his pillow and looked at me.

"What I was wonderin', Chief, are you biding your time towards the day you decide to lay into them?"

"No," I told him. "I couldn't."

"Couldn't tell them off? It's easier than you think."

"You're . . . lot bigger, tougher'n I am," I mumbled.

"How's that? I didn't get you, Chief."

I worked some spit down in my throat. "You are bigger and tougher than I am. You can do it."

"Me? Are you kidding? Criminy, look at you: you stand a head taller'n any man on the ward. There ain't a man here you couldn't turn every way but loose, and that's a fact!"

"No. I'm way too little. I used to be big, but not no more. You're twice the size of me."

"Hoo boy, you *are* crazy, aren't you? The first thing I saw when I came in this place was you sitting over in that chair, big as a damn mountain. I tell you, I lived all over Klamath and Texas and Oklahoma and all over around Gallup, and I swear you're the biggest Indian I ever saw."

"I'm from the Columbia Gorge," I said, and he waited for me to go on. "My Papa was a full Chief and his name was Tee Ah Millatoona. That means The-Pine-That-Stands-Tallest-on-the-Mountain, and we didn't live on a mountain. He was real big when I was a kid. My mother got twice his size."

"You must of had a real moose of an old lady. How big was she?"

"Oh—big, big."

"I mean how many feet and inches?"

"Feet and inches? A guy at the carnival looked her over and says five feet nine and weight a hundred and thirty pounds, but that was because he'd just *saw* her. She got bigger all the time."

"Yeah? How much bigger?"

"Bigger than Papa and me together."

"Just one day took to growin', huh? Well, that's a new one on me: I never heard of an Indian woman doing something like that."

"She wasn't Indian. She was a town woman from The Dalles."

"And her name was what? Bromden? Yeah, I see, wait a minute." He thinks for a while and says, "And when a town woman marries an Indian that's marryin' somebody beneath her, ain't it? Yeah, I think I see."

"No. It wasn't just her that made him little. Everybody worked on him because he was big, and wouldn't give in, and did like he pleased. Everybody worked on him just the way they're working on you."

"They who, Chief?" he asked in a soft voice, suddenly serious.

"The Combine. It worked on him for years. He was big enough to fight it for a while. It wanted us to live in inspected houses. It wanted to take the falls. It was even in the tribe, and they worked on him. In the town they beat him up in the alleys and cut his hair short once. Oh, the Combine's big— big. He fought it a long time till my mother made him too little to fight any more and he gave up."

McMurphy didn't say anything for a long time after that. Then he raised up on his elbow and looked at me again, and asked why they beat him up in the alleys, and I told him that they wanted to make him see what he had in store for him only worse if he didn't sign the papers giving everything to the government.

"What did they want him to give the government?"

"Everything. The tribe, the village, the falls . . ."

"Now I remember; you're talking about the falls where the Indians used to spear salmon—long time ago. Yeah. But the way I remember it the tribe got paid some huge amount."

"That's what they said to him. He said, What can you pay for the way a man lives? He said, What can you pay for what a man is? They didn't understand. Not even the tribe. They stood out in front of our door all holding those checks and they wanted him to tell them what to do now. They kept asking him to invest for them, or tell them where to go, or to buy a farm. But he was too little anymore. And he was too drunk, too. The Combine had whipped him. It beats everybody. It'll beat you too. They can't have somebody as big as Papa running around unless he's one of them. You can see that."

"Yeah, I reckon I can."

"That's why you shouldn't of broke that window. They see you're big, now. Now they got to bust you."

"Like bustin' a mustang, huh?"

"No. No, listen. They don't bust you that way; they work on you ways you can't fight! They put things in! They *install* things. They start as quick as they see you're gonna be big and go to working and installing their filthy machinery when you're little, and keep on and on and on till you're *fixed!*"

"Take 'er easy, buddy; shhh."

"And if you *fight* they lock you someplace and make you stop—"

"Easy, easy, Chief. Just cool it for a while. They heard you."

He lay down and kept still. My bed was hot, I noticed. I could hear the squeak of rubber soles as the black boy came in with a flashlight to see what the noise was. We lay still till he left.

"He finally just drank," I whispered. I didn't seem to be able to stop talking, not till I finished telling what I thought was all of it. "And the last I see him he's blind in the cedars from drinking and every time I see him put the bottle to his mouth he don't suck out of it, it sucks out of him until he's shrunk so wrinkled and yellow even the dogs don't know him, and we had to cart him out of the cedars, in a pickup, to a place in Portland, to die. I'm not saying they kill. They didn't kill him. They did something else."

I was feeling awfully sleepy. I didn't want to talk any more, I tried to think back on what I'd been saying, and it didn't seem like what I'd wanted to say.

"I been talking crazy, ain't I?"

"Yeah, Chief"—he rolled over in his bed—"you been talkin' crazy."

"It wasn't what I wanted to say. I can't say it all. It don't make sense."

"I didn't say it didn't make sense, Chief, I just said it was talkin' crazy."

He didn't say anything after that for so long I thought he'd gone to sleep. I wished I'd told him good night. I looked over at him, and he was turned away from me. His arm wasn't under the covers, and I could just make out the aces and eights tattooed there. It's big, I thought, big as my arms used to be when I played football. I wanted to reach over and touch the place where he was tattooed, to see if he was still alive. He's layin' awful quiet, I told myself, I ought to touch him to see if he's still alive. . . .

That's a lie. I know he's still alive. That ain't the reason I want to touch him.

I want to touch him because he's a man.

That's a lie too. There's other men around. I could touch them.

I want to touch him because I'm one of these queers!

But that's a lie too. That's one fear hiding behind another. If I was one of these queers I'd want to do other things with him. I just want to touch him because he's who he is.

But as I was about to reach over to that arm he said, "Say, Chief," and rolled in bed with a lurch of covers, facing me, "Say, Chief, why don't you come on this fishin' trip with us tomorrow?"

I didn't answer.

"Come on, what do ya say? I look for it to be one hell of an occasion. You know these two aunts of mine comin' to pick us up? Why, those ain't aunts, man, no; both those girls are workin' shimmy dancers and hustlers I know from Portland. What do you say to that?"

I finally told him I was one of the Indigents.

"You're *what?*"

"I'm broke."

"Oh," he said. "Yeah, I hadn't thought of that."

He was quiet for a time again, rubbing that scar on his nose with his finger. The finger stopped. He raised up on his elbow and looked at me.

"Chief," he said slowly, looking me over, "when you were full-sized, when you used to be, let's say, six seven or eight and weighed two eighty or so—were you strong enough to, say, lift something the size of that control panel in the tub room?"

I thought about that panel. It probably didn't weigh a lot more'n oil drums I'd lifted in the Army. I told him I probably could of at one time.

"If you got that big again, could you still lift it?"

I told him I thought so.

"To hell with what you think; I want to know can you *promise* to lift it if I get you big as you used to be? You promise me that, and you not only get my special body-buildin' course for nothing but you get yourself a ten-buck fishin' trip, *free!*" He licked his lips and lay back. "Get me good odds too, I bet."

He lay there chuckling over some thought of his own. When I asked him how he was going to get me big again he shushed me with a finger to his lips.

"Man, we can't let a secret like this out. I didn't say I'd tell you *how*, did I? Hoo boy, blowin' a man back up to full size is a secret you can't share with everybody, be dangerous in the hands of an enemy. You won't even know it's happening most of the time yourself. But I give you my solemn word, you follow my training program, and here's what'll happen."

He swung his legs out of bed and sat on the edge with his hands on his knees. The dim light coming in over his shoulder from the Nurses' Station caught the shine of his teeth and the one eye glinting down his nose at me. The rollicking auctioneer's voice spun softly through the dorm.

"*There* you'll be. It's the Big Chief Bromden, cuttin' down the boulevard—men, women, and kids rockin' back on their heels to peer at him: 'Well well well, what giant's this *here*, takin' ten feet at a step and duckin' for telephone wires?' Comes stompin' through town, stops just long enough for virgins, the rest of you twitches might's well not even line up 'less you got tits like muskmelons, nice strong white legs long enough to lock around his mighty back, and a little cup of poozle warm and juicy and sweet as butter an' honey. . . ."

In the dark there he went on, spinning his tale about how it would be, with all the men scared and all the beautiful young girls panting after me. Then he said he was going out right this very minute and sign my name up as one of his fishing crew. He stood up, got the towel from his bedstand and wrapped it around his hips and put on his cap, and stood over my bed.

"Oh man, I tell you, I tell you, you'll have women trippin' you and beatin' you to the floor."   –

And all of a sudden his hand shot out and with a swing of his arm untied my sheet, cleared my bed covers, and left me lying there naked.

"Look there, Chief. Haw. What'd I tell ya? You growed a half a foot already."

Laughing, he walked down the row of beds to the hall.

*T*wo whores on their way down from Portland to take us deep-sea fishing in a boat! It made it tough to stay in bed until the dorm lights came on at six-thirty.

I was the first one up out·of the dorm to look at the list posted on the board next to the Nurses' Station, check to see if my name was really signed there. SIGN UP FOR DEEP SEA FISHING was printed in big letters at the top, then McMurphy had signed first and Billy Bibbit was number one, right after McMurphy. Number three was Harding and number four was Fredrickson, and all the way down to number ten where nobody'd signed yet. My name was there, the last put down, across from the number nine. I was actually going out of the hospital with two whores on a fishing boat; I had to keep saying it over and over to myself to believe it.

The three black boys slipped up in front of me and read the list with gray fingers, found my name there and turned to grin at me.

Vhy, who you s'pose signed Chief Bromden up for this foolishness? Inniuns ain't able to write."

"What makes you think Inniuns able to *read?*"

The starch was still fresh and stiff enough this early that their arms rustled in the white suits when they moved, like paper wings. I acted deaf to them laughing at me, like I didn't even know, but when they stuck a broom out for me to do their work up the hall, I turned around and walked back to the dorm, telling myself, The hell with that. A man goin' fishing with two whores from Portland don't have to take that crap.

It scared me some, walking off from them like that, because I never went against what the black boys ordered before. I looked back and saw them coming after me with the broom. They'd probably have come right on in the dorm and got me but for McMurphy; he was in there making such a fuss, roaring up and down between the beds, snapping a towel at the guys signed to go this morning, that the black boys decided maybe the dorm wasn't such safe territory to venture into for no more than somebody to sweep a little dab of hallway.

McMurphy had his motorcycle cap pulled way forward on

his red hair to look like a boat captain, and the tattoos show-ing out from the sleeves of his T-shirt were done in Singapore. He was swaggering around the floor like it was the deck of a ship, whistling in his hand like a bosun's whistle.

"*Hit* the deck, mateys, *hit* the deck or I keelhaul the lot of ye from stock to stern!"

He rang the bedstand next to Harding's bed with his knuckles.

"*Six* bells and *all's* well. Steady as she goes. Hit the deck. Drop your cocks and grab your socks."

He noticed me standing just inside the doorway and came rushing over to thump my back like a drum.

"Look here at the Big Chief; here's an example of a good sailor and fisherman: up before day and out diggin' red worms for bait. The rest of you scurvy bunch o' lubbers'd do well to follow his lead. *Hit* the deck. Today's the day! Outa the sack and into the sea!"

The Acutes grumbled and griped at him and his towel, and the Chronics woke up to look around with heads blue from lack of blood cut off by sheets tied too tight across the chest, looking around the dorm till they finally centered on me with weak and watered-down old looks, faces wistful and curious. They lay there watching me pull on warm clothes for the trip, making me feel uneasy and a little guilty. They could sense I had been singled out as the only Chronic making the trip. They watched me—old guys welded in wheelchairs for years, with catheters down their legs like vines rooting them for the rest of their lives right where they are, they watched me and knew instinctively that I was going. And they could still be a little jealous it wasn't them. They could know because enough of the man in them had been damped out that the old animal instincts had taken over (old Chronics wake up sudden some nights, before anybody else knows a guy's died in the dorm, and throw back their heads and howl), and they could be jealous because there was enough man left to still remember.

McMurphy went out to look at the list and came back and tried to talk one more Acute into signing, going down the line kicking at the beds still had guys in them with sheets pulled over their heads, telling them what a great thing it was to be out there in the teeth of the gale with a he-man sea crackin' around and a goddam yo-heave-ho and a bottle of rum. "C'mon, loafers, I need one more mate to round out the crew, I need one more goddam volunteer. . . ."

But he couldn't talk anybody into it. The Big Nurse had the rest scared with her stories of how rough the sea'd been lately and how many boats'd sunk, and it didn't look like we'd get that last crew member till a half-hour later when George Sorensen came up to McMurphy in the breakfast line where we were waiting for the mess hall to be unlocked for breakfast.

Big toothless knotty old Swede the black boys called Rub-a-dub George, because of his thing about sanitation, came shuffling up the hall, listing well back so his feet went well out in front of his head (sways backward this way to keep his face as far away from the man he's talking to as he can), stopped in front of McMurphy, and mumbled something in his hand. George was very shy. You couldn't see his eyes because they were in so deep under his brow, and he cupped his big palm around most of the rest of his face. His head swayed like a crow's nest on top of his mastlike spine. He mumbled in his hand till McMurphy finally reached up and pulled the hand away so's the words could get out.

"Now, George, what is it you're sayin'?"

"Red worms," he was saying. "I joost don't think they do you no good—not for the Chin-nook."

"Yeah?" McMurphy said. "Red worms? I might agree with you, George, if you let me know what about these red worms you're speaking of."

"I think joost a while ago I hear you say Mr. Bromden was out digging the red worms for bait."

"That's right, Pop, I remember."

"So I joost say you don't have you no good fortune with them worms. This here is the month with one big Chinook run—su-ure. Herring you need. Su-ure. You jig you some herring and use those fellows for bait, *then* you have some good fortune."

His voice went up at the end of every sentence—for-*chune* —like he was asking a question. His big chin, already scrubbed so much this morning he'd worn the hide off it, nodded up and down at McMurphy once or twice, then turned him around to lead him down the hall toward the end of the line. McMurphy called him back.

"Now, hold 'er a minute, George; you talk like you know something about this fishin' business."

George turned and shuffled back to McMurphy, listing back so far it looked like his feet had navigated right out from under him.

"You bet, su-ure. Twenty-five year I work the Chinook trollers, all the way from Half Moon Bay to Puget Sound. Twenty-five year I fish—before I get so dirty." He held out his hands for us to see the dirt on them. Everybody around leaned over and looked. I didn't see the dirt but I did see scars worn deep into the white palms from hauling a thousand miles of fishing line out of the sea. He let us look a minute, then rolled the hands shut and drew them away and hid them in his pajama shirt like we might dirty them looking, and stood grinning at McMurphy with gums like brine-bleached pork.

"I had a good troller boat, joost forty feet, but she drew twelve feet water and she was solid teak and solid oak." He rocked back and forth in a way to make you doubt that the floor was standing level. "She was one good troller boat, by golly!"

He started to turn, but McMurphy stopped him again.

"Hell, George, why didn't you say you were a fisherman? I been talking up this voyage like I was the Old Man of the Sea, but just between you an' me an' the wall there, the only boat I been on was the battleship *Missouri* and the only thing I know about fish is that I like eatin' 'em better than cleanin' 'em."

"Cleanin' is *easy*, somebody show you how."

"By God, you're gonna be our captain, George; we'll be your crew."

George tilted back, shaking his head. "Those boats awful *dirty* any more—everything *awful* dirty."

"The hell with that. We got a boat specially sterilized fore and aft, swabbed clean as a hound's tooth. You won't get dirty, George, 'cause you'll be the captain. Won't even have to bait a hook; just be our captain and give orders to us dumb land-lubbers—how's that strike you?"

I could see George was tempted by the way he wrung his hands under his shirt, but he still said he couldn't risk getting dirty. McMurphy did his best to talk him into it, but George was still shaking his head when the Big Nurse's key hit the lock of the mess hall and she came jangling out the door with her wicker bag of surprises, clicked down the line with automatic smile-and-good-morning for each man she passed. McMurphy noticed the way George leaned back from her and scowled. When she'd passed, McMurphy tilted his head and gave George the one bright eye.

"George, that stuff the nurse has been saying about the bad sea, about how terrible dangerous this trip might be—what about that?"

"That ocean could be awful bad, sure, awful rough."

McMurphy looked down at the nurse disappearing into the station, then back at George. George started twisting his hands around in his shirt more than ever, looking around at the silent faces watching him.

"By golly!" he said suddenly. "You think I let her scare me about that ocean? You think *that?*"

"Ah, I guess not, George. I was thinking, though, that if you don't come along with us, and if there *is* some awful stormy calamity, we're every last one of us liable to be lost at sea, you know that? I said I didn't know nothin' about boating, and I'll tell you something else: these two women coming to get us, I told the doctor was my two aunts, two widows of fishermen. Well, the only cruisin' either one of them ever did was on solid cement. They won't be no more help in a fix than me. We *need* you, George." He took a pull on his cigarette and asked, "You got ten bucks, by the way?"

George shook his head.

"No, I wouldn't suppose so. Well, what the devil, I gave up the idea of comin' out ahead days ago. Here." He took a pencil out of the pocket of his green jacket and wiped it clean on his shirttail, held it out to George. "You captain us, and we'll let you come along for five."

George looked around at us again, working his big brow over the predicament. Finally his gums showed in a bleached smile and he reached for the pencil. "By golly!" he said and headed off with the pencil to sign the last place on the list. After breakfast, walking down the hall, McMurphy stopped and printed c-a-p-t behind George's name.

The whores were late. Everybody was beginning to think they weren't coming at all when McMurphy gave a yell from the window and we all went running to look. He said that was them, but we didn't see but one car, instead of the two we were counting on, and just one woman. McMurphy called to her through the screen when she stopped on the parking lot, and she came cutting straight across the grass toward our ward.

She was younger and prettier than any of us'd figured on. Everybody had found out that the girls were whores instead of aunts, and were expecting all sorts of things. Some of the religious guys weren't any too happy about it. But seeing her coming lightfooted across the grass with her eyes green all the way up to the ward, and her hair, roped in a long twist at the back of her head, jouncing up and down with every step like copper springs in the sun, all any of us could think of was that she was a girl, a female who wasn't dressed white from head to foot like she'd been dipped in frost, and how she made her money didn't make any difference.

She ran right up against the screen where McMurphy was and hooked her fingers through the mesh and pulled herself against it. She was panting from the run, and every breath looked like she might swell right through the mesh. She was crying a little.

"McMurphy, oh, you damned McMurphy . . ."

"Never mind that. Where's Sandra?"

"She got tied up, man, can't make it. But you, damn it, are you okay?"

"She got tied up!"

"To tell the truth"—the girl wiped her nose and giggled—"ol' Sandy got *married*. You remember Artie Gilfillian from Beaverton? Always used to show up at the parties with some gassy thing, a gopher snake or a white mouse or some gassy thing like that in his pocket? A real maniac—"

"Oh, sweet Jesus!" McMurphy groaned. "How'm I supposed to get ten guys in one stinkin' Ford, Candy sweetheart? How'd Sandra and her gopher snake from Beaverton figure on me swingin' *that?*"

The girl looked like she was in the process of thinking up an answer when the speaker in the ceiling clacked and the Big Nurse's voice told McMurphy if he wanted to talk with his lady friend it'd be better if she signed in properly at the main door instead of disturbing the whole hospital. The girl left the screen and started toward the main entrance, and McMurphy left the screen and flopped down in a chair in the corner, his head hanging. "Hell's *bells*," he said.

The least black boy let the girl onto the ward and forgot to lock the door behind her (caught hell for it later, I bet), and the girl came jouncing up the hall past the Nurses' Station, where all the nurses were trying to freeze her bounce with a united icy look, and into the day room just a few steps ahead of the doctor. He was going toward the Nurses' Station with some papers, looked at her, and back at the papers, and back at her again, and went to fumbling after his glasses with both hands.

She stopped when she got to the middle of the day-room floor and saw she was circled by forty staring men in green, and it was so quiet you could hear bellies growling, and, all along the Chronic row, hear catheters popping off.

She had to stand there a minute while she looked around to find McMurphy, so everybody got a long look at her. There was a blue smoke hung near the ceiling over her head; I think apparatus burned out all over the ward trying to adjust to her come busting in like she did—took electronic readings on her and calculated they weren't built to handle something like this on the ward, and just burned out, like machines committing suicide.

She had on a white T-shirt like McMurphy's only a lot smaller, white tennis shoes and Levi pants snipped off above her knees to give her feet circulation, and it didn't look like that was near enough material to go around, considering what it had to cover. She must've been seen with lots less by lots more men, but under the circumstances she began to fidget around self-consciously like a schoolgirl on a stage. Nobody spoke while they looked. Martini did whisper that you could read the dates of the coins in her Levi pockets, they were so tight, but he was closer and could see better'n the rest of us.

Billy Bibbit was the first one to say something out loud, not really a word, just a low, almost painful whistle that described how she looked better than anybody else could have. She laughed and thanked him very much and he blushed so red that she blushed with him and laughed again. This broke things into movement. All the Acutes were coming across the floor trying to talk to her at once. The doctor was pulling on Harding's coat, asking who *is* this. McMurphy got up out of his chair and walked through the crowd to her, and when she saw him she threw her arms around him and said, "You damned McMurphy," and then got embarrassed and blushed again. When she blushed she didn't look more than sixteen or seventeen, I swear she didn't.

McMurphy introduced her around and she shook everybody's hand. When she got to Billy she thanked him again for his whistle. The Big Nurse came sliding out of the station, smiling, and asked McMurphy how he intended to get all ten of us in one car, and he asked could he maybe *borrow* a staff car and drive a load himself, and the nurse cited a rule forbidding this, just like everyone knew she would. She said unless there was another driver to sign a Responsibility Slip that half of the crew would have to stay behind. McMurphy told her this'd cost him fifty goddam bucks to make up the difference; he'd have to pay the guys back who didn't get to go.

"Then it may be," the nurse said, "that the trip will have to be canceled—and *all* the money refunded."

"I've already rented the boat; the man's got seventy bucks of mine in his pocket right now!"

"Seventy dollars? So? I thought you told the patients you'd need to collect a hundred dollars plus ten of your own to finance the trip, Mr. McMurphy."

"I was putting gas in the cars over and back."

"That wouldn't amount to thirty dollars, though, would it?"

She smiled so nice at him, waiting. He threw his hands in the air and looked at the ceiling.

"Hoo *boy,* you don't miss a chance do you, Miss District Attorney. Sure; I was keepin' what was left over. I don't think any of the guys ever thought any different. I figured to make a little for the trouble I took get—"

"But your plans didn't work out," she said. She was still smiling at him, so full of sympathy. "Your little financial speculations can't *all* be successes, Randle, and, actually, as I think about it now, you've had more than your share of victories." She mused about this, thinking about something I knew we'd hear more about later. "Yes. Every Acute on the ward has written you an IOU for some 'deal' of yours at one time or another, so don't you think you can bear up under this one small defeat?"

Then she stopped. She saw McMurphy wasn't listening to her any more. He was watching the doctor. And the doctor was eying the blond girl's T-shirt like nothing else existed. Mc-Murphy's loose smile spread out on his face as he watched the doctor's trance, and he pushed his cap to the back of his head and strolled to the doctor's side, startling him with a hand on the shoulder.

"By God, Doctor Spivey, you ever see a Chinook Salmon hit a line? One of the fiercest sights on the seven seas. Say, Candy honeybun, whyn't you tell the doctor here about deep-sea fishing and all like that. . . ."

Working together, it didn't take McMurphy and the girl but two minutes and the little doctor was down locking up his office and coming back up the hall, cramming papers in a brief case.

"Good deal of paper work I can get done on the boat," he explained to the nurse and went past her so fast she didn't have a chance to answer, and the rest of the crew followed, slower, grinning at her standing in the door of the Nurses' Station.

The Acutes who weren't going gathered at the day-room door, told us don't bring our catch back till it's cleaned, and Ellis pulled his hands down off the nails in the wall and squeezed Billy Bibbit's hand and told him to be a fisher of men.

And Billy, watching the brass brads on that woman's Levis wink at him as she walked out of the day room, told Ellis to hell with that fisher of *men* business. He joined us at the door, and the least black boy let us through and locked the door behind us, and we were out, outside.

The sun was prying up the clouds and lighting the brick front of the hospital rose bed. A thin breeze worked at sawing what leaves were left from the oak trees, stacking them neatly against the wire cyclone fence. There was little brown birds occasionally on the fence; when a puff of leaves would hit the fence the birds would fly off with the wind. It looked at first like the leaves were hitting the fence and turning into birds and flying away.

It was a fine woodsmoked autumn day, full of the sound of kids punting footballs and the putter of small airplanes, and everybody should've been happy just being outside in it. But we all stood in a silent bunch with our hands in our pockets while the doctor walked to get his car. A silent bunch, watching the townspeople who were driving past on their way to work slow down to gawk at all the loonies in green uniforms. McMurphy saw how uneasy we were and tried to work us into a better mood by joking and teasing the girl, but this made us feel worse somehow. Everybody was thinking how easy it would be to return to the ward, go back and say they decided the nurse had been right; with a wind like this the sea would've been just too rough.

The doctor arrived and we loaded up and headed off, me and George and Harding and Billy Bibbit in the car with McMurphy and the girl, Candy; and Fredrickson and Sefelt and Scanlon and Martini and Tadem and Gregory following in the doctor's car. Everyone was awfully quiet. We pulled into a gas station about a mile from the hospital; the doctor followed. He got out first, and the service-station man came bouncing out, grinning and wiping his hands on a rag. Then he stopped grinning and went past the doctor to see just what was *in* these cars. He backed off, wiping his hands on the oil rag, frowning. The doctor caught the man's sleeve nervously and took out a ten-dollar bill and tucked it down in the man's hands like setting out a tomato plant.

"Ah, would you fill both tanks with regular?" the doctor asked. He was acting just as uneasy about being out of the hospital as the rest of us were. "Ah, would you?"

"Those uniforms," the service-station man said, "they're from the hospital back up the road, aren't they?" He was looking around him to see if there was a wrench or something handy. He finally moved over near a stack of empty pop bottles. "You guys are from that *asylum*."

The doctor fumbled for his glasses and looked at us too, like he'd just noticed the uniforms. "Yes. No, I mean. We, they *are* from the asylum, but they are a work crew, not inmates, of course not. A work crew."

The man squinted at the doctor and at us and went off to whisper to his partner, who was back among the machinery. They talked a minute, and the second guy hollered and asked the doctor who we were and the doctor repeated that we were a work crew, and both of the guys laughed. I could tell by the laugh that they'd decided to sell us the gas—probably it would be weak and dirty and watered down and cost twice the usual price—but it didn't make me feel any better. I could see everybody was feeling pretty bad. The doctor's lying made us feel worse than ever—not because of the lie, so much, but because of the truth.

The second guy came over to the doctor, grinning. "You said you wanted the Soo-preme, sir? You bet. And how about us checking those oil filters and windshield wipes?" He was bigger than his friend. He leaned down on the doctor like he was sharing a secret. "Would you believe it: eighty-eight per cent of the cars show by the figures on the road today that they need new oil filters and windshield wipes?"

His grin was coated with car from years of taking out spark plugs with his teeth. He kept leaning down on the doctor, making him squirm with that grin and waiting for him to admit he was over a barrel. "Also, how's your work crew fixed for sunglasses? We got some good Polaroids." The doctor knew he had him. But just the instant he opened his mouth, about to give in and say Yes, anything, there was a whirring noise and the top of our car was folding back. McMurphy was fighting and cursing the accordion-pleated top, trying to force it back faster than the machinery could handle it. Everybody could see how mad he was by the way he thrashed and beat at that slowly rising top; when he got it cussed and hammered and wrestled down into place he climbed right out over the girl and over the side of the car and walked up between the doctor and the service station guy and looked up into the black mouth with one eye.

"Okay now, Hank, we'll take regular, just like the doctor ordered. Two tanks of regular. That's all. The hell with that other slum. And we'll take it at three cents off because we're a goddamned government-sponsored expedition."

The guy didn't budge. "Yeah? I thought the professor here said you weren't patients?"

"Now Hank, don't you see that was just a kindly precaution to keep from *startlin'* you folks with the truth? The doc wouldn't lie like that about just *any* patients, but we ain't ordinary nuts; we're every bloody one of us hot off the criminal-insane ward, on our way to San Quentin where they got better facilities to handle us. You see that freckle-faced kid there? Now he might look like he's right off a *Saturday Evening Post* cover, but he's a insane knife artist that killed three men. The man beside him is known as the Bull Goose Loony, unpredictable as a wild hog. You see that big guy? He's an Indian and he beat six white men to death with a pick handle when they tried to cheat him trading muskrat hides. Stand up where they can get a look at you, Chief."

Harding goosed me with his thumb, and I stood up on the floor of the car. The guy shaded his eyes and looked up at me and didn't say anything.

"Oh, it's a bad group, I admit," McMurphy said, "but it's a planned, authorized, legal government-sponsored excursion, and we're entitled to a legal discount just the same as if we was the FBI."

The guy looked back at McMurphy, and McMurphy hooked his thumbs in his pockets and rocked back and looked up at him across the scar on his nose. The guy turned to check if his buddy was still stationed at the case of empty pop bottles, then grinned back down on McMurphy.

"Pretty tough customers, is that what you're saying, Red? So much we better toe the line and do what we're told, is that what you're saying? Well, tell me, Red, what is it *you're* in for? Trying to assassinate the President?"

"Nobody could *prove* that, Hank. They got me on a bum rap. I killed a man in the ring, ya see, and sorta got *taken* with the kick."

"One of these killers with boxing gloves, is that what you're telling me, Red?"

"Now I didn't say that, did I? I never could get used to those pillows you wore. No, this wasn't no televised main event from the Cow Palace; I'm more what you call a back-lot boxer."

The guy hooked his thumbs in his pockets to mock McMurphy. "You are more what I call a back-lot bull-thrower."

"Now I didn't say that bull-throwing wasn't also one of my abilities, did I? But I want you to look here." He put his hands up in the guy's face, real close, turning them over slowly, palm and knuckle. "You ever see a man get his poor old meathooks so pitiful chewed up from just throwin' the *bull*? Did you, Hank?"

He held those hands in the guy's face a long time, waiting to see if the guy had anything else to say. The guy looked at the hands, and at me, and back at the hands. When it was clear he didn't have anything else real pressing to say, McMurphy walked away from him to the other guy leaning against the pop cooler and plucked the doctor's ten-dollar bill out of his fist and started for the grocery store next to the station.

"You boys tally what the gas comes to and send the bill to the hospital," he called back. "I intend to use the cash to pick up some refreshments for the men. I believe we'll get that in place of windshield wipes and eighty-eight per cent oil filters."

By the time he got back everybody was feeling cocky as fighting roosters and calling orders to the service-station guys to check the air in the spare and wipe the windows and scratch that bird dropping off the hood if you please, just like we owned the show. When the big guy didn't get the windshield to suit Billy, Billy called him right back.

"You didn't get this sp-spot here where the bug h-h-hit."

"That wasn't a bug," the guy said sullenly, scratching at it with his fingernail, "that was a bird."

Martini called all the way from the other car that it couldn't of been a bird. "There'd be feathers and bones if it was a bird."

A man riding a bicycle stopped to ask what was the idea of all the green uniforms; some kind of club? Harding popped right up and answered him.

"No, my friend. We are lunatics from the hospital up the highway, psycho-ceramics, the cracked pots of mankind. Would you like me to d̶e̶c̶i̶p̶h̶e̶r̶ a Rorschach for you? No? You must hurry on? Ah, he's gone. Pity." He turned to McMurphy. "Never before did I realize that mental illness could have the aspect of power, *power*. Think of it: perhaps the more insane a man is, the more powerful he could become. Hitler an example. Fair makes the old brain reel, doesn't it? Food for thought there."

Billy punched a beer can for the girl, and she flustered him so with her bright smile and her "Thank you, Billy," that he took to opening cans for all of us.

While the pigeons fretted up and down the sidewalk with their hands folded behind their backs.

I sat there, feeling whole and good, sipping at a beer; I could hear the beer all the way down me—zzzth zzzth, like that. I had forgotten that there can be good sounds and tastes like the sound and taste of a beer going down. I took another big drink and started looking around me to see what else I had forgotten in twenty years.

"Man!" McMurphy said as he scooted the girl out from under the wheel and tight over against Billy. "Will you just look at the Big Chief slug down on that firewater!"—and slammed the car out into traffic with the doctor squealing behind to keep up.

He'd shown us what a little bravado and courage could accomplish, and we thought he'd taught us how to use it. All the way to the coast we had fun pretending to be brave. When people at a stop light would stare at us and our green uniforms we'd do just like he did, sit up straight and strong and tough-looking and put a big grin on our face and stare straight back at them till their motors died and their windows sunstreaked and they were left sitting when the light changed, upset bad by what a tough bunch of monkeys was just now not three feet from them, and help nowhere in sight.

As McMurphy led the twelve of us toward the ocean.

I think McMurphy knew better than we did that our tough looks were all show, because he still wasn't able to get a real laugh out of anybody. Maybe he couldn't understand why we weren't able to laugh yet, but he knew you can't really be strong until you can see a funny side to things. In fact, he worked so hard at pointing out the funny side of things that I was wondering a little if maybe he was blind to the other side, if maybe he wasn't able to see what it was that parched laughter deep inside your stomach. Maybe the guys weren't able to see it either, just feel the pressures of the different beams and frequencies coming from all directions, working to push and bend you one way or another, feel the Combine at work—but I was able to *see* it.

The way you see the change in a person you've been away from for a long time, where somebody who sees him every day, day in, day out, wouldn't notice because the change is gradual. All up the coast I could see the signs of what the Combine had accomplished since I was last through this country, things like, for example—a *train* stopping at a station and laying a string of full-grown men in mirrored suits and machined hats, laying them like a hatch of identical insects, half-life things coming pht-pht-pht out of the last car, then hooting its electric whistle and moving on down the spoiled land to deposit another hatch.

Or things like five thousand houses punched out identical by a machine and strung across the hills outside of town, so fresh from the factory they're still linked together like sausages, a sign saying "NEST IN THE WEST HOMES—NO DWN. PAYMENT

FOR VETS," a playground down the hill from the houses, behind a checker-wire fence and another sign that read "ST.
LUKE'S SCHOOL FOR BOYS"—there were five thousand kids in
green corduroy pants and white shirts under green pullover
sweaters playing crack-the-whip across an acre of crushed
gravel. The line popped and twisted and jerked like a snake, and
every crack popped a little kid off the end, sent him rolling up
against the fence like a tumbleweed. Every crack. And it was
always the same little kid, over and over.

All that five thousand kids lived in those five thousand
houses, owned by those guys that got off the train. The houses
looked so much alike that, time and time again, the kids went
home by mistake to different houses and different families.
Nobody ever noticed. They ate and went to bed. The only one
they noticed was the little kid at the end of the whip. He'd always be so scuffed and bruised that he'd show up out of place
wherever he went. He wasn't able to open up and laugh either.
It's a hard thing to laugh if you can feel the pressure of those
beams coming from every new car that passes, or every new
house you pass.

"We can even have a lobby in Washington," Harding was
saying, "an organization NAAIP. Pressure groups. Big bill-
boards along the highway showing a babbling schizophrenic
running a wrecking machine, bold, red and green type: 'Hire
the Insane.' We've got a rosy future, gentlemen."

We crossed a bridge over the Siuslaw. There was just enough
mist in the air that I could lick out my tongue to the wind
and taste the ocean before we could see it. Everyone knew we
were getting close and didn't speak all the way to the docks.

The captain who was supposed to take us out had a bald
gray metal head set in a black turtleneck like a gun turret on
a U-boat; the cold cigar sticking from his mouth swept over
us. He stood beside McMurphy on the wooden pier and looked
out to sea as he talked. Behind him and up a bunch of steps,
six or eight men in windbreakers were sitting on a bench along
the front of the bait shop. The captain talked loudly, half to
the loafers on his one side and half to McMurphy on the other
side, firing his copper-jacket voice someplace in between.

"Don't care. Told you specifically in the letter. You don't
have a signed waiver clearing me with proper authorities, I
don't go out." The round head swiveled in the turret of his
sweater, beading down that cigar at the lot of us. "Look
there. Bunch like that at sea, could go to diving overboard

like rats. Relatives could sue me for everything I own. I can't risk it."

McMurphy explained how the other girl was supposed to get all those papers up in Portland. One of the guys leaning against the bait shop called, "What other girl? Couldn't Blondie there handle the lot of you?" McMurphy didn't pay the guy any mind and went on arguing with the captain, but you could see how it bothered the girl. Those men against the shop kept leering at her and leaning close together to whisper things. All our crew, even the doctor, saw this and got to feeling ashamed that we didn't do something. We weren't the cocky bunch that was back at the service station.

McMurphy stopped arguing when he saw he wasn't getting any place with the captain and turned around a couple of times, running his hand through his hair.

"Which boat have we got rented?"

"That's it there. The *Lark*. Not a man sets foot on her till I have a signed waiver clearing me. Not a man."

"I don't intend to rent a boat so we can sit all day and watch it bob up and down at the dock," McMurphy said. "Don't you have a phone up there in your bait shack? Let's go get this cleared up."

They thumped up the steps onto the level with the bait shop and went inside, leaving us clustered up by ourselves, with that bunch of loafers up there watching us and making comments and sniggering and goosing one another in the ribs. The wind was blowing the boats at their moorings, nuzzling them up against the wet rubber tires along the dock so they made a sound like they were laughing at us. The water was giggling under the boards, and the sign hanging over the door to the bait shack that read "SEAMAN'S SERVICE—CAPT BLOCK, PROP" was squeaking and scratching as the wind rocked it on rusty hooks. The mussels that clung to the pilings, four feet out of water marking the tide line, whistled and clicked in the sun.

The wind had turned cold and mean, and Billy Bibbit took off his green coat and gave it to the girl, and she put it on over her thin little T-shirt. One of the loafers kept calling down, "Hey you, Blondie, you like fruitcake kids like that?" The man's lips were kidney-colored and he was purple under his eyes where the wind'd mashed the veins to the surface. "Hey you, Blondie," he called over and over in a high, tired voice, "hey you, Blondie . . . hey you, Blondie . . . hey you, Blondie . . ."

We bunched up closer together against the wind.

"Tell me, Blondie, what've they got *you* committed for?"

"Ahr, she ain't committed, Perce, she's part of the *cure!*"

"Is that right, Blondie? You hired as part of the *cure?* Hey you, Blondie."

She lifted her head and gave us a look that asked where was that hard-boiled bunch she'd seen and why weren't they saying something to defend her? Nobody would answer the look. All our hard-boiled strength had just walked up those steps with his arm around the shoulders of the bald-headed captain.

She pulled the collar of the jacket high around her neck and hugged her elbows and strolled as far away from us down the dock as she could go. Nobody went after her. Billy Bibbit shivered in the cold and bit his lip. The guys at the bait shack whispered something else and whooped out laughing again.

"Ask 'er, Perce—go on."

"Hey, Blondie, did you get 'em to sign a waiver clearing you with proper authorities? Relatives could sue, they tell me, if one of the boys fell in and drown while he was on board. Did you ever think of that? Maybe you'd better stay here with us, Blondie."

"Yeah, Blondie; my relatives wouldn't sue. I promise. Stay here with us fellows, Blondie."

I imagined I could feel my feet getting wet as the dock sank with shame into the bay. We weren't fit to be out here with people. I wished McMurphy would come back out and cuss these guys good and then drive us back where we belonged.

The man with the kidney lips folded his knife and stood up and brushed the whittle shavings out of his lap. He started walking toward the steps. "C'mon, now, Blondie, what you want to mess with these bozos for?"

She turned and looked at him from the end of the dock, then back at us, and you could tell she was thinking his proposition over when the door of the bait shop opened and Mc-Murphy came shoving out past the bunch of them, down the steps.

"Pile in, crew, it's all set! Gassed and ready and there's bait and beer on board."

He slapped Billy on the rear and did a little hornpipe and commenced slinging ropes from their snubs.

"Ol' Cap'n Block's still on the phone, but we'll be pulling off as quick as he comes out. George, let's see if you can get that motor warmed up. Scanlon, you and Harding untie that rope there. Candy! What are you doing off down there? Let's get with it, honey, we're shoving off."

We swarmed into the boat, glad for anything that would take us away from those guys standing in a row at the bait shop.

Billy took the girl by the hand and helped her on board. George hummed over the dashboard up on the bridge, pointing out buttons for McMurphy to twist or push.

"Yeah, these pukers, puke boats, we call them," he said to McMurphy, "they joost as easy like driving ottomobile."

The doctor hesitated before climbing aboard and looked toward the shop where all the loafers stood milling toward the steps.

"Don't you think, Randle, we'd better wait . . . until the captain—"

McMurphy caught him by the lapels and lifted him clear of the dock into the boat like he was a small boy. "Yeah, Doc," he said, "wait till the captain *what?*" He commenced to laugh like he was drunk, talking in an excited, nervous way. "Wait till the captain comes out an tells us that the phone number I gave him is a flophouse up in Portland? You bet. Here, George, damn your eyes; take hold of this thing and get us out of here! Sefelt! Get that rope loose and get on. George, come *on.*"

The motor chugged and died, chugged again like it was clearing its throat, then roared full on.

"*Hoowee!* There she goes. Pour the coal to 'er, George, and all hands stand by to repel boarders!"

A white gorge of smoke and water roared from the back of the boat, and the door of the bait shop crashed open and the captain's head came booming out and down the steps like it was not only dragging his body behind it but the bodies of the eight other guys as well. They came thundering down the dock and stopped right at the boil of foam washing over their feet as George swung the big boat out and away from the docks and we had the sea to ourselves.

A sudden turn of the boat had thrown Candy to her knees, and Billy was helping her up and trying to apologize for the way he'd acted on the dock at the same time. McMurphy came down from the bridge and asked if the two of them would like to be alone so they could talk over old times, and Candy looked at Billy and all he could do was shake his head and stutter. McMurphy said in that case that he and Candy'd better go below and check for leaks and the rest of us could make do for a while. He stood at the door down to the cabin and saluted and winked and appointed George captain and Harding second in command and said, "Carry on, mates," and followed the girl out of sight into the cabin.

The wind lay down and the sun got higher, chrome-plating the east side of the deep green swells. George aimed the boat straight out to sea, full throttle, putting the docks and that bait shop farther and farther behind us. When we passed the last point of the jetty and the last black rock, I could feel a great calmness creep over me, a calmness that increased the farther we left land behind us.

The guys had talked excitedly for a few minutes about our piracy of the boat, but now they were quiet. The cabin door opened once long enough for a hand to shove out a case of beer, and Billy opened us each one with an opener he found in the tackle box, and passed them around. We drank and watched the land sinking in our wake.

A mile or so out George cut the speed to what he called a trolling idle, put four guys to the four poles in the back of the boat, and the rest of us sprawled in the sun on top of the cabin or up on the bow and took off our shirts and watched the guys trying to rig their poles. Harding said the rule was a guy got to hold the pole till he got one strike, then he had to change off with a man who hadn't had a chance. George stood at the wheel, squinting out through the salt-caked windshield, and hollered instructions back how to fix up the reels and lines and how to tie a herring into the herring harness and how far back to fish and how deep:

"And take that number *four* pole and you put you twei\ ounces on him on a rope with a breakaway rig—I show you how in joost a minute—and we go after that *big* fella down on the bottom with that pole, by golly!"

Martini ran to the edge and leaned over the side and stared down into the water in the direction of his line. "Oh. Oh, my God," he said, but whatever he saw was too deep down for the rest of us.

There were other sports boats trolling up and down the coast, but George didn't make any attempt to join them; he kept pushing steadily straight on out past them, toward the open sea. "You bet," he said. "We go out with the commercial boats, where the real *fish* is."

The swells slid by, deep emerald on one side, chrome on the other. The only noise was the engine sputtering and humming, off and on, as the swells dipped the exhaust in and out of the water, and the funny, lost cry of the raggedy little black birds swimming around asking one another directions. Everything else was quiet. Some of the guys slept, and the others watched the water. We'd been trolling close to an hour when the tip of Sefelt's pole arched and dived into the water.

"George! Jesus, George, give us a hand!"

George wouldn't have a thing to do with the pole; he grinned and told Sefelt to ease up on the star drag, keep the tip pointed up, *up*, and work hell outa that fella!

"But what if I have a seizure?" Sefelt hollered.

"Why, we'll simply put hook and line on you and use you for a lure," Harding said. "Now work that fella, as the captain ordered, and quit worrying about a seizure."

Thirty yards back of the boat the fish broke into the sun in a shower of silver scales, and Sefelt's eyes popped and he got so excited watching the fish he let the end of his pole go down, and the line snapped into the boat like a rubber band.

"*Up*, I told you! You let him get a straight pull, don't you see? Keep that tip *up* . . . *up!* You had you one big silver there, by golly."

Sefelt's jaw was white and shaking when he finally gave up the pole to Fredrickson. "Okay—but if you get a fish with a hook in his mouth, that— ———— ᵗʰˡᵉssed fish!"

I was as excited as the rest. I hadn't planned on fishing, but after seeing that steel power a salmon has at the end of a line I got off the cabin top and put on my shirt to wait my turn at a pole.

Scanlon got up a pool for the biggest fish and another for the first fish landed, four bits from everybody that wanted in it, and he'd no more'n got his money in his pocket than Billy drug in some awful thing that looked like a ten-pound toad with spines on it like a porcupine.

"That's no fish," Scanlon said. "You can't win on that."

"It isn't a b-b-bird."

"That there, he's a *ling* cod," George told us. "He's one good eating fish you get all his warts off."

"See there. He is too a fish. P-p-pay up."

Billy gave me his pole and took his money and went to sit up close to the cabin where McMurphy and the girl were, looking at the closed door forlornly. "I wu-wu-wu-wish we had enough poles to go around," he said, leaning back against the side of the cabin.

I sat down and held the pole and watched the line swoop out into the wake. I smelt the air and felt the four cans of beer I'd drunk shorting out dozens of control leads down inside me: all around, the chrome sides of the swells flickered and flashed in the sun.

George sang out for us to look up ahead, that here come just what we been looking for. I leaned around to look, but all I saw was a big drifting log and those black seagulls circling and diving around the log, like black leaves caught up in a dust devil. George speeded up some, heading into the place where the birds circled, and the speed of the boat dragged my line until I couldn't see how you'd be able to tell if you did get a bite.

"Those fellas, those cormorants, they go after a school of *candle* fishes," George told us as he drove. "Little white fishes the size of your finger. You dry them and they burn joost like a candle. They are *food* fish, chum fish. And you bet where there's a big school of them candle fish you find the silver salmon feeding."

He drove into the birds, missing the floating log, and suddenly all around me the smooth slopes of chrome were shattered by diving birds and churning minnows, and the sleek silver-blue torpedo backs of the salmon slicing through it all. I saw one of the backs check its direction and turn and set course for a spot thirty yards behind the end of my pole, where my herring would be. I braced, my heart ringing, and then felt a jolt up both arms as if somebody'd hit the pole with a ball bat, and my line went burning off the reel from under my thumb, red as blood. "Use the star drag!" George yelled at me, but what I knew about star drags you could put in your eye so I just mashed harder with my thumb until the line turned back to yellow, then slowed and stopped. I looked around, and there were all three of the other poles whipping around just like mine, and the rest of the guys scrambling down off the cabin at the excitement and doing everything in their power to get underfoot.

"Up! Up! Keep the tip up!" George was yelling.

"McMurphy! Get out here and look at this."

"Godbless you, Fred, you got my blessed fish!"

"McMurphy, we need some help!"

I heard McMurphy laughing and saw him out of the corner of my eye, just standing at the cabin door, not even making a move to do anything, and I was too busy cranking at my fish to ask him for help. Everyone was shouting at him to do something, but he wasn't moving. Even the doctor, who had the deep pole, was asking McMurphy for assistance. And McMurphy was just laughing. Harding finally saw McMurphy wasn't going to do anything, so he got the gaff and jerked my fish into the boat with a clean, graceful motion like he's been boating fish all his life. He's big as my leg, I thought, big as a fence post! I thought, He's bigger'n any fish we ever got at the falls. He's springing all over the bottom of the boat like a rainbow gone wild! Smearing blood and scattering scales like little silver dimes, and I'm scared he's gonna flop overboard. McMurphy won't make a move to help. Scanlon grabs the fish and wrestles it down to keep it from flopping over the side. The girl comes running up from below, yelling it's her turn, dang it, grabs my pole, and jerks the hook into me three times while I'm trying to tie on a herring for her.

"Chief, I'll be damned if I ever saw anything so *slow!* Ugh, your thumb's bleeding. Did that monster bite you? Somebody fix the Chief's thumb—hurry!"

"Here we go into them again," George yells, and I drop the line off the back of the boat and see the flash of the herring vanish in the dark blue-gray charge of a salmon and the line go sizzling down into the water. The girl wraps both arms around the pole and grits her teeth. "*Oh* no you don't, dang you! *Oh* no . . . !"

She's on her feet, got the butt of the pole scissored in her crotch and both arms wrapped below the reel and the reel crank knocking against her as the line spins out: "*Oh* no you don't!" She's still got on Billy's green jacket, but that reel's whipped it open and everybody on board sees the T-shirt she had on is gone—everybody gawking, trying to play his own fish, dodge mine slamming around the boat bottom, with the crank of that reel fluttering her breast at such a speed the nipple's just a red blur!

Billy jumps to help. All he can think to do is reach around from behind and help her squeeze the pole tighter in between her breasts until the reel's finally stopped by nothing more than the pressure of her flesh. By this time she's flexed so taut and her breasts look so firm I think she and Billy could both turn loose with their hands and arms and she'd *still* keep hold of that pole.

This scramble of action holds for a space, a second there on the sea—the men yammering and struggling and cussing and trying to tend their poles while watching the girl; the bleeding, crashing battle between Scanlon and my fish at everybody's feet; the lines all tangled and shooting every which way with the doctor's glasses-on-a-string tangled and dangling from one line ten feet off the back of the boat, fish striking at the flash of the lens, and the girl cussing for all she's worth and looking now at her bare breasts, one white and one smarting red—and George takes his eye off where he's going and runs the boat into that log and kills the engine.

While McMurphy laughs. Rocking farther and farther backward against the cabin top, spreading his laugh out across the water—laughing at the girl, at the guys, at George, at me sucking my bleeding thumb, at the captain back at the pier and the bicycle rider and the service-station guys and the five thousand houses and the Big Nurse and all of it. Because he knows you have to laugh at the things that hurt you just to keep yourself in balance, just to keep the world from running you plumb crazy. He knows there's a painful side; he knows my thumb smarts and his girl friend has a bruised breast and the doctor is losing his glasses, but he won't let the pain blot out the humor no more'n he'll let the humor blot out the pain.

I notice Harding is collapsed beside McMurphy and is laughing too. And Scanlon from the bottom of the boat. At their own selves as well as at the rest of us. And the girl, with her eyes still smarting as she looks from her white breast to her red one, she starts laughing. And Selfelt and the doctor, and all.

It started slow and pumped itself full, swelling the men bigger and bigger. I watched, part of them, laughing with them— and somehow not with them. I was off the boat, blown up off the water and skating the wind with those black birds, high above myself, and I could look down and see myself and the rest of the guys, see the boat rocking there in the middle of those diving birds, see McMurphy surrounded by his dozen people, and watch them, us, swinging a laughter that rang out on the water in ever-widening circles, farther and farther, until it crashed up on beaches all over the coast, on beaches all over all coasts, in wave after wave after wave.

The doctor had hooked something off the bottom on the deep hole, and everybody else on board except George had caught and landed a fish by the time he lifted it up to where we could even see it—just a whitish shape appearing, then diving for the bottom in spite of everything the doctor tried to do to hold it. As soon as he'd get it up near the top again, lifting and reeling it it with tight, stubborn little grunts and refusing any help the guys might offer, it would see the light and down it would go.

George didn't bother starting the boat again, but came down to show us how to clean the fish over the side and rip the gills out so the meat would stay sweeter. McMurphy tied a chunk of meat to each end of a four-foot string, tossed it in the air, and sent two squawking birds wheeling off, "Till death do them part."

The whole back of the boat and most of the people in it were dappled with red and silver. Some of us took our shirts off and dipped them over the side and tried to clean them. We fiddled around this way, fishing a little, drinking the other case of beer, and feeding the birds till afternoon, while the boat rolled lazily around the swells and the doctor worked with his monster from the deep. A wind came up and broke the sea into green and silver chunks, like a field of glass and chrome, and the boat began to rock and pitch about more. George told the doctor he'd have to land his fish or cut it loose because there was a bad sky coming down on us. The doctor didn't answer. He just heaved harder on the pole, bent forward and reeled the slack, and heaved again.

Billy and the girl had climbed around to the bow and were talking and looking down in the water. Billy hollered that he saw something, and we all rushed to that side, and a shape broad and white was becoming solid some ten or fifteen feet down. It was strange watching it rise, first just a light coloring, then a white form like fog under water, becoming solid, alive. . . .

"Jesus God," Scanlon cried, "that's the doc's fish!"

It was on the side opposite the doctor, but we could see by the direction of his line that it led to the shape under the water.

"We'll never get it in the boat," Sefelt said. "And the wind's getting stronger."

"He's a big flounder," George said. "Sometimes they weigh two, three hundred. You got to lift them in with the winch."

"We'll have to cut him loose, Doc," Sefelt said and put his arm across the doctor's shoulders. The doctor didn't say anything; he had sweated clear through his suit between his shoulders, and his eyes were bright red from going so long without glasses. He kept heaving until the fish appeared on his side of the boat. We watched it near the surface for a few minutes longer, then started getting the rope and gaff ready.

Even with the gaff in it, it took another hour to drag the fish into the back of the boat. We had to hook him with all three other poles, and McMurphy leaned down and got a hand in his gills, and with a heave he slid in, transparent white and flat, and flopped down to the bottom of the boat with the doctor.

"That was something." The doctor panted from the floor, not enough strength left to push the huge fish off him. "That was . . . certainly something."

The boat pitched and cracked all the way back to shore, with McMurphy telling grim tales about shipwrecks and sharks. The waves got bigger as we got closer to shore, and from the crests clots of white foam blew swirling up in the wind to join the gulls. The swells at the mouth of the jetty were combing higher than the boat, and George had us all put on life jackets. I noticed all the other sports boats were in.

We were three jackets short, and there was a fuss as to who'd be the three that braved that bar without jackets. It finally turned out to be Billy Bibbit and Harding and George, who wouldn't wear one anyway on account of the dirt. Everybody was kind of surprised that Billy had volunteered, took his life jacket off right away when we found we were short, and helped the girl into it, but everybody was even more surprised that McMurphy hadn't insisted that he be one of the heroes; all during the fuss he'd stood with his back against the cabin, bracing against the pitch of the boat, and watched the guys without saying a word. Just grinning and watching.

We hit the bar and dropped into a canyon of water, the bow of the boat pointing up the hissing crest of the wave going before us, and the rear down in the trough in the shadow of the wave looming behind us, and everybody in the back hanging on the rail and looking from the mountain that chased behind to the streaming black rocks of the jetty forty feet to the left, to George at the wheel. He stood there like a mast. He kept turning his head from the front to the back, gunning the throttle, easing off, gunning again, holding us steady riding the uphill slant of that wave in front. He'd told us before we started the run that if we went over the crest in *front,* we'd surfboard out of control as soon as the prop and rudder broke water, and if we slowed down to where that wave *behind* caught up it would break over the stern and dump ten tons of water into the boat. Nobody joked or said anything funny about the way he kept turning his head back and forth like it was mounted up there on a swivel.

Inside the mooring the water calmed to a choppy surface again, and at our dock, by the bait shop, we could see the captain waiting with two cops at the water's edge. All the loafers were gathered behind them. George headed at them full throttle, booming down on them till the captain went to waving and yelling and the cops headed up the steps with the loafers. Just before the prow of the boat tore out the whole dock, George swung the wheel, threw the prop into reverse, and with a powerful roar snuggled the boat in against the rubber tires like he was easing it into bed. We were already out tying up by the time our wake caught up; it pitched all the boats around and slopped over the dock and whitecapped around the docks like we'd brought the sea home with us.

The captain and the cops and the loafers came tromping back down the steps to us. The doctor carried the fight to them by first off telling the cops they didn't have any jurisdiction over us, as we were a legal, government-sponsored expedition, and if there was anyone to take the matter up with it would have to be a federal agency. Also, there might be some investigation into the number of life jackets that the boat held if the captain really planned to make trouble. Wasn't there supposed to be a life jacket for every man on board, according to the law? When the captain didn't say anything the cops took some names and left, mumbling and confused, and as soon as they were off the pier McMurphy and the captain went to arguing and shoving each other around. McMurphy was drunk enough he was still trying to rock with the roll of the boat and he slipped on the wet wood and fell in the ocean twice before he got his footing sufficient to hit the captain one up alongside of his bald head and settle the fuss. Everybody felt better that that was out of the way, and the captain and McMurphy both went to the bait shop to get more beer while the rest of us worked at hauling our fish out of the hold. The loafers stood on that upper dock, watching and smoking pipes they'd carved themselves. We were waiting for them to say something about the girl again, hoping for it, to tell the truth, but when one of them finally did say something it wasn't about the girl but about our fish being the biggest halibut he'd ever seen brought in on the Oregon coast. All the rest nodded that that was sure the truth. They came edging down to look it over. They asked George where he learned to dock a boat that way, and we found out George'd not just run fishing boats but he'd also been captain of a PT boat in the Pacific and got the Navy Cross. "Shoulda gone into public office," one of the loafers said, "Too dirty," George told him.

They could sense the change that most of us were only suspecting; these weren't the same bunch of weak-knees from a nuthouse that they'd watched take their insults on the dock this morning. They didn't exactly apologize to the girl for the things they'd said, but when they asked to see the fish she'd caught they were just as polite as pie. And when McMurphy and the captain came back out of the bait shop we all shared a beer together before we drove away.

It was late when we got back to the hospital.

The girl was sleeping against Billy's chest, and when she raised up his arm'd gone dead holding her all that way in such an awkward position, and she rubbed it for him. He told her if he had any of his weekends free he'd ask her for a date, and she said she could come to visit in two weeks if he'd tell her what time, and Billy looked at McMurphy for an answer. McMurphy put his arms around both of their shoulders and said, "Let's make it two o'clock on the nose."

"Saturday afternoon?" she asked.

He winked at Billy and squeezed the girl's head in the crook of his arm. "No. Two o'clock Saturday night. Slip up and knock on that same window you was at this morning. I'll talk the night aide into letting you in."

She giggled and nodded. "You damned McMurphy," she said.

Some of the Acutes on the ward were still up, standing around the latrine to see if we'd been drowned or not. They watched us march into the hall, blood-speckled, sunburned, stinking of beer and fish, toting our salmon like we were conquering heroes. The doctor asked if they'd like to come out and look at his halibut in the back of his car, and we all started back out except McMurphy. He said he guessed he was pretty shot and thought he'd hit the hay. When he was gone one of the Acutes who hadn't made the trip asked how come McMurphy looked so beat and worn out where the rest of us looked red-cheeked and still full of excitement. Harding passed it off as nothing more than the loss of his suntan.

"You'll recall McMurphy came in full steam, from a rigorous life outdoors on a work farm, ruddy of face and abloom with physical health. We've simply been witness to the fading of his magnificent psychopathic suntan. That's all. Today he did spend some exhausting hours—in the dimness of the boat cabin, incidentally—while we were out in the elements, soaking up the Vitamin D. Of course, that may have exhausted him to some extent, those rigors down below, but think of it, friends. As for myself, I believe I could have done with a little less Vitamin D and a little more of his kind of exhaustion. Especially with little Candy as a taskmaster. Am I wrong?"

I didn't say so, but I was wondering if maybe he wasn't wrong. I'd noticed McMurphy's exhaustion earlier, on the trip home, after he'd insisted on driving past the place where he'd lived once. We'd just shared the last beer and slung the empty can out the window at a stop sign and were just leaning back to get the feel of the day, swimming in that kind of tasty drowsiness that comes over you after a day of going hard at something you enjoy doing—half sunburned and half. drunk and keeping awake only because you wanted to savor the taste as long as you could. I noticed vaguely that I was getting so's I could see some good in the life around me. McMurphy was teaching me. I was feeling better than I'd remembered feeling since I was a kid, when everything was good and the land was still singing kids' poetry to me.

We'd drove back inland instead of the coast, to go through this town McMurphy'd lived in the most he'd ever lived in one place. Down the face of the Cascade hill, thinking we were lost till ... we came to a town covered a space about twice the size of the hospital ground. A gritty wind had blown out the sun on the street where he stopped. He parked in some reeds and pointed across the road.

"There. That's the one. Looks like it's propped up outta the weeds—my misspent youth's humble abode."

Out along the dim six-o'clock street, I saw leafless trees standing, striking the sidewalk there like wooden lightning, concrete split apart where they hit, all in a fenced-in ring. An iron line of pickets stuck out of the ground along the front of a tangleweed yard, and on back was a big frame house with a porch, leaning a rickety shoulder hard into the wind so's not to be sent tumbling away a couple of blocks like an empty cardboard grocery box. The wind was blowing a few drops of rain, and I saw the house had its eyes clenched shut and locks at the door banged on a chain.

And on the porch, hanging, was one of those things the Japs make out of glass and hang on strings—rings and clangs in the least little blow—with only four pieces of glass left to go. These four swung and whipped and rung little chips off on the wooden porch floor.

McMurphy put the car back in gear.

"Once, I been here—since way the hell gone back in the year we were all gettin' home from that Korea mess. For a visit. My old man and old lady were still alive. It was a good home."

He let out the clutch and started to drive, then stopped instead.

"My God," he said, "look over there, see a dress?" He pointed out back. "In the branch of that tree? A rag, yellow and black?"

I was able to see a thing like a flag, flapping high in the branches over a shed.

"The first girl ever drug me to bed wore that very same dress. I was about ten and she was probably less, and at the time a lay seemed like such a big deal I asked her if didn't she think, *feel*, we oughta *announce* it some way? Like, say, tell our folks, 'Mom, Judy and me got engaged today.' And I meant what I said, I was that big a fool; I thought if you made it, man, you were legally *wed*, right there on the spot, whether it was something you wanted or not, and that there wasn't any breaking the rule. But this little whore—at the most eight or nine—reached down and got her dress off the floor and said it was mine, said, 'You can hang this up someplace, I'll go home in my drawers, announce it that way—they'll get the idea.' Jesus, nine years old," he said, reached over and pinched Candy's nose, "and knew a lot more than a good many pros."

She bit his hand, laughing, and he studied the mark.

"So, anyhow, after she went home in her pants I waited till dark when I had the chance to throw that damned dress out in the night—but you feel that wind? Caught the dress like a kite and whipped it around the house outa sight and the next morning, by God, it was hung up in that tree for the whole town, was how I figured then, to turn out and see."

He sucked his hand, so woebegone that Candy laughed and gave it a kiss.

"So my colors were flown, and from that day to this it seemed I might as well live up to my name—dedicated lover— and it's the God's truth: that little nine-year-old kid out of my youth's the one who's to blame."

The house drifted past. He yawned and winked. "Taught me to love, bless her sweet ass."

Then—as he was talking—a set of tail-lights going past lit up McMurphy's face, and the windshield reflected an expression that was allowed only because he figured it'd be too dark for anybody in the car to see, dreadfully tired and strained and *frantic*, like there wasn't enough time left for something he had to do. . . .

While his relaxed, good-natured voice doled out his life for us to live, a rollicking past full of kid fun and drinking buddies and loving women and barroom battles over meager honors— for all of us to dream ourselves into.

part 4

The Big Nurse had her next maneuver under way the day after the fishing trip. The idea had come to her when she was talking to McMurphy the day before about how much money he was making off the fishing trip and other little enterprises along that line. She had worked the idea over that night, looking at it from every direction this time until she was dead sure it could not fail, and all the next day she fed hints around to start a rumor and have it breeding good before she actually said anything about it.

She knew that people, being like they are, sooner or later are going to draw back a ways from somebody who seems to be giving a little more than ordinary, from Santa Clauses and missionaries and men donating funds to worthy causes, and begin to wonder: What's in it for them? Grin out of the side of their mouths when the young lawyer, say, brings a sack of pecans to the kids in his district school—just before nominations for state senate, the sly devil—and say to one another, *He's* nobody's fool.

She knew it wouldn't take too much to get the guys to wondering just what it was, now that you mention it, that made McMurphy spend so much time and energy organizing fishing trips to the coast and arranging Bingo parties and coaching basketball teams. What pushed him to keep up a full head of steam when everybody else on the ward had always been content to drift along playing pinochle and reading last year's magazines? How come this one guy, this Irish rowdy from a work farm where he'd been serving time for gambling and battery, would loop a kerchief around his head, coo like a teenager, and spend two solid hours having every Acute on the ward hoorahing him while he played the girl trying to teach Billy Bibbit to dance? Or how come a seasoned con like this— an old pro, a carnival artist, a dedicated odds-watcher gambling man—would risk doubling his stay in the nuthouse by making more and more an enemy out of the woman who had the say-so as to who got discharged and who didn't?

The nurse got the wondering started by pasting up a statement of the patients' financial doings over the last few months; it must have taken her hours of work digging into records. It showed a steady drain out of the funds of all the Acutes, except one. His funds had risen since the day he came in.

The Acutes took to joking with McMurphy about how it looked like he was taking them down the line, and he was never one to deny it. Not the least bit. In fact, he bragged that if he stayed on at this hospital a year or so he just might be discharged out of it into financial independence, retire to Florida for the rest of his life. They all laughed about that when he was around, but when he was off the ward at ET or OT or PT, or when he was in the Nurses' Station getting bawled out about something, matching her fixed plastic smile with his big ornery grin, they weren't exactly laughing.

They began asking one another why he'd been such a busy bee lately, hustling things for the patients like getting the rule lifted that the men had to be together in therapeutic groups of eight whenever they went somewhere ("Billy here has been talkin' about slicin' his wrists again," he said in a meeting when he was arguing aginst the group-of-eight rule. "So is there seven of you guys who'd like to join him and make it therapeutic?"), and like the way he maneuvered the doctor, who was much closer to the patients since the fishing trip, into ordering subscriptions to *Playboy* and *Nugget* and *Man* and getting rid of all the old *McCall's* that bloated-face Public Relation had been bringing from home and leaving in a pile on the ward, articles he thought we might be particularly interested in checked with a green-ink pen. McMurphy even had a petition in the mail to somebody back in Washington, asking that they look into the lobotomies and electro-shock that were still going on in government hospitals. I just *wonder*, the guys were beginning to ask, what's in it for ol' Mack?

After the thought had been going around the ward a week or so, the Big Nurse tried to make her play in group meeting; the first time she tried, McMurphy was there at the meeting and he beat her before she got good and started (she started by telling the group that she was shocked and dismayed by the pathetic state the ward had allowed itself to fall into: Look around, for heaven sakes; actual pornography clipped from those smut books and pinned on the walls—she was planning, incidentally, to see to it that the Main Building made an investigation of the *dirt* that had been brought into this hospital. She sat back in her chair, getting ready to go on and point out who was to blame and why, sitting on that couple seconds of silence that followed her threat like sitting on a throne, when McMurphy broke her spell into whoops of laughter by telling her to be sure, now, an' remind the Main Building to bring their leetle *hand* mirrors when they came for the investigation) —so the next time she made her play she made sure he wasn't at the meeting.

He had a long-distance phone call from Portland and was down in the phone lobby with one of the black boys, waiting for the party to call again. When one o'clock came around and we went to moving things, getting the day room ready, the least black boy asked if she wanted him to go down and get McMurphy and Washington for the meeting, but she said no, it was all right, let him stay—besides, some of the men here might like a chance to discuss our Mr. Randle Patrick McMurphy in the absence of his dominating presence.

They started the meeting telling funny stories about him and what he'd done, and talked for a while about what a great guy he was, and she kept still, waiting till they all talked this out of their systems. Then the other questions started coming up. What about McMurphy? What made him go on like he was, do the things he did? Some of the guys wondered if maybe that tale of him faking fights at the work farm to get sent here wasn't just more of his spoofing, and that maybe he was crazier than people thought. The Big Nurse smiled at this and raised her hand.

"Crazy like a fox," she said. "I believe that is what you're trying to say about Mr. McMurphy."

"What do you m-m-mean?" Billy asked. McMurphy was his special friend and hero, and he wasn't too sure he was pleased with the way she'd laced that compliment with things she didn't say out loud. "What do you m-m-mean 'like a fox'?"

"It's a simple observation, Billy," the nurse answered pleasantly. "Let's see if some of the other men could tell you what it means. What about you, Mr. Scanlon?"

"She means, Billy, that Mack's nobody's fool."

"Nobody said he wuh-wuh-wuh-*was*!" Billy hit the arm of the chair with his fist to get out the last word. "But Miss Ratched was im-implying—"

"No, Billy, I wasn't implying anything. I was simply observing that Mr. McMurphy isn't one to run a risk without a reason. You would agree to that, wouldn't you? Wouldn't all of you agree to that?"

Nobody said anything.

"And yet," she went on, "he seems to do things without thinking of himself at all, as if he were a martyr or a saint. Would anyone venture that Mr. McMurphy was a saint?"

She knew she was safe to smile around the room, waiting for an answer.

"No, not a saint *or* a martyr. Here. Shall we examine a cross section of this man's philanthropy?" She took a sheet of yellow paper out of her basket. "Look at some of these *gifts,* as devoted fans of his might call them. First, there was the gift of the tub room. Was that actually his to give? Did he lose anything by acquiring it as a gambling casino? On the other hand, how much do you suppose he made in the short time he was croupier of his little Monte Carlo here on the ward? How much did you lose, Bruce? Mr. Sefelt? Mr. Scanlon? I think you all have some idea what your personal losses were, but do you know what his total winnings came to, according to deposits he has made at Funds? Almost three hundred dollars."

Scanlon gave a low whistle, but no one else said anything.

"I have various other bets he made listed here, if any of you care to look, including something to do with deliberately trying to upset the staff. And all of this gambling was, is, completely against ward policy and every one of you who dealt with him knew it."

She looked at the paper again, then put it back in the basket.

"And this recent fishing trip? What do you suppose Mr. McMurphy's profit was on this venture? As I see it, he was provided with a car of the doctor's, even with money from the doctor for gasoline, and, I am told, quite a few other benefits without having paid a nickel. Quite like a fox, I must say."

She held up her hand to stop Billy from interrupting.

"Please, Billy, understand me: I'm not criticizing this sort of activity as such; I just thought it would be better if we didn't have any delusions about the man's motives. But, at any rate, perhaps it isn't fair to make these accusations without the presence of the man we are speaking of. Let's return to the problem we were discussing yesterday—what was it?" She went leafing through her basket. "What was it, do you remember, Doctor Spivey?"

The doctor's head jerked up. "No ... wait ... I think ..."

She pulled a paper from a folder. "Here it is. Mr. Scanlon; his feelings about explosives. Fine. We'll go into that now, and at some other time when Mr. McMurphy is present we'll return to him. I do think, however, that you might give what was said today some thought. Now, Mr. Scanlon ..."

Later that day there were eight or ten of us grouped together at the canteen door, waiting till the black boy was finished shop-lifting hair oil, and some of the guys brought it up again. They said they didn't agree with what the Big Nurse had been saying, but, hell, the old girl had some good points. And yet, damn it, Mack's still a good guy ... really.

Harding finally brought the conversation into the open.

"My friends, thou protest too much to believe the protesting. You are all believing deep inside your stingy little hearts that our Miss Angel of Mercy Ratched is absolutely correct in every assumption she made today about McMurphy. You know she was, and so do I. But why deny it? Let's be honest and give this man his due instead of secretly criticizing his capitalistic talent. What's wrong with him making a little profit? We've all certainly got our money's worth every time he fleeced us, haven't we? He's a shrewd character with an eye out for a quick dollar. He doesn't make any pretense about his motives, does he? Why should we? He has a healthy and honest attitude about his chicanery, and I'm all for him, just as I'm for the dear old capitalistic system of free individual enterprise, comrades, for him and his downright bullheaded gall and the American flag, bless it, and the Lincoln Memorial and the whole bit. Remember the Maine, P. T. Barnum and the Fourth of July. I feel *compelled* to defend my friend's honor as a good old red, white, and blue hundred-per-cent American con man. Good guy, my foot. McMurphy would be embarrassed to absolute *tears* if he were aware of some of the simon-pure motives people had been claiming were behind some of his dealings. He would take it as a direct effrontery to his craft."

He dipped into his pocket for his cigarettes: when he couldn't find any he borrowed one from Fredrickson, lit it with a stagey sweep of his match, and went on.

"I'll admit I was confused by his actions at first. That window-breaking—Lord, I thought, here's a man that seems to actually want to stay in this hospital, stick with his buddies and all that sort of thing, until I realized that McMurphy was doing it because he didn't want to lose a good thing. He's making the most of his time in here. Don't ever be misled by his backwoodsy ways; he's a very sharp operator, level-headed as they come. You watch; everything he's done was done with reason."

Billy wasn't about to give in so easy. "Yeah. What about him teaching me to d-dance?" He was clenching his fists at his side; and on the backs of his hands I saw that the cigarette burns had all but healed, and in their place were tattoos he'd drawn by licking an indelible pencil. "What about that, Harding? Where is he making muh-muh-money out of teaching me to *dance*?"

"Don't get upset, William," Harding said. "But don't get impatient, either. Let's just sit easy and wait—and see how he works it."

It seemed like Billy and I were the only two left who believed in McMurphy. And that very night Billy swung over to Harding's way of looking at things when McMurphy came back from making another phone call and told Billy that the date with Candy was on for certain and added, writing an address down for him, that it might be a good idea to send her a little *bread* for the trip.

"Bread? Muh-money? How muh-muh-much?" He looked over to where Harding was grinning at him.

"Oh, *you* know, man—maybe ten bucks for her and ten—"

"Twenty bucks! It doesn't cost that muh-muh-much for bus fare down here."

McMurphy looked up from under his hatbrim, gave Billy a slow grin, then rubbed his throat with his hand, running out a dusty tongue. "Boy, oh boy, but I'm terrible dry. Figure to be even drier by a week come Saturday. You wouldn't begrudge her bringin' me a little swallow, would you, Billy Boy?"

And gave Billy such an innocent look Billy had to laugh and shake his head, no, and go off to a corner to excitedly talk over the next Saturday's plans with the man he probably considered a pimp.

I still had my own notions—how McMurphy was a giant come out of the sky to save us from the Combine that was networking the land with copper wire and crystal, how he was too big to be bothered with something as measly as money—but even I came halfway to thinking like the others. What happened was this: He'd helped carry the tables into the tub room before one of the group meetings and was looking at me standing beside the control panel.

"By God, Chief," he said, "it appears to me you growed ten inches since that fishing trip. And lordamighty, look at the size of that foot of yours; big as a flatcar!"

I looked down and saw how my foot was bigger than I'd ever remembered it, like McMurphy's just saying it had blowed it twice its size.

"And that *arm!* That's the arm of an ex-football-playing Indian if I ever saw one. You know what I think? I think you oughta give this here panel a leetle heft, just to test how you're comin'."

I shook my head and told him no, but he said we'd made a deal and I was obligated to give it a try to see how his *growth* system was working. I didn't see any way out of it so I went to the panel just to show him I couldn't do it. I bent down and took it by the levers.

"That's the baby, Chief. Now just straighten up. Get those legs under your butt, there ... yeah, yeah. Easy now ... just straighten up. Hooeee! Now ease 'er back to the deck."

I thought he'd be real disappointed, but when I stepped back he was all grins and pointing to where the panel was off its mooring by half a foot. "Better set her back where she came from, buddy, so nobody'll know. Mustn't let anybody know yet."

Then, after the meeting, loafing around the pinochle games, he worked the talk around to strength and gut-power and to the control panel in the tub room. I thought he was going to tell them how he'd helped me get my size back; that would prove he didn't do everything for money.

But he didn't mention me. He talked until Harding asked him if he was ready to have another try at lifting it and he said no, but just because he couldn't lift it was no sign it couldn't be done. Scanlon said maybe it could be done with a crane, but no *man* could lift that thing by himself, and McMurphy nodded and said maybe so, maybe so, but you never can tell about such things.

I watched the way he played them, got them to come around to him and say, *No*, by Jesus, not a man alive could lift it—finally even suggest the bet themselves. I watched how reluctant he looked to bet. He let the odds stack up, sucked them in deeper and deeper till he had five to one on a sure thing from every man of them, some of them betting up to twenty dollars. He never said a thing about seeing me lift it already.

All night I hoped he wouldn't go through with it. And during the meeting the next day, when the nurse said all the men who participated in the fishing trip would have to take special showers because they were suspected of vermin, I kept hoping she'd fix it somehow, make us take our showers right away or something—anything to keep me from having to lift it.

But when the meeting was over he led me and the rest of the guys into the tub room before the black boys could lock it up, and had me take the panel by the levers and lift. I didn't want to but I couldn't help it. I felt like I'd helped him cheat them out of their money. They were all friendly with him as they paid their bets, but I knew how they were feeling inside, how something had been kicked out from under them. As soon as I got the panel back in place, I ran out of the tub room without even looking at McMurphy and went into the latrine. I wanted to be by myself. I caught a look at myself in the mirror. He'd done what he said; my arms were big again, big as they were back in high school, back at the village, and my chest and shoulders were broad and hard. I was standing there looking when he came in. He held out a five-dollar bill.

"Here you go, Chief, chewin'-gum money."

I shook my head and started to walk out of the latrine. He caught me by the arm.

"Chief, I just offered you a token of my appreciation. If you figure you got a bigger cut comin'—"

"No! Keep your money, I won't have it."

He stepped back and put his thumbs in his pockets and tipped his head up at me. He looked me over for a while.

"Okay," he said. "Now what's the story? What's everybody in this place giving me the cold nose about?"

I didn't answer him.

"Didn't I do what I said I would? Make you man-sized again? What's wrong with me around here all of a sudden? You birds act like I'm a traitor to my country."

"You're always . . . winning things!"

"Winning things! You damned moose, what are you accusin' me of? All I do is hold up my end of the deal. Now what's so all-fired—"

"We thought it wasn't to be *winning* things . . ."

I could feel my chin jerking up and down the way it does before I start crying, but I didn't start crying. I stood there in front of him with my chin jerking. He opened his mouth to say something, and then stopped. He took his thumbs out of his pockets and reached up and grabbed the bridge of his nose between his thumb and finger, like you see people do whose glasses are too tight between the lenses, and he closed his eyes.

"Winning, for Christsakes," he said with his eyes closed. "Hoo boy, winning."

So I figure what happened in the shower room that afternoon was more my fault than anybody else's. And that's why the only way I could make any kind of amends was by doing what I did, without thinking about being cagey or safe or what would happen to me—and not worrying about anything else for once but the thing that needed to be done and the doing of it.

Just after we left the latrine the three black boys came around, gathering the bunch of us for our special shower. The least black boy, scrambling along the baseboard with a black, crooked hand cold as a crowbar, prying guys loose leaning there, said it was what the Big Nurse called a *cautionary* cleansing. In view of the company we'd had on our trip we should get cleaned before we spread anything through the rest of the hospital.

We lined up nude against the tile, and there one black boy came, a black plastic tube in his hand, squirting a stinking salve thick and sticky as egg white. In the hair first, then turn around an' bend over an' spread your cheeks!

The guys complained and kidded and joked about it, trying not to look at one another or those floating slate masks working down the line behind the tubes, like nightmare faces in negative, sighting down soft, squeezy nightmare gunbarrels. They kidded the black boys by saying things like "Hey, Washington, what do you fellas do for fun the *other* sixteen hours?" "Hey, Williams, can you tell me what I had for breakfast?"

Everybody laughed. The black boys clenched their jaws and didn't answer; this wasn't the way things used to be before that damned redhead came around.

When Fredrickson spread his cheeks there was such a sound I thought the least black boy'd be blown clear off his feet.

"Hark!" Harding said, cupping his hand to his ear. "The lovely voice of an angel."

Everyone was roaring, laughing and kidding one another, until the back boy moved on and stopped in front of the next man, and the room was suddenly absolutely quiet. The next man was George. And in that one second, with the laughing and kidding and complaining stopped, with Fredrickson there next to George straightening up and turning around and a big black boy about to ask George to lean his head down for a squirt of that stinking salve—right at that time all of us had a good idea about everything that was going to happen, and why it had to happen, and why we'd all been wrong about Mc-Murphy.

George never used soap when he showered. He wouldn't even let somebody hand him a towel to dry himself with. The black boys on the evening shift who supervised the usual Tuesday and Thursday evening showers had learned it was easier to leave it go like this, and they didn't force him to do any different. That was the way it'd been for a long time. All the black boys knew it. But now everybody knew—even George, leaning backward, shaking his head covering himself with big oakleaf hands—that this black boy, with his nose busted and his insides soured and his two buddies standing behind him waiting to see what he would do, couldn't afford to pass up the chance.

"Ahhhh, bend you head down here Geo'ge. . . ."

The guys were already looking to where McMurphy stood a couple of men down the line.

"Ahhhh, c'mon, Geo'ge. . . ."

Martini and Sefelt were standing in the shower, not moving. The drain at their feet kept choking short little gulps of air and soapy water. George looked at the drain a second, as if it were speaking to him. He watched it gurgle and choke. He looked back at the tube in the black hand before him, slow mucus running out of the little hole at the top of the tube down over the pig-iron knuckles. The black boy moved the tube forward a few inches, and George listed farther back, shaking his head.

"No—none of that stoof."

"You gonna have to do it, Rub-a-dub," the black boy said, sounding almost sorry. "You gonna *have* to. We can't have the place crawlin' with *bugs,* now, can we? For all I know you got bugs on you a good *inch deep!*"

"No!" George said.

"Ahhh, Geo'ge, you jes' don't have no *idea.* These bugs, they very, very teeny—no bigger 'n a *pinpoint.* An', man, what they *do* is get you by the short hair an' hang on, an' drill, down inside you, Geo'ge."

"No bugs!" George said.

"Ahhh, let me tell you, Geo'ge: I seen cases where these awful bugs achually—"

"Okay, Washington," McMurphy said.

The scar where the black boy's nose had been broken was a twist of neon. The back boy knew who'd spoken to him, but he didn't turn around; the only way we knew he'd even heard was by the way he stopped talking and reached up a long gray finger and drew it across the scar he'd got in that basketball game. He rubbed his nose a second, then shoved his hand out in front of

George's face, scrabbling the fingers around. "A *crab* Geo'ge see? See here? Now you know what a *crab* look like, don't you? Sure now, you get crabs on that *fishin'* boat. We can't have crabs drillin' down into you, can we, Geo'ge?"

"No crabs!" George yelled. "No!" He stood straight and his brow lifted enough so we could see his eyes. The black boy stepped back a ways. The other two laughed at him. "Somethin' the matter, Washington, my man?" the big one asked. "Some-thin' holding up this end of the pro-ceedure, my man?"

He stepped back in close. "Geo'ge, I'm tellin' you: bend down! You either bend down and take this stuff—or I lay my *hand* on you!" He held it up again; it was big and black as a swamp. "Put this black! filthy! stinkin'! hand all over you!"

"No hand!" George said and lifted a fist above his head as if he would crash the slate skull to bits, splatter cogs and nuts and bolts all over the floor. But the black boy just ran the tube up against George's belly-button and squeezed, and George dou-bled over with a suck of air. The black boy squirted a load in his whispy white hair, then rubbed it in with his hand, smearing black from his hand all over George's head. George wrapped both arms around his belly and screamed.

"No! No!"

"Now turn around, Geo'ge—"

"I said that's enough, buddy." This time the way his voice sounded made the black boy turn and face him. I saw the black boy was smiling, looking at McMurphy's nakedness—no hat or boots or pockets to hook his thumbs into. The black boy grinned up and down him.

"McMurphy," he said, shaking his head. "Y'know I was be-ginnin' to think we might never get down to it."

"You goddamned coon," McMurphy said, somehow sound-ing more tired than mad. The black boy didn't say anything. McMurphy raised his voice. "Goddamned motherfucking nig-ger!"

The black boy shook his head and giggled at his two buddies. "What you think Mr. McMurphy is drivin' at with that kind of talk, man? You think he wants me to take the *initiative?* Hee-heehee. Don't he know we trained to take such awful-soundin' insults from these crazies?"

"Cocksucker! Washington, you're nothing but a—"

Washington had turned his back on him, turning to George again. George was still bent over, gasping from the blow of that salve in his belly. The black boy grabbed his arm and swung him facing the wall.

"Tha's right, Geo'ge now spread those cheeks."

"No-o-o!"

"Washington," McMurphy said. He took a deep breath and stepped across to the black boy, shoving him away from George. "Washington, all right, all right . . ."

Everybody could hear the helpless, cornered despair in Mc-Murphy's voice.

"McMurphy, you forcing me to protect myself. Ain't he forcing me, men?" The other two nodded. He carefully laid down the tube on the bench beside George, came back up with his fist swinging all in the same motion and busting McMurphy across the cheek by surprise. McMurphy nearly fell. He staggered backward into the naked line of men, and the guys caught him and pushed him back toward the smiling slate face. He got hit again, in the neck, before he gave up to the idea that it had started, at last, and there wasn't anything now but get what he could out of it. He caught the next swing blacksnaking at him, and held him by the wrist while he shook his head clear.

They swayed a second that way, panting along with the panting drain; then McMurphy shoved the black boy away and went into a crouch, rolling the big shoulders up to guard his chin, his fists on each side of his head, circling the man in front of him.

And that neat, silent line of nude men changed into a yelling circle, limbs and bodies knitting in a ring of flesh.

The black arms stabbed in at the lowered red head and bull neck, chipped blood off the brow and the cheek. The black boy danced away. Taller, arms longer than McMurphy's thick red arms, punched faster and sharper, he was able to chisel at the shoulders and the head without getting in close. McMurphy kept walking forward—trudging, flatfooted steps, face down and squinting up between those tattooed fists on each side of his head—till he got the black boy against the ring of nude men and drove a fist square in the center of the white, starched chest. That slate face cracked pink, ran a tongue the color of strawberry ice cream over the lips. He ducked away from McMurphy's tank charge and got in another couple of licks before that fist laid him another good one. The mouth flew open wider this time, a blotch of sick color.

McMurphy had red marks on the head and shoulders, but he didn't seem to be hurt. He kept coming, taking ten blows for one. It kept on this way, back and forth in the shower room, till the black boy was panting and staggering and working mainly at keeping out of the way of those clubbing red arms. The guys were yelling for McMurphy to lay him out. McMurphy didn't act in any hurry.

The black boy spun away from a blow on his shoulder and looked quick to where the other two were watching. "Williams ... Warren ... damn you!" The other big one pulled the crowd apart and grabbed McMurphy around the arms from behind. McMurphy shook him off like a bull shaking off a monkey, but he was right back.

So I picked him off and threw him in the shower. He was full of tubes: he didn't weigh more'n ten or fifteen pounds.

The least black boy swung his head from side to side, turned, and ran for the door. While I was watching him go, the other one came out of the shower and put a wrestling hold on me—arms up under mine from behind and hands locked behind my neck—and I had to run backward into the shower and mash him against the tile, and while I was lying there in the water trying to watch McMurphy bust some more of Washington's ribs, the one behind me with the wrestling hold went to biting my neck and I had to break the hold. He laid still then, the starch washing from the uniform down the choking drain.

And by the time the least black boy came running back in with straps and cuffs and blankets and four more aides from Disturbed, everybody was getting dressed and shaking my hand and McMurphy's hand and saying they had it coming and what a rip-snorter of a fight it had been, what a tremendous big victory. They kept talking like that, to cheer us up and make us feel better, about what a fight, what a victory—as the Big Nurse helped the aides from Disturbed adjust those soft leather cuffs to fit our arms.

*U*p on Disturbed there's an everlasting high-pitched machine-room clatter, a prison mill stamping out license plates. And time is measured out by the di-*dock*, di-*dock* of a Ping-pong table. Men pacing their personal runways get to a wall and dip a shoulder and turn and pace back to another wall, dip a shoulder and turn and back again, fast short steps, wearing crisscrossing ruts in the tile floor, with a look of caged thirst. There's a singed smell of men scared berserk and out of control, and in the corners and under the Ping-pong table there's things crouched gnashing their teeth that the doctors and nurses can't see and the aides can't kill with disinfectant. When the ward door opened I smelled that singed smell and heard that gnash of teeth.

A tall bony old guy, dangling from a wire screwed in between his shoulder blades, met McMurphy and me at the door \ the aides brought us in. He looked us over with yellow, scaled eyes and shook his head. "I wash my hands of the whole deal," he told one of the colored aides, and the wire drug him off down the hall.

We followed him down to the day room, and McMurphy stopped at the door and spread his feet and tipped his head back to look things over; he tried to put his thumbs in his pockets, but the cuffs were too tight. "It's a scene," he said out of the side of his mouth. I nodded my head. I'd seen it all before.

A couple of the guys pacing stopped to look at us, and the old bony man came dragging by again, washing his hands of the whole deal. Nobody paid us much mind at first. The aides went off to the Nurses' Station, leaving us standing in the day room door. Murphy's eye was puffed to give him a steady wink, and I could tell it hurt his lips to grin. He raised his cuffed hands and stood looking at the clatter of movement and took a deep breath.

"McMurphy's the name, pardners," he said in his drawling cowboy actor's voice, "an' the thing I want to *know* is who's the peckerwood runs the poker game in this establishment?"

The Ping-pong clock died down in a rapid ticking on the floor.

"I don't deal blackjack so good, hobbled like this, but I maintain I'm a fire-eater in a stud game."

He yawned, hitched a shoulder, bent down and cleared his

232

throat, and spat something at a wastepaper can five feet away; it rattled in with a *ting* and he straightened up again, grinned, and licked his tongue at the bloody gap in his teeth.

"Had a run-in downstairs. Me an' the Chief here locked horns with two greasemonkeys."

All the stamp-mill racket had stopped by this time, and everybody was looking toward the two of us at the door. Mc-Murphy drew eyes to him like a sideshow barker. Beside him, I found that I was obliged to be looked at too, and with people staring at me I felt I had to stand up straight and tall as I could. That made my back hurt where I'd fallen in the shower with the black boy on me, but I didn't let on. One hungry looker with a head of shaggy black hair came up and held his hand like he figured I had something for him. I tried to ignore him, but he kept running around in front of whichever way I turned, like a little kid, holding that empty hand cupped out to me.

McMurphy talked a while about the fight, and my back got to hurting more and more; I'd hunkered in my chair in the corner for so long that it was hard to stand straight very long. I was glad when a little Jap nurse came to take us into the Nurses' Station and I got a chance to sit and rest.

She asked if we were calm enough for her to take off the cuffs, and McMurphy nodded. He had slumped over with his head hung and his elbows between his knees and looked completely exhausted—it hadn't occurred to me that it was just as hard for him to stand straight as it was for me.

The nurse—about as big as the small end of nothing whittled to a fine point, as McMurphy put it later—undid our cuffs and gave McMurphy a cigarette and gave me a stick of gum. She said she remembered that I chewed gum. I didn't remember her at all. McMurphy smoked while she dipped her little hand full of pink birthday candles into a jar of salve and worked over his cuts, flinching every time he flinched and telling him she was sorry. She picked up one of his hands in both of hers and turned it over and salved his knuckles. "Who was it?" she asked, looking at the knuckles. "Was it Washington or Warren?"

McMurphy looked up at her. "Washington," he said and grinned. "The Chief here took care of Warren."

She put his hand down and turned to me. I could see the little bird bones in her face. "Are you hurt anywhere?" I shook my head.

"What about Warren and Williams?"

McMurphy told her he thought they might be sporting some

plaster the next time she saw them. She nodded and looked at her feet. "It's not all like her ward," she said. "A lot of it is, but not all. Army nurses, trying to run an Army hospital. They are a little sick themselves. I sometimes think all single nurses should be fired after they reach thirty-five."

"At least all single *Army* nurses," McMurphy added. He asked how long we could expect to have the pleasure of her hospitality.

"Not very long, I'm afraid."

"Not very long, you're *afraid?*" McMurphy asked her.

"Yes. I'd like to keep men here sometimes instead of sending them back, but she has seniority. No, you probably won't be very long—I mean—like you are now."

The beds on Disturbed are all out of tune, too taut or too loose. We were assigned beds next to each other. They didn't tie a sheet across me, though they left a little dim light on near the bed. Halfway through the night somebody screamed, "I'm starting to spin, Indian! Look me, look me!" I opened my eyes and saw a set of long yellow teeth glowing right in front of my face. It was the hungry-looking guy. "I'm starting to *spin!* Please look me!"

The aides got him from behind, two of them, dragged him laughing and yelling out of the dorm: "I'm starting to spin, Indian!"—then just *laugh*. He kept saying it and laughing all the way down the hall till the dorm was quiet again, and I could hear that one other guy saying, "Well . . . I wash my hands of the whole deal."

"You had you a buddy for a second there, Chief," McMurphy whispered and rolled over to sleep. I couldn't sleep much the rest of the night and I kept seeing those yellow teeth and that guy's hungry face, asking to Look me! Look me! Or, finally, as I did get to sleep, just asking. That face, just a yellow, starved need, come looming out of the dark in front of me, wanting things . . . asking things. I wondered how McMurphy slept, plagued by a hundred faces like that, or two hundred, or a thousand.

They've got an alarm on Disturbed to wake the patients. They don't just turn on the lights like downstairs. This alarm sounds like a gigantic pencil-sharpener grinding up something awful. McMurphy and I both sat bolt upright when we heard it and were about to lie back down when a loudspeaker called for the two of us to come to the Nurses' Station. I got out of bed, and my back had stiffened up overnight to where I could just barely bend; I could tell by the way McMurphy gimped around that he was as stiff as I was.

"What they got on the program for us now, Chief?" he asked. "The boot? The rack? I hope nothing too strenuous, because, man, am I stove up bad!"

I told him it wasn't strenuous, but I didn't tell him anything else, because I wasn't sure myself till I got to the Nurses' Station, and the nurse, a different one, said, "Mr. McMurphy and Mr. Bromden?" then handed us each a little paper cup.

I looked in mine, and there are three of those red capsules. This *tsing* whirs in my head I can't stop.

"Hold on," McMurphy says. "These are those knock-out pills, aren't they?"

The nurse nods, twists her head to check behind her; there's two guys waiting with ice tongs, hunching forward with their elbows linked.

McMurphy hands back the cup, says, "No sir, ma'am, but I'll forgo the blindfold. *Could* use a cigarette, though."

I hand mine back too, and she says she must phone and she slips the glass door across between us, is at the phone before anybody can say anything else.

"I'm sorry if I got you into something, Chief," McMurphy says, and I barely can hear him over the noise of the phone wires whistling in the walls. I can feel the scared downhill rush of thoughts in my head.

We're sitting in the day room, those faces around us in a circle, when in the door comes the Big Nurse herself, the two big black boys on each side, a step behind her. I try to shrink down in my chair, away from her, but it's too late. Too many people looking at me; sticky eyes hold me where I sit.

"Good morning," she says, got her old smile back now. McMurphy says good morning, and I keep quiet even though she says good morning to me too, out loud. I'm watching the black boys; one has tape on his nose and his arm in a sling, gray hand dribbling out of the cloth like a drowned spider, and the other one is moving like he's got some kind of cast around his ribs. They are both grinning a little. Probably could of stayed home with their hurts, but wouldn't miss this for nothing. I grin back just to show them.

The Big Nurse talks to McMurphy, soft and patient, about the irresponsible thing he did, the childish thing, throwing a tantrum like a little boy—aren't you *ashamed?* He says he guesses not and tells her to get on with it.

She talks to him about how they, the patients downstairs on our ward, at a special group meeting yesterday afternoon, agreed with the staff that it might be beneficial that he receive some shock therapy—unless he realizes his mistakes. All he has to do is *admit* he was wrong, to indicate, *demonstrate* rational contact, and the treatment would be canceled this time.

That circle of faces waits and watches. The nurse says it's up to him.

"Yeah?" he says. "You got a paper I can sign?"

"Well, no, but if you feel it nec—"

"And why don't you add some other things while you're at it and get them out of the way— things like, oh, me being part of a plot to overthrow the government and like how I think life on your ward is the sweetest goddamned life this side of Hawaii— you know, that sort of crap."

"I don't believe that would—"

"*Then*, after I sign, you bring me a blanket and a package of Red Cross cigarettes. Hooee, those Chinese Commies could have learned a few things from you, lady."

"Randle, we are trying to help you."

But he's on his feet, scratching at his belly, walking on past her and the black boys rearing back, toward the card tables.

"O-kay, well well well, where's this poker table, buddies . . . ?"

The nurse stares after him a moment, then walks into the Nurses' Station to use the phone.

Two colored aides and a white aide with curly blond hair walk us over to the Main Building. McMurphy talks with the white aide on the way over, just like he isn't worried about a thing.

There's frost thick on the grass, and the two colored aides in front trail puffs of breath like locomotives. The sun wedges apart some of the clouds and lights up the frost till the grounds are scattered with sparks. Sparrows fluffed out against the cold, scratching among the sparks for seeds. We cut across the crackling grass, past the digger squirrel holes where I saw the dog. Cold sparks. Frost down the holes, clear out of sight.

I feel that frost in my belly.

We get up to that door, and there's a sound behind like bees stirred up. Two men in front of us, reeling under the red capsules, one bawling like a baby, saying, "It's my cross, thank you Lord, it's all I got, thank you Lord. . . ."

The other guy waiting is saying, "Guts ball, guts ball." He's the lifeguard from the pool. And he's crying a little too.

I won't cry or yell. Not with McMurphy here.

The technician asks us to take off our shoes, and McMurphy asks him if we get our pants slit and our heads shaved too. The technician says no such luck.

The metal door looks out with its rivet eyes.

The door opens, sucks the first man inside. The lifeguard won't budge. A beam like neon smoke comes out of the black panel in the room, fastens on his cleat-marked forehead and drags him in like a dog on a leash. The beam spins him around three times before the door closes, and his face is scrambled fear. "Hut *one*," he grunts. "Hut *two!* Hut *three!*"

I hear them in there pry up his forehead like a manhole cover, clash and snarl of jammed cogs.

Smoke blows the door open, and a Gurney comes out with the first man on it, and he rakes me with his eyes. That face. The Gurney goes back in and brings the lifeguard out. I can hear the yell-leaders spelling out his name.

The technician says, "Next group."

The floor's cold, frosted, crackling. Up above the light whines, tube long and white and icy. Can smell the graphite salve, like the smell in a garage. Can smell acid of fear. There's one window, up high, small, and outside I see those puffy sparrows strung up on a wire like brown beads. Their heads sunk in the feathers against the cold. Something goes to blowing wind over my hollow bones, higher and higher, air raid! air raid!

"Don't holler, Chief. . . ."

Air raid!

"Take 'er easy. I'll go first. My skull's too thick for them to hurt me. And if they can't hurt me they can't hurt you."

Climbs on the table without any help and spreads his arms out to fit the shadow. A switch snaps the clasps on his wrists, ankles, clamping him into the shadow. A hand takes off his wristwatch, won it from Scanlon, drops it near the panel, it springs open, cogs and wheels and the long dribbling spiral of spring jumping against the side of the panel and sticking fast.

He don't look a bit scared. He keeps grinning at me.

They put the graphite salve on his temples. "What is it?" he says. "Conductant," the technician says. "Anointest my head with conductant. Do I get a crown of thorns?"

They smear it on. He's singing to them, makes their hands shake.

" 'Get Wildroot Cream Oil, Cholly. . . .' "

Put on those things like headphones, crown of silver thorns over the graphite at his temples. They try to hush his singing with a piece of rubber hose for him to bite on.

" 'Mage with thoothing lan-o-lin.' "

Twist some dials, and the machine trembles, two robot arms pick up soldering irons and hunch down on him. He gives me the wink and speaks to me, muffled, tells me something, says something to me around that rubber hose just as those irons get close enough to the silver on his temples—light arcs across, stiffens him, bridges him up off the table till nothing is down but his wrists and ankles and out around that crimped black rubber hose a sound like *hooeee!* and he's frosted over completely with sparks.

And out the window the sparrows drop smoking off the wire.

They roll him out on a Gurney, still jerking, face frosted white. Corrosion. Battery acid. The technician turns to me.

Watch that other moose. I know him. Hold him!

It's not a will-power thing any more.

Hold him! Damn. No more of these boys without Seconal.

The clamps bite my wrists and ankles.

e graphite salve has iron filings in it, temples scratching.

He said something when he winked. Told me something.

Man bends over, brings two irons toward the ring on my head.

The machine hunches on me.

AIR RAID.

Hit at a lope, running already down the slope. Can't get back, can't go ahead, look down the barrel an' you dead dead dead.

We come up outa the bullreeds run beside th... ailroad track. I lay an ear to the track, and it burns my cheek.

"Nothin' either way," I say, "a *hundred* miles. . . ."

"Hump," Papa says.

"Didn't we used to listen for buffalo by stickin' a knife in the ground, catch the handle in our teeth, hear a herd way off?"

"Hump," he says again, but he's tickled. Out across the other side of the track a fencerow of wheat chats from last winter. Mice under that stuff, the dog says.

"Do we go up the track or down the track, boy?"

"We go across, is what the ol' dog says."

"That dog don't heel."

"He'll do. There's birds over there is what the ol' dog says."

"Better hunting up the track bank is what your ol' man says."

"Best right across in the chats of wheat, the dog tells me."

Across—next thing I know there's people all over the track, blasting away at pheasants like anything. Seems our dog got too far out ahead and run all the birds outa the chats to the track.

Dog got three mice.

. . . man, Man, MAN, MAN . . . broad and big with a wink like a star.

Ants again oh Jesus and I got 'em bad this time, prickle-footed bastards. Remember the time we found those ants tasted like dill pickles? Hee? You said it wasn't dill pickles and I said it was, and your mama kicked the living tar outa me when she heard: Teachin' a kid to eat *bugs!*

Ugh. Good Injun boy should know how to survive on any-thing he can eat that won't eat him first.

We ain't Indians. We're civilized and you remember it.

You told me Papa When I die pin me up against the sky. Mama's name was Bromden. Still is Bromden. Papa said he was born with only one name, born smack into it the way a calf drops out in a spread blanket when the cow insists on standing up. Tee Ah Millatoona, the Pine-That-Stands-Tallest-on-the-Mountain, and I'm the biggest by God Injun in the state of Oregon and probly California and Idaho. Born right into it.

You're the biggest by God fool if you think that a good Christian woman takes on a name like Tee Ah Millatoona. You were born into a name, so okay, I'm born into a name. Brom-den. Mary Louise Bromden.

And when we move into town, Papa says, that name makes gettin' that Social Security card a lot easier.

Guy's after somebody with a riveter's hammer, get him too, if he keeps at it. I see those lightning flashes again, colors striking.

Ting. Tingle, tingle, tremble toes, she's a good fisherman, catches hens, puts 'em inna pens . . . wire blier, limber lock, three geese inna flock . . . one flew east, one flew west, one flew over the cuckoo's nest . . . O-U-T- spells out . . . goose swoops down and plucks *you* out.

My old grandma chanted this, a game we played by the hours, sitting by the fish racks scaring flies. A game called Tingle Tingle Tangle Toes. Counting each finger on my two outspread hands, one finger to a syllable as she chants.

Tingle, ting-le, tang-le toes (seven fingers) she's a good fisherman, catches hens (sixteen fingers, tapping a finger on each beat with her black crab hand, each of my fingernails looking up at her like a little face asking to be the *you* that the goose swoops down and plucks out).

I like the game and I like Grandma. I don't like Mrs. Tingle Tangle Toes, catching hens. I don't like her. I do like that goose flying over the cuckoo's nest. I like him, and I like Grandma, dust in her wrinkles.

Next time I saw her she was stone cold dead, right in the middle of The Dalles on the sidewalk, colored shirts standing around, some Indians, some cattlemen, some wheatmen. They cart her down to the city burying ground, roll red clay into her eyes.

I remember hot, still electric-storm afternoons when jackrabbits ran under Diesel truck wheels.

Joey Fish-in-a-Barrel has twenty thousand dollars and three Cadillacs since the contract. And he can't drive none of 'em.

I see a dice.

I see it from the inside, me at the bottom. I'm the weight, loading the dice to throw that number one up there above me. They got the dice loaded to throw a snake eyes, and I'm the load, six lumps around me like white pillows is the other side of the dice, the number six that will always be down when he throws. What's the other dice loaded for? I bet it's loaded to throw one too. Snake eyes. They're shooting with crookies against him, and I'm the load.

Look out, here comes a toss. Ay, lady, the smokehouse is empty and baby needs a new pair of opera pumps. Comin' at ya. *Faw!*

Crapped out.

Water. I'm lying in a puddle.

Snake eyes. Caught him again. I see that number one up above me: he can't whip frozen dice behind the feedstore in an alley—in Portland.

The alley is a tunnel it's cold because the sun is late afternoon. Let me . . . go see Grandma. Please Mama.

What was it he said when he winked?

One flew east one flew west.

Don't stand in my way.

Damn it, nurse, don't stand in my way Way WAY!

My roll. *Faw*. Damn. Twisted again. Snake eyes.

The schoolteacher tell me you got a good head, boy, be something. . . .

Be what, Papa? A rug-weaver like Uncle R & J Wolf? A basket-weaver? Or another drunken Indian?

I say, attendant, you're an Indian, aren't you?

Yeah, that's right.

Well, I must say, you speak the language quite well.

Yeah.

Well . . . three dollars of regular.

They wouldn't be so cocky if they knew what me and the *moon* have going. No damned regular Indian . . .

He who—what was it?—walks out of step, hears another drum.

Snake eyes again. Hoo boy, these dice are *cold*.

After Grandma's funeral me and Papa and Uncle Running-and-Jumping Wolf dug her up. Mama wouldn't go with us; she never heard of such a thing. Hanging a corpse in a *tree!* It's enough to make a person sick.

Uncle R & J Wolf and Papa spent twenty days in the drunk tank at The Dalles jail, playing rummy, for Violation of the Dead.

But she's our goddanged mother!

It doesn't make the slightest difference, boys. You shoulda left her buried. I don't know when you blamed Indians will learn. Now, where is she? you'd better tell.

Ah go fuck yourself, paleface, Uncle R & J said, rolling himself a cigarette. I'll never tell.

High high high in the hills, high in a pine tree bed, she's tracing the wind with that old hand, counting the clouds with that old chant: . . . three geese in a flock . . .

What did you say to me when you winked?

Band playing. Look—the *sky*, it's the Fourth of July.

Dice at rest.

They got to me with the machine again . . . I wonder . . . What did he say?

. . . wonder how McMurphy made me big again.

He said Guts ball.

They're out there. Black boys in white suits peeing under the door on me, come in later and accuse me of soaking all six these pillows I'm lying on! Number six. I thought the room was a dice. The number one, the snake eye up there, the circle, the white *light* in the ceiling . . . is what I've been seeing . . . in this little square room . . . means it's after dark. How many hours have I been out? It's fogging a little, but I won't slip off and hide in it. No . . . never again . . .

I stand, stood up slowly, feeling numb between the shoulders. The white pillows on the floor of the Seclusion Room were soaked from me peeing on them while I was out. I couldn't remember all of it yet, but I rubbed my eyes with the heels of my hands and tried to clear my head. I worked at it. I'd never worked at coming out of it before.

I staggered toward the little round chicken-wired window in the door of the room and tapped it with my knuckles. I saw an aide coming up the hall with a tray for me and knew this time I had them beat.

*T*here had been times when I'd wandered around in a daze for as long as two weeks after a shock treatment, living in that foggy, jumbled blur which is a whole lot like the ragged edge of sleep, that gray zone between light and dark, or between sleeping and waking or living and dying, where you know you're not unconscious any more but don't know yet what day it is or who you are or what's the use of coming back at all—for two weeks. If you don't have a reason to wake up you can loaf around in that gray zone for a long, fuzzy time, or if you want to bad enough I found you can come fighting right out of it. This time I came fighting out of it in less than a day, less time than ever.

And when the fog was finally swept from my head it seemed like I'd just come up after a long, deep dive, breaking the surface after being under water a hundred years. It was the last treatment they gave me.

They gave McMurphy three more treatments that week. As quick as he started coming out of one, getting the click back in his wink, Miss Ratched would arrive with the doctor and they would ask him if he felt like he was ready to come around and face up to his problem and come back to the ward for a cure. And he'd swell up, aware that every one of those faces on Disturbed had turned toward him and was waiting, and he'd tell the nurse he regretted that he had but one life to give for his country and she could kiss his rosy red ass befor. he'd give up the goddam ship. *Yeh!*

Then stand up and take a couple of bows to those guys grinning at him while the nurse led the doctor into the station to phone over to the Main Building and authorize another treatment.

Once, as she turned to walk away, he got hold of her through the back of her uniform, gave her a pinch that turned her face red as his hair. I think if the doctor hadn't been there, hiding a grin himself, she would've slapped McMurphy's face.

I tried to talk him into playing along with her so's to get out of the treatments, but he just laughed and told me Hell, all they was doin' was chargin' his battery for him, free for nothing. "When I get out of here the first woman that takes on ol' Red McMurphy the ten-thousand-watt psychopath, she's gonna light up like a pinball machine and pay off in silver dollars! No I ain't sacred of their little battery-charger."

He insisted it wasn't hurting him. He wouldn't even take his capsules. But every time that loudspeaker called for him to forgo breakfast and prepare to walk to Building One, the muscles in his jaw went taut and his whole face drained of color, looking thin and scared—the face I had seen reflected in the windshield on the trip back from the coast.

I left Disturbed at the end of the week and went back to the ward. I had a lot of things I wanted to say to him before I went, but he'd just come back from a treatment and was sitting following the ping-pong ball with his eyes like he was wired to it. The colored aide and the blond one took me downstairs and let me onto our ward and locked the door behind me. The ward seemed awful quiet after Disturbed. I walked to our day room and for some reason stopped at the door; everybody's face turned up to me with a different look than they'd ever given me before. Their faces lighted up as if they were looking into the glare of a sideshow platform. "Here, in fronta your very eyes," Harding spiels, "is the *Wild*man who broke the arm . . . of the black boy! Hey-ha, lookee, lookee." I grinned back at them, realizing how McMurphy must've felt these months with these faces screaming up at him.

All the guys came over and wanted me to tell them everything that had happened; how was he acting up there? What was he doing? Was it true, what was being rumored over at the gym, that they'd been hitting him every day with EST and he was shrugging it off like water, makin' book with the technicians on how long he could keep his eyes open after the poles touched.

I told them all I could, and nobody seemed to think a thing about me all of a sudden talking with people—a guy who'd been considered deaf and dumb as far back as they'd known him, talking, listening, just like anybody. I told them everything that they'd heard was true, and tossed in a few stories of my own. They laughed so hard about some of the things he'd said to the nurse that the two Vegetables under their wet sheets on the Chronics' side grinned and snorted along with the laughter, just like they understood.

When the nurse herself brought the problem of Patient Mc-Murphy up in group the next day, said that for some unusual reason he did not seem to be responding to EST at all and that more drastic means might be required to make contact with him, Harding said, "Now, that is possible, Miss Ratched, yes—

but from what I hear about your dealings upstairs with Mc-
Murphy, he hasn't had any difficulty making contact with
you."

She was thrown off balance and flustered so bad with everybody in the room laughing at her, that she didn't bring it up
again.

She saw that McMurphy was growing bigger than ever while
he was upstairs where the guys couldn't see the dent she was
making on him, growing almost into a legend. A man out of
sight can't be made to look weak, she decided, and started
making plans to bring him back down to our ward. She figured
the guys could see for themselves then that he could be as
vulnerable as the next man. He couldn't continue in his hero
role if he was sitting around the day room all the time in a
shock stupor.

The guys anticipated this, and that as long as he was on the
ward for them to see she would be giving him shock every time
he came out of it. So Harding and Scanlon and Fredrickson
and I talked over how we could convince him that the best
thing for everybody concerned would be his escaping the ward.
And by the Saturday when he was brought back to the ward—
footworking into the day room like a boxer into a ring, clasping
his hands over his head and announcing the champ was back—
we had our plan all worked out. We'd wait until dark, set a
mattress on fire, and when the firemen came we'd rush him
out the door. It seemed such a fine plan we couldn't see how he
could refuse.

But we didn't think about its being the day he'd made a date
to have the girl, Candy, sneak onto the ward for Billy.

They brought him back to the ward about ten in the morning—"Fulla piss an' vinegar, buddies; they checked my plugs
and cleaned my points, and I got a glow on like a Model T
spark coil. Ever use one of those coils around Halloween time?
Zam! Good clean fun." And he batted around the ward bigger
than ever, spilled a bucket of mop water under the Nurses'
Station door, laid a pat of butter square on the toe of the least
black boy's white suede shoes without the black boy noticing,
and smothered giggles all through lunch while it melted to
show a color Harding referred to as a "most suggestive yellow,"—bigger than ever, and each time he brushed close by a
student nurse she gave a yip and rolled her eyes and pitter-
patted off down the hall, rubbing her flank.

We told him of our plan for his escape, and he told us there
was no hurry and reminded us of Billy's date. "We can't dis-
appoint Billy Boy, can we, buddies? Not when he's about to

cash in his cherry. And it should be a nice little party tonight if we can pull it off; let's say maybe it's my going-away party."

It was the Big Nurse's weekend to work—she didn't want to miss his return—and she decided we'd better have us a meeting to get something settled. At the meeting she tried once more to bring up her suggestion for a more drastic measure, insisting that the doctor consider such action "before it is too late to help the patient." But McMurphy was such a whirligig of winks and yawns and belches while she talked, she finally hushed, and when she did he gave the doctor and all the patients fits by agreeing with everything she said.

"Y'know, she might be right, Doc; look at the good that few measly volts have done me. Maybe if we *doubled* the charge I could pick up channel eight, like Martini; I'm tired of layin' in bed hallucinatin' nothing but channel four with the news and weather."

The nurse cleared her throat, trying to regain control of her meeting. "I wasn't suggesting that we consider more shock, Mr. McMurphy—"

"Ma'am?"

"I was suggesting—that we consider an operation. Very simple, really. And we've had a history of past successes eliminating aggressive tendencies in certain hostile cases—"

"Hostile? Ma'am, I'm friendly as a pup. I haven't licked the tar out of an aide in nearly two weeks. There's been no cause to do any cuttin', now, has there?"

She held out her smile, begging him to see how sympathetic she was. "Randle, there's no cutting involv—"

"Besides," he went on, "it wouldn't be any use to lop 'em off; I got another pair in my nightstand."

"Another—pair?"

"One about as big as a baseball, Doc."

"Mr. McMurphy!" Her smile broke like glass when she realized she was being made fun of.

"But the other one is big enough to be considered normal."

He went on like this clear up to the time we were ready for bed. By then there was a festive, county-fair feeling on the ward as the men whispered of the possibility of having a party if the girl came with drinks. All the guys were trying to catch Billy's eye and grinning and winking at him every time he looked. And when we lined up for medication McMurphy came by and asked the little nurse with the crucifix and the birthmark if he could have a couple of vitamins. She looked surprised and said she didn't see that there was any reason why not and gave him some pills the size of birds' eggs. He put them in his pocket.

"Aren't you going to swallow them?" she asked.

"Me? Lord no, I don't need vitamins. I was just gettin' them for Billy Boy here. He seems to me to have a peaked look of late—tired blood, most likely."

"Then—why don't you give them to Billy?"

"I will, honey, I will, but I thought I'd wait till about midnight when he'd have the most need for them"—and walked to the dorm with his arm crooked around Billy's flushing neck, giving Harding a wink and me a goose in the side with his big thumb as he passed us, and left that nurse pop-eyed behind him in the Nurses' Station, pouring water on her foot.

You have to know about Billy Bibbit: in spite of him having wrinkles in his face and specks of gray in his hair, he still looked like a kid—like a jug-eared and freckled-faced and buck-toothed kid whistling barefoot across one of those calendars, with a string of bullheads dragging behind him in the dust—and yet he was nothing like this. You were always surprised to find when he stood up next to one of the other men he was just as tall as anyone, and that he wasn't jug-eared or freckled or buck-toothed at all under a closer look, and was, in fact, thirty-some years old.

I heard him give his age only one time, overheard him, to tell the truth, when he was talking to his mother down in the lobby. She was receptionist down there, a solid, well-packed lady with hair revolving from blond to blue to black and back to blond again every few months, a neighbor of the Big Nurse's, from what I'd heard, and a dear personal friend. Whenever we'd go on some activity Billy would always be obliged to stop and lean a scarlet cheek over that desk for her to dab a kiss on. It embarrassed the rest of us as much as it did Billy, and for that reason nobody ever teased him about it, not even McMurphy.

One afternoon, I don't recall how long back, we stopped on our way to activities and sat around the lobby on the big plastic sofas or outside in the two-o'clock sun while one of the black boys used the phone to call his bookmaker, and Billy's mother took the opportunity to leave her work and come out from behind her desk and take her boy by the hand and lead him outside to sit near where I was on the grass. She sat stiff there on the grass, tight at the bend with her short round legs out in front of her in stockings, reminding me of the color of bologna skins, and Billy lay beside her and put his head in her lap and let her tease at his ear with a dandelion fluff. Billy was talking about looking for a wife and going to college someday. His mother tickled him with the fluff and laughed at such foolishness.

"Sweetheart, you still have scads of time for things like that. Your whole life is ahead of you."

"Mother, I'm th-th-thirty-one years old!"

She laughed and twiddled his ear with the weed. *"Sweet-heart, do I look like the mother of a middle-aged man?"*

She wrinkled her nose and opened her lips at him and made a kind of wet kissing sound in the air with her tongue, and I had to admit she didn't look like a mother of any kind. I didn't believe myself that he could be thirty-one years old till later when I edged up close enough to get a look at the birth date on his wristband.

At midnight, when Geever and the other black boy and the nurse went off duty, and the old colored fellow, Mr. Turkle, came on for his shift, McMurphy and Billy were a̶r̶e̶a̶d̶y up, taking vitamins, I imagined. I got out of bed and put on a robe and walked out to the day room, where they were talking with Mr. Turkle. Harding and Scanlon and Sefelt and some of the other guys came out too. McMurphy was telling Mr. Turkle what to expect if the girl did come—reminding him, actually, because it looked like they'd talked it all over beforehand a couple of weeks back. McMurphy said that the thing to do was let the girl in the *window*, instead of risking having her come through the lobby, where the night supervisor might be. And to unlock the Seclusion Room then. Yeah, won't that make a fine honeymoon shack for the lovers? Mighty secluded. ("Ahh, McMurphy," Billy kept trying to say.) And to keep the lights out. So the supervisor couldn't see in. And close the dorm doors and not wake u̶p̶ ̶ ̶e̶ry slobbering Chronic in the place. And to keep *quiet̶*̶ ̶ ̶ ̶n̶'t want to disturb them.

"Ah, come on, M-M-̶ ̶ ̶k̶," Billy said.

Mr. Turkle kept nodding and bobbing his head, appearing to fall half asleep. When McMurphy said, "I guess that pretty well covers things," Mr. Turkle said, "No—not entiuhly," and sat there grinning in his white suit with his bald yellow head floating at the end of his neck like a balloon on a stick.

"Come on, Turkle. It'll be worth your while. She should be bringin' a couple of bottles."

"You gettin' closer," Mr. Turkle said. His head lolled and bobbled. He acted like he was barely able to keep awake. I'd heard he worked another job during the day, at a race track. McMurphy turned to Billy.

"Turkle is holdin' out for a bigger contract, Billy Boy. How much is it worth to you to lose your ol' cherry?"

Before Billy could stop stuttering and answer, Mr. Turkle shook his head. "It ain' *that*. Not money. She bringin' more than the bottle with her, though, ain't she, this sweet thing? You people be sharing more'n a bottle, won't you." He grinned around at the faces.

Billy nearly burst, trying to stutter something about not Candy, not *his* girl! McMurphy took him aside and told him not to worry about *his* girl's chastity—Turkle'd likely be so drunk and sleepy by the time Billy was finished that the old coon couldn't put a carrot in a washtub.

The girl was late again. We sat out in the day room in our robes, listening to McMurphy and Mr. Turkle tell Army stories while they passed one of Mr. Turkle's cigarettes back and forth, smoking it a funny way, holding the smoke in when they inhaled till their eyes bugged. Once Harding asked what manner of cigarette they were smoking that smelled so provocative, and Mr. Turkle said in a high, breath-holding voice, "Jus' a plain old cigarette. Hee hee, yes. You want a toke?"

Billy got more and more nervous, afraid the girl might not show up, afraid she might. He kept asking why didn't we all go to bed, instead of sitting out here in the cold dark like hounds waiting at the kitchen for table scraps, and we just grinned at him. None of us felt like going to bed; it wasn't cold at all, and it was pleasant to relax in the half-light and listen to McMurphy and Mr. Turkle tell tales. Nobody acted sleepy, or not even very worried that it was after two o'clock and the girl hadn't showed up yet. Turkle suggested maybe she late because the ward was so dark she couldn't *see* to tell which one to come to, and McMurphy said that was the obvious truth, so the two of them ran up and down the halls, turning on every light in the place, were even about to turn on the big overhead wake-up lights in the dorm when Harding told them this would just get all the other men out of bed to share things with. They agreed and settled for all the lights in the doctor's office instead.

No sooner did they have the ward lit up like full daylight than there came a tapping at the window. McMurphy ran to the window and put his face to it, cupping his hands on each side so he could see. He drew back and grinned at us.

"She walks like beauty, in the night," he said. He took Billy by the wrist and dragged him to the window. "Let her in, Turkle. Let this mad stud at her."

"Man, what you talkin'? I don't get too high, not on a little middlin' joint like that one." It was Mr. Turkle's voice somewhere in the dark latrine with us.

"Jesus, Turkle, what are you doing in here?" McMurphy was trying to sound stern and keep from laughing at the same time. "Get out there and see what she wants. What'll she think if she doesn't find you?"

"The end is upon us," Harding said and sat down. "Allah be merciful."

Turkle opened the door and slipped out and met her in the hall. She'd come over to see what all the lights were on about. What made it necessary to turn on every fixture in the ward? Turkle said every fixture wasn't on; that the dorm lights were off and so were the ones in the latrine. She said that was no excuse for the other lights; what possible reason could there be for all this light? Turkle couldn't come up with an answer for this, and during the long pause I heard the bottle being passed around near me in the dark. Out in the hall she asked him again, and Turkle told her, well, he was just cleanin' up, policing the areas. She wanted to know why, then, was the latrine, the place that his job description called for him to have clean, the only place that was dark? And the bottle went around again while we waited to see what he'd answer. It came by me, and I took a drink. I felt I needed it. I could hear Turkle swallowing all the way out in the hall, umming and ahing for something to say.

"He's skulled," McMurphy hissed. "Somebody's gonna have to go out and help him."

I heard a toilet flush behind me, and the door opened and Harding was caught in the hall light as he went out, pulling up his pajamas. I heard the supervisor gasp at the sight of him and he told her to pardon him, but he hadn't seen her, being as it was so dark.

"It isn't dark."

"In the latrine, I meant. I always switch off the lights to achieve a better bowel movement. Those mirrors, you understand; when the light is on the mirrors seem to be sitting in judgment over me to arbitrate a punishment if everything doesn't come out right."

"But Aide Turkle said he was cleaning in there . . ."

"And doing quite a good job, too, I might add—considering the restrictions imposed on him by the dark. Would you care to see?"

Harding pushed the door open a crack, and a slice of light cut across the latrine floor tile. I caught a glimpse of the super-

visor backing off, saying she'd have to decline his offer but she
had further rounds to make. I heard the ward door unlock
again up the hall, and she let herself off the ward. Harding
called to her to return soon for another visit, and everybody
rushed out and shook his hand and pounded his back for the
way he'd pulled it off.

We stood there in the hall, and the wine went around again.
Sefelt said he'd as leave have that vodka if there was something to mix it with. He asked Mr. Turkle if there wasn't something on the ward to put in it and Turkle said nothing but
water. Fredrickson asked what about the cough sirup? "They
give me a little now and then from a half-gallon jug in the drug
room. It's not bad tasting. You have a key for that room,
Turkle?"

Turkle said the supervisor was the only one on nights who
had a key to the drug room, but McMurphy talked him into
letting us have a try at picking the lock. Turkle grinned and
nodded his head lazily. While he and McMurphy worked at
the lock on the drug room with paper clips, the girls and the
rest of us ran around in the Nurses' Station opening files and
reading records.

"Look here," Scanlon said, waving one of those folders.
"Talk about complete. They've even got my first-grade report
card in here. Aaah, miserable grades, just miserable."

Bill and his girl were going over his folder. She stepped
back to look him over. "All these things, Billy? Phrenic this
and pathic that? You don't look like you have all these
things."

The other girl had opened a supply drawer and was suspicious about what the nurses needed with *all* those hot-water
bottles, a million of 'em, and Harding was sitting on the Big
Nurse's desk, shaking his head at the whole affair.

McMurphy and Turkle got the door of the drug room open
and brought out a bottle of thick cherry-colored liquid from
the ice box. McMurphy tipped the bottle to the light and read
the label out loud.

"Artificial flavor, coloring, citric acid. Seventy per cent inert
materials—that must be water—and twenty per cent alcohol—
that's fine—and ten per cent codeine Warning Narcotic May
Be Habit Forming." He unscrewed the bottle and took a taste
of it, closing his eyes. He worked his tongue around his teeth
and took another swallow and read the label again. "Well," he
said, and clicked his teeth together like they'd just been sharp-
ened, "if we cut it a leetle bit with the vodka, I think it'll be all
right. How are we fixed for ice cubes, Turkey, old buddy?"

Mixed in paper medicine cups with the liquor and the port wine, the sirup had a taste like a kid's drink but a punch like the cactus apple wine we used to get in The Dalles, cold and soothing on the throat and hot and furious once it got down. We turned out the lights in the day room and sat around drinking it. We threw the first couple of cups down like we were taking our medication, drinking it in serious and silent doses and looking one another over to see if it was going to kill anybody. McMurphy and Turkle switched back and forth from the drink to Turkle's cigarettes and got to giggling again as they discussed how it would be to lay that little nurse with the birthmark who went off at midnight.

"I'd be scared," Turkle said, "that she might go to whuppin' me with that big ol' cross on that chain. Wun't that be a fix to be in, now?"

"*I'd* be scared," McMurphy said, "that just about the time I was getting my jollies she'd reach around behind me with a thermometer and take my temperature!"

That busted everybody up. Harding stopped laughing long enough to join the joking.

"Or worse yet," he said. "Just lie there under you with a dreadful concentration on her face, and tell you— ﹏ Jesus, listen—tell you what your *pulse* was!"

"Oh don't . . . oh my Gawd . . ."

"Or even worse, just lie there and be able to calculate your pulse and temperature both—sans instruments!"

"Oh Gawd, oh please don't . . ."

We laughed till we were rolling about the couch and chairs, choking and teary-eyed. The girls were so weak from laughing they had to try two or three times to get to their feet. "I gotta . . . go tinkle," the big one said and went weaving and giggling toward the latrine and missed the door, staggered into the dorm while we all hushed one another with fingers to the lips, waiting, till she gave a squeal and we heard old Colonel Matterson roar, "The pillow is . . . a *horse!*"—and come whisking out of the dorm right behind her in his wheelchair.

Sefelt wheeled the colonel back to the dorm and showed the girl where the latrine was personally, told her it was generally used by males only but he would stand at the door while she was in there and guard against intrusions on her privacy, defend it against all comers, by gosh. She thanked him solemnly and shook his hand and they saluted each other and while she was inside here came the colonel out of the dorm in his wheelchair again, and Sefelt had his hands full keeping him out of the latrine. When the girl came out of the door he was trying to ward off the charges of the wheelchair with his foot while we stood on the edge of the fracas cheering one guy or the other. The girl helped Sefelt put the colonel back to bed, and then the two of them went down the hall and waltzed to music nobody could hear.

Harding drank and watched and shook his head. "It isn't happening. It's all a collaboration of Kafka and Mark Twain and Martini."

McMurphy and Turkle got to worrying that there might still be too many lights, so they went up and down the hall turning out everything that glowed, even the little knee-high night lights, till the place was pitch black. Turkle got out flashlights, and we played tag up and down the hall with the wheelchairs from storage, having a big time till we heard one of Sefelt's convulsion cries and went to find him sprawled twitching beside that big girl, Sandy. She was sitting on the floor brushing at her skirt, looking down at Sefelt. "I never experienced anything like it," she said with quiet awe.

Fredrickson knelt beside his friend and put a wallet between his teeth to keep him from chewing his tongue, and helped him get his pants buttoned. "You all right, Seef? Seef?"

Sefelt didn't open his eyes, but he raised a limp hand and picked the wallet out of his mouth. He grinned through his spit. "I'm all right," he said. "Medicate me and turn me loose again."

"You really need some medication, Seef?"

"Medication."

"Medication," Fredrickson said over his shoulder, still kneeling. "Medication," Harding repeated and weaved off with his flashlight to the drug room. Sandy watched him go with glazed eyes. She was sitting beside Sefelt, stroking his head in wonderment.

"Maybe you better bring me something too," she called drunkenly after Harding. "I never experienced anything to come even *close* to it."

Down the hall we heard glass crash and Harding came back with a double handful of pills; he sprinkled them over Sefelt and the woman like he was crumbling clods into a grave. He raised his eyes toward the ceiling.

"Most merciful God, accept these two poor sinners into your arms. And keep the doors ajar for the coming of the rest of us, because you are witnessing the end, the absolute, irrevocable, fantastic end. I've finally realized what is happening. It is our last fling. We are doomed henceforth. Must screw our courage to the sticking point and face up to our impending fate. We shall be all of us shot at dawn. One hundred cc's apiece. Miss Ratched shall line us all against the wall, where we'll face the terrible maw of a muzzle-loading shotgun which she has loaded with Miltowns! Thorazines! Libriums! Stelazines! And with a wave of her sword, *blooie!* Tranquilize all of us completely out of existence."

He sagged against the wall and slid to the floor, pills hopping out of his hands in all directions like red and green and orange bugs. "Amen," he said and closed his eyes.

The girl on the floor smoothed down her skirt over her long hard-working legs and looked at Sefelt still grinning and twitching there under the lights beside her, and said, "Never in my life experienced anything to come even *halfway* near it."

Harding's speech, if it hadn't actually sobered people, had at least made them realize the seriousness of what we were doing. The night was getting on, and some thought had to be given to the arrival of the staff in the morning. Billy Bibbit and his girl mentioned that it was after four o'clock and, if it was all right, if people didn't mind, they'd like to have Mr. Turkle unlock the Seclusion Room. They went off under an arch of flashlight beams, and the rest of us went into the day room to see what we could decide about cleaning up. Turkle was all but passed out when he got back from Seclusion, and we had to push him into the day room in a wheel chair.

As I walked after them it came to me as a kind sudden surprise that I was drunk, actually drunk, glowing and grinning and staggering drunk for the first time since the Army, drunk along with half a dozen other guys and a couple of girls— right on the Big Nurse's ward! Drunk and running and laughing and carrying on with women square in the center of the Combine's most powerful stronghold! I thought back on the night, on what we'd been doing, and it was near impossible to believe. I had to keep reminding myself that it had *truly* happened, that we had made it happen. We had just unlocked a window and let it in like you let in the fresh air. Maybe the Combine wasn't all-powerful. What was to stop us from doing it again, now that we saw we could? Or keep us from doing other things we wanted? I felt so good thinking about this that I gave a yell and swooped down on McMurphy and the girl Sandy walking along in front of me, grabbed them both up, one in each arm, and ran all the way to the day room with them hollering and kicking like kids. I felt that good.

Colonel Matterson got up again, bright-eyed and full of lessons, and Scanlon wheeled him back to bed. Sefelt and Mar-

tini and Fredrickson said they'd better hit the sack too. Mc-
Murphy and I and Harding and the girl and Mr. Turkle stayed
up to finish off the cough sirup and decide what we were going
to do about the mess the ward was in. Me and Harding acted
like we were the only ones really very worried about it; Mc-
Murphy and the big girl just sat there and sipped that sirup
and grinned at each other and played hand games in the
shadows, and Mr. Turkle kept dropping off to sleep. Harding
did his best to try to get them concerned.

"All of you fail to compren' the complexities of the situation," he said.

"Bull," McMurphy said.

Harding slapped the table. "McMurphy, Turkle, you fail to
realize what has occurred here tonight. On a mental ward. Miss
Ratched's ward! The reekerputions will be . . . devastating!"

McMurphy bit the girl's ear lobe. Turkle nodded and opened
one eye and said, "Tha's true. She'll be on tomorrow, too."

"I, however, have a plan," Harding said. He got to his feet.
He said McMurphy was obviously too far gone to handle the
situation himself and someone else would have to take over.
As he talked he stood straighter and became more sober. He
spoke in an earnest and urgent voice, and his hands shaped
what he said. I was glad he was there to take over.

His plan was that we were to tie up Turkle and make it look
like McMurphy'd snuck up behind him, tied him up with oh,
say, strips of torn sheet, and relieved him of his keys, and after
getting the keys had broken into the drug room, scattered
drugs around, and raised hell with the files just to spite the
nurse—she'd believe *that* part—then he'd unlocked the screen
and made his escape.

McMurphy said it sounded like a television plot and it was
so ridiculous it couldn't help but work, and he complimented
Harding on his clear-headedness. Harding said the plan had
its merits; it would keep the other guys out of trouble with
the nurse, and keep Turkle his job, and get McMurphy off the
ward. He said McMurphy could have the girls drive him to
Canada or Tiajuana, or even Nevada if he wanted, and be completely safe; the police never press too hard to pick up AWOLs
from the hospital because ninety per cent of them always show
back up in a few days, broke and drunk and looking for that
free bed and board. We talked about it for a while and finished the cough sirup. We finally talked it to silence. Harding
sat back down.

McMurphy took his arm from around the girl and looked
from me to Harding, thinking, that strange, tired expression

on his face again. He asked what about us, why didn't we just up and get our clothes on and make it out with him?

"I'm not quite ready yet, Mack," Harding told him.

"Then what makes you think I am?"

Harding looked at him in silence for a time and smiled, then said, "No, you don't understand. I'll be ready in a few weeks. But I want to do it on my own, by myself, right out that front door, with all the traditional red tape and complications. I want my wife to be here in a car at a certain time to pick me up. I want them to know I was *able* to do it that way."

McMurphy nodded. "What about you, Chief?"

"I figure I'm all right. Just I don't know where I want to go yet. And somebody should stay here a few weeks after you're gone to see that things don't start sliding back."

"What about Billy and Sefelt and Fredrickson and the rest?"

"I can't speak for them," Harding said. "They've still got their problems, just like all of us. They're still sick men in lots of ways. But at least there's that: they are sick *men* now. No more rabbits, Mack. Maybe they can be well men someday. I can't say."

McMurphy thought this over, looking at the backs of his hands. He looked back up to Harding.

"Harding, what is it? What happens?"

"You mean all this?"

McMurphy nodded.

Harding shook his head. "I don't think I can give you an answer. Oh, I could give you Freudian reasons with fancy talk, and that would be right as far as it went. But what you want are the reasons for the reasons, and I'm not able to give you those. Not for the others, anyway. For myself? Guilt. Shame. Fear. Self-belittlement. I discovered at an early age that I was—shall we be kind and say different? It's a better, more general word than the other one. I indulged in certain practices that our society regards as shameful. And I got sick. It wasn't the practices, I don't think, it was the feeling that the great, deadly, pointing forefinger of society was pointing at me—and the great voice of millions chanting, 'Shame. Shame. Shame.' It's society's way of dealing with someone different."

"I'm different," McMurphy said. "Why didn't something like that happen to me? I've had people bugging me about one thing or another as far back as I can remember but that's not what—but it didn't drive me crazy."

"No, you're right. That's not what drove you crazy. I wasn't giving my reason as the sole reason. Though I used to think at one time, a few years ago, my turtleneck years, that society's chastising was the sole force that drove one along the road to crazy, but you've caused me to re-appraise my theory. There's something else that drives people, strong people like you, my friend, down that road."

"Yeah? Not that I'm admitting I'm down that road, but what is this something else?"

"It is us." He swept his hand about him in a soft white circle and repeated, "Us."

McMurphy halfheartedly said, "Bull," and grinned and stood up, pulling the girl to her feet. He squinted up at the dim clock. "It's nearly five. I need me a little shut-eye before my big getaway. The day shift doesn't come on for another two hours yet; let's leave Billy and Candy down there a while longer. I'll cut out about six. Sandy, honey, maybe an hour in the dorm would sober us up. What do you say? We got a long drive tomorrow, whether it's Canada or Mexico or wherever."

Turkle and Harding and I stood up too. Everybody was still weaving pretty much, still pretty drunk, but a mellow, sad feeling, had drifted over the drunk. Turkle said he'd boot Mc-Murphy and the girl out of bed in an hour.

"Wake me up too," Harding said. "I'd like to stand there at the window with a silver bullet in my hand and ask 'Who *wawz* that'er masked man?' as you ride—"

"The hell with that. You guys both get in bed, and I don't want to ever see hide nor hair of you again. You get me?"

Harding grinned and nodded but he didn't say anything. Mc-Murphy put his hand out, and Harding shook it. McMurphy tipped back like a cowboy reeling out of a saloon and winked.

"You can be bull goose loony again, buddy, what with Big Mack outa the way."

He turned to me and frowned. "I don't know what you can be, Chief. You still got some looking to do. Maybe you could get you a job being the bad guy on TV rasslin'. Anyway, take 'er easy."

I shook his hand, and we all started for the dorm. Mc-Murphy told Turkle to tear up some sheets and pick out some of his favorite knots to be tied with. Turkle said he would. I got into my bed in the graying light of the dorm and heard Mc-Murphy and the girl get into his bed. I was feeling numb and warm. I heard Mr. Turkle open the door to the linen room out in the hall, heave a long, loud, belching sigh as he pulled the door closed behind him. My eyes got used to the dark, and I could see McMurphy and the girl snuggled into each other's shoulders, getting comfortable, more like two tired little kids than a grown man and a grown woman in bed together to make love.

And that's the way the black boys found them when they came to turn on the dorm lights at six-thirty.

I've given what happened next a good lot of thought, and I've come around to thinking that it was bound to be and would have happened in one way or another, at this time or that, even if Mr. Turkle had got McMurphy and the two girls up and off the ward like was planned. The Big Nurse would have found out some way what had gone on, maybe just by the look on Billy's face, and she'd have done the same as she did whether McMurphy was still around or not. And Billy would have done what he did, and McMurphy would have heard about it and come back.

Would have *had* to come back, because he could no more have sat around outside the hospital, playing poker in Carson City or Reno or someplace, and let the Big Nurse have the last move and get the last play, than he could have let her get by with it right under his nose. It was like he'd signed on for the whole game and there wasn't any way of him breaking his contract.

As soon as we started getting out of bed and circulating around the ward, the story of what had taken place was spreading in a brush fire of low talk. "They had a *what?*" asked the ones who hadn't been in on it. "A *whore?* In the dorm? Jesus." Not only a whore, the others told them, but a drunken blast to boot. McMurphy was planning to sneak her out before the day crew came on but he didn't wake up. "Now what kind of crock are you giving us?" "No crock. It's every word gospel. I was in on it."

Those who had been in on the night started telling about it with a kind of quiet pride and wonder, the way people tell about seeing a big hotel fire or a dam bursting—very solemn and respectful because the casualties aren't even counted yet —but the longer the telling went on, the less solemn the fellows got. Everytime the Big Nurse and her hustling black boys turned up something new, such as the empty bottle of cough syrup or the fleet of wheelchairs parked at the end of the hall like empty rides in an amusement park, it brought another part of the night back sudden and clear to be told to the guys who weren't in on it and to be savored by the guys who were. Everybody had been herded into the day room by the black boys, Chronics and Acutes alike, milling together in excited confusion. The two old Vegetables sat sunk in their bedding, snapping their eyes and their gums. Everybody was still in pajamas and slippers except McMurphy and the girl; she was dressed, except for her shoes and the nylon stockings, which now hung over her shoulder, and he was in his black shorts with the white whales. They were sitting together on a sofa, holding hands. The girl had dozed off again, and Mc-Murphy was leaning against her with a satisfied and sleepy grin.

Our solemn worry was giving way, in spite of us, to joy and humor. When the nurse found the pile of pills Harding had sprinkled on Sefelt and the girl, we started to pop and snort to keep from laughing, and by the time they found Mr. Turkle in the linen room and led him out blinking and groaning, tangled in a hundred yards of torn sheet like a mummy with a hangover, we were roaring. The Big Nurse took our good humor without so much as a trace of her little pasted smile; every laugh was being forced right down her throat till it looked as if any minute she'd blow up like a bladder.

McMurphy draped one bare leg over the edge of the sofa and pulled his cap down to keep the light from hurting his reddened eyes, and he kept licking out a tongue that looked like it had been shellacked by that cough syrup. He looked sick and terrifically tired, and he kept pressing the heels of his hands against his temples and yawning, but as bad as he seemed to feel he still held his grin and once or twice went so far as to laugh out loud at some of the things the nurse kept turning up.

When the nurse went in to call the Main Building to report Mr. Turkle's resignation, Turkle and the girl Sandy took the opportunity to unlock that screen again and wave good-by to all and go loping off across the grounds, stumbling and slipping on the wet, sun-sparkle grass.

"He didn't lock it back up," Harding said to McMurphy. "Go on. Go on after them!"

McMurphy groaned and opened one eye bloody as a hatching egg. "You kidding me? I couldn't even get my *head* through that window, let alone my whole body."

"My friend, I don't believe you fully comprehend—"

"Harding, goddam you and your big words; all I fully comprehend this morning is I'm still half drunk. And sick. Matter of fact, I think you're still drunk too. Chief, how about you; are you still drunk?"

I said that my nose and cheeks didn't have any feeling in them yet, if this could be taken to mean anything.

McMurphy nodded once and closed his eyes again; he laced his hands across his chest and slid down in his chair, his chin settling into his collar. He smacked his lips and smiled as if he were napping. "Man," he said, "everybody is still drunk."

Harding was still concerned. He kept on about how the best thing for McMurphy to do was get dressed, quickly, while old Angel of Mercy was in there calling the doctor again to report the atrocities she had uncovered, but McMurphy maintained that there wasn't anything to get so excited about; he wasn't any worse off than before, was he? "I've took their best punch," he said. Harding threw up his hands and went off, predicting doom.

One of the black boys saw the screen was unlocked and locked it and went into the Nurses' Station for the big flat ledger, came back out running his finger down the roll and lipping the names he read out loud as he sighted the men that matched up with them. The roll is listed alphabetically backwards to throw people off, so he didn't get to the Bs till right at the last. He looked around the day room without taking his finger from that last name in the ledger.

"Bibbit. Where's Billy Bibbit?" His eyes were big. He was thinking Billy'd slipped out right under his nose and would he ever catch it. "Who saw Billy Bibbit go, you damn goons?"

This set people to remembering just where Billy was; there were whispers and laughing again.

The black boy went back into the station, and we saw him telling the nurse. She smashed the phone down in the cradle and came out the door with the black boy hot after her; a lock of her hair had broken loose from beneath her white cap and fell across her face like wet ashes. She was sweating between her eyebrows and under her nose. She demanded we tell her where the Eloper had gone. She was answered with a chorus of laughter, and her eyes went around the men.

"So? He's not gone, is he? Harding, he's still here—on the ward, isn't he? Tell me. Sefelt, tell me!"

She darted the eyes out with every word, stabbing at the men's faces, but the men were immune to her poison. Their eyes met hers; their grins mocked the old confident smile she had lost.

"Washington! Warren! Come with me for room check."

We rose and followed as the three of them went along, unlocking the lab, the tub room, the doctor's office. . . . Scanlon covered his grin with his knotty hand and whispered, "Hey, ain't it gonna be some joke on ol' Billy." We all nodded. "And

Billy's not the only one it's gonna be a joke on, now that I think about it; remember who's in there?"

The nurse reached the door of the Seclusion Room at the end of the hall. We pushed up close to see, crowding and craning to peep over the Big Nurse and the two black boys as she unlocked it and swung it open. It was dark in the windowless room. There was a squeak and a scuffle in the dark, and the nurse reached out, flicked the light down on Billy and the girl where they were blinking up from that mattress on the floor like two owls from a nest. The nurse ignored the howl of laughter behind her.

"William Bibbit!" She tried so hard to sound cold and stern. "William . . . Bibbit!"

"Good morning, Miss Ratched," Billy said, not even making any move to get up and button his pajamas. He took the girl's hand in his and grinned. "This is Candy."

The nurse's tongue clucked in her bony throat. "Oh, Billy Billy Billy—I'm so ashamed for you."

Billy wasn't awake enough to respond much to her shaming, and the girl was fussing around looking under the mattress for her nylons, moving slow and warm-looking after sleep. Every so often she would stop her dreamy fumbling and look up and smile at the icy figure of the nurse standing there with her arms crossed, then feel to see if her sweater was buttoned, and go back to tugging for her nylon caught between the mattress and the tile floor. They both moved like fat cats full of warm milk, lazy in the sun; I guessed they were still fairly drunk too.

"Oh, Billy," the nurse said, like she was so disappointed she might break down and cry. "A woman like *this*. A cheap! Low! Painted—"

"Courtesan?" Harding suggested. "Jezebel?" The nurse turned and tried to nail him with her eyes, but he just went on. "Not Jezebel? No?" He scratched his head in thought. "How about Salome? She's notoriously evil. Perhaps 'dame' is the word you want. Well, I'm just trying to *help*."

She swung back to Billy. He was concentrating on getting to his feet. He rolled over and came to his knees, butt in the air like a cow getting up, then pushed up on his hands, then came to one foot, then the other, and straightened. He looked pleased with his success, as if he wasn't even aware of us crowding at the door teasing him and hoorahing him.

The loud talk and laughter swirled around the nurse. She looked from Billy and the girl to the bunch of us behind her. The enamel-and-plastic face was caving in. She shut her eyes and strained to calm her trembling, concentrating. She knew this was it, her back to the wall. When her eyes opened again, they were very small and still.

"What worries me, Billy," she said—I could hear the change in her voice—"is how your poor mother is going to take this."

She got the response she was after. Billy flinched and put his hand to his cheek like he'd been burned with acid.

"Mrs. Bibbit's always been so proud of your discretion. I know she has. This is going to disturb her terribly. You know how she is when she gets disturbed, Billy; you know how ill the poor woman can become. She's very sensitive. Especially concerning her son. She always spoke so proudly of you. She al—"

"Nuh! Nuh!" His mouth was working. He shook his head, begging her. "You d-don't n-n-need!"

"Billy Billy Billy," she said. "Your mother and I are old friends."

"No!" he cried. His voice scraped the white, bare walls of the Seclusion Room. He lifted his chin so he was shouting at the moon of light in the ceiling. "N-n-*no!*"

We'd stopped laughing. We watched Billy folding into the floor, head going back, knees coming forward. He rubbed his hand up and down that green pant leg. He was shaking his head in panic like a kid that's been promised a whipping just as soon as a willow is cut. The nurse touched his shoulder to comfort him. The touch shook him like a blow.

"Billy, I don't want her to believe something like this of you—but what am I to think?"

"Duh-duh-don't t-tell, M-M-M-Miss Ratched. Duh-duh-duh—"

"Billy, I have to tell. I hate to believe you would behave like this, but, really, what else can I think? I find you alone, on a mattress, with this sort of woman."

"No! I d-d-didn't. I was—" His hand went to his cheek again and stuck there. "She did."

"Billy, this girl could not have pulled you in here forcibly." She shook her head. "Understand, I would like to believe something else—for your poor mother's sake."

The hand pulled down his cheek, raking long red marks. "She d-did." He looked around him. "And M-M-McMurphy! He did. And Harding! And the-the-the rest! They t-t-teased me, *called* me things!"

Now his face was fastened to hers. He didn't look to one side or the other, but only straight ahead at her face, like there was a spiraling light there instead of features, a hypnotizing swirl of cream white and blue and orange. He swallowed and waited for her to say something, but she wouldn't; her skill, her fantastic mechanical power flooded back into her, analyzing the situation and reporting to her that all she had to do was keep quiet.

"They m-m-made me! Please, M-Miss Ratched, they may-may-*MAY*—!"

She checked her beam, and Billy's face pitched downward, sobbing with relief. She put a hand on his neck and drew his cheek to her starched breast, stroking his shoulder while she turned a slow, contemptuous look across the bunch of us.

"It's all right, Billy. It's all right. No one else is going to harm you. It's all right. I'll explain to your mother."

She continued to glare at us as she spoke. It was strange to hear that voice, soft and soothing and warm as a pillow, coming out of a face hard as porcelain.

"All right, Billy. Come along with me. You can wait over here in the doctor's office. There's no reason for you to be submitted to sitting out in the day room with these . . . friends of yours."

She led him into the office, stroking his bowed head and saying, "Poor boy, poor little boy," while we faded back down the hall silently and sat down in the day room without looking at one another or speaking. McMurphy was the last one to take a seat.

The Chronics across the way had stopped milling around and were settling into their slots. I looked at McMurphy out of the corner of my eye, trying not to be obvious about it. He was in his chair in the corner, resting a second before he came out for the next round—in a long line of next rounds. The thing he was fighting, you couldn't whip it for good. All you could do was keep on whipping it, till you couldn't come out any more and somebody else had to take your place.

There was more phoning going on in the Nurses' Station and a number of authorities showing up for a tour of the evidence. When the doctor himself finally came in, every one of these people gave him a look like the whole thing had been planned by him, or at least condoned and authorized. He was white and shaky under their eyes. You could see he'd already heard about most of what had gone on here, on his ward, but The Big Nurse outlined it for him again, in slow, loud details so we could hear it too. Hear it in the proper way, this time, solemnly, with no whispering or giggling while she talked. The doctor nodded and fiddled with his glasses, batting eyes so watery I thought he must be splashing her. She finished by

telling him about Billy and the tragic experience we had put
the poor boy through.

"I left him in your office. Judging from his present state, I
suggest you see him right away. He's been through a terrible
ordeal. I shudder to think of the damage that must have been
done to the poor boy."

She waited until the doctor shuddered too.

"I think you should go see if you can speak with him. He
needs a lot of sympathy. He's in a pitiful state."

The doctor nodded again and walked off toward his office.
We watched him go.

"Mack," Scanlon said. "Listen—you don't think any of us
are being taken in by this crap, do you? It's bad, but we know
where the blame lies—we ain't blaming you."

"No," I said, "none of us blame you." And wished I'd had
my tongue pulled out as soon as I saw the way he looked at me.

He closed his eyes and relaxed. Waiting, it looked like. Harding got up and walked over to him and had just opened his
mouth to say something when the doctor's voice screaming
down the hall smashed a common horror and realization onto
everybody's face.

"Nurse!" he yelled. "Good lord, *nurse!*"

She ran, and the three black boys ran, down the hall to
where the doctor was still calling. But not a patient got up.
We knew there wasn't anything for us to do now but just sit
tight and wait for her to come to the day room to tell us what
we all had known was one of the things that was bound to
happen.

She walked straight to McMurphy.

"He cut his throat," she said. She waited, hoping he would
say something. He wouldn't look up. "He opened the doctor's
desk and found some instruments and cut his throat. The poor
miserable, misunderstood boy killed himself. He's there now,
in the doctor's chair, with his throat cut."

She waited again. But he still wouldn't look up.

"First Charles Cheswick and now William Bibbit! I hope
you're finally satisfied. Playing with human lives—gambling
with human lives—as if you thought yourself to be a *God!*"

She turned and walked into the Nurses' Station and closed
the door behind her, leaving a shrill, killing-cold sound ringing
in the tubes of light over our heads.

First I had a quick thought to try to stop him, talk him into
taking what he'd already won and let her have the last round,
but another, bigger thought wiped the first thought away
completely. I suddenly realized with a crystal certainty that

neither I nor any of the half-score of us could stop him. That Harding's arguing or my grabbing him from behind, or old Colonel Matterson's teaching or Scanlon's griping, or all of us together couldn't rise up and stop him.

We couldn't stop him because we were the ones making him do it. It wasn't the nurse that was forcing him, it was our need that was making him push himself slowly up from sitting, his big hands driving down on the leather chair arms, pushing him up, rising and standing like one of those moving-picture zombies, obeying orders beamed at him from forty masters. It was us that had been making him go on for weeks, keeping him standing long after his feet and legs had given out, weeks of making him wink and grin and laugh and go on with his act long after his humor had been parched dry between two electrodes.

We made him stand and hitch up his black shorts like they were horsehide chaps, and push back his cap with one finger like it was a ten-gallon Stetson, slow, mechanical gestures—and when he walked across the floor you could hear the iron in his bare heels ring sparks out of the tile.

Only at the last—after he'd smashed through that glass door, her face swinging around, with terror forever ruining any other look she might ever try to use again, screaming when he grabbed for her and ripped her uniform all the way down the front, screaming again when the two nippled circles started from her chest and swelled out and out, bigger than anybody had ever even imagined, warm and pink in the light—only at the last, after the officials realized that the three black boys weren't going to do anything but stand and watch and they would have to beat him off without their help, doctors and supervisors and nurses prying those heavy red fingers out of the white flesh of her throat as if they were her neck bones, jerking him backward off of her with a loud heave of breath, only then did he show any sign that he might be anything other than a sane, willful, dogged man performing a hard duty that finally just had to be done, like it or not.

He gave a cry. At the last, falling backward, his face appearing to us for a second upside down before he was smothered on the floor by a pile of white uniforms, he let himself cry out:

A sound of cornered-animal fear and hate and surrender and defiance, that if you ever trailed coon or cougar or lynx is like the last sound the treed and shot and falling animal makes as the dogs get him, when he finally doesn't care any more about anything but himself and his dying.

I hung around another couple of weeks to see what was to come. Everything was changing. Sefelt and Fredrickson signed out together Against Medical Advice, and two days later another three Acutes left, and six more transferred to another ward. There was a lot of investigation about the party on the ward and about Billy's death, and the doctor was informed that his resignation would be accepted, and he informed them that they would have to go the whole way and can him if they wanted him out.

The Big Nurse was over in Medical for a week, so for a while we had the little Jap nurse from Disturbed running the ward; that gave the guys a chance to change a lot of the ward policy. By the time the Big Nurse came back, Harding had even got the tub room back open and was in there dealing blackjack himself, trying to make that airy, thin voice of his sound like McMurphy's auctioneer bellow. He was dealing when he heard her key hit the lock.

We all left the tub room and came out in the hall to meet her, to ask about McMurphy. She jumped back two steps when we approached, and I thought for a second she might run. Her face was bloated blue and out of shape on one side, closing one eye completely, and she had a heavy bandage around her throat. And a new white uniform. Some of the guys grinned at the front of it; in spite of its being smaller and tighter and more starched than her old uniforms, it could no longer conceal the fact that she was a woman.

Smiling, Harding stepped up close and asked what had become of Mack.

She took a little pad and pencil from the pocket of her uniform and wrote, "He will be back," on it and passed it around. The paper trembled in her hand. "Are you sure?" Harding wanted to know after he read it. We'd heard all kinds of things, that he'd knocked down two aides on Disturbed and taken their keys and escaped, that he'd been sent back to the work farm —even that the nurse, in charge now till they got a new doctor, was giving him special therapy.

"Are you quite positive?" Harding repeated.

The nurse took out her pad again. She was stiff in the joints, and her more than ever white hand skittered on the pad like one of those arcade gypsies that scratch out fortunes for a penny. "Yes, Mr. Harding," she wrote. "I would not say so if I was not positive. He will be back."

Harding read the paper, then tore it up and threw the pieces at her. She flinched and raised her hand to protect the bruised side of her face from the paper. "Lady, I think you're full of so much bullshit," Harding told her. She stared at him, and her hand wavered over the pad a second, but then she turned and walked into the Nurses' Station, sticking the pad and pencil back down in the pocket of her uniform.

"Hum," Harding said. "Our conversation was a bit spotty, it seemed. But then, when you are told that you are full of bullshit, what kind of written comeback *can* you make?

She tried to get her ward back into shape, but it was difficult with McMurphy's presence still tromping up and down the halls and laughing out loud in the meetings and singing in the latrines. She couldn't rule with her old power any more, not by writing things on pieces of paper. She was losing her patients one after the other. After Harding signed out and was picked up by his wife, and George transferred to a different ward, just three of us were left out of the group that had been on the fishing crew, myself and Martini and Scanlon.

I didn't want to leave just yet, because she seemed to be too sure; she seemed to be waiting for one more round, and I wanted to be there in case it came off. And one morning, after McMurphy'd been gone three weeks, she made her last play.

The ward door opened, and the black boys wheeled in this Gurney with a chart at the bottom that said in heavy black letters, MCMURPHY, RANDLE P. POST-OPERATIVE. And below this was written in ink, LOBOTOMY.

They pushed it into the day room and left it standing against the wall, along next to the Vegetables. We stood at the foot of the Gurney, reading the chart, then looked up to the other end at the head dented into the pillow, a swirl of red hair over a face milk-white except for the heavy purple bruises around the eyes.

After a minute of silence Scanlon turned and spat on the floor. "Aaah, what's the old bitch tryin' to put over on us anyhow, for crap sakes. That ain't him."

"*Nothing* like him," Martini said.

"How stupid she think we are?"

"Oh, they done a pretty fair job, though," Martini said, moving up alongside the head and pointing as he talked. "See. They got the broken nose and that crazy scar—even the sideburns."

"Sure," Scanlon growled, "but *hell!*"

I pushed past the other patients to stand beside Martini. "Sure, they can do things like scars and broken noses," I said. "But they can't do that *look*. There's nothin' in the face. Just like one of those store dummies, ain't that right, Scanlon?"

Scanlon spat again. "Damn right. Whole thing's, you know, too *blank*. Anybody can see that."

"Look here," one of the patients said, peeling back the sheet, "tattoos."

"Sure," I said, "they can do tattoos. But the arms, huh? The arms? The couldn't do those. His arms were *big!*"

For the rest of the afternoon Scanlon and Martini and I ridiculed what Scanlon called that crummy sideshow fake lying there on the Gurney, but as the hours passed and the swelling began subsiding around the eyes I saw more and more guys strolling over to look at the figure. I watched them walk by acting like they were going to the magazine rack or the drinking fountain, so they could sneak another look at the face. I watched and tried to figure out what he would have done. I was only sure of one thing: he wouldn't have left something like that sit there in the day room with his name tacked on it for twenty or thirty years so the Big Nurse could use it as an example of what can happen if you buck the system. I was sure of that.

I waited that night until the sounds in the dorm told me everybody was asleep, and until the black boys had stopped making their rounds. Then I turned my head on the pillow so I could see the bed next to mine. I'd been listening to the breathing for hours, since they had wheeled the Gurney in and lifted the stretcher onto the bed, listening to the lungs stumbling and stopping, then starting again, hoping as I listened they would stop for good—but I hadn't turned to look yet.

There was a cold moon at the window, pouring light into the dorm like skim milk. I sat up in bed, and my shadow fell across the body, seeming to cleave it in half between the hips and the shoulders, leaving only a black space. The swelling had gone down enough in the eyes that they were open; they stared into the full light of the moon, open and undreaming, glazed from being open so long without blinking until they were like smudged fuses in a fuse box. I moved to pick up the pillow, and the eyes fastened on the movement and followed me as I stood up and crossed the few feet between the beds.

The big, hard body had a tough grip on life. It fought a long time against having it taken away, flailing and thrashing around so much I finally had to lie full length on top of it and scissor the kicking legs with mine while I mashed the pillow into the face. I lay there on top of the body for what seemed days. Until the thrashing stopped. Until it was still a while and had shuddered once and was still again. Then I rolled off. I lifted the pillow, and in the moonlight I saw the expression hadn't changed from the blank, dead-end look the least bit, even under suffocation. I took my thumbs and pushed the lids down and held them till they stayed. Then I lay back on my bed.

I lay for a while, holding the covers over my face, and thought I was being pretty quiet, but Scanlon's voice hissing from his bed let me know I wasn't.

"Take it easy, Chief," he said. "Take it easy. It's okay."

"Shut up," I whispered. "Go back to sleep."

It was quite awhile; then I heard him hiss again and ask, "Is it finished?"

I told him yeah.

"Christ," he said then, "she'll know. You realize that, don't you? Sure, nobody'll be able to prove anything—anybody coulda kicked off in post-operative like he was, happens all the time—but her, she'll know."

I didn't say anything.

"Was I you, Chief, I'd breeze my tail outa here. Yessir. I tell you what. You leave outa here, and I'll say I saw him up and moving around after you left and cover you that way. That's the best idea, don't you think?"

"Oh, yeah, just like that. Just ask 'em to unlock the door and let me out."

"No. He showed you how one time, if you think back. That very first week. You remember?"

I didn't answer him, and he didn't say anything else, and it was quiet in the dorm again. I lay there a few minutes longer and then got up and started putting on my clothes. When I finished dressing I reached into McMurphy's nightstand and got his cap and tried it on. It was too small, and I was suddenly ashamed of trying to wear it. I dropped it on Scanlon's bed as I walked out of the dorm. He said, "Take it easy, buddy," as I walked out.

The moon straining through the screen of the tub-room windows showed the hunched, heavy shape of the control panel, glinted off the chrome fixtures and glass gauges so cold I could almost hear the click of it striking. I took a deep breath and bent over and took the levers. I heaved my legs under me and felt the grind of weight at my feet. I heaved again and heard the wires and connections tearing out of the floor. I lurched it up to my knees and was able to get an arm around it and my other hand under it. The chrome was cold against my neck and the side of my head. I put my back toward the screen, then spun and let the momentum carry the panel through the screen and window with a ripping crash. The glass splashed out in the moon, like a bright cold water baptizing the sleeping earth. Panting, I thought for a second about going back and getting Scanlon and some of the others, but then I heard the running squeak of the black boys' shoes in the hall and I put my hand on the sill and vaulted after the panel, into the moonlight.

I ran across the grounds in the direction I remembered seeing the dog go, toward the highway. I remember I was taking huge strides as I ran, seeming to step and float a long ways before my next foot struck the earth. I felt like I was flying. Free. Nobody bothers coming after an AWOL, I knew, and Scanlon could handle any questions about the dead man—no need to be running like this. But I didn't stop. I ran for miles before I stopped and walked up the embankment onto the highway.

I caught a ride with a guy, a Mexican guy, going north in a truck full of sheep, and give him such a good story about me being a professional Indian wrestler the syndicate had tried to lock up in a nuthouse that he stopped real quick and gave me a leather jacket to cover my greens and loaned me ten bucks to eat on while I hitchhiked to Canada. I had him write his address down before he drove off and I told him I'd send him the money as soon as I got a little ahead.

I might go to Canada eventually, but I think I'll stop along the Columbia on the way. I'd like to check around Portland and Hood River and The Dalles to see if there's any of the guys I used to know back in the village who haven't drunk themselves goofy. I'd like to see what they've been doing since the government tried to buy their right to be Indians. I've even heard that some of the tribe have took to building their old ramshackle wood scaffolding all over that big million-dollar hydroelectric dam, and are spearing salmon in the spillway. I'd give something to see that. Mostly, I'd just like to look over the country around the gorge again, just to bring some of it clear in my mind again.

I been away a long time.